P9-CEC-725

BORDERLINE

GERRY BOYLE

To Tom and Donne,
all the very best,
Gerry Boyle
1998

Berkley Prime Crime Books by Gerry Boyle

DEADLINE

BLOODLINE

LIFELINE

POTSHOT

BORDERLINE

BORDERLINE

GERRY BOYLE

BERKLEY PRIME CRIME, NEW YORK

BORDERLINE

A Berkley Prime Crime Book
Published by The Berkley Publishing Group,
a Member of Penguin Putnam Inc.,
200 Madison Avenue, New York, NY 10016

The Putnam Berkley World Wide Web site address is
http://www.berkley.com

Copyright © 1998 by Gerry Boyle
Book design by Erin L. Lush

All rights reserved. This book, or parts thereof, may not be
reproduced in any form without permission.

First edition: March 1998

Library of Congress Cataloging-in-Publication Data

Boyle, Gerry, 1956–
Borderline / Gerry Boyle.
p. cm.
ISBN 0-425-16147-1
I. Title.
PS3552.0925B67 1998
97–24629
CIP

813'.54—dc21

Printed in the United States of America

10   9   8   7   6   5   4   3   2   1

For Emmet Jeremiah Boyle, 1912–1991
He loved history and felt its mystery.

Acknowledgments

For my knowledge of Benedict Arnold and his overland trek, I am indebted to Willard Sterne Randall and his book, *Benedict Arnold: Patriot and Traitor;* the works of Kenneth Roberts, and the Maine State Museum.

The lunch stop was over, and the tour bus heaved its way out of the parking lot and headed north. I stood in the diesel haze with the Chamber of Commerce lady, Sandy something-or-other, and a big guy on a small bicycle, who, with the patience of a scavenger, sat ten feet away and listened.

Sandy had me by the left upper arm. She was telling me that I should write a story about her little shoe-factory town, Scanesett, Maine.

I listened. Smiled. Tried to break her grip but couldn't. I explained that my story, for *Historic Touring* magazine, was supposed to be about Benedict Arnold and his march to Québec. Arnold went through Scanesett, at least what there was of it in 1775, but he didn't stay long. If it hadn't been for the falls, he wouldn't have gotten out of his boat. I just wanted to know if there were any historical museums in town. Scanesett might get a couple of sentences. It might get a paragraph.

"But maybe another time," I said.

Sandy held tight. Smiled her best cheerleader's smile. The heat shimmered off the asphalt. The big guy on the bicycle moved closer. Sandy turned toward him.

"Robie, do you mind?" she hissed. He rolled back and she switched her smile back on.

"We have two major motels, one has Triple-A rat-ing, and a heated indoor pool, and there's all kinds of fishing, and every August at the fairgrounds—this would be perfect for a magazine—they have the custom-car show. People come from, like, Massachusetts and Connecticut, just for that. I could put you in touch with this friend of mine. He's in charge of the whole thing. I could take you to his office. It's right around the corner. I just saw him at lunch, he'd be glad to—''

And then the bus was back.

Sandy paused and loosened her grip. The bus, which had left bound for Québec City from Boston, belched and roared, then pulled back into the parking lot and stopped in front of us. The door hissed open. The driver, a blond machine-tanned guy who only minutes ago had been Mr. Geniality as he tried to look down the front of Sandy's blouse, bounded out.

''You seen him?'' he snapped.

''Seen who?'' I said.

''The bozo who isn't on the bus. I get a mile up the goddamn road and this lady says this guy's not in his seat. God almighty, I gotta be in Québec City, at the hotel, at seven. Now I'm gonna be baby-sitting all afternoon, hanging around this dump just because some guy—''

This dump. Sandy winced.

''What does he look like?'' I asked.

''How the hell should I know? Just some guy. Nobody's been here?''

I shook my head.

''Goddamn it,'' the driver said.

Robie, the guy on the bicycle, rolled closer. We looked around, and then a gray-haired woman appeared at the top of the bus steps, turned sideways, and eased her way down.

''He got back on,'' she said, starting right in with the chronology. ''He was at lunch and then he got back on and sat down, and then he said he was going to go to the men's room. He said he didn't feel well. Not that I cared where he was going. I said to myself, 'You don't need to tell me your every move. Go to the men's room. What do I care?' ''

"And he never came back?" I said.

"Well, no. I figured he was still in the john. But he wasn't in his seat, either. So I sat there—what do I care, right?—and then people keep getting on and the bus is filling up and then off we go."

"I asked if that was everybody," the driver said, glaring up and down the block.

"I thought he was in the bathroom, but then I saw this other woman go back there and go right in, so I figured he wasn't in there. But he wasn't in his seat, and where else can you go on a bus?"

"You sure he didn't just sit down in another seat?" Sandy asked.

"Yeah, I'm sure," the driver said, scowling so that his cheeks dimpled. "I did a head count."

I wondered what the bus company did when a driver lost a passenger. Probably you had to fill out a lot of forms. I looked at the driver. There was perspiration running down his neck in shiny rivulets that disappeared under his white collar.

"So he was gone when you pulled out of here?" I said.

"Unless he beamed his way out. Son of a bitch."

The driver strode to the rear of the bus and looked around. Sandy looked in the other direction, toward the downtown block. The gray-haired woman shaded her eyes with her hand and looked that way, too. Her fingers were bony and strung with jewels.

"What's he look like?" I asked.

She put her hand down.

"Well, he's not a big man. A little smaller than you."

"How old?"

"Well, I would say fifty. But it's hard to tell sometimes. Sometimes people look fifty and they're forty. Sometimes they look fifty and they're sixty. So gee, I wouldn't want to be quoted on this, but I'd say fifty. Give or take because—''

''Dark hair? Light hair? Fat, skinny? Glasses? Bald? Black, white?''

She closed her eyes and put her jeweled fingers to her temples, as if the answer required the assistance of a higher power.

''Oh, white. No glasses. Not fat, but not skinny. And his hair, it was short and sort of, well, I guess it was just brown. And he was wearing shorts. Sort of tan shorts.''

The gray-haired woman opened her eyes and looked at me.

''But his legs weren't tanned. They were very pale. And a polo shirt. The shirt was a dark color. Red or maroon or something.''

She looked at me. I looked back and smiled. She looked a little flushed, maybe from the heat, but also relieved, as if there had been a surprise quiz and she'd passed. The driver came back. He was glowering.

''Five minutes and we're gone,'' he said.

''You just leave him?'' I said.

''I got forty-three other paying passengers who are going to Québec. I can't play games.''

''What if he got really sick?'' I said. ''Tried to find a hospital or something. Or, I don't know. Maybe he's got some sort of mental illness.''

''Hey, I can't chase some wingnut all over the place. These people have to get to Québec City. They got dinner reservations.''

''Seven-thirty,'' the gray-haired woman said, her humanitarian duty fulfilled.

''Yeah, well, it appears like he isn't here,'' the driver said. ''Maybe he heard somebody talking French and he thought we were there already. Not my problem, *n'est-ce pas*?''

''It's going to be somebody's,'' I said. ''Don't you think

you should leave his name with the police or something? In case they find him in a ditch?''

Sandy winced again, then brightened.

''Maybe we could find him—I mean, not in a ditch or anything—and the whole town could turn out to help him. Give him the key to the town. Put him up for the night. Give him dinner and some gift items. The businesses could donate things. Didn't they do that for some lost foreign person in Bangor once?''

''This man wasn't foreign,'' the gray-haired woman said. ''He was a regular person.''

''Any bars around here?'' I said.

''He wasn't drinking. I can smell it a mile away,'' the gray-haired woman said.

''Maybe he just didn't want to use the bus bathroom,'' Sandy said. ''You know how gross they are.''

She left the phrase hanging, her payback for the ''dump'' remark.

''It's not gross,'' the driver said.

''Maybe he thought he could find a real bathroom and then the bus left,'' Sandy went on. ''If he wasn't feeling well.''

''I'd wait a few minutes,'' I said.

''It's gonna take me ten minutes to find his name,'' the driver sputtered.

''Oh, I know his name,'' the gray-haired woman said. ''He told me. It was Ron. Or maybe Don. Don or Ron.''

The driver rolled his eyes. I noticed he was wearing a gold chain around his neck and it was caught in the creases of flab. The gray-haired woman said, ''Well, that's all I can tell you,'' and started back up the bus steps. The driver shook his head in disgust and started up after her. Sandy was saying something about turning this into good news for Scanesett. Robie, the guy on the bicycle, sat there looking straight ahead, hands on his handlebars, big sneakered feet planted on the pavement.

I glanced at him. He was in his early twenties, big and

paunchy under his T-shirt. There was something not quite right about him, a thickness in his mouth, or maybe just a vagueness in his eyes.

"Well, he's got to be someplace, doesn't he," I said.

Robie turned quickly and looked at me. For a moment, our eyes locked. His gaze seemed to sharpen, like a lens twisting into focus, and then he looked away, embarrassed or rattled. He gave a shove with his feet, wheeled around and pedaled off across the parking lot. As he rode away, I noticed there were odd attachments coming off the back axle of his bicycle.

"What's his story?" I asked Sandy.

She looked distracted, her mind probably spinning with the possibilities for this next public relations coup: the rescue of the man with the runs.

"Who, Robie?" Sandy said.

"Yeah."

"Oh, I've known him since grade school," she said. "Him and his sister. They're just, well, I shouldn't say this, but they're just sort of, well . . ."

I waited.

"Well, sort of numb," Sandy said.

She gave an apologetic shrug, though I couldn't tell whether she was apologizing for her bluntness or Robie's condition. I followed his pedaling figure until it disappeared down an alley between Scanesett House of Pizza and an empty storefront.

"Is that right?" I said. "He didn't look so numb to me."

2 There was a museum, an old brick Cape Cod house that overlooked the Kennebec just north of Scanesett's downtown. The handpainted sign beside the front door said the museum was open Tuesday and Thursday, from noon to 3 P.M., Saturday from 10 A.M. until noon, or by appointment. This was Friday. There was a number to call, so I walked back to the truck and dialed. A man answered. He sounded startled.

"This is Jack McMorrow," I said. "Is this the right number to call about the museum?"

There was a fumbling noise. A muttered curse.

"Okay," the man said. "I got it now."

I tried again.

"I'm Jack McMorrow. I'm writing a magazine story about the Arnold Trail. Benedict Arnold. I wondered if your museum here would have anything of interest."

"Yup," the man said.

I waited. That was it.

"So I thought I might look around, if that would be possible. It says on the sign to call for an appointment."

"You want to make an appointment?"

"Yes, I would."

"For when?"

"How 'bout right now?" I said.

"Where're you?"

"At the museum."

"Well, hell," the man said. "Sit tight and I'll be right over."

So I sat in a rickety Adirondack chair on the museum's back lawn, against a thicket of spent lilacs. It was hot and close, the way inland Maine can be, but the chair was in the shade. I sat back and looked out at the river, which was still and wide here because it was dammed a few hundred yards downstream. The dam crossed the throat of a deep stone gorge, and above the gorge, the waters coasted slowly before slipping over the brink and cascading down over the rocks and around the red-brick jumble of the town.

Of course, when Arnold had come up the river that fall, on his doomed mission to capture Québec City, there had been no town, no dam, just Scanesett Falls, named by the Abenakis. Arnold and his five hundred men had hauled their heavy *bateaux* out of the river, heaved them up the rocks and around the torrent. That done, they'd gamely continued on their way, not knowing that most of them would soon be dead of exposure, starvation or bayonet.

They probably came through here singing.

I knew this because I'd been doing some reading. To write a story for a magazine called *Historic Touring,* you had to know something about history. The editor at *Historic Touring,* a voice over the phone from Delaware, had told me that. Her name was Allison Smythe, pronounced as it was spelled, and she'd asked me if I'd ever done any travel writing. I said not really. Actually, I'd always looked down on it. When you're a metro reporter at the *New York Times,* you don't get too revved up about describing menus and scenery. In those days, the travel stuff had always seemed so decadent and presumptuous. Eat well, dicker hard, and don't look the beggars in the eye.

But those days were long gone, and money was money. I'd figured I'd read the encyclopedia and get to work. One day of research. A couple of days on the road checking out museums and bed-and-breakfasts. A day to write it. Hit the fax button and wait for the check. And a thousand dollars

in a week would make up for the month I'd spent on sab-
batical. And a week or two before that.

It had been three weeks since I'd accepted my assignment. I hadn't written a word.

Day after day, I'd sat in a chair out behind my house in
Prosperity, Maine, books stacked beside me, one always in
my lap. When the bugs came out, I went in. I ate out of
cans. Got ketchup on the pages. Let full bottles of ale get
warm and flat as I tunneled through the past. The battles
and bravery. The conspiracies and intrigue. The brutality
and tragedy. The people, real people, who had lived all of
it.

So as I sat out behind the Scanesett museum, slouched
in the chair, I looked out on the river. The opposite shore
was unbroken gray-green tree line, hazy in the heat, and I
could picture those men, now long dead, poling and paddling their boats past this very place. It was October 1775
and the shore must have been lined with yellow and crim-
son, the river filled with fish, the woods rustling with birds.
Their voices must have rung across the water. Jokes and
songs, conversation and curses.

And now, more than two hundred years later, they were
forgotten, as if they'd never existed. All those lives lost.
All that perseverance and courage. All for nothing, and
none of it remembered, except by a handful of tweedy professors, and a few old coots in little backwater towns like
this one.

"You the writer fella who called?"

I turned and stood up.

"Yes," I said. "Jack McMorrow."

He was white-haired, red-nosed, stooped over an aluminum cane. I held out my right hand. He took it in his
left, awkwardly hooking his fingers over mine. A stroke?
He didn't introduce himself.

"Thanks for coming down," I said. "I know it was short
notice."

"Wasn't any notice," the man said, turning and heading

for the building. "But no matter. Wasn't doing anything anyway, 'cept sitting on my duff. You gotta go in the front door. Back door's locked and the key's lost."

He limped to the front walk, shuffled up the granite steps and, letting his cane rest against his leg, unlocked the door. It swung open and he went inside. I followed him into the cool, dead air.

"So you're just after Arnold stuff?"

"Well, yeah," I said. "That's what the story's about."

"Want the nickel tour anyway?"

"Sure."

"Close that door. Keep the heat out."

I did, then looked around as my eyes adjusted to the dimness. The house was a center-hallway Cape and the hall was hung with yellowed samplers, framed in glass. The room to the right was packed with antique furniture: a pine cupboard with old blue paint, a pine harvest table, some Shaker-looking ladderback chairs. There was a settee sort of thing that looked Victorian.

The man glanced at it, too.

"Some of the stuff's just old. Not period. But some big-wig family leaves it to the museum, and they want it displayed."

"Hard to say no?" I said.

"Not for me, it wouldn't be. But all the muck-a-mucks around here are thick as thieves. They run the place. I'm sort of the caretaker. Want to see any more?"

"Lead the way."

So he did. There was a lot of town history. Blank-eyed boys and girls in front of the high school. Sepia photos of log drives on the Kennebec. A complete bedroom from the early nineteenth century, with a four-poster bed, pillows like grain sacks. In the cradle, there was an antique doll, with human hair and staring eyes that made the doll look like a corpse.

There were old dresses, laid across the bed, somebody's wire-rimmed glasses open on a delicate writing desk that looked valuable. A fireplace with a Dutch oven and old iron implements. Part of one room was the century-old equipment of a town doctor.

The man reached into the black medical bag and pulled out a pair of forceps.

"For delivering babies," he said.

"Huh," I said.

We circled back to the front of the house, where the man read my mind.

"But you wanted Arnold, right?"

"Right."

"As far as artifacts, we don't have much. A powder horn that one of the soldiers must've dropped. I'm trying to remember where that is. I think they loaned it to the Maine State Museum. And a canteen they found after the soldiers went through. That's here."

He walked to the cupboard and swung open a door. There were dishes and pottery bowls. The canteen, too. He took it out and handed it to me.

"Feel that."

I did. It was heavy.

"Lead. Whole thing's lead. They had to lug that and a ten-pound musket and all their powder and bullets and food and flints and who knows what else. Going up this river in these goddamn rowboats, and it wasn't a pond back then, the way it is now. Rocks and rapids and waterfalls and them going twenty miles a day. Bunch of farmers. You couldn't get anybody to do it for a day nowadays, never mind months."

"No, you couldn't."

"One other thing you might want to see."

He went to a big oak case and slid open a drawer. Closed that one and opened another one. Then a third. He took out something that looked like a pamphlet. It was old and yellowed and he handed it to me.

The Arnold Expedition and Scanesett, it said on the cover.

"That might be of some help," the man said.

I opened the brittle pages gingerly.

"Can I make copies and bring it back?"

"Hell, you can take it. Where do you live?"

"Prosperity."

"Waldo County, huh? Nice country. Used to hunt there, once upon a time. Nah, just take it and bring it back. My number's on the sign."

"You know my name. Jack McMorrow?"

"Yup."

"And your name is?"

"Horace."

"You want my number or anything?" I said.

Horace gave me an assessing glance.

"Nope. No need," he said.

He drove off in an old Dodge pickup, painted pale green. I sat in my truck, a Toyota four-wheel-drive, red and rust, and skimmed the crackling pages.

The pamphlet was published in 1875, for some sort of 100-year commemoration. There was a summary: the infantry marching from Boston to Newburyport, in Massachusetts. Sailing up the coast to the Kennebec River. Picking up their boats near Pittston, Maine, south of Augusta, and setting off up the Kennebec in the leaky *bateaux*.

The page opened to an entry from the journal of a Captain Thayer, who camped right here in Scanesett: "Last night our clothes being wet were frozen a pane of glass thick, which proved very disagreeable, being obliged to lie in them."

Very disagreeable. Sitting there in the truck in the August heat, I shivered.

I put the pamphlet down and scrawled a few notes: a description of the museum building, the hours, the contents. I reminded myself to make a point to mention the view of the river, and the one Adirondack chair. Maybe Scanesett would get two paragraphs after all.

Putting the pamphlet carefully in my briefcase, I headed back into the downtown. The road slipped between the brick buildings, stores and offices, coffee shops and video stores. There was a fire station and then a big metal factory building where they made shoes. The road east, and eventually to Prosperity, was to the left.

I took a right.

 The Chamber of Commerce office was closed, and the parking lot was deserted, except for a couple of punky-looking kids leaning against the wall of the hardware store. They were probably waiting to buy eightpenny nails so they could stick them through their lips.

I circled the block and meandered on until I came upon a three-story brick building that held the Scanesett town offices. Turning into the parking lot, I paused and looked, and drove a little farther. Outside the back door to the place, at the far end of the building, was a small glass-and-wrought-iron sign that said ''Police.'' There was a blue globe over a light. Just past the light, two police cars were parked against the building: one marked, a blue-and-white Chevy, and one unmarked, a Chevy in plain blue. I parked my truck next to the patrol car in a slot marked, ''12-minute parking.''

Plenty of time.

Inside, a short flight of stairs led to a glass partition, behind which sat a dispatcher. The glass had a metal disk in the center. I put my mouth close to it and spoke.

"I'm here about the bus," I said. "The guy who didn't make the bus."

The dispatcher was a balding man with glasses. He looked up at me but I couldn't tell if he had heard. Then he leaned toward the microphone on his console and his lips moved. I couldn't hear them, or read them, either.

But then a door swung open to my right. A big cop came out. Mustached. Silver hair. An arrogant smirk.

"You're a little late," he said, walking right up to me, chest first. I read his gold nameplate. Chief Dale Nevins. How unfortunate, I thought.

"Late for what?" I said.

He gave a little snort.

"For the bus *au* Canada."

He leaned closer.

"I don't smell booze, so it must have been a piece of tail," this Nevins said.

He gave me a conspiratorial wink, a good old boy of the first order, a dying breed.

"Hope she was worth it, mister—what'd the report say your name was? Mantis?"

"It's McMorrow."

"That isn't what the report—"

"I'm not the guy who missed the bus," I said, smiling as I broke the news.

Chief Nevins frowned.

"He said you were here because you—"

"I wanted to inquire about the guy who missed the bus."

"Who are you?"

"A reporter."

"Jesus. A reporter for what?"

"I freelance. I live in Maine but I string a little for the *Boston Globe*. I'm in town for something else and I just happened to be standing there when the bus came back short a passenger. I was wondering if they'd found him."

"Friggin' A," Nevins said. "That ain't news. Guy

latches on to some barfly and decides to bag his trip. They don't want to read about that in the goddamn *Boston Globe*.''

He gave me a dismissive wave and started backing toward the door.

''Oh, I don't know,'' I said, moving with him. ''I thought it was sort of interesting. Guy gets off a tour bus for lunch and disappears.''

''And tomorrow morning he comes to and looks across the pillow at some horror show and skedaddles out of town. Short story.''

''Maybe.''

He stopped backpedaling.

''What'd you say your name was?''

''Jack McMorrow.''

''You live around here?''

''Waldo County.''

''What're you after here? Besides the bus, I mean.''

None of your business, I thought.

''Oh, nothing much, Chief. What do you got?''

''Nothing at all. Things are quiet and that's the way I like 'em. The less I see of the goddamn media the better. Nine times out of ten, it's nothing but trouble.''

I smiled.

''No kidding. Must have some regular Woodwards and Bernsteins around here, huh?''

''They all want to be, in the beginning. We got a little paper here. Local rag, comes out on Tuesday. Gets these kids right out of grade school who think they're working for the goddamn *National Enquirer*. Until I straighten 'em out.''

''So the local paper will do the story on the guy who fell off the bus?''

''What story?''

''He hasn't turned up yet?''

''How the hell should I know? If he does, he probably won't be dragging his ass in here.''

"Unless he gets rolled," I said. "Or worse."

I looked around. There were some framed certificates of appreciation on the wall. The Lions Club. Rotary. A dusty glass-fronted case in which marijuana pipes and roach clips were displayed.

"Got some rough customers around here, I'll bet," I said.

"Nothing we can't handle," the chief said.

He reached for the doorknob, and a buzzer sounded. He pushed the door open.

"Chief, if you want Bell to talk to him, she's on her way in," I heard the dispatcher say. "She took the report."

The door started to swing closed.

"That isn't the guy from the bus. That's some goddamn reporter from the *Boston Globe* or some goddamn place. What do you got? Shit for brains? God almighty, sometimes I—"

The door closed.

"Have a nice day," I said, and sauntered outside to wait for Bell, so I could ask her a couple of questions. I wondered if she would have as delicate a sensibility. A piece of tail. Nice.

I stood by my truck, hoping that this Officer Bell would arrive before the sergeant came out and tried to engage me in further discussion of the media and its place in a democratic society. Leaning against the hood, I looked at the old pigeon-spackled building, watched the birds launch themselves from the third-floor pediments. I walked across the driveway and peered down through the trees toward the Kennebec, which was far below, at the bottom of a steep gully. This was below the dam, a stretch of rocky river that was more like what Arnold and his men had struggled against. I could barely see the water through the foliage, but the river was a presence here. Even when it couldn't be seen, it could be sensed, like the ocean in a town on the coast.

I decided that if Bell didn't come soon, I'd go find some

way for my readers to get close to that stretch of river.
After five minutes, I went back and sat in the truck. Five
more minutes and I turned on the radio. Started to take out
the pamphlet again. Put it back as the cruiser rounded the
corner of the building, drove up and parked beside me.

I got out and stood. The cop got out, too. I smiled. She
didn't.

"You're Officer Bell?" I said.

"What can I do for you?"

"I had a question about the bus. They told me you took
the report."

Bell came around the front of the car and stopped. She
was thirtyish, with flushed cheeks and wavy red hair that
looked unruly. Under her blue uniform shirt, even in this
heat, she wore a flak jacket. Apparently Bell took no
chances.

She looked at me.

"You the guy?" Bell said.

"No. I was standing there with Sandy from the Chamber
of Commerce when the driver came back looking for him.
I just wondered what happened. Did he turn up?"

"Why do you want to know?"

"Curious."

Her expression said that wasn't good enough.

"I'm a reporter. Freelance. My name's Jack McMorrow.
I was in town for another story."

"So you want to write about this, too?"

Her radio crackled a message in police code. I took it to
mean that she was wanted inside. She leaned to her shoulder mike and said "Ten-four," but didn't move.

"I don't know if I want to write about it," I said. "But
it is sort of interesting. If the guy hasn't turned up, where
is he?"

"What newspaper do you write for?"

"*Boston Globe,* once in a while. That's probably where
I'd pitch this, if it amounted to anything."

"We're not allowed to talk to the press," Bell said. "If were up to me, I would."

"I met your chief." I smiled.

Her eyebrows gave a little twitch.

"Yeah, well, that's the way it is."

"He didn't seem to think there was a story there, but I think there could be," I said. "The guy steps off the bus in this little town in Maine and disappears. Who is he? Where is he? As time goes by, it gets more curious, don't you think?"

I tried to sound amiable. Bell started to answer, then caught herself.

"What newspapers have you worked for? I mean, any in Maine or around here?"

"Well, the paper in Kennebec, the *Observer,* but that was only part-time. A weekly in Androscoggin. Most of my newspaper career was elsewhere."

"Oh, yeah? Like where?"

"Here and there."

I hesitated. Sometimes it was helpful to be more specific. Sometimes it wasn't. I took a chance.

"I ended up at the *New York Times.*"

Bell looked curious. Not impressed, just curious. She eyed me more closely.

"What'd you do there?"

"Reporter. Right in the city."

"Cover the cops?" she asked.

"Oh, yeah."

"Name one."

"One what? A cop?"

"Yeah."

"You think I'm making this up?"

Bell gave a little shrug. I grinned.

"If you don't believe me, that's fine. You don't have talk to me."

I stopped there, and waited. Bell eyed me, the way cops

do as they look for the telltale fidget, the barely visible quiver of guilt. And then she relaxed. I could see it in her eyes.

"I believe you," Bell said. "But I still can't tell you anything."

"The report is public record."

"Yup."

"I don't want to turn this into a big deal. I just want to know if the guy turned up."

"Off the record, Mr.—"

"McMorrow."

"Mr. McMorrow, if you tell anybody I told you, I'll call you a liar. No, he hasn't turned up."

"Got a name?"

"Off the bus list."

"Real name?"

"You tell me."

"What is it?"

"Mantis. P. Ray Mantis," Bell said slowly.

"P-ray-ing Mantis?"

She shrugged.

"A phony name?"

I don't know," Bell said. "Would you name your kid P. Ray Mantis?"

"Kids are stuck with a lot of foolish names. Their parents are self-indulgent. Address?"

"A town in Massachusetts that doesn't exist. Harkley or Harclay. Something like that."

"I guess it wasn't a woman," I said.

"What?"

"Your chief's theory. He got picked up. Shacked up somewhere. The bus guy, I mean."

"I don't know," Bell said. "The guy's just gone."

"Don't you think it's sort of strange?"

She started moving toward the door.

"Yup."

"How hard are you going to push it?" I asked, moving with her.

"I don't know."

"But you're not going to just file it."

"It's an active investigation," Bell said, one hand on the doorknob.

She paused.

"Give me your name and number."

"You gonna call me if there's a break in the case?"

"No. I just want to know where to find you, just in case. You ask an awful lot questions."

"It's an old habit," I said. "Kind of hard to break."

I took out my wallet and fingered through it until I found a card. It read, "Jack McMorrow. Prosperity, Maine," with my telephone number below it. Bell looked at the card, then unbuttoned the left-hand pocket on the front of her shirt and dropped the card in. I noticed she was wearing a gold wedding band on her left hand, but no diamond.

She held the doorknob again.

"One thing," I said quickly. "You know this guy named Robie, who rides the bike?"

"Yeah."

"What's his last name?"

"Robie Roberts?"

"Is Robie short for Robert? Robert Roberts?"

"No, I think it's just Robie."

"Nice name," I said. "Well, anyway, he was there when the bus came back and, I don't know. I'm not sure why I think this, but he seemed to know something. It was just, I don't know. It's hard to explain."

"What'd he say?"

"He didn't say anything. He just had this look."

"Robie always has that look," Bell said.

"No," I said. "He just seemed to be aware of something. I'd talk to him."

"You would."

''Well, yeah.''

''If you were me,'' she said, looking amused.

''Right,'' I said, as the door closed. ''And even if I were not.''

 The road home followed the river, at least until the town of Winslow, where the Kennebec continued to the southeast, on its tireless way to the sea. I veered to the southeast, passed through the little crossroads towns of East Vassalboro and South China, and skirting the south end of China Lake, joined the tourists on Route 3, the pipeline to Belfast and Bar Harbor.

I drove slowly, hanging to the right lane and letting the cars with the out-of-state plates—New York, Pennsylvania, Connecticut, New Jersey—zoom by in their frenzied rush to get to their camps and cottages, where they would screech to a halt and contemplate the serenity of nature. I was not in a hurry, because I knew nature would be waiting with open fields and dark woods, when I turned off the main road and made my way back into the hills that surrounded Prosperity.

It was a sleepy sort of hollow, the town where I lived. The natives ran a few farms, sold vegetables and milk, cut and hauled pulp and firewood. Some of them raised sheep or bees, sold jam and honey. Some sold off chunks of land to supplement their Social Security. Mostly they traded news of their children, who had moved far away. The hippies, who had landed here thirty years ago, were getting gray, and their children moved away, too.

In modern times, love of these poor, shadowed hills was not something easily passed from generation to generation.

It was a circuitous route that had taken me here. A decision here. Indecision there. Hesitation and a stumble on the treadmill that had taken me to the top of the newspaper world. If you stumbled, you didn't always get back on. If you retreated to the mill towns and hand-to-mouth hollows that had become my world since those days in New York, you were suspect. Heretical. The door didn't necessarily slam behind you, but it didn't stay open, either. And after a while, that old world became a gauzy memory. It was somebody else who had dogged those stories, wandered those streets. It was somebody else who had worked the phones frantically, who had schmoozed until the oil ran out of his pores. It was somebody else who wouldn't take no for an answer, ever, who had written clearly and concisely, who, at a succession of newspapers, always seemed to come out on top.

Almost always.

It was at the *Times* that my best just didn't seem to be the best. Everyone was driven, everyone was talented, everyone was very, very tough. And after a while—what was it, four years or five?—I realized I wasn't climbing anymore. When the executive editor came into the newsroom, when the editors and top-gun reporters huddled about something very big, I was at left at my terminal. I wasn't the go-to guy, as they said in sports. So I went. And I'd ended up here.

I didn't think about the old days very often, but that cop in Scanesett had awakened the ghosts. Detectives. Editors. Reporters. Acquaintances from the past. Men and women.

As I drove, they slipped back at random, the way memories do. A reporter named Wharton who didn't make it through his probation and went back whence he came. Miami, I thought. A woman I'd been with for several months.

Cassandra, but she was called Cassie. She had been very smart and very pretty, but underneath it all, she hadn't liked herself. I remembered her making love, all fits and false starts, as if she didn't even deserve that pleasure.

I shook my head.

They trotted through my head, all those people from the past, until I slipped them them off as I rolled through Prosperity village. There were a few trucks pulled up to the store, like horses hitched to posts. A couple of guys in green work clothes stood by the door. I waved. They recognized the truck and waved back.

I drove on. Enough socializing for one day.

My road was called the Dump Road, but the dump had been closed for years, traded for a place in the next town where trash was squished into containers and hauled off to be burned in a power plant near Bangor. That kept the road very quiet and in the past month, since the college kids had locked up their house and gone back home, it had been positively still.

I drove into the yard and shut off the motor, rolling to a stop by the shed. Sitting in the seat, I looked around and listened. Heard the hum of cicadas, the general buzz and chirp of the woods. After a moment, I got out of the truck and went inside.

The big room was cool. I went to the refrigerator and took out a can of ale, then checked my watch. It was four forty-six. I put the can back, adhering to my recent regimen. No ale before five or after seven. It was either that or no ale at all, if I wanted to live long. And I did, for any number of reasons.

I checked the answering machine, hit the button. One of those reasons had had called.

On the tape, Roxanne sounded weary, even more so than usual. I pushed number one on the speed dial do-jigger. It beeped. Rang. She answered.

"Hey," I said gently.

"Hey, baby," Roxanne said.

"Bad day?"

"Oh . . . yeah, I guess. It's a hundred degrees and humid. I don't know how people live in Florida."

I knew that wasn't what she meant.

"How is she?"

Roxanne took a breath.

"Not good. Not good. This morning she tried to leave the place. She did leave. She said she had to get her good clothes and she got halfway across the parking lot and, oh, God, she was in her nightgown and she was trying to get into these cars and she was headed for the road, which is like a highway and . . ."

She broke off. I heard the sob.

"I'm sorry. You want me to come down?"

"Oh, Jack, I don't know."

I could picture her fighting back tears.

"Jack, I got there and . . . and she was back in her room and, the nurses, they're so nice to her. The one, Janey, from St. Lucia? Oh, she's great. But . . ."

Roxanne paused again.

"Jack, she kept calling me Sarah. She thought I was her sister."

She sobbed again, deeper, just once.

"I'm saying, 'Mom, it's Roxanne. Mom, it's me. Roxanne.' And she's saying, 'Sarah, you didn't need to come. Where are the children? Does Peter have the children? You can't leave them alone in a hotel, you know.'"

Roxanne was crying.

"I'm sorry, honey."

"Oh, Jack, is this what it was all for? Is this what her life comes to, not knowing her daughter, lost inside her head? Oh, God."

"I'll come down. I can get a flight out of Portland in the morning, I'm sure."

She pulled herself together.

"No, I'll be okay. It was just a bad one. It's hard and it's your mother and I think, 'Well, where were you when she was okay?' All those years I missed. Damn it.''

Roxanne caught herself.

"Sometimes it just gets to me."

"I know it does. But I'll come. I can be there tomorrow."

"No, I'm all right. It won't be much longer."

"What'd the people in South Portland say? Did you talk to them today?"

"Yeah, a couple of weeks, maybe. No guarantees, though."

"Of a vacancy at all? Would it go to somebody else?"

"No, but I guess the person has to get bad enough that they have to go to the hospital. And you know how Alzheimer's is. It's hard to predict how fast it will progress. So they're not sure exactly when that'll be."

"But they're holding the place for you? For your mother?"

"Yeah, I guess. I don't know. It was hard to pin them down. I guess she's all set, that way."

"But you're not," I said.

"It's just hard. It's hard and I miss you."

"I could—"

"No. Just be waiting for me when I get back. Give me the biggest hug you've ever given."

"I will."

"Now, tell me what you've been doing. I need to hear about something else."

So standing there by the counter, I told her about my day. I'd told her I talked to Clair in North Carolina. He'd said he was ready to walk to Maine, gallbladder or no gallbladder.

"He doesn't like the heat, either," I said. "And he said the air-conditioning makes him feel like he's living in a milk cooler."

"Doesn't his daughter live in some sort of development?"

"Yeah. It's nice but all the houses look the same, I guess.

He said if he went for a walk, he'd take a hatchet and leave blaze marks on the little trees in the yards so he could find his way back.''

Roxanne almost chuckled. Almost. I continued talking before she could slide back down, telling her about the drive up the Kennebec to Scanesett. The old guy, Horace, at the museum. Sandy from the Chamber of Commerce. The man who jumped ship, except it was a bus.

"P. Ray Mantis?" Roxanne said.

"Yeah," I said. "Whoever he is, he has a sense of humor."

"Sort of an expensive joke. Don't you have to pay for those trips in advance?"

"I don't know. I suppose so. If I were going to write something, I'd find out. How did he pay? What kind of ID do you have to show? After all, they are crossing the Canadian border. They must have to document themselves somehow."

"You'd think," Roxanne said.

Her voice was brighter, at least for the moment. I went on.

"It was sort of an odd scene. Me and Sandy and this strange guy, I'd say he was in his twenties, sitting on a bicycle. And the bicycle was too small for him and it had some sort of equipment bolted to the back. So he's there, they call him Robie, and it sounded like everybody in town knew him."

"What was the matter with him?"

"I don't know. Maybe just slow or something. Because he didn't miss a word. And I said something, I don't know, that the guy couldn't just disappear, he had to be someplace, and this Robie turned and looked at me and, at least for that moment, he looked as sharp as anybody."

"Huh," Roxanne said.

"It was strange. Hard to explain. I tried telling this local cop there, a woman named Bell, and she didn't get it."

"She's probably known him for years. After a while, you stop seeing people."

"And this guy's part of the landscape," I said. "I don't know, but I can picture him scrounging cans and bottles and riding around this little town. Probably born there. Probably hasn't been twenty miles in any direction in his whole life. Whole family probably lives in the same block."

"Something to be said for that," Roxanne murmured.

I understood. It was guilt about always living so far from her mother. But they hadn't been close. For some reason, there had always been a barrier between them. From what I could tell, Roxanne's mother had been a little too self-centered, self-absorbed. When she snapped out of herself, her first reaction was to criticize whatever it was that her daughter was doing, saying or wearing. When Roxanne was able to get out of reach, she did. And now that she was back, it was too late. Her mother was gone.

"So what's next for your story?" Roxanne said.

"Well, I guess tomorrow I'll head downriver to the mouth of the Kennebec. I probably should have started there but I didn't. I'll go down to Popham and back. And I should make a run up to Québec City at some point. I had thought we could go. Spend a night at the Château Frontenac."

"That would have been nice."

She said it as though it were a dream. Nice to win the lottery, too. "I could wait for you," I said.

"No, you have to get it done, don't you?"

"A couple of weeks isn't going to make or break me," I said. "I'll leave that for last."

"It might be longer," Roxanne said.

"It'll be worth it."

"We'll see."

"I'll make sure the room is on the river side."

"We'll see."

"We'll find a great place for dinner. Walk on the promenade."

"We'll see."

"Veux-tu coucher avec moi?"

"Let me think," Roxanne said.

"You have to think?"

"About the French, I mean. How do you say in French?"

"Oui, certainement?"

"Non. Peut-être," she said.

"What do you mean, 'perhaps'?"

"Je joue très difficile obtenir."

I laughed. Roxanne did, too, and then seemed to catch herself. She sighed.

"I have to get ready to go back," she said.

"Call me when you get back tonight. And call me tomorrow in the truck."

"Oui," Roxanne said. *"Je t'aime."*

"I love you, too," I said, and we hung up.

At 5:11 P.M., the ale tasted good. I poured it into a chilled mug, and sat down at the big oak table. The table was spread with maps, a Maine atlas, books about Arnold and the Revolutionary War. I sipped and sat, then sipped again. I thought about Roxanne and her tears, and her mother, whom I'd met only once.

It had been three years ago, maybe four, at the airport in Boston. She had been en route to England from Washington and, for some reason, had ended up with a layover. I was in Portland with Roxanne, and when her mother had called from D.C., as if Portland, Maine, were a Boston suburb, I'd gone along. Karleena Masterson had not seemed pleased to meet her daughter's new beau. She had not seemed particularly pleased to see Roxanne.

We'd eaten dinner in an airport restaurant because she didn't want to let the airplane out of her sight. She complained about the airline food, the fat man in the seat next to her, the rambunctious children in the seat in front, the cost of taxis in Washington, where she'd been visiting a friend, crime in Florida, and the dampness in Massachusetts, though she hadn't set foot outdoors, how things hadn't been the same since Roxanne's father had died, and what had it been? Fifteen years?

Just as it occurred to her to ask about Roxanne's life, her flight had been called. Roxanne had gotten a cold peck on the cheek. I'd carried the bag.

"Well?" Roxanne had said as the plane took off with her mother, the fat man, and the rambunctious children on board.

"I don't know," I'd said diplomatically. "She didn't really ask how you were doing."

I still remembered what Roxanne had said.

"My mother is the most self-absorbed person I know. She doesn't even know me. And she doesn't even know that."

And now she didn't know Roxanne at all.

So it was a sad end to a sad story, but it was one of many. Happy endings were random occurrences, nothing more. When ants cross a road, some of them don't make it. A typhoon washes away a village on some island in Indonesia. A bus goes off the road in India. Mudslides kill ten thousand people at a whack in China and Bangladesh.

I sat there and sipped my ale, looked down at my books, maps and papers. Most of the men who followed Arnold up the Kennebec, across to the Dead River, through the frozen, trackless bogs, didn't live. They drowned. Froze to death. Died of starvation. Were shot down in Québec City, or wasted away on English prison ships delirious with fever. And none of them thought it would end like that, the only life they had.

Well, a life is sacred only to the person who happens to be living it. That's what it came down to, when you stripped away all of the elaborate myths and decorations. Some ants don't make it.

I sat and drank my ale, feeling myself slide down the chute into the blackness below. I heard Roxanne sobbing. I sighed. It occurred to me that this probably wasn't the best frame of mind to take into the *Historic Touring* story.

"For your next vacation, follow the trail of death!"

I grinned blackly. And the phone rang.

"Jack," a voice rang out. "It's Sandy."

She said it as if I should be elated to hear from her.

"Hi," I said.

"How are you?"

"Good," I said. "How are you?"

"Great. Just great. Hey listen, I'm truly sorry to bother you. What are you doing? Getting the kids supper?"

"No. Not really."

"Oh, I guess it is early."

"Right. And I don't have any."

"Don't have any—no children?"

She sounded incredulous. A virile guy like me.

"Gosh, well, I guess a lot of couples are waiting longer now. I had my first when I was nineteen. Three by the time I was twenty-three."

"That's nice," I said, taking another ale from the refrigerator. "How are they doing?"

"Good. Eleven, nine, and seven. They're at my ex's this week. He takes them a lot in the summer because they're with me a lot during the school year. The school bus works out better."

I pressed the receiver against my chest so she wouldn't hear the can whoosh open. When I put it back on my ear, Sandy was still going.

". . . fine, really. We were just too young, you know? Just kids. We didn't know what love was."

"Yeah," I said. "Well, that happens."

"Yes, it sure does. But hey, I didn't call to talk about my life."

Hey, why not? I thought.

"I called to talk about yours," Sandy chittered. "I talked to Hope Bell this afternoon. I had no idea I was talking to a national journalist."

"Yeah, well—"

"Hope told me. *New York Times*? I didn't know we had a celebrity coming through Scanesett."

"It was a few years ago. I've been in Maine six years now."

"Well, still," Sandy said. "I wouldn't have let you get away that easy. A guy who was a journalist at the *New York Times*? I said to Hope—I've known her since she was this little redheaded kid. I crack up every time I see her in her policeman's uniform. I said to her, 'Hey, that doesn't happen every day in Scanesett, Maine. A story in the *New York Times* would . . . ' "

She paused. Changed tack.

"Well, maybe I can help you more with your history story there. You know, Benedict Arnold came up the Kennebec right through our town. That's why we have the Arnold Motel. And the museum, it has stuff from when he came through. I'm not sure exactly what, but a picture of the museum and the motel."

"So what was Hope doing?" I interrupted. "Checking out my story?"

"Oh, no. I mean, she just—"

"That's okay. That's what she's supposed to do. It's her job."

"Well, she did ask if I'd talked to you. You know, where you were when the bus came back. I said, 'He was right here talking to me. If I'd known he was a national journalist, I would have held on a little tighter.' " She laughed.

"Uh-huh."

"You don't realize what a stir you made, Jack. Even Robie. He came by later, well, he didn't really come by. I was walking down Main Street and he came riding up and he said, 'Who was that guy?' I said, 'Robie, what guy?'

Because with him, you never know what he means. I mean, he's a little off the wall, no offense intended. The sister's a little more in tune with reality, but they're both sort of out there. Some gene thing, probably, what with both of them being—''

"What guy did he mean?'' I asked.

"Well, you, Jack. He said, 'Who was that guy?' I said, 'What guy?' He said, 'The guy you was talking to.' ''

Sandy said it in a low monotone.

"I said, 'That was a national journalist, Robie. And don't you ever interrupt me when I'm talking to someone on behalf of the Chamber.' Just because he knows you, he thinks he can ride right up on that crazy-looking bicycle and—''

"What else did he say?''

"Who, Robie? Oh, he wanted to know what you wanted. I told him it really wasn't any of his business, but you were in town to do a story for a national magazine. I told him to stay out of your way, too. He has this way of following people, just sort of always being there when you don't want him to be.''

I took a long swallow of ale.

"So then what happened, Sandy?''

She hesitated.

"Well, nothing really happened. Really. He just sort of jabbered away a little. Were you from Washington? You have to know Robie. Really. Did you have a car with license plates from another state? Then he started in with, 'Where is he now?' I said, 'Robie, if you bother Mr. McMorrow, I'll have your hide.' But he kept at it: He said, 'Where did he go?' I said, 'I don't know. He left. Do you see him here?' He said, 'Did he have a hearing thing?' Something like that. I don't know what he was talking about. I said, 'Robie, if you aren't out of here by the time I count to three, I'm gonna kick you where the sun don't shine.' ''

"So?''

"So he left. Got this real serious look on his face and pedaled off. I mean, you try to improve a town's image and then you've got people like Robie bothering everybody. What is some businessperson from some other town going to think when they see somebody like that, right on Main Street like he owns the place?"

"That Scanesett is a nice place that takes care of its own," I said.

Sandy didn't say anything for a moment, but when she spoke, she had regrouped.

"Right. It's a nice town. A lot of people from the city, they come here to the lakes or come up snowmobiling or passing through or whatever, and they tell me about the crime down there. They can't believe it when I say we never have a murder. Well, almost never. And then it's always somebody who knows the person. A husband killing a wife or something. There are no gangs in the schools. You don't have to worry—"

"What was it he said? The ear thing?"

She paused.

"Oh, Jack, I don't know. It's just Robie. I don't know. 'Did he have an ear thing like the guys on TV?' I told him—"

"Sandy," I said, "tell me something. Just one more thing about that. Did Robie ask about the guy on the bus? Whether they'd found him or he'd turned up?"

"Well, let me think."

She thought. I waited.

"No," Sandy said. "He didn't ask about that."

5

Roxanne called late that night. Her mother had eaten and then had slept. Roxanne said she had fallen asleep in the chair beside her mother's bed at the nursing home. I pictured the two of them there sleeping, mother and daughter, as close as they'd been in twenty-five years.

But Roxanne seemed better, so I felt better, too. I decided I wouldn't go to Florida; I'd drive south to the mouth of the Kennebec at Popham Beach. Then I'd work my way back up, looking for historic stuff along the way. That much was settled, so I went to bed early. I read about Arnold for an hour, about how he was politically pummeled by the radicals in the Revolution. And then I turned off the only light on the entire road, lay there in the dark, and thought, not about Roxanne or Benedict, but about Robie and the bus man.

Where was the guy? What was the "ear thing" Robie had asked about? Why would he ask if I was from Washington, D.C.? What did Robie know?

And then it was dawn.

I was ready to roll by five-thirty. It had clouded over during the night and the sky to the southeast was dark over the green bank of maples and oaks across the dirt road. Out behind the house, the leaves on the poplars at the edge of the field were fluttering, palms-up to the breeze. I brought my stuff out to the truck—camera, notebooks, tape recorder, bread and cheese—and went back in to close the windows. With only rain threatening, I didn't lock the door.

My first stop was the Prosperity General Store, where by twenty to six, some of the regulars were already in place. They stood outside the front door with foam coffee cups in their hands and rocked on their heels. When I pulled up to the gas pumps, a couple of them nodded. I got out and nodded back, and started pumping.

''Morning, boys,'' I said.

''How's Jack?'' one of them said.

He was an older man, a friend of Clair's. His hair was white under his red tractor-dealer cap, his shirt and work pants uniformly green.

''Fair,'' I said. ''How are you doing, Clarence?''

''Can't complain. Don't do no good. Speaking of no good, what do you hear of that carpetbagger?''

''Going batty,'' I said. ''Says the air-conditioning down there has him feeling like he's living in a milk cooler.''

That brought grins.

''I told him they were still smarting down there,'' Clarence said. ''He'd better keep his Yankee mouth shut or he'd be getting in trouble.''

''Leave it to a marine to get himself in a jam,'' one of the other men said. ''Have to get the army in and get him out.''

''He's outnumbered down there,'' Clarence said.

''Southerners?'' a younger, bearded guy said.

''Women,'' Clarence said. ''All his grandkids are girls. Mary and the daughter there. Won't be able to spit.''

''Well, you ain't allowed to spit, Clarence,'' the bearded guy said. ''And you're one to one.''

''Listen to 'em,'' Clarence said.

He smiled. I grinned back and went into the store and paid for the gas and a foam cup of tea. Virginia behind the counter said, ''Morning, Jack.'' I said, ''Good morning, Virginia.'' Back out the door, Clarence told me to ''keep it under eighty.'' I saluted and pulled out, and headed out of town. My town.

Five miles east, I took a right onto Route 3. It was start-ing to rain, a silvery mist that coated the roadway and showed tire tracks like snow. It was Saturday and the only traffic was a few early-rising tourists, starting the long trek home. They hurtled south, just as they'd hurtled north a week or two before. I hurtled with them, all the way to Augusta, where they swung west toward the interstate and home. I drove south, along the Kennebec and the past.

In Augusta, from the bridge, the river showed as a stream snaking through a wide but shallow trough of mud. It was low tide, even here, thirty-five miles from the ocean, and both the mud and the water were dark gray. The shore was tree-lined and there were stone cairns every few hundred yards, little islands of piled rock that dated to the days when logs were floated down the river in rafts and the stone pil-ings were used to store and guide them.

I followed the road along the west side of the Kennebec, past the capital building, massive and stately under its golden dome. The road led past government offices, de-serted on weekends, and car dealers and pizza shops. I drove south to Hallowell, the entire main street of which was lined with antiques shops and restaurants. The history buffs would like this, I told myself, and as I coasted slowly through, I took notes on the cassette recorder.

A haven for antiquers. The perfect place to spend a rainy day. Don't miss Hallowell, one of Maine's best-known an-tiques centers. And be sure to examine the high-water mark on Main Street.

As I shut off the recorder, I thought of Sandy—"and then there's the car show"—and winced. Was this what I had come to?

But I swallowed hard and things looked up. Below Hal-lowell, tucked against the bushes, was a peeling sign mark-ing the Arnold Trail. It showed cartoonish men getting off their sloops here and climbing up the riverbanks with their guns. I noted that, and big nineteenth-century mansions overlooking the river in Gardiner. The riverside brick buildings in Gardiner had the look of a medieval walled city, with pigeons clinging to steeply pitched roofs. A few sailboats swinging on moorings in the brackish water gave the town the look of an odd little port.

And then it was over the concrete bridge at Gardiner and down the river on the east side. I noted the big antiques dealers, with their gold-lettered signs and meticulously restored Federal-period houses. Just the thing for people who read *Historic Touring*.

I meandered south through Pittston, past trailers, woods, hilly pastures with knobs of sheep. There was supposed to be an Arnold museum along there and I found it, in a vintage red colonial house once owned by Major Reuben Colburn. I pulled into the driveway and stopped. The sign said the house was built in 1765. It didn't say that Arnold thought the boats built by Colburn, heavy *bateaux* made of green pine, were junk, that they leaked like sieves.

The place looked closed but I got out and walked around, peered in the windows. There was a display of old stuff in a glass case. I could make out powder horns. What looked like arrowheads. The next window faced a massive fireplace, fronted by a pine harvest table.

I told my tape recorder, ''The historic tourers will love this.''

But as I walked around the yard in the mist, looked out on the river, which swept past far below, I began to feel something. I felt a reverence for the past, for the people who had lived here before. I felt like I was more than a hired gun, a shill enticing tourists to shops and restaurants. I was viewing history. Reaching back and touching the past.

So as I drove on, hugging the river, I saw more than just trailers and fields and trucks in yards. I saw woods where Arnold and his men had seen woods. I saw the river, a rippling presence behind the trees, where Arnold and his men had ridden up on the tide. I felt an odd sense of wonder.

Maybe I was turning into one of those old coots.

Me and Horace. Peas in a pod.

I drove south to Dresden, right along the river, and it started to rain, big drops that flicked the leaves like rifle shots. The woods were more dense here, and the Kennebec appeared suddenly, through clearings, behind houses. Then the river disappeared again, and there was a blue state sign that pointed to a historic place. It was something called Pownalborough Courthouse, 1761. Spanking new when Arnold came through. I turned.

The drive was lined with beautiful old maples. It ended in front of a massive three-story colonial house, bristling with chimneys, with windows of old rippled glass. I put on a hat and jacket, got out of the truck and walked up to the sign. It said the courthouse opened at ten o'clock. It was eight-fifteen, so I read and then walked some more.

It was the courthouse and tavern for Lincoln County and first owned by a Major Samuel Goodwin, a grand place at a time when settlers were hacking their homesteads out of the woods. I looked in the window and saw displays of colonial-era clothes and boots and shoes. I tried the door. It was locked.

Out back, there were massive pines and hemlocks, direct descendants of the trees used to build this place. The clearing was still, except for the rain, and the river below was patterned with the drops. I turned and looked the place over again, then went back to the truck.

I meant to turn around and keep going, but then I noticed that the drive didn't end beyond the house. Twin tracks continued on into the woods, and I put the truck in gear and followed them. The tracks grew fainter and the road narrower and branches scraped the sides of the cab. It was darker in the woods, and as I drove, I wondered if there would be a turnaround, whether I'd have to back out the whole way. And then, behind big white pines, was an old stone wall. Behind the wall was a cemetery.

There was a rusty iron gate but it was chained and locked, so I put a hand on the top of the waist-high wall and vaulted over. Inside, the grass was tangled and oak saplings grew up between the stones. The saplings were ten and twenty years old. The graves dated to the early nineteenth century.

I walked from stone to stone, my hands folded in front of me. There were Johnsons. Goodwins. The son of the major died when he was thirty-four, in 1838. It seemed 1838 was a bad year. Several people had died, including a little girl named Angelina, who was two. I looked at her stone and then back at the woods. I pictured the family, what was left of it, walking down that same path from the big house, carrying her tiny coffin.

Somebody had said prayers and then they'd lowered the little girl into the ground and covered her up. I pictured the silent walk back to the house. Perhaps one of them—a mother, a father—had remained at the grave after everyone else had left. Maybe it was then that they had broken down and cried.

I thought of Roxanne and her mother. I thought of my mother, with a stone of her own in Manhasset, New York. I thought of myself as a little boy, of Roxanne as a little girl. It was troubling, all this mortality, all the flailing we do in our short time on the planet.

A wind had come up off the river, and the water came down from the branches in little showers. I looked at Angelina's mossy stone, then up at the trees. I looked behind me, past the truck and into the woods. I looked up into the trees again.

It was silent, but it wasn't. I listened. Heard the tree sound. The rain. I felt like there was something just beyond my hearing. I felt a chill. I felt like being there was some sort of sacrilege.

I turned slowly and walked back to the wall. Eased my way over and got back into the truck. Looked around the dark woods once more, and backed the truck all the way out.

This place would not be mentioned in *Historic Touring*.

•   •   •

The road followed the Kennebec south, the river always a presence. Above the shipbuilding city of Bath, it was too my right; below Bath, to my left. Talking into the tape recorder as I drove, I described the pale green wild-rice shores of Swan Island, where the Abenaki Indians watched Arnold's ships pass, and the spread of Merrymeeting Bay. I noted a narrow sluiceway called The Chops, and Day's Ferry, another colonial village. Then I crossed the metal bridge into Bath, where moored boats were all turned downriver into the incoming tide. I described the steeples and cranes, the towers on the frigates in the shipyard, the Maine Maritime Museum.

It wasn't Arnold but, hey, they were on vacation.

From Bath, I followed Route 209 down the Phippsburg peninsula. The shore of the river was all rock here, with channels cut between little spruce-topped islands. The tide was running now, and you could see the power of it as it moved up the reaches and around the heads. It was entrancing and I had to force myself to notice the colonial houses, the bed-and-breakfasts.

I frowned and pictured the paycheck.

And then there was the ocean, or at least signs of it. Campgrounds with pickups and campers. Painted lobster pot buoys hanging on signposts. Cars with kids who wanted to be at the beach. And the beach itself.

The lot at Popham Beach was mostly empty in the rain. I parked close to the outhouses, and used one, which was smelly inside. Then I walked down the path through the asters and bayberries and scrub oaks and pines and there was the ocean, the point Arnold had found with his little flotilla. Now it was marked with a lighthouse, on Seguin Island, three miles offshore. I stood on the gray-sand beach and watched the tide rips, the waves cresting a sandbar from both directions. I walked with the rest of the beach-combers, and plovers and sandpipers scuttled away from me. I could have stayed for hours, watching the ocean, but the business called.

The check.

Fort Popham was around the point, an empty stone shell built for the Civil War. The sign said there was a British emplacement here in 1775 but the British burned it. I read the sign and then made room for a family in yellow slickers and black rubber boots. They gave up quickly, though, and I was left to watch the tide and the lobster boats, and a big sailboat with rich people on it.

And then I talked into the tape recorder some more and went back to the truck. I turned the key. The motor ticked. The phone rang.

"Hey," I said.

"Where are you?" Roxanne said.

"Fort Popham."

"How is it?"

"Damp and sort of dreary," I said, as a lobsterman in a truck gave me and the phone the eye. "How are you?"

"Okay. Better," Roxanne said.

"How is she today?"

"Okay. We had breakfast. She knew me, but she keeps saying she wants to go home."

"Oh, boy."

"Yeah. But we'll get through it. I'm better than yesterday. I wouldn't have called, because I know these calls are expensive. But I wanted to make sure you knew that."

"I did, but I'm still glad you called."

"You lonesome?" Roxanne asked.

"I don't know. A little. I'm not sure I'm doing this right. You think I'm supposed to be checking the sheets in bed-and-breakfasts?"

"Not without me."

"Okay. I'll tell the editor that. I have to bring my sheet checker."

I paused.

"You okay?" Roxanne asked.

"I'm supposed to be asking that. But yeah, I'm fine. It's just—do you ever have that feeling that you don't quite know what you're doing? I saw some interesting places today. The house where the guy lived who had Arnold's boats built. The *bateaux.* It's a museum, but it was closed.''

"Huh.''

"I don't know. I guess my mind's not a hundred percent on this. Part of me's somewhere else.''

The lobsterman, small but hard, with a drinker's flush, started loading traps into his truck.

"I'd like to be somewhere else,'' Roxanne said.

"We could both be somewhere else together.''

"Soon.''

"Yup.''

"I've got to go,'' Roxanne said. "Where are you off to from there?''

"I don't know,'' I said, but in the back of my mind, I knew that wasn't true.

6 It took me two hours to get to Scanesett, twenty minutes to spot Robie.

I saw him as I pulled out of McDonald's, where I'd bought a cup of tea. He was in the right lane on the main drag, off to the side, and cars and trucks were swerving around him. Probably the story of his life.

He was pedaling hard, up a long grade, and his big legs were whirling. Behind his bike, he was towing some sort of homemade cart. The cart had red lights, but they were painted on. So was the license plate, which said ''Maine'' above what appeared to be randomly selected numbers. It was raining, not hard but a heavy drizzle, and the spray from his back tire had made a dark, wet splotch running up the back of his shirt.

I followed him, pulling up close, then dropping back. But he was going too slow for the traffic and soon the cars and trucks were swerving to pass me, too. I sped up and went by him, but he didn't seem to notice me, just stared straight ahead under his baseball hat. Watching him in the rearview mirror, I drove for a few hundred yards, then pulled off into the lot of an auto parts store. I waited, waited some more, and then there he was, flashing by in the mirror. After a five-count, I backed out and followed.

The next time I passed, he seemed to turn his head. I thought he'd glanced at me, and then, in the mirror, the bike and cart suddenly swerved left and crossed the road, slipping between the cars and down a side street.

''Whoops,'' I said.

I turned around in the parking lot of an insurance office, then waited for traffic to break so I could pull back out. When I turned down the side street, Robie wasn't in sight. It was a short dead-end street with small, closely set bungalows and an old factory building at the end. Coasting slowly, I looked in the yards and driveways for the bike, and got stares from a woman, a couple of kids. I drove on, into the dirt parking lot of the factory, which was half filled with cars and pickups. Made a loop. Saw a path through the brush.

It wasn't a dead end, after all.

The path paralleled the main drag. I pulled back out and drove north, slowly in the left lane. Cars passed me on the right as I peered down the next two side streets, and then the road veered and there weren't any more turnoffs until I came to a shopping center. I turned in.

It was called the Scanesett Mall, but it was really just a

supermarket and a discount store linked by a row of shops, some dingy, some vacant. I drove to the supermarket end and turned on to an access road that led out back behind the building. When I got to the corner, I stopped the truck. Then pulled out.

There were Dumpsters, piles of broken pallets, unmarked metal doors leading to the shops. I eased the truck along, thinking that he could have stopped at a house. He could be in a garage. He could be out in the woods.

And there he was.

The bike was parked. Robie was picking through a pile of junk, his back to me. He turned with a piece of metal in his hand. Looked at me and froze. I stopped the truck. He leaped on his bike and went by me, cart and all.

"Robie," I called out the window.

He stood up on the pedals.

I put the truck in gear and followed, and then he turned down a path through the sumac scrub. The cart bounced and he was gone.

"What's his problem?" I said.

I drove back out to the front parking lot, and out on to the road, back the way I had come. At the first side street, I slowed and looked. Nothing.

At the next street, I looked again. Still no sign of him. I drove on and then there he was, crossing the road five hundred yards behind me, and disappearing from sight.

I drove a couple of more blocks, then turned left. At the first cross street, I stopped and sat. Cracked open the plastic top on my tea and sipped. Sipped again. And there he was again, a block down. I followed.

Robie wound through the streets, slipped through a trailer park that had front and rear entrances. I didn't pursue him, but drove in the general direction he seemed to be taking, which was back toward the center of downtown, back toward the river. Just when I thought I'd lost him, he would reappear, bent to his bike, legs churning.

I drove slowly on until I hit East Street, where the police

station was. I drove past it, looking to my left and then took a left, in the direction from which Robie would be coming. The sign said Covey Street, which turned out to be two rows of run-down houses, with the occasional big Victorian chopped into apartments. I looked left and right, up the driveways.

And saw the cart disappear.

It had gone around the corner of the building. I stopped the truck and backed up. Got out and looked the place over. Broken windows on the first floor. Rotting steps. There was some bamboo-looking stuff growing up along the foundation and, in the thicket, was a shopping cart.

I looked up. In the two third-floor windows on the front there were screens, the kind you prop under the sash. In the right window, somebody moved. I hesitated, but only for a moment, then started up the driveway.

The bike was there, parked just around the corner. The backyard was piled with bicycle parts, wheels, frames, chains, sprockets, all old and rusted, all neatly stacked. The back stairs ran up the outside of the building, with a little open porch at each back door. There were wooden railings with rungs, many of which were broken out. Some sections were patched with plywood, but not many. It was not a place for small children.

I went up the stairs to the first landing. Bicycle wheels— spokes and mags—hung on nails driven into the wall. There were cartons of empty bottles on the floor, most of them dirty, the kind scrounged from roadsides.

I considered the door. A broken window with cardboard instead of glass. A hasp that hung loose. I walked over and listened. There was nothing. No appliance hum. Nothing. I looked up the stairs, then started up.

The second-floor landing was more of the same. Bike parts. More bottles. Pizza boxes stacked like record albums. Names scribbled on the clapboards with crayon.

Nobody I knew.

The door was shut, with a sheet held tight over the window. There was another window to the right of the door and that was covered with a sheet, too. I leaned toward it, then decided it would be better to just knock. There are places where peeking in windows can get you shot. This felt like one.

I knocked three times on the wood, just below the glass. The door felt old and loose and made a rattling noise that resonated like a snare drum. I waited. Thought I heard something. Knocked again. This time I made it four.

"Hey, Robie," I said.

I listened. I thought I heard a slip. A single shuffle.

"Hey, Robie. This is Jack McMorrow. I was with Sandy at the bus stop."

I paused.

"Hey, man, I didn't mean to sneak up on you like that out behind the store. I saw you riding by and I just wanted to ask you if you'd heard anything about the guy. The guy who got off the bus. I didn't mean to startle you."

The tip of a finger slipped around the far edge of the sheet on the window to the right of the door. The dark opening widened. I kept talking.

"So Robie, have you heard anything? I'm just curious. I thought I'd write something for the newspaper about the guy. That's what I do. I'm a newspaper reporter. I thought it might make—"

The doorknob, a brown ceramic-looking knob, began to turn.

"—a good story. Maybe not, but I figured I'd at least look into—"

There was a click and the door began to open.

"—it and see what it was all about."

The door opened. It was a woman. Young and heavy.

"He ain't here," she said.

"Oh, I saw his bike. I thought—"

"He's got lots of bikes. He took another one."

Her face was plain and round, just a face. No makeup

or earrings. The sleeve of something that looked like a white T-shirt. A haircut that could have been Robie's. Her eyes, which were small and brown, showed fright bordering on panic.

"I didn't mean to scare him," I said. I smiled gently.

"You didn't scare him."

"Good, because the way he took off, and I just wanted to talk to him, I just thought I'd scared him or something."

"He just was late."

"For dinner?"

"No. For . . . he was just late. Late for something."

I moved closer, so I was almost between the door and the jamb.

"I hope I didn't make him late. I didn't want to bother him. But Sandy said he was asking about me. She said he had some questions. Maybe I could answer them myself."

She looked like she might fall backward. Her sneakered foot appeared. They were old sneakers. But white. Beyond her, the apartment was dark but I could smell something cooking. Something like bacon. Or sausage.

"I'm Jack McMorrow. Are you Robie's sister?"

"Hi. I mean, yeah. But you can't come in. I'm busy."

"I'm sure. I didn't mean to barge in on you. I was just wondering if Robie had heard anything about the guy on the bus. You know, the guy who they were looking for. Me and Robie were right there when the bus guy came running out. He was all upset. It was kinda funny. Did he tell you about—"

"No," she said. "I mean, they don't know. He left."

"Who?" I said.

"Who?"

"Who left? Robie?"

"The man on the bus."

"Robie didn't leave?"

"No. I mean, he, uh, had to go."

"Because he was late?"

"Yeah."

I smiled.

"So did Robie hear anything since we left the parking lot yesterday? I guess he hears a lot of things, being out and about the way he is."

"No, he doesn't hear anything."

I smiled again.

"Well, gee, I'm sorry I missed him. And I'm sorry if I scared him. What's your name?"

"My name?"

She looked at me as if it were a nonsensical question.

"Yeah," I said.

I waited.

Her eyes went left and right, as though she were looking for help.

"Um, my name's Rob-ann."

"Huh," I said. "That's a nice name. Is your father named Robert or something, and that's how you got to be Rob-ann and Robie?"

"No," Rob-ann said. "He's dead."

"Oh. I'm sorry."

Her eyes were darting more now, mostly to her left. I figured Robie was against the wall beside the door. I was beginning to get the feeling that he didn't want to talk to me.

"Listen, Rob-ann," I said. "When Robie gets back could you give him my card?"

I fished one from my pants pocket. It was bent but legible. She peered at it, turned it over and turned it back, then peered at it some more. Then she looked up at me.

"He can call collect. Or he can call me in my truck. Let me write that number down for you."

I reached for the card and she flinched, pulling back. Then she understood and held the card out for me. I took it and wrote the number, holding the card to my leg. I handed it back. She reached for it and I heard something from inside the door.

A sniff.

Rob-ann's eyes went wide.

I looked at her and smiled.

"It's okay," I said. "He doesn't have to talk to me if he doesn't want to. I just thought the two of us kind of came in on this thing together. And I heard he had questions. I was passing through, that's all. I'll catch him next time."

"Um, well, I don't—"

"Tell him to call me if he changes his mind. Or I'll stop by again. I live in Prosperity. Waldo County. I've lived there for years. I'm harmless. It's no big deal, either way."

But Rob-ann's eyes, unblinking, riveted to mine, told me it was. For some reason, it was.

I figured Hope Bell would work Saturdays and her chief would stay home. I was right.

It took a half hour but I finally spotted the Scanesett police cruiser on East Street, just beyond the downtown. It was coming toward me and I flashed my lights. Bell turned in a driveway and came after me. I pulled into a little park with wrought-iron gates and lawns that, like everything else around here, overlooked the river. Bell followed and we both got out and stood in the rain, which had subsided to a drizzle. I leaned against the cruiser fender. Some cops didn't like it when you did that. If Bell minded, she didn't say anything.

"I just wanted to ask you, did you talk to Robie?"

"No," Bell said. "I've been busy. And he wasn't on the top of my list."

"I just tried to and he bolted like a rabbit. Then I stopped at his apartment and his sister barely opened the door. She was petrified. She tried to tell me he wasn't there, but he was. He was hiding."

"Well, Mr. McMorrow, you know they aren't the most polished people around. And you're a stranger."

"He didn't seem to mind when we were in the parking lot. He was right in the middle of it. Sandy Chamber of

Commerce had to chase him off. And he's always riding around town. It's not like he's some kind of recluse.''

"But he's not a back-slapper, either," Bell said.

"I didn't want him to join the Rotary Club. I just wanted to ask him if he'd heard anything.''

"Why?''

"Because.''

It sounded more flip than I'd intended, so I grinned. Bell tried not to, but she smiled, too.

"Because why?" she said.

"Because I was curious. And because he's been asking about me.''

"Asking who?''

"Asking Sandy. Who I am. Do I have an ear thing like the guys on TV?''

"What's that mean?" Bell asked.

"I don't know. Maybe the *Times* stuff in his mind means Dan Rather or something. And he wanted to know if I was from Washington, what kind of plates I had on my car. I think the guy knows something.''

"So you went over and demanded to know what it was?''

"I didn't demand. I asked. I made myself available for an interview. And I did everything I could to calm old Rob-ann there, but when I left, she was still bug-eyed. Something's going on there.''

"Whatever you say, McMorrow. Maybe we ought to deputize you and give you a badge.''

"Nah, then I'd have to have a warrant or probable cause or something. A reporter can go more places.''

"I thought you were writing about Benedict Arnold," Bell said.

"I write about anything that seems halfway interesting. I did Arnold stuff this morning.''

"And now you're working your second job?''

"There's a story here," I said.

"Maybe.''

The drizzle seemed to strengthen. There were droplets on Bell's red hair. She seemed to be mulling something.

"You might want to call the bus company," Bell said, looking away. "Off the record, see if they'll tell you how this guy paid for his ticket."

"Cash?"

"Nope."

"Stolen credit card?"

"Nope. A check. It bounced."

"From what bank?"

"A little savings bank in Gardiner."

"Gardiner, Maine?"

"Yeah."

"But the bus company, where are they?"

"Boston."

"But he's from Gardiner?"

"I didn't say that. I said the check was from that bank."

"What name was on it?" I asked.

"Same name. Mantis. P. Ray Mantis."

"So that's really his name?"

Bell looked at me.

"I didn't say that, Mr. McMorrow."

She looked away again, as if that made her tip more confidential.

"Phony address on the checks. Nobody by that name in the phone book. I asked the Gardiner P.D. to check. The street's real but the number is wrong. One of the detectives down there knew a guy, he's lived on the street for forty years or something. He called him and the guy never heard of any Mantis."

I smiled.

"So he planned this. Didn't he have to show ID at the bank?"

"The bank's closed on Saturday. I'm gonna check Monday."

"I think they need a driver's license," I said. "And a Social Security card. Don't you think so?"

Bell shrugged.

"Maybe they were phony, too."

"God," I said. "If that's the case . . . why would he do all that, and then step off a tour bus up here?"

"Wanted to disappear, I guess."

"There are easier ways than that. You just get in your car and get on the interstate and keep going. How did he get to Boston to get on the bus? He'd have to leave a car or have somebody drop him."

"I don't know, McMorrow," Bell said.

She looked at me and smiled. It occurred to me that she had an interesting face. The hair and the green eyes and a quiet, small-town confidence.

"Maybe he took a bus," she said.

Bell turned toward her car, then turned back.

"All of that is off the record, right?"

"Right."

"You didn't hear it from me, or from 'one police officer' or anything like that. A reporter tried pulling that one on me and I got reamed out like you wouldn't believe. 'One police officer.' That day there was only one police officer. So no games?"

"I don't play games," I said. "Not that kind."

"Good," Bell said.

She opened the cruiser door and got in. Buzzed the window down.

"So," I said. "If I were you, I'd—"

"Right, McMorrow. I'll see what I can do."

She paused. A garbled voice blurted something on her radio and she turned it down, then looked at me again, started to say something. Just then the phone rang in the truck.

"Car phone. Must be nice," Bell said.

"I deduct it," I said.

I went to the truck and she backed the cruiser away, toward the street. I pulled the truck door open and grabbed the receiver off the dash.

"Hello," I said, standing there untangling the cord.
There was no answer.
"Hello?"
Still nothing.
"Hello," I said, one last time.
I listened.
And then I heard something.
A sniff.

"Robie?" I said.
   For a moment, there was no reply. Then another sniff.
"Yeah," a voice said. It was low. Hesitant.
"This is Jack McMorrow."
"Yeah?"
"How are you?" I said.
"Um," Robie said. "Good."
"So what's happening? I didn't mean to startle you when you were on your bike."
"Yeah, well, I wasn't scared."
"Good. I didn't mean to sneak up on you. I just couldn't catch you. You sure move on that bike."
"Yeah."
"Find anything good back there?"
"No," Robie said.
" 'Cause I interrupted you?"
"No."
I waited.

"There wasn't anything good. No aluminum."

"That's what you were looking for?"

"It's lighter. For trailers and stuff."

"You make those, huh?"

"Yeah. Some."

He didn't say anything.

"So, Robie," I said, "I heard you had some questions about what I do or something. I'd be glad—"

"No," Robie said.

" 'No,' what?"

"No, you don't have to come here any more."

"I don't?"

" 'Cause I was just wondering, that's all."

"Wondering what?"

"I was just wondering. Before I was just wondering. You don't have to come over."

"Well, I don't mind. We could meet someplace else. Have a cup of coffee or a Pepsi or something. I'm still in town. I could just meet—"

"No," Robie said, a little more agitated. "I don't want to talk. I . . . no comment. I gotta go."

"Okay," I said, and then I covered my other ear and listened.

There was a clattering noise.

"I told him," I heard Robie say.

Another clatter. Then Robie, again.

"I told him to stay away from here."

And then Rob-ann.

"How was that?" she was saying.

The phone went dead.

I sat up the street from Robie's building for twenty minutes and watched. The bike and cart were still in the backyard, but there was no movement, no sign of life. It was late afternoon and still raining and the second-floor apartment was still dark. Finally, at four-thirty, there was a faint blue television glow. So they were in there. From the truck, I called the Scanesett police and left a message for Officer Bell.

"Could you ask her to call Jack?" I told the man on the phone, leaving both my numbers. "Yes, she'll know what it's regarding."

But Bell didn't call, so I only had myself to ask the question: Who was Rob-ann talking to? Who was the third person in the apartment?

I assumed Robie had called from home. He'd told me to stay away from "here." And then as the receiver jiggled in the cradle, Rob-ann asked, "How was that?" Would she have asked Robie that? Or was she asking him how the conversation had gone? Maybe he hadn't wanted to call and she had wanted him to, and she had meant, "How was that?" As in, "That wasn't so bad, was it?"

It was possible. But I didn't think so.

As I followed the gray river south, past the massive paper mill at Hinckley, past the brick blocks of Waterville and across the bridge, my mind revolved, turning around and around but always stopping at the same place. What if it was Mantis? What if he was in there?

Through the mill town of Winslow and on toward the coast, I drove slowly and absently, going over everything Robie had done.

He'd behaved oddly when the bus driver had come off the bus, but then he behaved oddly most of the time. His questions to Sandy had been odd, but were they out of character? It had been hard to tell from what Sandy had said, but it seemed to me that Robie was more of a silent presence, someone who loitered on the edge of things but didn't insert himself into the action.

That might explain why he'd been so uncomfortable on the telephone. Maybe Robie just didn't like this kind of direct scrutiny. Maybe he was just embarrassed that Sandy had passed his questions on to me.

Or maybe not.

"How was that?" Rob-ann had said.

I mulled it over and over, and by the time I turned off Route 3 and headed up through the glistening green hills, I'd decided I just didn't know enough. I didn't know Robie and his sister well enough to judge their behavior. I didn't even know who Mantis was, or what his reason was for stopping in Scanesett. Maybe he was just nuts?

I'd done a story at the *Times* about a man who rode Greyhound buses all over the country. He was in his twenties, on disability for some sort of mental handicap, but he could read bus schedules like brokers scan the board. Every month he'd set out from the Port Authority, and he'd ride all over the country, sitting there in his seat, watching the landscape roll by, quiet and content. No luggage. No money. No destination.

Sanity was a relative thing.

And then a year or so later, his landlady had called to tell me he'd been murdered outside a bus station in Texas. Austin or Houston. I couldn't recall which.

I'd written that story, too.

And I'd like to write this one but I had a feeling it still was unfolding. On Monday, I'd call the *Globe*. If Tom Wellington, the New England editor, was interested, I'd call the bus company and the bank. I'd talk to the Gardiner cops and get Bell's chief to say something for the record. The "piece of tail" quote would be a nice touch.

But this was Saturday night, early. Monday seemed a long way off. I pulled into the yard, shut off the truck, and went inside to start counting the minutes.

Roxanne had called, just to say hello. I took an ale from the refrigerator and went to the counter and dialed the number in Florida. It was busy. I shuffled through the papers next to the phone and found the number in North Carolina. I dialed that one and it rang and Mary answered.

"Mary, this is Jack," I said.

"Jack, dear," Mary said. "Good to hear your voice. We miss you."

"Me, too."

"How's the road?"

"Quiet," I said.

"Oh, it must be. You must be getting lonesome. Roxanne still in Florida?"

"Yeah. For a couple of more weeks, anyway."

"How's her mother?"

"Well," I said. "Not very good. Rox is waiting for the room to open up at the place in South Portland. Then at least she can get back to her life."

"Oh, that's sad," Mary said. "That's so sad. You never know what life has in store for you, do you?"

"No," I said. "You don't."

"That Alzheimer's is a terrible thing."

"Yes, it is. It's very hard."

"And we take so much for granted, don't we, Jack? Our health, our families. I look at these grandchildren and I just want to squeeze them. They get sick of me pawing at them, but I just want to hold on to every minute."

"How are they doing?"

"Good. They're beautiful. And Susan and Jeff are taking great care of you know who."

Mary hesitated.

"Well, I think he's a little down in the dumps. It'll cheer him up to talk to you. You give my love to Roxanne. Tell her we'll all get together before the summer's over."

"I will."

So she told me to "take care of yourself, dear," and went to get Clair. I waited and sipped my ale, stared out at the rain.

"Goddamn high-tech phones. Shoving these things in your face. How's a man supposed to get any sleep around here?"

"A real man wouldn't be lying around in bed at five in the afternoon," I said. "What you won't do to get out of doing your chores. There was nothing wrong with that gallbladder and you know it."

"Sure there was," Clair said. "When I get back I'll

show you. I've got it in a jelly jar on the mantle.''

''God, what a showboat,'' I said. ''I suppose you're inviting neighborhood kids in to look at it.''

''Not for free. Costs them a dollar. Little monsters.''

''Except your grandchildren.''

''Well, they're perfect,'' Clair said.

''Take after their grandmother.''

''No doubt. How goes the battle?''

''How goes yours?'' I said.

So Clair told me everything was fine, that he was being waited on hand and foot, moving a little slow but that would pass. I could hear a television in the background and he sensed that I could hear it, and he seemed embarrassed.

''I couldn't read anymore,'' he said. ''My eyes were dropping out of my head.''

I felt bad, like I'd walked in on him in the bathroom. But also, I felt like I was seeing a chink in the armor of my ex-marine friend. Clair was rarely ill, almost never discouraged. Now he seemed to be both. Nothing like sickness to make somebody seem old.

''So how's my girl?'' he said.

''She's okay. It's getting to her, though.''

''You tell her that if I was able, I'd be down there helping her.''

''I will. But there's nothing anybody can do.''

''Stinks,'' Clair said.

''Yup.''

''Well, when these things all settle down, we'll have a rip-roarer.''

''Three ales instead of two?''

''You betcha,'' Clair said, but it seemed forced.

He asked about his house and barn and I said they were fine. He asked if I'd been having any trouble starting the tractor and I said, no, and the mower bar was working fine. He asked if the asparagus was done for the year and I said, yes, just about. He asked if it looked like the apples were doing well, and I said yes to that, too.

Then I told him about my trip down to the mouth of the Kennebec and he perked up. Clair knew about Arnold like he knew about a lot of things, and he asked if I knew that it was politics that had spoiled Arnold's bid to take Québec. I did but I let him tell me anyway. The politicians had hemmed and hawed so much that Arnold didn't get started until October, he said.

"That's what got him caught in the cold," Clair said. "Six weeks earlier, and Québec would be the fifty-first state. The French up there wanted us. Politicians were mucking things up for soldiers, even then."

"What a waste," I said.

"History keeps repeating itself."

But Clair seemed better for talking, so I kept on. I told him about the bus man, and Robie and Rob-ann, Sandy and Bell. I told him about the bad check and my conversation on the phone. It was all very curious, I said. Why would somebody go to all that trouble?

For a moment or two, Clair said nothing. I waited.

"This bike kid and his sister," he said. "They threatening at all?"

"Oh, no. Just misfits. Probably been pushed around a lot over the years. You know. A rough time on the playground."

Clair thought some more.

"Sounds to me like there was a plan, to a point," he said. "And something went wrong."

"How do you figure that?"

"A phony check. Maybe a phony license. Nobody would do all that so they could end up running into the Bobbsey Twins there."

"Why not?"

" 'Cause they sound like a couple of loose cannons," Clair said. "They're not criminals. They don't have anything, right?"

"A bunch of old bike parts. Just junk. An apartment in a house that ought to be condemned."

"What would this guy want with them?"

"I don't know," I said. "I don't know that he does want anything with them. I don't know who he is. I don't know much about them, for that matter."

"Gonna be one of those Swiss cheese stories, huh?" Clair said.

"What's that?"

"Full of holes."

But holes and all, it was on my mind all weekend.

When I called Roxanne that night, I talked about it: Robie leading me across town, Rob-ann in the doorway, Robie on the phone, Rob-ann saying, "How was that?"

Roxanne listened but I realized I'd gone on too long about Scanesett, and hadn't gone on long enough about her situation. Her mother was in the throes of this terrible mind-stealing disease, and I wanted to talk about some guy who had jumped from a bus, some . . . some what?

I couldn't even describe him. Another gaping hole.

It was one of those conversations that start with a missed beat and never find their rhythm. After ten minutes, Roxanne said she'd had a long day, that she was very tired and just wanted to climb into bed with a book.

I said I'd probably do the same, and I did. As the rain drummed the roof, I read about Arnold sailing up the coast from Newburyport, Massachusetts, to the Kennebec. They slipped a British blockade of Massachusetts, in dense fog found the point that marked the river's mouth, but discovered that a drought had left the inland waters of the Kennebec shallow and rocky.

From that point, for Arnold, the river would bring nothing but trouble. As I dozed off, I wondered if it would do the same for me.

I fell asleep with the lamp on and slept in spurts. A June bug slamming the screen woke me at two. A noise downstairs jarred me awake at three-forty, but I listened and concluded that it was the refrigerator faking death throes. I dozed off again but dreamed of frightening things: I was sitting on a bus and the people kept jumping out the windows and I tried to tell the driver but no sound would come from my mouth; I went to visit Roxanne, and her condo had turned into a nursing home.

She didn't know who I was; she said her name was Angela. I awoke drenched with sweat.

My neck was stiff from the dreams, the sweat, the damp breeze from the window. Pulling on a sweatshirt and shorts, I went down the loft stairs to the kitchen and put water on for tea. It was still raining, a drenching downpour that spattered the deck and splashed in the birdbath on the railing. Still groggy, I went into the bathroom and brushed my teeth, putting my toothbrush back in the cup next to Roxanne's. That reminded me of our last conversation. That made me wince.

Looking up, I peered into the mirror. Saw a fortyish guy with reddening cheeks, once of which showed a jagged three-inch scar, a souvenir of another story gone sour. I wondered if the guy who did it was out of jail yet. Probably.

I winced again.

Breakfast was cereal turned soggy in the package by the dampness. I made a cup of tea but discovered it was the last bag in the box. That meant I had to make a run to the general store. I had a bad tea habit, Roxanne said. Among others.

So I made the tea run at midmorning. The store was busy and I stood in line and glanced through the *Maine Sunday Telegram* and the *Globe*. There wasn't anything in the *Telegram* about anybody missing from Gardiner, or from Scanesett. Nothing in the *Globe* about a bus company losing a passenger. Not yet.

It was the first I'd considered that I might get scooped on this one. A report to the local cops by the bank security people. A remark from the bus driver to somebody in a bar. The somebody tells his brother-in-law. The brother-in-law works with somebody whose sister works at the *Globe*. The sister is in classifieds but she sees this guy on the elevator who she thinks is an editor. He's a clerk but he tells an editor who tells a reporter. The reporter gets on the phone, the bus company talks, and I'm out two hundred bucks.

It didn't make Sunday go by any faster.

Back at home, I made a pot of tea and, sitting at the big table, typed out my notes from the Popham Beach trip (*Fort is fifteen miles from Bath. Built in 1759 by Massachusetts royal governor Thomas Powell. British burned it in 1775. . . .*). I added to a list of possible photos, as instructed by the editor at *Historic Touring*. She would pass it on to the photographer they were using, who lived someplace near Boston.

That done, I got out my maps and notes and made a plan for the week.

I'd do the Maine State Museum on Monday. Tracking the Arnold route to Canada would take two trips because Arnold's route went cross-country, from the road to Jackman to the road to Coburn-Gore, a more remote border station to the west. I'd make the Coburn-Gore loop—to Lac Megantic, west along the Chaudière River to Beauceville, back into the States at Jackman—on Tuesday. Realistically, it looked like I'd have to go to Québec City alone.

How did they say ''lonely'' in French? *Solitaire*?

So with a wet walk in the woods, a stroll around Clair's silent barn, the day passed. It was a day I would have liked to talk to a brother or a sister, if I'd had one. It was a day I would have liked to call someone and say I was a little down. The only person I could say that to was down herself and didn't need me to drag her deeper. That night I considered having four ales instead of three, but didn't.

8 The Maine State Museum is a big modern concrete building directly across from the State Office Building in Augusta. The office building is attached to the State House by a tunnel. It's a busy place when the legislature is in session, a little quieter in the summer, when it's not. But I knew something was wrong when I pulled into the parking lot at nine-thirty Monday morning and it was empty.

I parked by the glass museum doors, which were dark. After a moment, I got out and walked over and gave them a shake. They were locked. Turning back to the car, I saw a capital security van approaching. I waved. It stopped.

"State shutdown day," the gray-haired guy at the wheel said.

"Shoot," I said.

"All that budget crap," he said. "Everything's coming apart."

He smiled. I nodded. He drove away.

Well, I thought. What now?

Every day that I spent on this story reduced my take. A thousand dollars for fifteen hundred words was sixty-seven cents a word. But about now, it was also sixty-seven cents an hour. And dwindling.

I got back in the truck and pondered the map, and Plan B.

The route north ran along the Kennebec, but the river took a jog to the southwest and passed through towns such as Norridgewock, a big Abenaki Indian settlement in Arnold's time, and on past Madison and Anson and North Anson. Arnold had followed the Kennebec to what was now the tiny town of The Forks, a place that catered to whitewater rafters and bear hunters. There Arnold and the boys dragged their boats overland to the west. They caught another river and followed it northwest, poling wading and trudging fifty miles through the unforgiving wilderness all the way to Canada. That river was called the Dead, which was just what many of those farm boys and sailors ended up, without firing a shot.

So I could go northwest through Carrabassett Valley or north up Route 201. Either way, I had to pass through Scanesett, and as I put the truck in gear and pulled out of the State House lot, I knew what that meant.

The sun broke through just as I came into town, coming in on the east side of the river, where its banks were hung with big pines and white-barked birches that arched over the water like the pale arms of ballerinas. I eyed the river as I drove, felt the sun pulling steam from the woods. Then I was up above the river, in town, passing the park where I'd talked to Bell. I slowed and took a right, went up two blocks and slowed again. I looked to my left, up the driveway. The bike and cart were there.

I parked three houses up and walked back. Shoved my notebook into the back pocket of my khakis. As I walked up the driveway, Robie emerged from behind the house and got on his bike.

"Hey, Robie," I said.

He turned quickly, looked like he might get off the bike and run for the house. But then I was there, between him and the stairs. I smiled.

"Where you headed, Robe?" I said.

He looked away.

"Downtown," he said. "I gotta go."

I kept smiling.

''That's a nice bike. And the trailer thing is a good idea. You do that yourself?''

He nodded. He was wearing a red T-shirt that said Scanesett Track in white letters, dungaree shorts, and big basketball shoes with no socks. Clenched on the handlebars, his fists were grubby.

''You run track?''

''No.''

''Oh. Just wear the shirt, huh?''

''Yeah.''

''Hey, what are those things on your trailer? Springs?''

''Yeah.''

''Why'd you do that?''

''Keeps stuff from breaking. Sometimes I carry some heavy stuff. Sometimes bottles.''

I looked at his legs. They were enormous, like a football lineman's.

''You must be in shape,'' I said.

He looked down.

''I guess so.''

''Well, listen, I just wanted to tell you—''

A screen slid up in a window of the house next door, fifteen feet away. A woman's head popped out. She was fiftyish. Smoking a cigarette. She glared at me.

''You okay, Robie?'' she said.

''Yeah,'' Robie said.

She glared at me again, then withdrew.

''Friend of yours?''

''No. I just know her, that's all.''

''Well, listen, I just wanted to tell you I didn't mean to bother you. Or to bother your sister. But I write for newspapers, you know? I'm a reporter. I thought this thing with the guy on the bus might make a good story. Didn't you think it was interesting? You were there. You heard it all, too. Got any idea of what might have happened?''

Still looking away, he shook his head. Beads of perspiration popped out on his big forehead.

"No?"

Robie's head kept shaking. Behind his armpits, his shirt was darkening.

"Well, I thought you might have seen something. You seem to see a lot, riding around. You seem to always have your eyes and ears open."

He didn't say anything.

"Well, I won't keep you. I know you have to go. But no hard feelings?"

I held out my hand.

He considered it. Hesitated. Took his big hand off the handlebar and gave mine a fleeting, tepid squeeze. Then he put his sneaker on the pedal and scuffed the bike and cart around, and started to coast down the driveway. A voice came from the house.

"Robie. Come here, please."

He heard her. The bike skidded to a stop, and he got off of it, leaving it standing in the driveway, held upright by the trailer. When he started for the stairs, I followed.

Robie lumbered up, bending the stair treads with his weight. I waited until he hit the second-floor landing and started up. When I reached the second floor, the door was open. I stood for a moment, then took a couple of steps inside.

The door opened into a hall, with cracked white linoleum, jackets all hung in a row. There was a broom standing in the corner with a dustpan clipped to the shaft. To the right, through an open doorway, was the kitchen. I could see part of a menu stuck to the door of the refrigerator. Magnets in the shape of cats and dogs. A white cat started around the corner, saw me, and fled.

"Pepsi, and I need that white tape," Rob-ann was saying. "In the blue-and-white package. It's next to the Band-Aids. Blue and white. Don't forget. Get the big bottles and get one diet. And some hot dogs and hot-dog rolls. And macaroni and cheese. Get five boxes. The blue and gold kind, not the yellow."

It struck me that Robie was illiterate.

"I don't have any more stamps," I heard him say.

"Take twenty then. It's a twenty-dollar bill. A lot of money. Bring back the change, now."

I heard feet shuffling. I knocked on the wall.

"Hey, guys?"

They appeared, two big quizzical faces.

"What—"

"Hi. I just wondered if I could talk to you some more."

"Um—" Robie said. He looked to his sister. She was wearing blue sweatpants and a T-shirt. Her feet were big and bare.

"About what?" she said.

"About the bus. The man on the bus. I mean Robie."

"I talked to you."

He looked to Rob-ann.

"This is the guy. The guy talking to Sandy."

"He don't know anything," Rob-ann said.

"That's okay," I said. "You didn't see him get off the bus, Robe?"

He looked to her again.

"No, he didn't see nothin'."

"Okay," I said. "I didn't, either. And I was standing right there. Talking to Sandy about Benedict Arnold. Did you know he came right through here? On the way to Québec?"

"Yeah," Rob-ann said. "There's a rock thing in the park. But I don't know—"

"That park down by the police station? I didn't know that."

I took out my notebook.

"Yup," Rob-ann said.

"By the water where the kids drink," Robie said. "Lotsa bottles."

"Yeah, but mister, he's gotta go," Rob-ann said.

She'd started to herd him toward me when there were footsteps on the stairs. I turned. Two guys came through the doorway. One tall, thirties, with a dark beard. One shorter and younger, wearing a tank top and a baseball hat on backward over long, dirty-blond hair.

"What the hell?" the taller guy said, looking at me.

"How you doing?" I said.

"Who's he?" he asked Robie and Rob-ann.

"The writer guy," Robie said apologetically.

"I'm Jack McMorrow."

"What the hell's he doing in here?"

"Talking to Robie and Rob-ann," I said. "What are you doing here?"

"We was just talking," Robie began. "We was telling him about the rock in the—"

"Get outta here," the tall guy said. The short guy was trying to see around him.

"Who are you?" I said.

"I'm their friggin' cousin. Get outta here."

I looked at him.

"I don't hear them asking me to leave."

"I'm telling you. Gimme that."

He reached out and grasped my notebook. I pulled it back. He pulled, too, then started to shove me with his other hand. I put my foot against the wall and shoved back. He smelled.

"Gimme that," he was muttering. "Gimme it, you son of a—"

"Howard, no," Rob-ann shouted. "Stop it. Let him—"

The short guy shoved me in the shoulder. I swung around and my back hit the wall beside Howard.

"Hey," Robie said.

"This is my house!" Rob-ann shouted.

"Stop," Robie said.

Howard still had one end of the notebook. The short guy lunged and wrapped his forearm around my neck. I tensed and got a knee up and shoved him back. He snarled and came at me again but Howard lost his grip on the notebook and I fell back toward the next room, with the short guy still coming toward me. Robie stepped in and wrapped his big arms around the short guy and knocked off his hat. The hat was underfoot and the short guy was looking down to find it.

"Get out of my house!" Rob-ann screamed.

"Get outta here!" Howard yelled.

"Okay," I said, but they were all blocking the way. I glanced around. Bike parts laid out on newspapers. A TV. Shelves of videos. There were two or three other doors but they were closed. Howard came around Robie and caught me by the shirt and started dragging me back down the hall. I did a couple of stutter steps and bulled into him and he went down on his back and I kept going over him, stepping on his chin or his face or something on the way by.

"You want the cops here again?" Rob-ann said behind me, and as I reached the porch, I looked back. She was leaning over Howard, her teeth and fists clenched. He looked up at her but said nothing.

"Nice family," I said, and I started down the stairs, not running, but walking slowly. It was a dignified retreat, but no one came out of the door as I crossed the dooryard. There was a beat-up Chevette parked there, copper with a blue hood, dented in front. No one followed me down the driveway. There were no taunts, no threats.

Not a sound, not a sign of anyone, as I started the truck and drove past the house and away.

The dispatcher, the same guy whom the big chief laid into, said Bell wasn't on duty. Driving toward Scanesett's downtown, I asked when she'd be back. He said she wasn't scheduled until Wednesday. I thanked him and leaned down to dig a phone book off of the floor. Looked up and had to stand on the brakes to stop for a stop sign and a car crossing in front of me.

"Jeez," I said.

I pulled past the stop sign and stopped to look at the phone book. It showed there were three Bells in Scanesett.

Two just listed roads, without numbers, probably on the outskirts of town. A third was on Pleasant Street, number forty-six. Hope Bell seemed like a person who would live on a Pleasant Street. Wholesome and honest and hardworking. I pictured a Cape Cod house with a picket fence. When I found it, after three sets of directions from three different people, it turned out to be a ranch with a big attached garage, built on a wooded lot between two older houses, on a side street off of the main drag heading north. There was a Toyota station wagon in the driveway. The fence was split rail and ran across the front of the yard. Bell was kneeling on the grass, digging in the garden that ran in front of the fence.

When the truck approached, she stood up. I parked in the street and got out.

"Sorry to bother you," I said.

She was standing there in shorts and a white V-neck T-shirt, with a little speaker thing tucked into her waistband. Her hands were dirty and so were her knees. She didn't say it wasn't a bother.

"I called and they said you wouldn't be back until Wednesday."

"I get Monday and Tuesday off," she said.

"Sorry," I said. "You probably don't like to talk business on your day off."

Bell shrugged. She didn't disagree.

"But I just had a strange thing happen at Robie and Robann's. Did I tell you he called me?"

"No."

She dropped back on her knees and started digging between the plants with a hand trowel.

"I don't mean to be rude, but I've got a baby asleep, for the minute."

She touched the speaker thing.

"That's what this is. And my other daughter gets home from kindergarten in a half hour. And my husband's doing an addition on the next street, so he'll be home for lunch. This is my big chance of the day.''

''Sorry. How old's the baby?''

''Nine months,'' Bell said.

''Well, I'll make it quick.''

She kept digging.

''I stopped there a little while ago. Robie called Saturday. Called me in the truck as I was headed out of town. He said I didn't need to talk to him, not to bother. I don't know. Something to that effect. And then when he was about to hang up, I heard Rob-ann say, 'How was that?' To somebody else. As though somebody else had told Robie to call. And was listening.''

''Yeah,'' Bell said. The trowel hacked at a clump of weed.

''What are these? All perennials?''

''Yup. It's my other life.''

''Nice,'' I said. ''Well, anyway, I stopped there. Just a little while ago. I'm on my way up north.''

''I thought he told you he didn't want you to.''

''I wanted to see if he really meant it,'' I said.

''Did he?''

''Well, I don't know. He didn't chase me away. I talked to him a little outside in the driveway. He didn't say much.''

''Never has,'' Bell said, scrunched down in front of me.

''But he didn't run away, either. I think he was pretty surprised to see me standing there.''

''I know the feeling.''

''Oh,'' I said. ''Sorry.''

She turned and smiled.

''Just kidding. Go on.''

''Well, so Rob-ann called him and he went inside. He was heading off somewhere on his bike and he stopped. So I sort of followed him up the stairs—''

Bell turned again. There was smudge of soil on her forehead.

"Sort of followed him?"

"Followed him."

"You are pushy, aren't you? Is that what it takes to make it as a big-city reporter?"

"That times a hundred. I've mellowed."

"No kidding."

A car went by and the driver, a young woman, beeped. From the ground, Bell raised her trowel in a wave. Then she listened to the speaker on her belt, and troweled some more.

"So this is what happened. I walked into the apartment—I really just wanted to get a look at it—and they were standing there, talking about a grocery list or something, and they looked at me and, I don't know, they seemed a little panicky. She was immediately on the defensive. 'He doesn't know anything.' That sort of thing. And then all of a sudden these two guys came up the stairs and came in."

"What'd they look like?"

"Thirties, the taller one. His name was Howard. Beard. Kind of scroungy. Shorter one was younger. Maybe mid-twenties. Long hair and a hat on backward. Probably saw it on TV."

"No doubt," Bell murmured.

"So these two guys, especially the older one, they just go berserk. 'What's he doing in here? Get outta here.' Older guy tried to grab my notebook. We're in this tug-of-war and the younger guy is trying to jump in on it and it's just chaos. Screaming and yelling."

Bell had stopped and was turned toward me, listening, sitting on her haunches.

"So finally Robie grabbed the shorter guy and I kind of ran over the taller guy and got out of there. And, oh, yeah, Rob-ann is screaming at the taller guy when he's on the floor, I mean, right in his face, 'You want the cops here again?' "

Bell stood up. The speaker at her waist gave a little murmur. She listened but after that it just hissed.

''That was me,'' she said. ''I stopped and talked to them.''

''How were they?''

''Nervous.''

''More than usual?''

''I'd say so. But they have good days and bad days. They're kind of hard to figure.''

''Who would these guys have been?'' I asked.

She was moving toward the driveway.

''Oh, I'd say Howard and Damian. They're cousins. I mean, they're brothers but they're cousins to Robie and Rob-ann.''

''What kind of family is this?''

Bell smiled.

''I don't know. I suppose you could call it a family. Robie and Rob-ann get checks. SSI or something. The rest of the crew sponges off them. Bunch of dirtbags, mostly. Howard and Damian are in jail one year out of three. Damian's been to Windham. Howard, I think, has done mostly county time. They're thieves. Drunks. Damian has a couple of gross sexual misconducts. Underage girls. I don't know about Howard for that sort of thing. But Robie and Rob-ann are their golden geese. Guaranteed money, first of the month.''

''So they leech off them?''

''Sure. Borrow twenty bucks. More if they can get it. Go get drunk. That's how we know about it. The cousins get any kind of cash and you can bet they're going to get picked up for something. Get tossed out of a bar. Get in a fight. We say, 'Where'd you get the money?' They say, 'Robie and Rob-ann gave it to us,' like it's somehow Robie and Rob-ann's fault. They're bad news, those two. Yup. Howard and Damian. Some nasty assaults, back when they were dealing drugs. Howard almost gouged a guy's eye out once. They're the kind who, once you're down, keep on stomping.''

''Nice,'' I said.

We stood at the end of the driveway. The speaker murmured again.

"She's waking up," Bell said.

My exit cue. I hurried.

"Well, what about Robie and Rob-ann? What happened to them?"

Bell took a step toward the house, turned back to me.

"No father. Mother was a drunk. I think Robie has some sort of mental disability. Maybe some learning thing. The sister's a little better but something's still not right. Maybe just their upbringing. They were behind me in school, but I remember the two of them there. She was older. Picked on like you wouldn't believe. Sort of stuck together. Kids used to say they were, you know, jokes about incest. And then they stopped going to school much, finally stopped altogether. I don't think Robie can read."

"So what did they do, if they didn't go to school?"

"Took care of Mom," Bell said. "What was her name? Rolene. She's dead but they used to stay home and keep house, make the meals for each other, wipe up the vomit, and other stuff, I guess. Toward the end. I heard Rob-ann used to impersonate her mother on the phone when her mother was too drunk to talk."

"God," I said.

"Yeah," Bell said, inching toward the house. "They didn't really have a childhood. Just them and Mom and then her liver went and she died and it was just them. Except they never learned to be grown-ups. And they never learned to be just kids, either. Stuck in never-never land. Kinda sad."

"And they've got these hangers-on who come around?"

"First of the month," Bell said.

"But it's July seventeenth," I said. "What were they there for today?"

She stopped. Looked like she was thinking about it.

"I don't know, McMorrow. That's a good question."

Her speaker started to cry. She tossed the trowel on the lawn.

"And what about all that today? How did they know about me? And why did they get so wound up about it?"

Bell was walking away.

"Those are good questions, too," she said.

"And who was Rob-ann talking to on the phone?"

"Could've been the Tooth Fairy."

I took two steps after her.

"But I don't think so," I said. "You know what I think?"

She turned.

"Yeah, I do."

"I think the bus man is in there."

Bell sighed. The baby was screeching.

"Can you get a warrant?"

"Based on what? Your intuition?"

"Based on their odd behavior."

"Robie and Rob-ann? You've got to be kidding," Bell said.

"Odd, even for them."

"Yeah, right. The chief is really gonna like that one. I'll tell him it was the reporter's idea."

"What about the bad check?"

Bell's hand was on the doorknob.

"I don't know. I'll see. I'll be back Wednesday. If the guy's there, and I don't know why on earth he would be, he'll still be there."

"What if he isn't?" I said.

"God, McMorrow," Bell said, going through the doorway toward the baby's cries. "You sure know how to ruin a day off."

9

A day off? I didn't want one.

For reasons I couldn't quite identify, I was driven. From Bell's neat little house, I proceeded directly to Robie and Rob-ann's. I drove by once, slowly, and saw that the bike was gone. Circling the block, I parked three houses away and watched. Nothing stirred. Not the warm, still air. Not the street. Not the dreary house. Not the tattered shades in its windows.

I waited and watched. Sitting there in the truck, I felt like I was the only living thing in sight. After fifteen minutes in the hot, noonday sun, I started the truck and left, looking up at the second-floor windows as I passed.

What if he was in there? If he was, what was he doing? Why?

As I drove, the questions floated in front of me, like mist on the windshield. Distracted, I drove through the side streets until I ran into Route 201, then turned north. A mile up the road, I pulled into a supermarket and went in to buy something for lunch. I gathered two apples, two oranges, a bag of pretzels and a quart of orange juice.

As I stood in the checkout line, I wondered why he would be there. Who was he? What could the connection be?

''Paper or plastic?'' the checkout girl said.

If there was one, I thought.

''Sir?'' the girl said.

• • •

I ate in the truck, parked in the shade of an oak at the back of the parking lot. On the seat next to me were a detailed state atlas called a *Maine Gazeteer,* notebooks, the tape recorder, and a book about Benedict Arnold that had a map that showed his route in little dots, like bread left behind by Hansel and Gretel. I shook Robie and Rob-ann from my mind and traced his path.

Arnold and his men went straight up the river until they were just below what is now the village of Caratunk, thirty-five miles to the north. There they went overland, catching rides on three small ponds, stopping to build a hospital, not a good sign. The men then dragged their boats across Bigelow Mountain and became desperately mired in a boggy marsh east of what is now Flagstaff Lake. The lake is a wide, shallow backwater held back by a small hydroelectric dam. The historic tourers could drive this part of the route, crossing a causeway at the lake's southwest tip. They could picture Arnold's struggles, his plight as he and his troops were mired in this Maine morass. It would take some imagination. For me, with Robie and the rest of them tugging at me, it was taking less and less.

But Robie didn't pay bills, at least not yet, so the apple cores and the orange juice carton went through the sliding window into the bed of the truck. I headed west, past old farms cut into house lots, former pastures where used cars now were lined up under plastic pennants. The road slipped through the little town of Norridgewock, where a French missionary was massacred by the English along with most of his Abenaki congregation. They made shoes in Norridgewock now.

And then it was on to Madison, where they made magazine paper, and the mill, with its steam-cloud pennant, dwarfed the game little downtown. From there, it was across a bridge and the Kennebec, and then the river stayed on the right, looping around low, wooded islands. I drove slowly and chatted with my tape recorder past the tiny town of Embden, across the river at Solon.

Researching away, I continued north. I noted a sign that said, "Moose next 35 miles," or, *en français, "Moose sur soixante kilometres."* English or French, I wasn't sure what I was supposed to do for the next thirty-five miles. Perhaps they should have put a sign up where the moose were not.

The road was a straight shot to the next town, Bingham, ten miles away, but to the west, the mountains could be seen beyond the tree-covered hills, as if heaving themselves up onto their elbows. There was just a hint of wildness here, something that told you that you would soon be in territory that was, if not hostile, at least ambivalent.

The only other traffic was log trucks, which popped up over the crest of approaching hills like locomotives. Headed south, they were loaded, tree-length logs piled fifteen feet high, secured with winched chains that seemed like threads as the trucks thundered by.

Like programmed missiles, they couldn't stop. It was like a building passing, missing my truck by five feet. It was a near miss, a dodging of instant death, and I covered my ears and winced as the log trucks passed in a gust of grit. My truck began to feel very small.

But I made it to Bingham, where there were white clapboard houses, a post office, and a sign that said I was halfway between the equator and the North Pole. Maybe Santa stopped here to gas up.

It was in Bingham that I saw the first of the whitewater outfitter buses, which hauled rafters to the river. The rafters rode the rapids after the power company opened its dam. Tourists had a good time on this giant water slide, and more importantly, they spent money, which in this country of woods and rugged hills, was sorely needed. Only so many people could be depended upon to come here to hunt bear.

So today's adventurers rode down the river in rubber rafts, shrieking with glee. In 1775, Arnold's army went up the river in leaky wooden boats. A few of them may have shrieked, but it would have been in pain. The rafters stayed in lodges with restaurants and bars with karaoke music.

Arnold's men slept on the ground in wet clothes in the cold. They didn't have much to eat, and many of them were very sick. I'd just read about one guy who was left behind because he was dying of dysentery and was "covered with vermin."

And not just Howard and Damian.

With Robie and Rob-ann, they crept back into my thoughts as I drove. What would excite them enough to light into me like that? Money. Booze. Maybe cocaine. Stuff they could sell for money to buy booze and cocaine. Was it just that they saw me as some sort of threat to Robie and Rob-ann? But if they were just a source of cash on check day, how could I get in the way? The cousins had to be seeing them as something more than that. What had changed? Who was in those rooms with the closed doors?

I drifted, then pulled myself back. Just outside of Bingham there was a rest area, and a marker that said Arnold Trail. I pulled in and saw that there was a billboard sort of thing that showed Arnold's route. I got out and read it, standing there in the hot sun. It said the trip took six weeks, that it included "great hardship and extremely difficult travel." I guessed the sign people didn't want to come right out and say the men were reduced to eating candles and their shoes.

But I would, because that was the story. These woodsmen and farmers and fisherman who risked their lives for what they thought was a just cause. Life and liberty, and being able to tell the king to go scratch. I thought about this as I drove north. It was a different time then, with so many people ready to die for what they thought was right. Nothing gets Americans that fired up anymore. That's what we've got the army for, right? If somebody's bothering us, they'll take—

"Whoa," I said.

Above Bingham, the road swerved sharply up and to the left, with a rock wall on my right. A loaded log truck was just there, coming at me, three feet over the center line. I jerked the wheel.

"God almighty," I said as the truck's roar subsided. I told myself I'd better warn the historic tourers about this one. Gawk at your own risk.

There was plenty to gawk at. Above the town of Moscow, the Kennebec was dammed. Above the dam, the river was called Wyman Lake. In the sun, the water was a shimmering deep blue, against steep walls of trees that melded into green wooded hills and ridges. I glanced out as I followed the still-twisting road, then up at the mirror.

A log truck was gaining.

I sped up a little, but the Toyota was short and high and seemed to lean on the corners. The tractor behind me kept gaining until I could just see the grille, windshield, the word "Freightliner" and a Québec plate. I tried to go faster but the truck stayed just off my bumper.

To my right was sheer rock wall. To the left was the other lane, a guardrail, then a steep pitch down to the water. An oncoming truck roared by and I swerved and slowed. Now the mirror showed just grille, no windshield.

"What's your problem?" I shouted.

There was no place to pull over. What did he want?

I hung on and drove, eyes locked on the road, hands gripping the wheel. Through another set of S-turns, braking to keep from swinging too wide. The truck downshifted and accelerated and then the road suddenly dropped and turned to the left. The river was slipping by in blue-black flashes but I couldn't look. Another oncoming truck, coming, coming. Blasting by, a wind-tunnel whoosh, logs wavering in the wind. I looked for a turnoff, a logging road, a clearing in the woods, a break in the rocks.

Nothing.

An Arnold sign flashed by. For what? It was somewhere along here that the army had left the river and headed east. I looked in the mirror and saw more grille, heard the diesel skip as the driver downshifted.

It was a straight stretch now, coming into Caratunk. The river on the left, a few camp cottages high on the right. I put on my turn indicator. The truck drew closer. I put on my flashers. He still didn't back off. I turned the flashers off, left the right turn signal on, and turned hard onto the gravel shoulder in front of a camp.

He went by in a cloud of dust and smoke. I slid to a stop.

"Son of a bitch," I said.

The gray-haired history buffs would love this one. What was the hurry? Did he want to get back to get another load? To have an ale? Next time I'd bring a bazooka. Maybe a couple of water balloons.

But that was what this north country was like, in some ways. Unforgiving. Unsentimental. You still could die up here, if you got lost in the wrong place, at the wrong time of year. Freeze to death just like Arnold's men. In the deep woods, you still could trip and break your ankle or your leg, and then bet your life on how far you can crawl.

I didn't get into the deep woods that day. I did drive the twisting turns back to Bingham, and then cross the timber bridge over the Kennebec. The gravel logging road on the west side ran north along the river for six or seven miles before it swung away toward the carry ponds that Arnold used. I drove to Middle Carry, through an unlocked paper company gate. And then I hiked a mile through the woods to a spot that showed on the map as Arnold's Point.

It was a small pond, a mile across, surrounded by spruce hills. The trail was part of the Appalachian Trail, tiny red dots on the map, like a trail of ants. In real life, it was a narrow path with orange blazes on the tree trunks. It led to a hut, and perhaps because it was a Monday, I was the only one there. I walked out on Arnold's Point, and stood and looked at the pond and the hills, with the sun starting to fall in the west. I saw an osprey fly over, a great blue heron. I thought I heard the whine of a Canada jay, but it might have been a catbird.

I stood there and wondered what Arnold had thought when he'd stood at this spot. A sense of foreboding? A sense that something was going to go very wrong? That plans would begin to unravel?

Or was that just me?

The feeling followed me out of the woods, to the truck, to the road. It clung to me all the way back down Route 201, where I blasted along at sixty miles an hour, looking at the range settings on the phone. In Caratunk, out of range of the dishes or transmitters or whatever it was that made the thing work, they'd been near zero.

By the time I reached Madison, the range was up to three, four on the crests of the hills. I waited until I was in Scanesett to try it, dialing as I drove. The phone beeped and I waited and then it beeped again and hung itself up. I was staring down at it when I almost rear-ended a car stopped for a light.

I didn't try again until I was on Robie and Rob-ann's dreary little street, this time parked four houses down. The phone beeped and then it rang. Rang some more. It was four thirty-five and there was no answer. Roxanne wasn't back. I hung up and looked up at the house. There was a light on in what I thought was the main room, the room into which I'd fallen. Two of the closed-door rooms were on this side of the house. Both were dark. The third was on the other side, which I couldn't see. I'd make a loop in a minute and check it.

So I waited. Sorted through my books and notes. Labeled the cassette from my recorder. Opened the pretzels and crunched a few down. Wished I had a drink. Looked around.

The house closest to me was an old gray place, with asbestos siding and a glassed-in front porch full of trash. There was a wood-and-wire fence around the front yard and some sort of vine had swarmed all over it and, along with age, pulled it down. But the front yard, which showed signs of care and design, was overgrown. Maples were growing up in the corners of what had been the lawn. English sparrows slipped from the maples to the sidewalk by the truck. I tossed out a piece of pretzel and they attacked it, and each other.

That kind of town, I thought.

And then I saw him.

It was Robie. He was behind me, behind the trees at the corner of the yard. I could see him in the side mirror. I tossed another pretzel out. He was crouched down, peering around the corner at me. The sparrows fluttered and chittered. A pigeon arrived from somewhere. I picked up the receiver again and pretended to dial. Pretended to talk. I talked loudly, said things were okay but it had been a long day. I'd been to Caratunk and out in the woods. Log trucks just blasted up and down that road, which made it kind of hairy. But the story would be fun—I could see Robie looking at me—and I should have it done on time.

And then I got out of the truck, still talking. Tossed pretzels on the sidewalk, and then turned and started walking, slowly at first, then more quickly and he was jumping on his bike when I stepped up and grabbed the handlebars.

"Mister, I didn't do nothing," Robie blurted.

"I know that. I didn't say you did."

"Yeah, well, I gotta go."

"Just talk to me for a second, Robie," I said, trying to calm him. "What are you afraid of?"

"I ain't afraid."

His hands twisted on the handgrips. The fingers were stained with grease. I looked at him. He had very bad teeth, blackened near the gums.

"Then what is it?" I said gently. "What was that all about today?"

"Nothing."

"Those guys, your cousins, why'd they want me out of your house?"

"They weren't my cousins," Robie said, looking down at his front wheel.

"Sure they were, Robe."

"How do you know?"

"I asked. I asked Officer Bell. She told me who they were."

"Why'd you ask her?"

"Because I wanted to know. If you hadn't been there to help me, I might have gotten my clock cleaned. Two on one."

"Yeah, well—"

"Thanks," I said. "You helped me out."

"Yeah," Robie said.

His hands slowed on the handgrips.

"But I didn't do nothin'," he said.

"Who said you did?"

"Why you chasin' me?"

"I'm not."

"Why you got my house under surveyance?"

"I don't. I'm just wondering what happened to the bus guy, that's all. I'm going to write a story about it this week. Maybe for a big paper. But if the guy's just sitting here, visiting relatives or something, I'd like to know. If it's something like that, I probably won't write a story."

"He ain't my relative."

"No?"

"I don't even know him. I didn't do nothing."

"Well, you and your sister—"

"She didn't do nothing."

His eyes went wide.

"I didn't say that."

"Yeah, well, she didn't know him, either. We don't know him."

I looked at him. He looked up the block. The woman from the window of the house was coming down the street, pulling a wire shopping cart. She looked up and saw me. I made sure to smile at Robie. The woman approached. Glared at me, but looked kindly at Robie.

"You okay, Robe?" she said, slowing as she reached us.

"Yeah," he said. "Sure. I'm okay, Darlene. You okay?"

"Yeah," she said.

She looked at me suspiciously and I smiled at her. I noticed that she was big and stocky and her eyes were made up oddly. The black eyeliner was on the bottom, but not the top. Her eyebrows were drawn with pencil. One had more of an arch than the other.

"How are you today?" I said.

"Fine," she said.

She looked me up and down.

"You're not bothering him, are you?"

"No," I said. "Of course not."

"Yeah, well," she said, and she slowly walked away, sandals scuffing on the sidewalk, leaving the threat unsaid but hanging.

"Hey, I gotta go," Robie said.

"Friend of yours?"

"What? Darlene. Oh, she's okay. She works. She works in the shoe shop."

That was all. In Robie's circle of intimates, a job was a defining characteristic.

"So did Rob-ann see him?" I said, absently. "Is that how you know she didn't know him?"

"Yeah," Robie said, then thought. "She never seen him. I never seen him, neither. She never seen him, my sister."

"No?"

"Uh-uh."

"Well, you know he's wanted by the police."

Robie looked at me, then looked away. He looked agitated.

"I didn't know that. I didn't know nothin'."

"Yeah, well, the police say he wrote a bad check for his bus ticket. Used a fake name and everything."

"He didn't tell me no name."

"I thought you said you hadn't seen him," I said.

"Yeah. I never seen him."

I waited. He had started to roll back and forth on his bike. The seat creaked under his weight.

"You aren't gonna take us away?" Robie said suddenly, rolling back and forth faster. " 'Cause my sister, she gets a check, and um, I get a check and we sorta . . ."

He trailed off.

"Sorta what?" I said softly.

"Yeah, well, we sorta stay together and if we was in jail, they got the girls' jail and the boys' jail and we, like, we gotta stay together. We gotta. Like, I have to sorta watch out for her, 'cause we get checks, you know? The third, every month, and if she was in the girls' jail, I couldn't see her and how would she get her check? Somebody might steal it. They steal things around here, they're like—"

"Robie. I'm a reporter. I write stories. I don't put people in jail."

He looked at me doubtfully.

"That's not what—"

He paused.

"Not what?" I said.

"I gotta go," Robie said.

"Don't get yourself in trouble," I said. "You think you're getting in trouble, or your sister, call Officer Bell."

He looked at me.

"Yup," he said.

"Because you're right about those jails. The boys and the girls are separate."

I smiled.

"Or you can call me. I'll give you a card with my number. I gave one to your sister, too."

I took a card out and handed it to him. He peered at it.

"It says I'm a writer," I said.

"Yeah," Robie said.

He scuffed his feet and rolled the bike backward to pull

around me. Stopped. Looked at me, looked away, and looked at me again.

"Yeah, well, what're you gonna do to him when you catch him?" Robie said.

"Do to who?"

"The guy."

"The bus guy?"

"Uh-huh."

"I don't know," I said truthfully. "I guess I'll ask him if he'll talk to me."

"I don't think he'll wanna."

"Well, then, Robe, I guess he'll just have to say, 'No comment.' "

Robie rode around the corner, but like a grouse luring a fox away from its chicks, he turned right, away from home. Clever.

I walked back to the truck, started it and drove slowly toward the house. I looked up at the windows, where I was sure Mantis was or had been. I pulled over and stared up. Felt an urge to just walk through the doorway and search the place, room by room. But it subsided, and I put the truck in gear and started off.

The Chevette rolled down the driveway and followed.

It was Howard at the wheel. Damian beside him. In the mirror, it looked like they were grinning. Maybe they were going to let me in on the joke.

I drove to the stop sign at the next cross street and

stopped. When the Chevette was fifty yards back, I pulled out and turned right. The Chevette rolled right through and followed.

There were three blocks of residential before the road ran into Route 2, a fast two-lane highway that ran along the Kennebec. I knew my truck could outrun their old beater on the highway, so I took a right at the next stop sign and began threading my way through the streets of tenements. I zigzagged toward the downtown, with the Chevette following behind like I was towing it with a hundred-yard chain. Left, right, left, straight. Once when I was at a stop sign and a little urchin girl kid walked in front of me, they stopped in the middle of the street, fifty yards back. When the little girl had passed, I still sat there. They sat, too. A big pickup swerved around them and the driver gave them the horn and the finger. They didn't budge until I did.

I led them through the downtown, then up Route 201. At McDonald's, I turned in. Coasted through the lot with my eye on the mirror. The Chevette turned in, too. I pulled into the drive-through lane and a car slipped out of a space and got between us. I sat and then it was my turn and the voice on the little box asked if she could take my order. I said no and accelerated, past the second window and around the restaurant again. They were sitting there in the order line when I pulled up behind them.

Howard's eyes met mine in the mirror. Damian turned and looked. They looked at each other and said something. I stared at Howard's eyes in the mirror. The Chevette suddenly lurched forward and pulled into a parking space.

They got out. I reached under the seat for a lug wrench and rolled the truck out of the lane and off to the side.

It was Howard who approached first, scuffing along in his unlaced basketball shoes. He lit a cigarette along the way, cupping it in his hands as he held up his lighter. Damian was three feet behind him and looked pumped up. Neither showed a knife or a club or a gun. I slid the wrench under the atlas on the passenger seat and waited.

Howard came to the window.

"What the hell you think you're doing?" he said.

"Just what I was going to ask you."

"Yeah, well, you better leave my friggin' cousins alone, you got that? Back off."

I smiled.

"Oh, yeah? Why's that?"

" 'Cause they ain't all that friggin' swift, you know what I'm saying?"

"So leave 'em alone," Damian piped in.

I looked at him.

"He already said that."

Howard leaned closer, stuck a finger in my face. The nails were dirty, the finger was nicotine yellow.

"And I mean it, Mr. Newspaperman, or whatever you say you are. Point that truck out of town and keep right on going. I don't want to see you here again."

I looked at him. Swallowed the urge to tell him to stick it. I wanted to know more.

"Why's that, Howard?" I said. "Damian, you feel free to chime in."

"How do you know our names?" Howard said.

"Rob-ann was yelling them. Kind of hard to miss."

"What the hell do you want here?"

"Yeah," Damian said.

I looked at him, then turned back to big brother.

"I'm thinking of doing a story. I write stories. This one would be about the guy who left the bus. That's what I do for a job."

"Stay away from my cousins," Howard said. "They don't know nothing about any goddamn bus. Leave 'em alone."

"I think they do know."

"I'm telling you they don't. So leave 'em alone. They don't know nothin'."

"Leave 'em alone," Damian said, leaning toward me chin first, his fists clenched.

"Why?"

" 'Cause I said so," Howard said.

" 'Cause he friggin' said so," Damian said.

"So?"

"So you don't go near 'em," Howard said.

"Not good enough," I said.

"Yes, good enough," he said.

"Sorry, boys," I said, reaching for the gearshift. "This isn't going anywhere. And I'll go wherever I damn well—"

Damian lunged. Got me by the front of the shirt and started pulling but the seat belt held me in.

"No," Howard said.

"I'm gonna kill this son of a—"

Damian pulled. I grabbed his wrist with my left hand, but he was strong. My shirt ripped and he lunged and got my throat. Howard was saying, "Dame, not here, the cops'll—" and was pulling on Damian's shirt. Damian had his left hand on the door, the right starting to squeeze my throat. "I'm gonna kill this bastard."

Tighter. Tighter. I couldn't breathe. Couldn't swallow. Started to gag, felt a rush of panic. I grabbed the wrench and swung as hard as I could, slamming his knuckles against the door.

"Aaaaah!" Damian screamed.

He fell away, still screaming, holding his hand.

"It's broke." Damian was crying. "It's broke."

"I told you not to," Howard said, pulling him away. "These guys are trained. I told you."

"Oh, it's broke. Oh, man, oh, man, oh, man."

They lurched toward their car, Howard holding Damian, Damian holding his smashed hand. A car full of kids pulled up to the drive-through speaker, and the kids stared. A little bald guy in a McDonald's outfit came out of the side door and stood with his hands on his hips.

"I called the cops!" he shouted. "Now you guys get the hell out of here!"

I put the truck in gear and headed for the exit, fast. As I pulled out, a cruiser skidded into the entrance, bouncing up the ramp. I headed north, trying to clear my throat. It was sore to swallow. I wondered if he'd bruised my trachea, what that was all about, what he meant, "These guys are trained." Trained for what?

And then there were lights flashing, coming up fast, then locking on behind me like a fighter jet.

I pulled over.

I was sitting at a table in what passed for a squad room at the Scanesett P.D. There was a coffee machine, a box of doughnuts with one doughnut left. It was chocolate. There were wanted posters, showing real criminals from places such as Texas and California. An old calendar from a police uniform company. The woman in the picture was wearing a police shirt, half buttoned, and apparently nothing else.

Progress was slow in reaching this stretch of the frontier.

The young cop who had pulled me over had left. Damian was at the hospital having his hand X-rayed. Big brother Howard had gone with him for moral support. I was at the station for questioning. Chief Dale Nevins was standing over me, holding my driver's license in his hand.

"I thought I told you there wasn't any story here," Nevins said.

He seemed more exasperated than angry, as though he couldn't understand why I hadn't heeded his advice.

"You did," I said. "But it isn't up to you to make that determination. I don't tell you who to arrest."

"You're lucky I'm not arresting you, Mr. McMorrow."

"Just defending myself. Like I said, he had me by the throat and I couldn't breathe. I've heard either of those guys will stomp you if you go down."

"Where'd you hear that?" Nevins asked.

"Around town."

"You hear an awful lot for somebody who's only passing through."

I didn't say anything.

"I knew your name sounded familiar. You were the goddamn reporter hooked up with those goddamn pot growers. I told Bell who you were. Warned her in case you came around asking questions."

"Thanks," I said.

"Seems to me you have a talent for stirring up trouble. I told Bell that. You really smashed Damian's hand all to hell."

"Look at the bruises on my throat."

"He won't be using that hand for a long, long time."

"That's why God gave him two," I said.

My voice was scratchy. I was tired. Nevins seemed in no hurry.

"Howard says they just wanted to talk to you and you began acting in a threatening manner."

"Howard said that? He's cleaned up his grammar since we last spoke."

"He says you threatened them with that wrench."

"So they reached in the car and got me by the throat to protect themselves."

"That wrench is a deadly weapon," Nevins lectured.

I looked at him. Rolled my eyes.

"This is a serious matter," he said.

"And if that son of a bitch had strangled me, it'd be even more serious."

"You want to file a complaint?"

"Nope."

"Why not?"

"Hey. He grabbed me, I whacked him to get him off. What are they gonna do? Howard and Damian?"

"I don't know. Nothing, probably. Howard and Damian have a thing about the legal system. Usually they're on the receiving end, bent right over. And this time, I'll tell you something. Howard seemed a little spooked."

"Why?" I said.

"I don't know."

He looked at my license one more time, then flipped it onto the table. I picked it up, took out my wallet and tucked the license in.

Nevins stepped back from the table.

"Well, consider this a warning, Mr. McMorrow. And I've got a suggestion for you. Stay away."

"Kind of hard to do this story over the phone," I said, getting up. Nevins faced me, chest out, man to man.

"Try it."

"Can't be done."

"Then do it somewhere else, whatever this history crap is. Do it someplace else."

"I was talking about the bus story."

"That's nothing," Nevins said.

"If it's nothing, why did they try to chase me away from it?"

"Because they don't like you. They don't like anybody new."

"Why did Howard say 'These guys are trained' when he was trying to pull Damian off me?"

"How the hell should I know? Because he's a goddamn idiot. He's fried."

"Nope. Something's going on with this. A real police department would want to know what it was."

He gave me his hard look.

"You just crossed the line, McMorrow."

"What if they've got him buried in the cellar? What if they killed him for his watch and the cash in his wallet? What if he was carrying cocaine? Who the hell is he? Where did he go?"

"I don't know, McMorrow. But I know he's gone. He's somebody else's problem. And I want the same thing for you. Go play reporter someplace else."

"So you can play policeman?"

Nevins stepped closer. His head tipped back, his chin out. I could see the hair in his nostrils.

"You got an attitude problem, sir."

"No, I really don't," I said, a touch of conciliation in my voice. "I'm just tired. It's been a long day. I don't like these guys touching me. I don't like having to hit them, either. Makes me feel kind of sick."

He relaxed. Backed off.

"And I want this story," I said.

"I can't stop you from writing some bullshit story," Nevins said. "But let me tell you. If you end up in here again, I'll fry your ass."

It was a somber ride home. I took the road down the east side of the Kennebec. It led past old farmhouses, empty chicken barns, trailers and riverbank camps. The river was on my right, a constant presence.

I barely noticed any of it.

As I drove, slowly and absently, I puzzled over it all. What was happening in Scanesett was very strange. I felt like I was playing a game but I had come in too late to hear the instructions. I'd missed a key element, something that was fundamental to understanding the rest of the rules, rules that Robie and Rob-ann, Howard and Damian, seemed to understand. And if they understood, how complicated could it be? Robie was simple and literal; Rob-ann, too. They didn't seem to be afflicted with some delusional mental illness. And Howard and Damian, they operated purely on instinct, like sharks. If they wanted something, they took it. If they were threatened, they lashed out. If they were outgunned or outnumbered, they backed off.

What had I done to threaten them? I'd asked about the bus man. He was the missing piece, the paper on which the instructions were written, the rules to the game. How had Robie put it? "What are you gonna do when you catch him?" And Howard, "These guys are trained." And then

Robie, when he talked to Hope Bell: "Did he have one of those ear things like on TV?"

Did they think I was a cop? A drug agent? Was this Mantis a drug runner? Was he trying to smuggle something into Canada? Did he get spooked on the bus for some reason? What had he told Robie or Rob-ann? Because they definitely knew something about him. Had they talked to him? Had he threatened them? Used their phone or holed up in their apartment?

I mulled it all the way through Clinton, Benton and Winslow, past the sprawling paper mills, with their steam plumes lifting straight up into the sky. Behind the steam plumes, there were cloud banks approaching from the southeast. There was no wind and the air had turned heavy, the way it does in the late afternoon. I looked at my watch. It was four thirty-five. I picked up the phone receiver and hit the button for Roxanne's number in Florida. It beeped its discordant little tune and then rang busy. I hung it up and kept driving, the implacable river on my right, the puzzle pieces shuffling and shifting in my head.

All the way up Route 3. All the way into Prosperity. All the way home, where I pulled into the yard and sat in the truck, and watched the rain start to fall, still mulling. I sat and thought, and the rain came down steadily, tapping on the hood, on the windshield. I concluded that it was all very simple. They knew something I didn't know.

When I went inside, I left the map on the seat, and the wrench under the map.

There were four calls on the answering machine. One was from Roxanne. She sounded cool and distant, telling me to call her after seven. The second was from Sandy-at-the-Chamber. Her little-girl voice spilled from the phone like a gurgling mountain stream as she said she had a great idea for a story, and it was really awesome, and I just had to call her.

Au contraire.

And the remaining calls were from Allison Smythe at the magazine. She sounded anxious, telling me to call as soon as possible, which meant after an ale.

"Jack," she said, picking up after one ring.

"Hi," I said.

"We've got a problem."

"You don't want Benedict Arnold?"

"No, I want him more than ever. I want him quick."

"How quick?"

"Our November cover, wild turkey country, just went belly up. The writer's husband had a massive heart attack."

"That's too bad," I said.

"Yeah, because we had the cover all designed. We'll have to plug with Arnold."

"When do you need it?"

"A week. And I mean that. Seven days, in my hands. Can you do that?"

I thought.

"Yeah, I guess—"

"Cover story means you can go longer. Up to twenty-five-hundred words. Also, it pays another three hundred bucks."

"Thirteen hundred?"

"In seven days. If you don't deliver it . . . well, you'll just have to deliver it. Come hell or high water. Our third choice is Revisiting Route 66."

"That's been done to death, hasn't it?" I said.

"It's not a cover. And Arnold, that's November, right? When he marched up there?"

"October, November. The attack was New Year's Eve."

"Fine. So can I count on it?"

I thought.

"Yeah. I'll have to go to Québec City. Make a couple of quick trips. When's your photographer coming?"

"As soon as you give me a list. Or how 'bout if I give you his number? He's in Boston. You can call him."

"Okay."

"Seven days."

"Okay."

"Not ten," Smythe said. "Not nine."

"Okay."

"And you'll call Kevin."

"Who's Kevin?"

"The photographer."

"Oh, okay."

"Here's his number."

She read it to me, said she had to go, and hung up.

"Huh," I said.

I drank another ale as I adjusted to the new reality, which came down to the fact that I'd have to crank it up. A morning at the state museum. A day to drive up through Coburn-Gore, across the border, then over to Québec City. A night there, and part of the next day. Somewhere in there, call the photographer. I could be back on Thursday. Write it Friday and Saturday. Fed-ex the disk so it would be there Monday morning.

It could be done, but it would have to be done without Roxanne. So much for the Château Frontenac.

I looked at the phone and my watch. Five-thirty. An hour and a half to wait to talk to her. I went out to the truck in the rain and brought in the atlas, leaving the wrench tucked into the passenger seat. When I came back I put the map down on the table, started to open it, then hesitated.

The rain drummed on the deck outside. The woods behind the house were still, but with leaves flicking, ticked by the drops. I walked to the window and looked out. There was nothing but rain and woods. No other sound, here on this deserted back road in a backwoods town. Nobody out there. Birds. Maybe a bear, once in a while. But nobody else in these woods.

I went to the closet anyway.

The rifle, a Remington thirty-ought-six, was in the back, behind the brooms. I took it out and laid it across the maps and notes on the table. The shells were in the drawer by the kitchen sink, under the dish towels. I took the box out and loaded the rifle, five in the magazine, one in the chamber, safety on. Then I stood it in the corner by the stairs, went back to the window and watched some more. Listened. Was I nuts? There was nobody out there. There was no one for miles. What was bothering me? A couple of numskulls who couldn't find Prosperity on a map? A guy who would have to ride here on his bike? A woman who probably thought a big adventure was going to get groceries at—

The phone rang. I jumped.

"Jeez," I said.

I went and picked up the receiver.

"Hello," I said.

There was a rattling noise.

"Hello," I said again.

I listened.

Heard breathing. Soft and slow.

"Hello," I said. "Hello. Anybody there?"

The person exhaled. I listened. The same sound. Somebody short of breath? Somebody there.

I waited. Neither of us spoke. I heard more breathing. Then a sniff. Then nothing. Then a creak, like a chair shifting. Then another sniff.

"So what is it?" I said.

Nothing. I waited, listened intently. There was the sound of the exhalation again. Another creak. A barely audible click. A rub. The sounds of someone sitting still.

I listened. The other person, presumably, listened, too. The sounds would stop and then start again, as if the person were putting a hand over the receiver, then removing it. I waited, the receiver pressed hard against my ear, my hand over my other ear.

The caller sniffed again. Then nothing. Then a sound, so faint I wasn't sure I was hearing it, then still faint but more real, then muffled again, but for a moment, still there.

A siren.

The phone clicked. The caller had hung up.

I stood there with the receiver in my hand. Looked at it, then reached for the phone book. I looked up Scanesett, the police department. The emergency number was 911. I dialed the other number. He answered, my buddy the dispatcher.

"Scanesett Police," he said.

Hi," I said. "Was that a police car, the siren I just heard near—Park Street?"

"Just now?" he said.

"Yeah. Ten seconds ago."

"No, sir. That is a rescue unit. Woman having a seizure. Park Street, corner of Park and—Grand. Can I get your name, sir? And could you state the nature of your problem?"

"No," I said. "There's no problem."

Or maybe there was. I looked up Robie Roberts, but there was nothing listed. There was an A. Roberts on Covey Street. I called that number. It rang. Three. Four. Five times.

Click.

"Yeah?"

It was Rob-ann's voice, but even more hesitant and timid than when we'd spoken before.

"Hi," I said. "This is Jack McMorrow."

"Oh," she said.

"What does he want?" I said.

Rob-ann didn't answer.

"What?" she said after a moment.

"What does he want?" I repeated.

"Um. Who?"

I paused. I didn't know who. It could have been her. It could have been Robie, or Howard. Damian couldn't stay quiet that long, so he was out. Or it could have been . . .

"Mantis," I said. "What's he want?"

"Shit," Rob-ann said, and hung up.

I put the phone down. It rang again. I picked it up, slowly. I listened. Heard a clattering sound, like silverware.

"Hello," I said.

"Jack. You all right?"

It was Roxanne, but terse.

"Yeah," I said. "Fine. How are you doing?"

"Not so great. You sure you're okay? You sound, I don't know, you sound strange."

I tried to brighten up.

"No, I'm fine. I just got off the phone. I thought you might be someone else."

"Is this a bad time?" Roxanne said.

There was a chill in her voice.

"No, it's fine. It was just sort of a crank call. Nothing at all. How are you?"

"Well, if you really want to know—"

"Of course, I do," I said.

"Because I could call you another time," Roxanne said.

"What's the matter?"

"Nothing. I just don't want to bother you if you're in the middle of something."

"I'm not. And even if I was, it wouldn't matter. What's going on? What's the matter?"

"Well, what do you think?" Roxanne said. "I've spent half the day with a lawyer and the other half with this jerky real-estate lady, trying to sell the condo, and I think she's trying to screw my mother out of money, so I've got to get rid of her, but there's a contract. And my mother, she's in there, and she was trying so hard, oh, God, and she tried to go to the bathroom and it was all over the place, and I'm trying to clean her up and it got all over my blouse, which is silk, because I was supposed to see this goddamn lawyer over this guardianship stuff and the money for the nursing home, and Jesus Christ, Jack, I called you for about two hours this afternoon, because I needed somebody to talk to, and you weren't in your truck and you weren't at home, and I didn't know where the hell you were, driving all over the state for some goddamn story about Benedict Arnold, and goddamn it, Jack, sometimes I need you, can't you understand that?''

''I do understand that,'' I said quietly.

''Well, then, why am I—''

Roxanne's voice cracked.

''Why do I—''

She started to sob, but caught herself.

''Why do I feel so—''

She sobbed again.

''So goddamn alone?''

And then the dam broke and Roxanne sobbed and sobbed, and cried and sobbed. I listened with the stupid receiver in my hand, a stupid receiver when I should have been there to hold her. But if I'd been there she wouldn't have had to do all this herself, but she'd said not to come, that she'd need me when she and her mother got back.

''Rox,'' I said, ''I love you.''

She just kept crying, then sniffing and crying some more.

''Hon, it's okay. It's going to be okay. It really will be okay. I promise.''

''Oh, God almighty.''

''Honey, it's okay.''

''Oh, Jack. She's there today and she's all, she's all soiled and she doesn't know what the hell is going on, and all I can think of is this picture of her and my father and me, and we were going to the Nutcracker, and we're all dressed up and, there I am, so happy, and my mother, oh, God, she could be so elegant, you know? My dad in black tie and my mother in this black gown, God, I still remember it, all beaded, and these gloves, and her furs, she looked like a movie star, and my dad, he was so big and handsome.''

Roxanne sighed.

''It's okay,'' I said.

''And today, I mean, she's in the bathroom, and these

nurses and aides are in there, and they're calling her
'honey,' and she's fighting them and, oh, God, is this what
it comes to? Is this what it was all for? Oh, Jack, I'm sorry.
I just needed you.''

''I would have come,'' I said, staring out at the rain.

''I know.''

''You told me not to.''

''I know. But you had your work to do.''

''It could have waited,'' I said. ''But now, they just
called. They want to use it for a cover, which means they
have to have it in a week. Something else fell through.''

''Oh,'' Roxanne said, her voice trailing off.

''You want me to come down? I can just tell them to
forget it. Tell them I had an emergency. The deal's off.''

''No. You've already worked on this so much. You can't
just drop it. I'm fine. I just was at one of those, I don't
know, those low points. It just got to me, that's all.''

''I understand.''

''But I'll be okay.''

''I can still come.''

''No. It isn't worth it. I'll wrap things up here and I'll
be back. You just hold me when I get there.''

''I will,'' I said.

''A week,'' Roxanne said. ''That means you have to go
to Québec City by yourself?''

''I guess so. We'll save the Château for when you get
home.''

''It's a date.''

''So what's the story with the condo?'' I asked.

''Oh, God, this woman says she has a buyer, but I think
they take me for some sort of rube. Think they're going to
pick it up cheap and resell it for a fat profit.''

''Your mother wouldn't have let that happen.''

''My mother? Are you kidding? She took three hundred
thousand from my dad's insurance and lived on it for
twenty years. With the condo, now it's closer to six hundred. And she lived well, too. And now these bloody vul-

tures down here . . . Anyway, tell me what you've been doing. I need a break.''

I stood there by the counter with the receiver in my hand. Walked over, trailing the cord, and took the box of shells off the table and stuck it back in the towel drawer.

''Oh, the usual,'' I said.

I told her about the museum being closed, about going up Route 201 to Caratunk. I told her about Arnold cutting across to the Dead River, how I found Arnold Pond, where he stood as he and his men carried their canoes west. How he got lost and so many of his men nearly starved or died of the cold.

''I hope you had a better time,'' Roxanne said.

''It was fine. Now it's all log trucks and white water-rafting. Still some beautiful rugged country, though. Off to the west, just beautiful mountains. Arnold ended up around Bigelow, northeast of Sugarloaf. Cutting across there. That's my next trip. I'll scout it out and then we can go in the fall together. Make a foliage run.''

''I'd love that,'' she said, but ruefully, as though the idea of something pleasurable only reminded her of all the sadness she would have to deal with first.

''And finish up with three days at the Château,'' Roxanne said bravely.

''And never leave the room,'' I said.

''Never leave the bed,'' Roxanne said.

''Never come back.''

''They'd report us missing. Hey, speaking of missing, was there any more about the guy on the bus? Did they find him?''

''No,'' I said. ''But I think I have.''

11   Roxanne thought it all very strange.
"What's in it for them?" she said.
"For who?"

"For the two leeches. Or the brother and sister. What would they get out of it?"

I told her I didn't know, but I was sure there had been some contact. And now the cousins were afraid of something. Getting caught. Being exposed in some way. But if it had been Mantis who had called me, why were they protecting him? Roxanne, as usual, got to the heart of the matter.

What was in it for them?

She had to go back to the nursing home, so we said good-bye, among other things, promising to call the next day. Roxanne told me to take care of myself. I told her to do the same, and to call me if she changed her mind about me coming there to help her. She said she would, but by then her strength and composure had returned and I knew she would try to handle it all on her own.

And I was relieved.

I knew I wasn't handling this well, the whole matter of Roxanne and her mother's illness. But the truth was, I didn't do illness well. I didn't do death well, either, and Karleena Masterson was headed for both. She was headed for both in a very sad way, and I didn't want to think about that.

When my father had died, when I was twenty-five, I had

numbed myself for a long time after, escaping to packed pubs, all-night parties, a succession of women. When my mother had gone, when I was twenty-nine, I'd thrown myself into my job like a dervish. I'd tackled every story with ferocity. If a story called for empathy, I would be ferociously empathetic. If a story called for toughness, I'd walk through doors. If a story demanded good writing, I would slave over my copy like some possessed composer. If a story called for persuasion, I could convince Adam and Eve to chomp that apple. If a story called for pursuit, leaping from lead to lead, I was relentless as a hound.

In a way, my denial of death had propelled me to the top of my profession. Hand over hand, I'd climbed journalism's ladder, with the Grim Reaper one rung behind.

Standing there by the window with a can of ale in my hand, I smiled at the thought. What was I afraid of? What kept me from running to Roxanne's side as she watched her mother's terrible decline? Why did I find these passages in the Benedict Arnold books, the names of the dead and dying, so poignant? Why was I so compelled to chase down the bus man?

Because if I couldn't face the answer to the big mystery—after this, what?—I could at least distract myself with the little ones.

So that night, with the house, the road, this whole stretch of woods in absolute darkness, I lay in bed in the loft and listened to the rain on the roof. As it drummed steadily, I thought about Roxanne and her mother, the picture of the happy family, at least back then. I thought about my father, a big, gentle, quiet man who I had come to appreciate too late. About my mother, who, when I was at the *Times,* put my clips on her refrigerator with magnets, like papers brought home from first grade.

I thought about good luck and bad luck, and Benedict Arnold and people who gave their lives for causes that were soon forgotten. I thought about my good friend Clair, whom I had thought was impervious to doubt, but seemed shaken by the sudden symptoms of approaching old age. I thought about Robie and Rob-ann and their lives, which were obscure by almost every definition. I thought about the bus man, and how our paths had crossed by pure chance. And as I grew more and more drowsy, I reached down and touched my rifle, on the floor by the bed, and felt reassured.

"God almighty," the voice barked. "I leave and you turn into some kinda slug, sleeping the day away. What time is it? Almost seven o'clock?"

Standing at the kitchen counter in my shorts, I looked at my watch.

"Clair," I rasped, "it's six forty-one."

"And don't try to tell me I didn't wake you. The phone rang twenty-three times. And I can tell by your voice. You sound like you got a hairball. No self-discipline. That's your problem. Probably up all night watching videos or some goddamn thing."

"You sound like you're feeling better."

"The body's recovering. The mind is going nuts. I gotta get out of here."

"You want me to come down and break you out?"

"Pretend you're here to clean the goddamn pool or something. I'll hide in your truck."

"Place is getting to you, huh?"

"Jeez, it's good to see the kids, but God almighty, if I hear another conversation about underground lawn sprinklers, mark my words, I'll strangle somebody."

"With a hose."

"Good idea," Clair said. "I like irony."

"Lawn sprinklers a big topic down there?"

"Hell, yes. That and goddamn golf. All these flabby guys, couldn't lift a chainsaw over their knees, stand around and talk about this shot and that shot and what club they used, and I've got teeth marks in my tongue trying not to say anything. And this goddamn suburbia goes on forever.

And you're driving through it, and then there's some mall that wasn't there last week. And then there's more suburbia. All looks the same, disorienting as the Sahara. What I'd give to be out on the ridge right now. How's the tractor?''

''Fine. I think I've got that mower bar totally mastered.''

''I hope so. Summer's half over.''

''How's Mary?''

''Fine. She'd like to be home, too, though. How's her gardens?''

''Blooming up a storm. How are those grandkids?''

''Nothing wrong with 'em that a summer in Waldo County wouldn't cure. They're getting soft, all this god-damn television. They just stare at screens all day. Got eyes like owls.''

''They're toddlers, Clair. One's just a baby.''

''You gotta catch it early.''

''Surprised you don't have them out on maneuvers. Fill their backpacks with rocks.''

''That's an idea,'' Clair said. ''Double time around the neighborhood.''

''Get that baby crawling on her belly.''

''Right. Under razor wire.''

''Live rounds, over their heads.''

''Now you're talking,'' Clair said.

He paused.

''How's it going?''

I put a teabag in a mug of water and slipped it into the microwave. Reached down and brushed crumbs off of the soles of my feet.

''Okay, I guess,'' I said.

''Roxanne?''

''About the same.''

''Sorry.''

''She'll get through it. We'll get through it. But it's hard on her. Hard as hell.''

''You going down?''

''Oh, I would, but I've got to finish this story by Monday. The Benedict Arnold thing. They want it earlier because another story fell through.''

''Did I tell you about the politics behind all that?'' Clair said.

''Yeah,'' I said. ''The more things change—''

''Yup. He was one hell of a soldier. Got greedy in the end. Big ego, too.''

''Yeah,'' I said, waiting for the tea. ''But I don't think he was in the Revolution for the same reasons as the democracy types. He just wanted free enterprise. Get the king off his back so he could make more money. And then the hard-core lefties wanted to get on his back, too.''

''Boy,'' Clair said, ''things don't change at all, do they? Find your AWOL bus passenger?''

I took the tea out, turned to the refrigerator for the milk.

''Not yet. But it's been interesting. I think I'm getting closer. And I've got to call the *Globe* one of these days. I just keep waiting to have more to tell them.''

''You think he's still there?''

''If he isn't, he was. And he fraternized with the locals for some reason.''

I sipped my tea.

''You want to hear about it?'' I said.

''Is there anything in the story about golf?''

''Not that I know of.''

''Okay, then. Shoot.''

So I shot. Robie on the sidewalk. The psycho brothers in the parking lot. The phone call. Rob-ann's reaction when I guessed and said, ''Mantis.'' When I finished, I could almost hear Clair thinking.

''Why would the guy call you if he was hiding from you?''

''I don't know. Why would he call and not say anything?''

''If it was him.''

''Right,'' I said.

''And the cop went there and didn't find anything?''

"That's what she said. I don't know how hard she was able to look. There isn't enough for a warrant or anything. Her sergeant thinks it's nothing, thinks I'm just being a pain in the neck."

"He's got that right."

"Thanks."

I sipped the tea. I was beginning to feel better. Outside, the sun had broken through and the wet trees were gleaming. A yellow warbler flitted by, disappearing into the green.

"Two things," Clair said, his military, guerrilla-warfare mind in gear. "These people think you're something you're not. A cop, undercover. A secret agent. I don't know, some kind of enforcer. You say they're not really whacked out, but from the sounds of it, they're probably easily led. So they're getting it from someplace."

"I'd say so."

I drank my tea.

"But the cousins are getting it, too. So it must be sort of convincing. And if they're trying to protect somebody or something, they must stand to gain from it. Money. Maybe the promise of money. Drugs. A couple of guys like that would probably do a lot for an ounce of cocaine."

"Kill their mother," I said.

"Torture her first. But the brother and sister, they're different types, right?"

"I don't think they'd hurt anybody."

"And they don't want cocaine," Clair said. "What about money?"

I considered it.

"No," I said. "They're just not the type. They don't need money. They have their apartment. He has his old bicycles, this routine he goes through, collecting stuff. They have a TV, I saw a lot of videos. I'd say they have pretty simple needs."

"But they're all in it together, for some reason."

"Maybe different reasons," I said.

"Maybe," Clair said.

He paused. Somewhere in the background, I heard a baby cry.

"They have trash?" Clair said suddenly.

"What do you mean?"

"Trash. Household stuff. Garbage."

"I suppose."

"If he's in there, he's probably not wearing gloves. See if you can get hold of their trash. Bottles, jars. He says, 'Please pass the ketchup,' and they hand it to him and, *voilà*, there's your print. Look for the one that doesn't belong."

"And have the cops run it?"

"They can send it to the FBI."

"Scanesett? I don't know if they've even heard of the FBI. This is very small-town stuff."

"This cop, the woman, she sounds reasonable," Clair said. "Ask her to do it."

"Dust their trash?"

I thought about it all the way down Route 3 to Augusta.

With the reassuring light of day, the rifle had gone back in the closet. I'd jumped in and out of the shower, put on hiking boots, a polo shirt and shorts with lots of pockets, and pulled in to grab a coffee from the Prosperity General Store. Ready for the wilderness, ready for the library, ready for Howard and Damian, ready for whatever else Scanesett could bring on, I drove, sipped my coffee and wondered.

How could I get a print out of that apartment? Would the police have prints of Robie and Rob-ann? What if the bus man wasn't on file anywhere? Would Hope Bell be willing or able to do anything like this, or had I already pushed her to the limit? If she wasn't interested, I didn't really have any right, or need, to go much farther. I needed to be able report the results of an investigation. Ideally, it wouldn't be only my own.

I was still mulling it all as I crossed the Augusta bridge,

high over the Kennebec. The tide was low again and the river was glittering in the morning sun, like a long sluice full of silver. A couple of big powerboats were moored just upriver from the bridge, out behind the rust-stained, fire-scarred brick walls of the old downtown. I glanced down at the boats as I drove, picturing their owners, sitting in offices in those buildings, standing at windows and watching their dreams turning on the mooring lines. Back on the desk, there would be forms to fill out, reports to finish, financials to work up.

And they would look down at those boats and tell themselves that one day, a summer day like this, they would leave for work, for another day of forms and reports, and they would keep right on going. Down to the landing, the little ramp by the town park. Get in the dinghy and row out to the boat and start the motor and head downriver. Keep going all the way past Swan Island, past the rocky heads, past the shipyard at Bath and out the Kennebec. Past the little figures on Popham Beach, out into the swells and maybe turn northeast, up the coast.

With a gold card for gas, a two-foot chop, hopping from point to point, harbor to harbor, all the way up the coast. Past Acadia, past the tourists, past Machiasport and Cutler and Eastport, all the places that had been just words on the charts, places out of reach of the little day trips that the office job allowed, the job that dragged the boat back up the Kennebec like an eel every Sunday afternoon, because there were forms to be filled out every Monday morning. Forms and reports and phone calls, but not this time; this time the boat wouldn't ever come back upriver. It would slip into the fog and just disappear.

I wondered as I drove. Was that what Mantis had planned? To just disappear? Step off of a bus and never be seen again? Had that been the plan?

If so, what had gone wrong?

I pulled into the museum parking lot, rolled into a space and shut off the motor. The cooling motor ticked. The sun beat down on my left arm, resting on the door. I sat.

What had gone wrong? Certainly the plan hadn't been to find some local misfits and their hair-trigger cousins. Move in for the weekend. Drink some beer, watch some videos. That wasn't the kind of plan that included fake checking accounts and phony licenses. Those things indicated a need for secrecy. Who would trust Robie and Rob-ann with a secret? Who would trust Howard and Damian at all? Who?

I sat for another minute, then still pondered it as I gathered my equipment. Who would trust that crew? Nobody. Nobody in his right mind. Nobody who had a choice.

As I walked up to the library building, an image slipped into my mind. A man in a room. A man tied to a chair. A man waiting for someone to come. A man whose plan had come apart, for some odd reason, in a very odd place, and now there was no plan at all.

That image faded as I went down the stairs to the library. The central room was big and airy, a two-story atrium with tall indoor birch trees that grew futilely toward the light, blind to their captivity. I stopped at the bottom of the stairs, saw a sign that said "reference desk," and walked over. A woman, gray-haired and smiling with both her mouth and eyes, turned to me and asked if she could help. I told her what I needed. She directed me to the catalog computer terminals, and when I came back, five minutes later, she was still smiling. I showed her the entries I had marked.

"This one's in the safe," she said.

"Can I see it?"

"It can't be photocopied. It's special handling."

"I'll be careful," I said.

"And your name is?" she asked, taking out a form.

"Jack McMorrow."

"This can't leave the room, Mr. McMorrow."

"That's fine."

"And you'll have to wear gloves."

"Really?"

"We supply them," she said reassuringly, and took the

computer printout and hurried off, bound for the catacombs. I waited but looked around so I could describe the place to my readers. The tables were filled singly, one reader for each, like diners who wanted to eat alone. They were mostly older people, probably retired. Some in shorts, like me. A lot of polo shirts. Sneakers with white ankle socks. No one spoke, but they rustled pages. Someone coughed and it echoed across the room. A man in a plaid sports shirt blew his nose, and that echoed, too. The ventilation system made a quiet hiss, and the leaves on the indoor trees trembled, as if a storm were coming, blowing in from the lobby upstairs.

I watched and waited, and then there she was, holding a folder in her hands like a priest holds a Bible. We went to a table and she showed me how to use the gloves. She reminded me again about the photocopying and I told her I'd brought a camera. Could I just photograph the pages? She'd check. I put on my plastic gloves and unfolded the cardboard cover and the white protective paper, peeling away the modern trappings to reveal the yellowed, fragile ''Journal of Isaac Senter.''

I'd read about Senter in my history books. He was a physician from Rhode Island, one of the hundreds of volunteers on the march. Senter lived through it but he wrote through it as well, and his notes were published under the title *On a Secret Expedition Against Québec.* This particular copy had been printed in Philadelphia in 1846. I sat down at the library table, opened the book with reverence and read.

Once again, it was October 1775.

Saturday, 14th.—Returned again to my boat, and continued carrying over the remainder with all possible speed. The army was now much fatigued, being obliged to carry all the batteaux, barrels of provisions, warlike stores, &e., over on their backs through a most terrible piece of woods conceiva-

ble. Sometimes in the mud knee deep, then over ledgy hills, &e. The distance was three and three-quarter miles. Was obliged to encamp between the river and pond, not being able to get quite over with the last load.

This was near Caratunk, at the beginning of the death march to the Dead River. The next day, Senter waited for the stragglers.

Sunday, 15th.—Many of us were now in a sad plight with the diarrhea. Our water was of the worst quality. The lake was low, surrounded with mountains, situate in a low morass. Water was quite yellow. With this we were obliged not only to do all our cooking, but use it as our constant drink. Nor would a little of it suffice, as we were obliged to eat our meat exceeding salt. This with our constant fatigue called for large quantities of drink. No sooner had it got down than it was puked up by many of the poor fellows.

They named that place "Camp Disaster." Two weeks later, more than a third of the farmers, woodsman, sailors, all turned soldiers, had drowned or starved or simply disappeared in the bitter-cold wilderness. The survivors were slogging along the Chaudière River in Québec.

Wednesday, Nov. 1.—Our greatest luxuries now consisted of a little water, stiffened with flour, in imitation of shoemaker's paste . . . Instead of diarrhea, which tried our men most shockingly in the former part of our march, the reverse was now the complaint, which continued for many days. We had now arrived as we thought to almost the zenith of distress. Several had been entirely destitute of either meat or bread for many days. These chiefly consisted of those who devoured their provision immediately, and a number who were in the boats. The voracious disposition many of us had now arrived at, rendered almost anything admissible. Clean and unclean were forms now little in use. In company was a poor dog [who had] hitherto lived through all the tribulations, became a prey for the sustenance of the assassinators. This poor animal was instantly devoured, without leaving any vestige of the sacrifice. Nor did the shaving soap, pomostum, and even the lip salve, leather of their shoes, cartridge boxes, &e., share any better fate; passed several poor fellows, truly commiserating [with them].

I'd read about the dog in my books. It was a Newfoundland, belonging to an officer. I pictured a big, loyal and finally bewildered dog, hacked to death by his supposed benefactors. And in the quiet, sunny room, with the people bent silently over their rustling books, I read on.

Senter wrote of the mountains, bogs, small ponds and streams, "the most execrable bogmire imaginable," all of which had to be crossed in the icy winter weather. He mentioned the army's "pretended pilot," who led them this way and that, their number dwindling day by day.

In this condition we proceeded with as little knowledge of where we were, or where we should get to, as if we had been in the unknown interior of Africa, or the deserts of Arabia.

Two days later, an estimated 675 of the original 1,100 men—and a handful of women—who had left Cambridge for the march were met by French Canadians, who had been dispatched southward by Arnold's advance scouts. The Canadians were driving cattle, which were devoured, like the dog, on the spot.

The march continued up the Chaudière to the St. Lawrence River, with long days of misery instead of daily brushes with death. Well fed by the French Canadians, the army camped for almost two months within site of the stone walls of Québec City. On New Year's Eve they attacked the ramparts, and many of the survivors of the long march got their reward, cut down on the snowy streets. Arnold was shot, too, but refused to give up the fight, even from his hospital bed, where Dr. Senter treated him.

He would neither be removed, nor suffer a man from the Hospital to retreat. He ordered his pistols loaded, with a sword on his bed, adding that he was determined to kill as many as possible if they came into the room. We were now all soldiers. . . .

I looked up from the page. It was all for naught. All of the suffering, the starvation, the cold, miserable deaths. All of the lives sucked into oblivion, by this march, this battle, this war and countless others like it. Territory seized and lost, kings crowned and dethroned, causes embraced but now long forgotten, people stamped out like bugs, ground into dust as though they'd never existed. Roxanne's mother, once regal, wrestling with nurse's aides on the floor of a nursing home bathroom.

"God," I said aloud.

At the next table, a white-haired woman looked up from a book about genealogy.

"Sorry about that," I said, smiling at her.

She pursed her thin, gray lips and went back to her search for a pedigree.

I thumbed through the fragile pages, and then went to the shelves and found other journals in newer volumes. I read about an Indian "Sataness," about men "seized by the cramp" and dying, about floods and snowstorms. After an hour or so, I took my camera out of its bag and laid the pages open on the table. The librarian hadn't come back, but she hadn't said no, so I photographed most of Senter's journal, and a few pages of the diary of another marcher, one Simeon Thayer. The shutter snapped and the library patrons looked up. The pedigree lady gave me another dirty look.

This time I didn't apologize.

When I left, I returned the journal to the librarian and thanked her. She said I was very welcome and headed for the safe, somewhere away from public view. I climbed the stairs out of the library, out of the past, where Dr. Senter and Arnold and all of the others had lived and died, and into the present. When I pushed the door, a wave of heat enveloped me and I squinted in the sun. I walked to the truck, started it, and was digging around for my sunglasses when the car phone rang. Startled, I grabbed the receiver.

"Roxanne?" I said. "I mean, hi."

"This Jack McMorrow?" a voice said.

A man. Older.

"Yeah," I said. "Who's this?"

"It don't matter who I am. I just want to help you out, buddy."

"Yeah?"

"He's gone."

"Who?"

"The guy. The guy on the bus. He ain't here."

"He ain't where?" I said.

"He ain't here. He left."

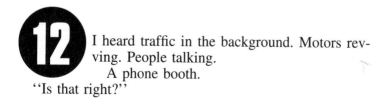

I heard traffic in the background. Motors revving. People talking.

A phone booth.

"Is that right?"

"Yeah. He's gone," the voice said.

I dug in my camera bag for my tape recorder. Fished out the little suction cup microphone from Radio Shack. As I talked, I stuck the suction cup on the receiver, the plug into the jack. I hit record.

"Where'd he go?"

"He said he was going to New Hampshire."

He pronounced it New Hamp-sheer.

"When did he leave?" I said.

"A coupla days ago. He didn't stay here long."

A car drove by. I pressed my hand over my left ear.

"How'd he leave?" I said.

"Um, he hitchhiked."

"To New Hampshire?"

"Yeah. He said he knew somebody there. And then he was gonna go to Boston. After that he was going to Boston."

The guy said it like he was reading from notes.

"Huh," I said. "So he's gone?"

"Yeah. Long gone."

"Why'd he get off the bus?"

There was a muffled pause, like he'd covered the receiver.

"He changed his mind," the guy said. "He said he didn't want to go to Canada."

"Then why did he sign up for a trip to Québec?"

"I got no friggin' idea. He didn't tell me."

"Talk to him much?"

More muffle.

"A little."

"Did he say why he changed his mind in Scanesett?"

"He didn't feel good."

"Oh, yeah?"

"He said he had a headache. He didn't want to ride on the bus no more."

"How'd you meet him?"

"I just met him."

"Just met him?"

"Yeah. Around town."

"What did you do?"

Pause.

"I run into him. I bought him a coupla beers."

"That made his head feel better?"

"Yeah, it did. So then he felt good enough to leave. He ain't coming back, neither."

A van pulled into the spaces next to mine. A woman got out and slammed her door shut. She opened the sliding door and a bunch of little kids spilled out. I shut my window.

"So you bought him a coupla beers?"

"Yeah."

"Where?"

"Um, just in a bar."

"Which one?"

"Um, just a bar. It don't matter."

"What'd he look like?" I said. "Just so I know we're talking about the same guy."

Traffic noise. Then the muffled pause. Then more traffic noise.

"Just a guy. Kind of average."

"How old?"

"I don't know."

He paused.

"Maybe forty. I don't know. I suck at ages."

"Fat? Skinny?"

Pause.

"Kind of chubby."

"Shorts? Long pants?"

Pause again.

"Shorts."

"Did he have any money?"

No pause this time.

"No, he didn't have no money. He was broke. That's why I bought him the beers."

"You must be a nice guy."

He didn't say anything.

"To buy this stranger beers, I mean."

"Yeah, well . . ."

"He have any bags with him?"

"Nope."

"Tell you his name?"

"Um, yeah. Manter."

He covered the phone. The mother and kids headed for the museum, and I opened the window.

"Mantis. He said 'Mantis.' "

"Like the bug?" I asked.

"What?"

"Like the bug. P. Ray Mantis. Get it? Praying mantis?"

"Oh," the guy said. "Whatever. I don't know nothing 'bout that. I just wanted to tell you he's outta here."

"It's a phony name," I said. "The cops are looking for him. Did you know that? Looking for anybody who's seen him, too. I think there might be a reward."

"Yeah, well, um, they better go looking in friggin' New Hampshire, 'cause he's gone."

"How 'bout I meet you someplace? You don't have to tell me your name or anything. I just need to know more about him. I might write a story about—"

"Yeah, right. Well, he's history. He's in Manchester, New Hampshire. You can look for him there. I gotta go."

And he hung up.

It wasn't Howard. It wasn't Damian. It wasn't Robie, either, so it seemed that the Mantis affair was spreading through Scanesett. How many more people were in on this well-kept secret? Who the hell was that?

He was making it up as he spoke, or at best, was being coached. If Mantis had grabbed a couple of beers and hitch-hiked out of town, why were Robie and Rob-ann so connected to him? Why were Howard and Damian so worked up? Manchester, New Hampshire? Give me a break.

Sitting there in the truck, with cars coming and going

around me, I rewound the tape. When I played it back, it was so faint as to be almost inaudible, at least here. Maybe if I played it at home, on a big tape deck with filters, I'd be able to hear it. Maybe if I played it for Hope Bell.

It was Tuesday, and she'd be off again. I looked at my watch. It was only ten-thirty and I could be up there before noon. What else did I have to do? Drop off my film. Write out my notes from the trip up Route 201 to Caratunk. That wouldn't take all day. I could do that after supper.

What else was there? Call Roxanne, of course. She'd be at the nursing home until at least four. I could call her there. And I was going to call the Gardiner police to see if I could find out anything about Mantis and his bad check. Maybe make an initial inquiry at the *Globe*. But if I went to Scanesett, I could make a run for the Canadian border at Coburn-Gore. I could check out Eustis and Stratton, where Arnold caught the north branch of the Dead River. If I didn't stay in Scanesett too long, I could be at the border crossing by three or four. That way I could make the Québec City trip through Jackman, and have more time to spend in the city itself.

It made perfect sense, once you rationalized a bit. I put the truck in gear and headed up the Kennebec, knowing what Arnold probably had known as well: The perfect antidote for all those existential doubts was a mission.

I drove fast, out of Augusta and up Route 201, windows open, hot breeze blowing through.

In Vassalboro, there were dairy farms; in Waterville, red-brick mills. More dairy farms in Benton and Clinton, where I had to lock up the brakes to avoid hitting a tractor pulling a wagon of manure. And then there was the big paper mill at Hinckley, massive and ominous and smelling of dampness and sulfur. Then more woods, and scraggly fields and the pine-bordered Kennebec off to my right. In the mill town of Skowhegan, there was a factory that turned bolts of birch into toothpicks, and the workers were on a break, sitting at picnic tables, smoking in the heat.

They looked at me as I drove past. They looked tired.

Then there was a stretch of trailers and houses and hair salons in converted garages, and then I coasted down a long hill into the town of Scanesett, past the shoe shop, over the bridge and the Kennebec, and down Main Street.

I looked for two things as I drove through the downtown: one was the Chevette, and the other was Robie. I didn't see either one, so I kept going past the municipal building and the police station, and then off to the left to Robie's street and then his building. I slowed and looked but the bike and trailer weren't in sight out back. I took a left and headed across town toward Hope Bell's house. It was eleven thirty-five and I wondered what her husband would think if I interrupted his dinner break. Probably not much, no matter how pressing the case, and I had a feeling that, to a contractor with a wife and a couple of kids, the bus man wouldn't seem pressing.

I hoped he'd be civil. I really hoped he wouldn't be home at all. Bell could listen to the tape. I could give the baby a bottle. Open wide for Uncle Jack, that's a good . . .

There was the bike, hitched to the trailer.

It was parked outside a corner grocery, a store built into the first floor of a tenement house. I slowed as I passed it, then pulled into a driveway. A man mowing the lawn looked up. I nodded and put the truck into reverse and pulled back out. Robie's bike still was there. I parked beside it and got out.

The trailer was half filled with grocery bags. The bags were filled with empty cans and bottles. I stood there, leaning against the truck, and waited.

In a moment, the door pushed open, and two little kids came out, tearing wrappers off of candy bars.

"Thanks, Robie," one of them said, hopping off the step, and then there was big Robie, coming through the door and looking up and seeing me. And stopping in his tracks.

"Robie," I said. "What's going on?"

He took a couple of steps toward the trailer.

"I gotta bring in my bottles."

"I'll help you," I said.

He picked up two bags, and I picked up two more. I followed him to the door and he held it open for me with his shoulder. We both went into the store and a young woman came out from behind the counter and pointed to a place between the counter and the milk coolers.

She looked at me curiously and smiled.

"Hi," she said.

"Hello," I said, putting the bags down.

"Thanks," she said. "You count 'em, Robe?"

"Six seventy-five," he said, putting his bags down. "But you have to minus the candy bars for B. J. and Jason."

"That's eighty-three, but we'll call it six even," the young woman said, going back to the register. She hit the buttons and the drawer slid open. She took out a five and a one and held them out for Robie. He took them and slid them into the front pocket of his jeans.

"Bye, Annie," Robie said.

"Take her easy, Robe," the woman said.

I held the door for him on the way out, and he didn't stop until he'd mounted his bike.

"What's going on, Robe?" I said, standing in front of him. "I've got your loony relatives chasing me around. People calling me on the phone. This morning some guy called me in my truck and told me Mantis was in Manchester, New Hampshire."

He looked at me and shrugged.

"You and Rob-ann are the only ones who had that number. Is this another one of your relatives?"

He looked around uncomfortably.

"I don't know."

"Well, God, Robe, it's making it hard for me to do my job. Should I give up on the guy here? I'd hate to have to chase him around New England, and then find out he was right here the whole time.''

Robie rocked on his bike.

''I don't know,'' he said again.

''Listen, Robie,'' I said, lowering my voice. ''I don't know how you got involved in this, whatever it is. But you're not getting into any trouble, are you? The police are looking for this guy, you know. Hope Bell is talking to other police departments. This guy may not be what you think he is.''

Robie looked at me. He was listening.

I changed tacks.

''Those little kids friends of yours?''

''Jason and B. J.? Yeah, they're friends of mine. I got a lotta friends.''

''So you buy them stuff?''

''Yeah. They're only little. They don't have any money.''

''So you buy them candy? Sort of take care of them?''

''Sorta.''

I paused. He was looking away now, watching the cars go slowly by.

''You've taken care of a lot of people, haven't you? You and your sister.''

Robie shrugged. Hands twisted back and forth on the grips.

''Hope Bell was telling me you took care of your mother. You and Rob-ann. That was good of you.''

He nodded, still looking away.

''How long ago did she die, Robie? If you don't mind my asking.''

''June eleventh, nineteen-ninety. And my daddy died March twenty-second, nineteen-seventy-nine.''

His pedigree. Short and sad.

''You were—''

''I was four and three-quarters when my daddy died, but I can remember him. When my mother died, June eleventh, nineteen-ninety, I was fifteen and then in a couple of days after that, I was sixteen. I didn't have a party.''

''Did you want one?''

He thought.

''No, I didn't feel like having one. The funeral was that day. We didn't have time to have a party, too. It was a while after that, Rob-ann made me the cake.''

''A birthday cake?''

''Yup. She makes all the cakes. She's the cook in the family. I'm the fix-it man.''

We stood there, the two of us. There was a big silver maple in front of the store and we were in its shade. The woman in the store came to the door and looked, then went back to whatever it was she had been doing.

''So you take care of people, huh, Robie?''

''Yeah.''

''That's nice of you.''

He didn't say anything.

''You know, you're a nice guy, but sometimes being nice can get you into trouble. Like the bus guy. Let's say you were taking care of him. Maybe he needed help. And he told you some things about what he was doing, or what he'd done. Let's say he told you the truth, then what? Then you know something that maybe you shouldn't know. That can get you in trouble.''

I looked at him. He was chewing on his lower lip. The hands were twisting faster, working the handgrips.

''I didn't mean to know nothin','' Robie said, softly, almost in a murmur.

''I know that. But it won't make any difference.''

I paused. Let it sink in.

''You know what Hope Bell needs?'' I said. ''She needs a fingerprint. Something he's handled. Anything. She'll take that and find out if he is who he says he is. If he is, then . . . well, I guess we'll see what happens. But if he's doing bad things here, or if he's in trouble from someplace else, and you're helping him . . . and Rob-ann . . . well,

Robe, you could get in trouble. You both could.''

Robie looked away. His big sneaker slipped off of the pedal, and it spun.

"I wouldn't do nothin' wrong."

"But your cousins? They would. They have already."

He looked at me, his eyes flickering.

"And if you're there, you could get blamed, too. The younger one tried to choke me yesterday. Did you know that?''

He shook his head.

"I don't know, but I have a feeling that, if he got caught, he might try to blame you and Rob-ann. But if you had done something, if you helped Officer Bell, then she'd know that you didn't mean to get mixed up in it. You didn't want to get in trouble. She'd know—''

Robie swung his leg over the bike, got off and started for the door. He went inside and I waited, and in a minute or so he came out. He was carrying an empty soda bottle.

It was Diet Pepsi, caffeine-free. Robie was carrying it by the neck.

Bell's Toyota was parked in her driveway. Beside it was a big red Ford pickup, with ladders on racks and steel toolboxes, one on each side. The logo on the door said, "Bell Bros. Const." There was a big white bell over the words.

"Damn," I said.

I parked in the street and walked up the drive to the side

door. As I approached it, I could hear utensils scraping on plates. Then Hope's voice, saying, "Megan, no. Oh, honey, I just got you changed. Oh, lord. You stay here, and I'll go pound nails."

"That would be fine, wouldn't it, Megsy?" a man's voice said, deep but doing baby talk. "We'd have lots of fun. Make all the messes we want. All the messes we want. Right, honey bun?"

The baby chortled. I took a deep breath and tapped on the aluminum door. Hope Bell's husband filled the screen. He was blond and wide and he looked down at me.

"Hi," I said. "I'm Jack McMorrow. I'm looking for Officer Bell."

"She isn't working today," he said, stern, no more baby talk. "You can call her at the station tomorrow."

He started to turn away.

"Listen, I'm sorry to bother you at home. I know she's off-duty. But I have something I think she'd like to have, and I'm going to be in Canada tomorrow, and I didn't want to—"

"Hey," Hope's husband started to say. "I'm sorry, sir, but she's not—"

"It's okay, Ray," I heard Bell say. "I know him. I'll talk to him."

"But goddamn it, it never ends. You open the door and before you know it, you're working seven days a week. Hope, you said it yourself, you said—"

"It's okay. Here, take her. I'll just be a minute."

"Jesus," Ray Bell sputtered, and then Hope Bell came to the door and stepped outside.

"Sorry," I said. "Really, I am."

"It's okay. What is it?"

She was barefoot, wearing shorts and a loose white blouse over a bathing suit top. There were orange stains on the front of the blouse. She caught my glance.

"Carrots," Bell said. "She throws her food."

I tried not to look again.

"I really am sorry, but I'm going to Québec tomorrow and I might be there for the rest of the week."

"Must be nice."

"It's for work."

"Even nicer."

We stood in the driveway. I wondered if the pavement was burning her feet, but it didn't seem to be.

"I got something you might be interested in."

Bell looked unimpressed.

"You heard about my run-in with the cousins?"

"Yeah. I heard you guys didn't hit it off. A little scuffle, Devins said."

"The younger one got me by the throat. He's like a pit bull. I had to hit him with a tire iron to to get him off."

She looked at me. Protectively fingered the opening of her blouse.

"I just hit him on the hand. The other hand," I said.

Bell looked at me.

"I didn't know reporters did that," she said.

"It's the exception, not the rule."

"Good."

"Anyway, I got a call this morning, in the truck. Some guy—not Robie or the cousins—telling me the bus guy was in Manchester, New Hampshire. Only I think he was making it up as he went. Kept covering the receiver up, calling from a phone booth. He told me I didn't need to look 'here' anymore."

"Where's 'here'?" Bell said.

Inside the house, the baby squealed. I could hear her husband's voice, teasing now.

"Here, I think. Scanesett. I think he got my number from Robie or Rob-ann. Had to be. I didn't give the car phone number to anybody else. Except you. Did I give it to you?"

"No."

"Well, I will."

"Don't do me any favors," Bell said, but she smiled.

"Be that way," I said. "Anyway—"

The baby started to cry.

"You can't eat that," Ray Bell said.

"So what I had to tell you was, I think he's still here. Someplace. I saw Robie at this store and I stopped and talked to him. I don't think he knows what's going on about a lot of this. But I told him this guy might be wanted, that he could get in trouble. Robie, I mean. And Rob-ann."

"You could do my job, McMorrow," Bell said.

"Yeah."

"But I don't get to run off to Québec in the middle of the week."

I grinned, but tried to keep to the subject.

"But what I told him was, if we had something with prints, the police could find out who Mantis really is."

Bell looked more serious.

"Hope," Ray Bell called. "I gotta get back."

"I'll be right there," she called back.

"So anyway, he listened to my spiel about the prints, and then, he all of a sudden gets up and goes in the store. He'd just turned in all these bags of bottles. And he comes out with one and he's holding it by the top, the screw-top thing."

"And you've got it?" Bell said, very serious now.

"In the truck," I said. "Can you dust it and run them?"

She was thinking.

"I don't know . . . I'll find a way. I'll figure it out."

"Do you have known prints for the rest of the crew?"

"Hope," Ray Bell called again.

"Just a sec."

We walked down the driveway to my truck.

"I know we have the cousins. I think we have Robie. The only one I don't know about is Rob-ann. Robie slugged some kids who were picking on him a couple of years ago. Actually, I think they hit him first but Devins arrested him. DA tossed it out, but the prints should still be there. Rob-ann, I don't think so."

We stopped at the truck. I opened the passenger door,

leaned in and stuck a pencil in the Pepsi bottle. I handed it to Bell, pencil and all.

"How long?" I said.

"It's the FBI that does it," she said, standing there with the food stains on her shirt. "It could be a couple of weeks, if I can get a rush on it."

"Jeez. A couple weeks is a rush?"

"This isn't exactly a mass murder, McMorrow."

"I know, but a couple weeks, the guy could be in Guatemala. And maybe he is a mass murderer. We don't know."

"And maybe he's just some flake," Bell said.

In front of her, the bottle rotated on the pencil.

"I don't think so. Too many people are interested. The cousins. The guy on the phone this morning. I've got a tape of that, if you want it."

"A tape?"

"I use a tape recorder to take notes while I drive," I said. "I hooked up the microphone to the phone. It's pretty fuzzy."

"Better luck next time, James Bond," Bell said.

I smiled.

"What if Gardiner P.D. ordered the prints? With that case, it might be faster."

Bell shook her head.

"It's mine. I've got a guy I know in Augusta. He owes me one for this junkyard chop-shop case I helped him with. I'll call him."

Behind us, the door opened. Ray Bell came out, holding the baby. He was tall and rangy. In his big tanned arms, the baby looked like a doll.

"Hope. Gotta go," he said.

We walked toward the house. Ray Bell walked toward us. He kissed the baby on the cheek. Truly secure men don't have to be macho.

He started to hand the baby to his wife, then noticed the

bottle on the pencil. Hope handed it to me and took the baby.

"I'll get a Baggie," she said, and went inside.

When she came back out, it was with the baby in the crook of one arm, a plastic bag in the other. I dropped the bottle in. Ray Bell came out of the garage with a big lunch pail, and got in his truck and started it. The motor roared, then rumbled. He sat, and I realized he was waiting for me to leave first.

Hope Bell and the baby turned toward the door.

"I'll call you," I said.

"Better not leave your real name. Say you're—"

She thought.

"Sam Alexander," Bell said.

"Okay," I said.

"In a day or two?"

"I don't know. I have to go through Augusta later. Going to the mall in South Portland with my sister. Maybe I could drop it. I'm curious," I said.

"Me, too," she said.

I took a couple of steps toward the truck, then stopped. Ray Bell was still waiting, his big arm on the back of the seat, his truck still rumbling, exhaust huffing into the heat.

"One more thing. You hear what Howard said to Damian after he tried to choke me and I had to hit him? I put it in my statement."

"I never saw it," Bell said.

She shifted the baby to her other arm.

"He said something like, 'I told you these guys were trained.' "

"Weird," Bell said. "What's that supposed to mean?"

"I don't know."

She started to turn, then turned back.

"I guess I'll just have to ask him," she said.

• • •

There are two border crossings to Canada from western Maine. One is in Sandy Bay Township, north of Jackman. The road that leads to it, Route 201, is a straight shot north from Wyman Lake, a trucking road that, in its lonely northern stretches, is lined with moose-grazed spruce, stunted trees gnawed eight feet from the ground. It's a road meant to be driven fast, like a highway through the desert. The Canadian log trucks, the semitrailers, their cabs carrying names of companies in places like Beauceville and Linière, blast up and down this asphalt chute as fast as the moose and frost heaves will allow. Meandering tourists pass at their own risk.

The second route forces you to meander.

It threads its way between rugged hills and mountains, from Madison and Anson, in Somerset County, through the ski country of Carrabassett Valley, northwest along the Dead River. The settlements beyond the ski country are Eustis and Stratton, which cling to the river and the road, Route 27. Away from the road are the big mountains—Bigelow, Crocker, Sugarloaf—and smaller, more forgotten places, whose names ring from the past. Lookout Hills. Poison Pond. Picked Chicken Hill. Caribou Mountain.

There are places like Holeb and Skinner townships, where people tried to settle but gave up. Their names are attached to rectangular plots that give order to this still-wild country, but only on maps.

I had one of those maps spread on the passenger seat of the truck. Arnold's route was shown in pink highlighter: west from the Kennebec across Carrying Place Township, just north of Bigelow Mountain range, along Flaggstaff Lake, then up the north branch of the Dead River to Chain of Ponds, across what is now the Canadian border to Lac aux Araignees and Lac Megantic, and down the winding Rivière de la Chaudière to the St. Lawrence.

In two hours, I could be at the border. In four, I could be well on my way to Québec City, doing in a few hours what Arnold and his ragged troops did in weeks. But then, I didn't have to walk.

I sat there, in the parking lot of a sub shop in downtown Scanesett, ate my tuna sandwich and looked at the map with wonder. If you hiked that far today, they'd do a story about you in the little newspapers along the way. They'd take your picture, in your Gore-Tex jacket and insulated mittens, lightweight waterproof boots. If you tried to hike dragging a sixteen-foot wooden boat, they'd lock you up. Sure as hell, they wouldn't let you through at the border.

My plan was to meander to the border, talking to my tape recorder the whole way. I'd try to get to Lac Megantic, maybe get a look at the Chaudière, see if it still was worthy of its name, French for cauldron. If time permitted, I'd try to make it across to Route 173, the north–south route to Québec City. Then I could make the straight run south, through Jackman and home to Prosperity. If I'd been thinking, I would have thrown an overnight bag in the truck and made the run all the way to Québec City.

Well, I had been thinking. About Roxanne. About Clair. About what Clair had said. I still was thinking. About the guy on the phone and Robie, and about Bell and the Pepsi bottle, her husband and her little kid.

Maybe I was thinking too much.

I finished the sandwich, crumpled the wrapper and tossed it out the rear window into the truckbed. When I looked back, I saw a Ballantine ale can in the rubble back there. Not a good thing to show at the border. I got out and walked around and reached that can out, then another. They were worth a dime, but I didn't want to go back into the store, so I decided to just leave them on the step for some kid to find and cash. As I put the cans down and turned, I heard my name.

"Jack."

I looked up. She hurried toward me. Her legs were tanned, her dress was short and white.

"Sandy," I said. "How are you?"

"Jack, where on earth have you been keeping yourself? I called your house."

She was smiling exuberantly, even joyously, as if I were a friend long lost and presumed dead. She took my arm and squeezed it, as if to make sure I were real.

"I've been busy," I said.

"Well, boy, oh, boy, do I have a story for you," Sandy said, still hanging on. She was staring at me intently, unblinking, an amphetamine stare she'd probably learned from a self-help book. An old man walked by and she moved to the side, but still hung on.

"I already talked to him, and he said he'd be glad to talk to you. He's been written up in the local paper, but the *New York Times*? He said that would be great."

"But I don't work there anymore, Sandy."

She dug in her purse with her left hand.

"Here's his card. His company, it employs, like, thirty-five people. But he's gonna be expanding. It's one of those small-town bootlace stories. Oh, I think it's just great. Lon, that's his name, he's a good friend. He just got this contract, I mean, if it works out, it could be great for the town."

"What's he do?"

"I don't know exactly. But it's this chemical thing. Sort of like a plastic. But he said—this is your angle—Lon said his company could be making the clear stuff that goes over the things that go on the hood of Cadillacs."

She looked at me triumphantly.

"Really," I said.

"Yeah. You know the Cadillac thing. The thing that flips down because it's on a spring? 'Cause kids steal them? The clear stuff that goes over it. You buy a Cadillac in, like, Boston or Texas or someplace, and the clear stuff will be from Scanesett, Maine. Even if you bought your Cadillac in Utah. Or Canada. Or even in Europe. They sell some in Europe, don't they?"

"I'm sure."

Sandy beamed. Gave my arm an extra squeeze.

"Great," I said.

"It's not a sure thing, but Lon says he thinks he has the contract."

"Well, maybe it's too soon, then."

"He said he'll talk to you now. And then, when he gets the word, he could, like, call you. It's a story about how a small-town businessman is about to hit it big."

"I don't write much business stuff, really."

"But it's a good story, don't you think? Horatio what's-his-name."

"Alger."

"Right."

"Hey, I gotta go. I'm late for Rotary. But I'm so glad I spotted you. It was your truck. I said, 'That's Jack's truck.' I knew it because you have that piece of metal on the side. You'd never know you were a big-time reporter driving that truck."

I smiled.

"What do they call it? Incognito?" Sandy said.

She grinned.

"Gotta run."

Sandy let go of my arm and started for her car, a sporty red two-door, American-made. Her skirt was sort of ruffly and it did a little flip.

"Hey, Sandy," I said.

She turned.

"Talk to Robie lately?"

"No," she said. "But you know what? This is kind of weird, but I was just driving down East Street by the dry cleaners. And Robie was riding this way, coming toward me. And you know what? I couldn't tell for sure, but I think—and this isn't like him at all. I mean, he's weird and all, but not in all the years I've known him."

She paused.

"What?" I said.

"I think he was crying."

14 It was out of character. Robie was one of those people who have been so beaten up, physically and psychologically, that they grow a very hard shell. They don't open up because when they did, early on, they were betrayed.

Tell your father you love him, and he doesn't say it back. Tell your mother you're unhappy, and she tells you to leave her the hell alone. Come home elated, and get cold stares. Come home and find that Mommy or Daddy are gone. Or both.

After a while, you know better.

So what had happened to make Robie break down? I considered going looking for him but then decided against it. If he wanted to hide, I wouldn't be able to find him. And I had a story to do, I reminded myself. A real story, for cash money. I glanced at my maps one more time, and drove out of town.

With Robie still somewhere in the back of my mind, I headed northwest, through Norridgewock, then through the countryside for fifteen minutes and into the paper-mill town of Madison, where steam wafted from a giant stack like a smoke signal. I crossed the Kennebec on the green metal bridge and then headed upriver, past low scrubby islands and rock pilings, log-drive remnants where alder sprouted like whiskers from a mole.

The Kennebec was wide here and the land was flood-plain, planted in corn, but with mountains beginning to rear up on the horizon to the northwest. There were houses here and there, mostly small, square to the road. As I drove, I noticed that the houses seemed to be getting smaller, but the trucks parked beside them were bigger. I was wondering if this could be some sort of natural law—the harsher the elements, the smaller the house and bigger the truck—when I noticed one in the rearview mirror.

It was a pickup, an old one, full-size, dark blue or maybe black. It was five hundred yards behind me, and holding steady. I was poking along at forty-five and the road was straight, flat and, and at this point, deserted. I would have expected the driver of the truck to take the opportunity to blast by me, but the truck matched my speed. I watched, as I slowed to forty and the other truck slowed, too. I sped up to fifty-five and the distance between us stayed the same. Slowed again. Sped up. The truck followed.

Coming into the village of North Anson, I crossed the bridge over the Carrabassett River, turned left onto Route 16, and pulled over. I counted. At ten, the truck turned the corner, then passed me.

An old Ford. Black and beat-up. Two-wheel-drive. Two men in it. When the truck went by, they held their hands up alongside their faces. I saw beards. Longish hair on one, short on the other. I wrote the license number in my notebook.

There was a corner store just up the road. The truck pulled into the parking lot, just beyond a van. I watched to see if someone got out. A man went into the store, but I couldn't tell from which truck he'd come. I waited. Put the truck in gear and drove.

I passed the store at forty, then put my foot to the floor as the road left the town. It was a long, straight stretch, more cornfields, with the Carrabassett on the left. I was doing seventy when the Ford grew in the mirror. It was gaining. I passed a big farmyard and a flock of pigeons burst into the air. An oncoming log truck spattered my windshield with sand. I hit a pothole and slowed. The truck was five hundred yards back and holding steady.

It followed me through North New Portland and across the bridge into Kingfield. I took a right and drove slowly through the semideserted main street, past the off-season ski shops and cafés. The truck reappeared.

I watched. Waited. Hoped it would pull in, and I could chalk the whole thing up to my own paranoia.

It followed.

North of Kingfield, the road moves into the mountains. There are steep pitches on the west side, the Carrabassett on the right. Like most mountain roads, there is a touch of danger here, no room for error, as the road pitches up and down, left and right. I downshifted for the turns, saw the Ford behind me on the straightaways.

Through Carrabassett Valley, past the locked chalets, the ski motels and restaurants, the truck followed. I passed the Sugarloaf ski-area access road and headed for Stratton, the bristly mountains looming on both sides. The Bigelow range was on my right. To the left was Sugarloaf, with its now grassy trails showing in the woods like lava paths.

I glanced up. And in the mirror, glanced back.

There were moose signs, warning of danger. Tell me about it, I thought. Five miles from Stratton, the road began to climb and there were two lanes, one for the slower trucks. I looked up and saw that the pickup was gaining. I slammed from fifth gear to fourth and put the pedal to the floor. Damn, if only the truck weren't so old. Damn, if it weren't a four-cylinder.

The Ford kept coming. I was in the right lane, then swung to the left. It drifted right and I did, too. It went left and I swung back.

A hundred yards now. Seventy-five. My leg was aching from pushing the pedal so hard. The little motor was screaming.

Left lane, then right. Right lane, then left. Fifty yards. He swung right and I did, too. Saw the sign showing that the lanes would merge. A log truck was careening down the grade the other way, loaded. The Ford was on the left side. I drifted right to give him an opening, then swung back to cut him off.

A horn blasted from the log truck. The Ford started to swerve left into the other lane, then whipped to the right, onto the shoulder, gaining, then coming alongside. The shoulder ended and there was an awful clatter and the Ford hit the gravel. The log truck roared by, horn blaring. I looked over.

They had ski masks on. There was a gun. I hit the seat. Heard the blast. Felt a slap, then the truck yawing.

I pulled myself back up by the steering wheel as the truck started to slide to the left, sideways. Yanked it back. Too much and it slid the other way, then back again, schussing from side to side, then the brakes and a screech and dust and it stopped.

In the mirror, I saw the black Ford make a U-turn and head south.

I dialed *77, the cellular phone number for the Maine state police. It rang and a dispatcher answered. I told him someone had just shot at my truck, on Route 16, south of Stratton. He asked me my name. I told him. He asked me my cellular number. I gave him that, too. He asked me if I'd been hit. I said, no, I didn't think so. He asked me when this had happened. I told the smoke still hadn't cleared. He asked me if the perpetrator was still in the area. I said he was heading back toward Carrabassett. He asked me if I could describe their vehicle. I said I could, and did. He asked me if I'd gotten the license number, and I gave it to him. He told me to stay put. I did.

The trooper took twenty-eight minutes to get there. That gave me time to look myself over and see that I didn't have a scratch. I stood by the driver's door of the truck for a minute, looking down the road and listening. I didn't hear anything. Birds. The breeze. No truck.

I walked around to the other side of the truck to check

for a bullet hole, which would have been this truck's second. The last time had been a .22, a kid feeling playful. This time it had been a big rifle, thankfully not a shotgun. There was no sign that the truck had been hit, but I was almost sure I'd felt a slug go by. Maybe it had gone in one open window and out the other. Maybe my guardian angel had taken it in the chest.

After I'd walked around, I got back in the truck and called the Scanesett police. The same dispatcher answered, and if he recognized me, he didn't let on. I told him I needed to talk to Bell. He said she was off. I said it was very important, something she'd want to know as soon as possible. He asked for my number, but in a tone that said, "Yeah, right."

But she called three minutes later, her voice faint and crackly.

"McMorrow, what's up?"

"Somebody took a shot at me."

"A shot? You okay?"

"Fine. They missed."

"Where are you?"

"On Route 16, about five miles south of Stratton."

"Who was it?"

"I don't know. Two guys in an old black pickup. A Ford. State police have the number. They're looking for them."

"Howard and Damian?"

"I don't know. I almost don't think so. They seemed bigger, but I only got a glance. They wore masks. They pulled alongside me and let go."

"What'd you do?" Bell asked.

"I ducked."

"Jeez," she said.

"Exactly."

"What the hell's going on?"

"I don't know. Maybe they're serious students of American history. Don't want me besmirching Benedict Arnold."

"Yeah, right," Bell said.

"People get all worked up about this old stuff. You wouldn't believe it."

"No, I wouldn't."

"Would you believe that there's more to this bus thing?" The phone got fuzzy.

"I guess I'd better start," Bell said faintly. "Unless there's something about you I don't know about."

"Lots of things, but they've got nothing to do with this."

"You think somebody was trying to scare you?"

"No," I said. "I think they were trying to kill me, but they missed."

"Why didn't they try again?"

"I don't know. Maybe they just panicked. I would think that shooting a rifle at somebody's head is a pretty scary thing, unless you do it all the time."

"We don't have anybody like that around here," Bell said.

"Yeah, well, you know what they say about bad things from away."

"What's that?"

"They all move north," I said. "Eventually."

Bell said she'd put a rush order on the fingerprinting of the bottle, and call the trooper assigned to the case. He turned out to be a tall, thin kid, new to the state police and assigned to the boonies. After he searched me, and my truck, he let me sit beside him in his Chevy cruiser and give my statement. I told him what happened, and he wrote it out longhand on a form on a clipboard. When I politely asked him if it wouldn't be a good idea to try to find the black pickup, rather than wait to fill out the form, he said they would find the truck.

The kid, baby-faced with a wisp of sideburn, waved an arm at the wilderness all around us.

"Where they gonna go, sir?" the kid asked.

I looked around at the mountains, too, but didn't feel reassured.

And then the trooper left, roaring southward in his blue cruiser. I sat there for a moment and considered heading for home. It was two-thirty, and it had been a long day. But then I thought of Benedict and the boys and how they wouldn't have let a single shot make them turn tail. So I started the truck, pumped the brakes a couple of times, and off to Canada I went, pretending to be brave.

As I drove slowly north, my mind raced. What had I stumbled into? Who was it? Why did they think of me as such a threat? What did they think I was going to take away from them? How could I hurt them when I didn't know who they were? Why was Robie crying? Who was this guy from the bus who had started all this?

The Pepsi bottle would tell, I said. They'd rub the Pepsi bottle and the genie would come out.

I eyed the mountains, still pondering it all, then forced myself to take out the tape recorder and start talking. I described the rocky faces of the mountains, the Bigelow range, seen beyond shelves of spruce and birch and maple. Peaks and ridges, some craggy, some rounded like fists. This hadn't changed much since Arnold had struggled through. You could picture it, except that back then, the wilderness went on almost forever. And even now, there was a sense that this country hadn't yet surrendered, that there was a larger purpose to it all, and people were just incidental, crawling through the woods like fleas on a dog.

The settlements here were just that, like something you'd see in Alaska. First there was Stratton, which consisted of a post office, a gas station, a fire station, three or four streets, some garages and houses, a few seasonal cabins. It was set at the southwestern tip of Flagstaff Lake, the man-made widening of the Dead River where Arnold's troops, close to starvation, pitched and tripped their way through that October. In the center of town was the Dead River Area Historical Society, an old clapboarded building with a *bateau* under a canopy out front. I pulled over and got out.

The *bateau* was a replica. I looked it over and then went to the front door, but it was locked. There was a sign with a number to call to have the place opened. I rattled the door and looked around. The building was silent and, after a truck had coasted past, so was the town, baking in the silent summer heat. I walked back to my truck and dialed the number. Waited as it rang. An older man answered, but then I realized it was a machine. He said he was out, probably fishing, but he'd call back. I hung up, wrote the number in my notebook, with a star for the photo list, and continued north.

After Stratton, the road crossed the low, wide Dead River basin and then hugged the river's north branch. This was fishing and hunting country, with signs for taxidermists and Maine guides. And it was Arnold country.

I passed under the towering Cathedral Pines, where Arnold camped. Then I drove through Eustis, which was like Stratton, except smaller. A mile up the road, a sign said I was approaching Chain of Ponds, a historic site. There was the Natanis Point campground, the site of the hunting camp of the Abenaki chief who slipped ahead of Arnold's troops as they blundered their way toward the Chaudière River, and signed on for the attack on Québec. It was Natanis who named Arnold ''Dark Eagle'' and predicted that he would soar to great heights but also fall.

Even today, some of the country belonged to the Penobscots.

North of Eustis, I pulled off on to a gravel road to relieve myself. A piece of plywood told me that I was in Penobscot Territory, that the moose season at Alder Stream was limited to bulls, that I needed permission to cut spruce or fir tips for wreaths. Grouse season was two weeks later than on surrounding land.

And then off I went again, and the road began to twist and turn, following the Dead River to the northwest. The road seemed to follow the crest of a ridge and I was looking down on treetops on both sides. There were rocky crags above the trees to the west, cliffs only a falcon would like. It was here, somewhere off to my right in these Boundary Mountains, that Arnold's men floundered through icy bogs, made stew of their cartridge cases, complained that they were as lost as they could have been in deepest Africa. Even today, the road wound through sheer precipices, past country that was an odd mix of bog and mountain. Here, in the dense growth of Hathan Bog and its surrounding ridges, that hundreds of troops wandered north into Canada, lost and frozen.

I pictured them as I looked off to my right, where the shoulder slipped away, and then the road dropped and twisted to the left and a log truck came at me, half in my lane, and I swore and swerved.

You could die here still. I was living proof.

And then the road suddenly widened and a sign said Coburn Gore, and there it was, a desolate little place with a row of peeling bungalows, a gas station, a liquor store, a tiny grocery with a sign advertising cold beer and pizza, coffee and dougnuts.

The essentials.

I coasted past and approached the border stations. Trucks were pulled up at the U.S. Customs building across the way, idling under a canopy. I headed for the canopy on my side, where the sign said, *"Attendez dans l'auto."* I braked, stopped under the canopy, and waited.

A door swung open. A kid came out, skinny and young, the Canadian version of my state trooper. He opened the passenger door of the truck and leaned in.

"Bonjour, monsieur," he said.

"Bonjour," I said.

"You are from Maine?"

"Oui."

"Which place?"

"Prosperity," I said.

"And where are you going?"

"To Lac Megantic."

"Why?" he said.

He was polite, but direct.

"I'm a writer," I said. "I'm doing a piece on Benedict Arnold."

The customs kid looked at me more curiously. He looked at the notes and maps spread on the seat.

"Do you have liquor?"

"Non," I said fluently.

"Cigarettes?"

"Non."

He looked at the gun rack.

"Firearms?"

"Non," I said.

He looked at me for a moment, his face revealing nothing.

"What do you have in here?" he said.

"Rien," I said. *"Les chose usuelles."*

He stared at me again, then gave an almost imperceptible shrug.

"Okay," he said, still inside the truck, but then the door to the station swung open. A woman, same uniform but older, spoke to him in a burst of French. I caught the words *noir* and *camion* and "pickup." He stood, with my door open but turned toward her, and said, *"Mais rouge?"* The woman officer said something else and he turned to me.

"Could you please step out of the truck, sir," he said.

"Mais oui," I said. *"Certainment."*

I started to dig under the maps for my wallet and the skinny kid reached out and grabbed my wrist. He was stronger than he looked. It was one of those days.

15 The Canadian customs station was air condi-
tioned, almost cold enough to see your breath.
I sat in a room that contained a metal table and
plastic chairs. There was an ashtray on the table and a color
photo of a bull moose on the wall. I stared at it as the older
woman customs officer stood over me and tried to decide
whether I was a threat to Québec Province. The younger
guy and his buddies were searching my truck.

"So you don't know why these men shot a rifle at you?"
she said, her French accent pronounced but not thick.

"No," I said.

"But you think it might have something to do with some
of your inquiries about a man from the this town of Scanesett, Maine, who is missing?"

"He's not from there. I don't know where he's from.
But yeah, I think it might have to do with that."

"And now you want to enter Canada to do a story on
Benedict Arnold?"

"Right. I want to go along the Chaudière, and I need to
go to Québec City, too. But not today."

"Today, where do you want to go?"

"Just up to Lac Megantic. Along Route 204 a little way,
maybe. Just to get a feel for it. It's a travel magazine and
I have to be able to tell people what they'll see if they take
this trip."

"For the tourists?" she said.

"Right. For tourists who like history. That's what this

magazine is for. It's a national magazine. Published in Delaware. You can call them if you want. I've got the editor's number.''

''But you also write about missing persons?''

''For newspapers. I write different things. I'm a freelancer. I used to work for the *New York Times*.''

If that impressed her, she didn't show it. She considered me. I considered her back. Her name plate said M. Toulouse. Her hair was neat, short, swept away from her face. She was fiftyish and fit, carefully made up. Handsome in a metallic sort of way.

''So the tourist magazine would be promoting trips to Québec?''

''Yeah. It would tell people how they can take a trip to learn more about Benedict Arnold and his march to Québec. I'm going to suggest that's where they end up.''

''Visit the historic sites?''

''Right.''

''Have you been to Quebec?''

''Not recently, but years ago.''

''It's the only walled city in North America.''

''I read that,'' I said, relieved. She wouldn't be giving me a tourist talk if she were going to turn me away.

''Very beautiful,'' she said.

''I'm sure. I can't wait to get there.''

''Very historic.''

''Do you think I could leave soon?'' I said.

''I don't know, Monsieur McMorrow. Your Officer Bell hasn't called back.''

''She's off today,'' I said. ''And she's got a baby. She might be busy.''

''Well, if the state trooper calls, maybe we'll see.''

''What if he doesn't?''

''We'll see.''

I sat some more. Looked at the moose. She looked at my driver's license, my card, and my old *Times* ID, then flipped them back on the table.

"You have the number of this magazine?" she said.

"Yeah," I said, and dug in my wallet for the right slip of paper. I found it, put my thumbnail on the number.

"Ask for Allison Smythe," I said. "At *Historic Touring.*"

She put her thumbnail, painted blood red, on the same spot. Just then my truck pulled up outside the window, the skinny kid at the wheel. He got out and came inside.

"Telephone for you, *monsieur,*" the kid said. "In the truck."

I looked to M. Toulouse.

"You are not in custody," she said.

"Who was that?" Roxanne said, her voice faint and fuzzy.

"I don't know his name," I said, sitting in the driver's seat on the hot pavement, with the motor running. The seat felt funny, like they'd rearranged the stuffing.

"But he's in your truck?"

"He's some Canadian customs guy," I said.

"Customs. Are you in Canada?" Roxanne said.

"Not yet. They're trying to decide whether to let me into their country. How are you doing?"

"Fine. I mean, not so fine. Why won't they let you in?"

"It's a long story."

"It's always a long story with you, Jack."

"The gift of gab," I said.

The static clouded over Roxanne's voice. I thought I heard her ask what had happened. Or maybe it was, "Where are you?" I played it safe.

"I'm in Coburn Gore. Up above Kingfield. Following the Arnold highway."

The static subsided.

"But what happened, Jack? Are you okay?"

"Fine, except they rearranged this seat and it's poking me in the *derrière*. That's French. Did you know I'm fluent?"

"Jack."

"It's amazing how fast it came back," I said. "I was just talking in French with the customs guys. About Sartre and Camus and stuff. Kind of an existential job, sitting up here at this remote border outpost."

"Jack."

"Now I'm going to Lac Megantic. See if I can order a Big Mac."

"Jack."

"Une Mac grand? Une burger gigantesque?"

Silence.

"You're supposed to say, 'Jack,' " I said.

More silence. A station wagon with Québec plates drove by me. Kids stared out the window.

"Somebody took a shot at me."

I waited.

"Are you okay?" Roxanne said slowly.

"Yeah, I'm fine. They missed."

"How close did they come?"

Her tone was measured, resigned.

"I don't know. It's hard to tell."

"Why's that?"

"Because I ducked. I think the bullet went in one window and out the other."

"One window of what?" Roxanne asked.

"My truck," I said.

"And where were you?"

"I was driving. But I ducked."

I thought I heard her sigh.

"And where was this?" she asked.

"Between Carrabassett and Stratton. A couple of hours ago. It was a black pickup. Two guys wearing ski masks. They took off, headed south. I don't know, they seemed like they sort of panicked. Amateurs, you know?"

A pause.

"No, I don't know. Did you call the police?"

"Yeah. A state trooper came. I called Hope Bell in Scanesett, too. I figure it's got to have something to do with the bus guy. I've been getting calls.''

''Saying what?'' Roxanne said flatly.

''That he's gone. He's in New Hampshire. He's left. I think he's right there. But you know what?''

''What?''

The same tone of voice.

''I think we're going to be able to ID him. I got a bottle that's supposed to have his prints. Once I have a name, I can really write the story. You know, 'Where is Joe Schmo, and why did he step off this bus?' ''

''That's great,'' Roxanne said, as if she didn't think so at all. ''But you know what I know?''

''What's the matter?'' I said.

''I know that I'm going to have a very hard time if I have to deal with this, with my mother and everything, all by myself.''

''You won't have to. I'll be with you.''

As I spoke, the static rose and then fell.

''What if next time you don't duck?'' Roxanne said.

''Oh, come on, Rox. There probably won't be a next time. These are small-towners. Keystone kops types. I mean, they were probably drunk.''

''Sounds like they didn't miss by much.''

''Next time I'll know better. I'll be more careful.''

''Jack, I'm going to need you. I don't have anybody else. This could go on for, I don't know, for years, and I am just going to need to have you to . . .''

She faltered. I sat there and waited.

''To love you?'' I said. ''Well, I do. You know that.''

''Well, sometimes it means more than just saying it.''

A truck went by, a Lac Megantic chip hauler heading home. I waited as it ran through the gears.

''I don't just say it,'' I said.

''What if they'd shot you, Jack?'' Roxanne said, her voice breaking. ''I can't handle two of these. I just can't take any more. I just . . .''

She sobbed.

"Just can't."

She cried, her jagged sobs cutting through the static. I sat there in the parking lot and waited for her to stop. I was waiting when the customs woman suddenly stuck her hand in the passenger window. She pointed toward Canada and gave me a thumb-and-forefinger okay. I nodded and she turned and left, leaving me to listen to Roxanne cry.

"It's okay," I said.

She cried. I said it again.

"It'll be all right. It will."

"Oh, Jack. What if something happened?"

"But it didn't."

"But it could."

"I'm here for you," I said. "I'll come tomorrow. I would have come last week."

"It's more than just you," Roxanne said. "You're responsible for more than that. You're responsible for me, too. You're responsible for the people you love. You can't keep taking these chances. God, I don't know what I'd do. I mean, what would I do? Come back to Maine and arrange your funeral? Jack, there's only so much—"

"I know. It's okay. I'm fine. I didn't know it was going to happen. I had no way—"

"I can take care of this if I know you're there to take care of me," Roxanne said. "If I think I'm going to lose you, then that's just too much."

Another truck went by. I waited.

"You're not going to lose me. I'll be more careful now. Police are involved all over the place. They'll take care of it. And I'll fly down tomorrow."

"No," Roxanne shot back. "You stay there and you finish your story about Benedict Arnold and when I come back with my mother, probably next week, I'm going to need you to help me. To help me get through it. That's why you have to be there. That's why, Jack, my baby, that's why you can't let anything happen. Promise?"

"I promise. Cross my heart and—"
I caught myself.
"Don't say it," Roxanne said.
So I didn't.

Roxanne hung up, still shaken. I promised I'd call her when I got back to Prosperity, no matter how late it was. She didn't tell me what had happened with her mother to upset her so much. She said it was just more of the same. Before I hung up, she told me to promise again that I wouldn't take any chances. She said to do it for her sake, not for mine. So I did.

And then I followed the highway as it swung west into Canada, past the signs that told me the signs were metric, that I had to wear my seat belt, that *"Vous souhaite la bienvenue."* I was welcome in Québec. That made one place.

With the Boundary Mountains left behind, the road flattened out and so did the countryside. I drove absently, thoughts of Roxanne and Robie and masked men crisscrossing my mind as I spoke into the tape recorder in a monotone. I noted that the trees looked more tame here, that Woburn, four miles up the road, was an industrial-looking little frontier town. The houses were modest and modern, lined up next to sprawling sawmills and massive stacks of two-by-eight lumber. Everything was neat and orderly but hot and desolate, with steam belching from the kiln-dryers, rising into the gray-blue sky. There was a bar motel with Christmas lights across the front, a shop that advertised chainsaws. And then I was beyond the town and into farmland, dairy country with pastures around big gambrel-roofed barns. A sign said "Rivière Arnold." I was hot on the trail.

The river was like a canal, running alongside the pastures, and it seemed almost a relief after the twists and turns on the American side of the border. Three miles north of Woburn, I took a hard right to follow Route 161, then a couple of miles after that, a hard left. Then the road was one long straight shot between fields and neatly trimmed spruce and tamarack. Le Rivière Arnold was off to my left someplace. I found myself drifting, back to Roxanne and Robie and said, ''Come on'' and ''Pay attention'' out loud. That worked until I passed Lac aux Araignees and then Lac Megantic. It was here that Arnold and the men knew they'd been saved.

I had no such revelation.

But I did see Lac Megantic, long and narrow to my left. The map showed it to be about seven miles long, to us a hard row, to Benedict and the boys, saved from starvation, a quick blast. I drove the length of the lake, and into the city of Lac Megantic. Like Arnold's men, I was thirsty and hungry. Pulling on to the main drag, I found a pizza shop and stopped and went inside. I bought pretzels and a Pepsi and left, saying only one word to the smiling high-school girl behind the counter: *''Merci.''*

I was in a hurry when I should have wanted to linger. I didn't want to speak to anyone, to inquire about historic sites. I could feel myself sinking, knowing deep inside that I felt I was failing Roxanne. I was floundering around Scanesett. I was afraid I wasn't going to do this story—or any of it—justice.

With the Pepsi between my legs, I shot out of town, headed east, passing an oncoming city police cruiser, which braked but didn't follow. Relieved, I sped through the farm country, following Route 204 to the tiny hamlet of Audet. There I took a left and drove north toward the Rivière de la Chaudière, which the road followed to the east. This was Arnold's route, a twisting, turning narrow river that doubled back on itself as it snaked through its valley. The towns were small and neatly dispersed, each one anchored by a church, the houses lined up like seats, the church spire rising like the pole of an invisible circus tent.

In St. Ludger I turned off the main road and coasted

down into the villages, toward the river. Sitting in the truck, I spoke into the tape recorder.

"Close-packed houses on steep treeless streets, like terraces easing their way down to the Chaudière. In each one, a salon, a bar, a small sign.... Everyone in town knows where it is. There is no need to advertise.... A river at the foot of a pastured plain ... serious farms here ... towns that look European, charmingly Old World. People walking ... Kids in concrete playgrounds of church schools ... old nuns watching their lay replacements ... a sense of unchanging community."

I clicked the tape recorder off.

It was so starkly beautiful in these little villages, something simple and paternal, but also very sad. I sat there in my truck and watched a little boy walking down the road toward me. He was wearing shorts and a blue and white striped shirt, black socks and black sneakers. When he passed the truck, he looked at me with solemn dark eyes and kept going. In the side mirror, I saw him slip through the chain-link fence around the little asphalt schoolyard. There was one swing dangling from the metal swing set and he ran to it and jumped on and started swinging, like a lonely little pendulum.

Oh, Jesus, I thought. There was something isolated and melancholy about these little places. Little salons. Little schools. Little kids with their big dark eyes.

Was it obscurity or oblivion?

Or was it just me?

And so with the boy watching me, I drove back up the hill to the main road, turned left and headed east, as fast as the traffic would allow. Through St. Gédéon and St. Martin, and then, with the sinking sun glaring from the rearview mirror, on to Route 173, the main north–south highway, the commercial strip, the route to Québec. I took a left, and drove five fast miles north to Beauceville, the bustling little city that services all of the villages named for saints. There was a McDonald's, a Dunkin' Donuts, a Pizza Hut. I bought gas in a Petro Canada station, a cup of tea in a Burger King. I forgot to pronounce it "tay" and the girl behind the counter smirked.

Then, with the sun settling into the mountains to my left, I drove south. Through Linière and Armstrong, with their roadside mills, into the scrubby no-man's-land above the border. At the border station, the American guard asked the usual questions but seemed to know nothing about the shooting, and waved me through.

I began the long and lonely ride home. Trucks on my tail and in my face. The tea spilled in my lap. Driving hard along the twisting and turning Kennebec, past the pizza-and-beer sign sentinels that passed for civilization, along roads that seemed too familiar. And finally, at seven forty-five, rolling into Scanesett's brick-mill downtown, where I watched for the black Ford truck as I slipped across the bridge. I reached for the phone receiver, then put it down, then picked it up again. I dialed. The dispatcher answered. I asked for Bell. He didn't answer, but there was a click, and then she did.

"This is Jack McMorrow," I said. "I didn't think you were working."

"I wasn't but I decided to come in," she said.

"Because of what happened to me?"

"No, but we did run the plate on your buddies in the truck. Came off a '93 Chevy Cavalier. Owner is from Scanesett. Myrtle Street. She's eighty-three years old, doesn't drive much. Car's in her garage. Didn't know the plate was even missing."

"And the truck?"

"No sign of it. Could be back behind a barn someplace."

"Until the next time," I said. "Great."

There was a pause. I cradled the receiver on my shoulder as I shifted the truck.

"So you want to know why I did come in?" Bell asked.

"Sure."

I shrugged, one hand on the steering wheel.

"Because I got a call," Bell said. "Somebody beat the hell out of Robie."

16

Actually, the beating wasn't that bad. What brought Bell in on her day off were the burns on Robie's forearm.

"Cigarette," she said. "Three of 'em. Not real deep, but deep enough."

We were sitting in her station wagon in the parking lot of the Scanesett municipal parking lot. Bell was wearing jeans and a white T-shirt and sandals. There was a baby seat in the back. My truck was three spaces over. It was her idea; Nevens didn't like me.

"What'd Robie say about it?" I asked.

"Nothing at all, at first. Just sat there with his mouth glued shut," Bell said. "Then when he realized I wasn't going to let him off the hook that easy, he said he was working on a bike. Heating up some part. An axle or something, and it burned him."

"Three times?" I said.

"Yeah, I know."

"What about the bruises?"

"Cheeks. Above the eyebrow. But not like a fight, you know? With cuts and scrapes? Just the bruises, like he was just sitting there, taking it."

"And couldn't defend himself," I said.

"Right. Not rolling around on the ground."

"Which would match with the burns."

"Yeah," Bell said. "Lady next door. She called because she was worried about him 'cause his face was bruised, so she went to talk to him and she saw the burns. She was a nurse's aide or something, and she knew what she was looking at. Round as a dime. Three of them. Identical."

"What about Rob-ann?"

"I made the mistake of letting him go before I talked to her. By that time, he was home. She gave me the same bunch of bull. He was working on his bikes and he hurt himself. Except she added this part about how she shouldn't have let him have a propane torch."

"Not a bad touch. Are they good liars?"

Bell looked away. Reached to brush a moth off of her forearm, which was out the window.

"I don't think so. Not spontaneous enough. They're so—what's the word?—routine about everything. Robie goes to the store. Rob-ann cooks the meals. He goes around looking for junk. Every night, they watch a couple of videos. Kind of depressing, in a way."

I flicked at the plastic vent handle with my finger.

"But they don't improvise well," I said.

"Not like some people. You know, the kind who don't even know what the truth is, they've been lying so long."

"Robie would have to have it all planned in his mind. All mapped out."

"Yup."

"So who do you think mapped it out for him?"

"One of his poor relations would be my guess," Bell said.

"Like Howard and Damian?"

"Yeah, or others. There's no shortage of dirtbags in the family tree."

"I noticed," I said. "You think it was them with the rifle?"

"Probably. You made any other enemies lately?"

"Not lately. Anything that happens has to come from right here. This is it, unless I made too much noise at the state library."

I picked at the glove compartment latch and it fell open. Inside there was a diaper and a pacifier, still in the package.

"For emergencies," Bell said.

"I figured you'd carry extra ammo or something."

"You've been watching too much television."

I smiled. Bell did, too. It occurred to me that I liked her. I wondered if it had occurred to her that she liked me, too.

"So," I said. "You think Howard and Damian could do something like that? The cigarette burns?"

She looked out at the parking lot. A car and a pick-up pulled in, both full of teenage kids. They parked window-to-window and killed the lights. "Easy," Bell said. "But they'd only do it if there was a heck of an incentive, you know what I'm saying? I mean, Robie and Rob-ann are their meal ticket every month. Their beer ticket."

"Yeah."

"They wouldn't screw that up unless it was for something better."

"Like the bus man," I said.

"Yeah," Bell said. "He's got to be calling the shots, whoever he is."

"How soon can you get the fingerprints?"

"I already called. I'm going to Augusta first thing in the morning. Usually it takes a couple weeks, anyway. But I called in those favors and then some. They'll scan the prints in and run it through their system. Same-day service. I'll take it to the state, too, but that takes longer."

"So if we get lucky, he'll be in the FBI system?"

"AFIS—Automated, or automatic, Fingerprint Identification System," Bell said. "Something like that. They say it works like the things they use to check out groceries. If the print's in there, it kicks it right back out."

"That would be nice. To know, I mean."

"To know who we're dealing with."

"Is that what we're doing?" I said.

I wasn't sure then. An hour later, I still wasn't sure as I sat in the truck in the dark, sipping McDonald's tea, four houses down and just around the corner from Robie and Rob-ann's.

From where I sat, I could see one side and the front of their building. Their lights were on, in every room, but the sheets were pulled over the windows. All of them.

I sat there and wondered what they were doing. Making tawdry videos? Showing the place to prospective tenants? Looking for a lost contact lens? Waxing the floors? Rolling up their sleeves and really making the place spic and span? Not a spot. Not a stain.

Not a fingerprint.

As I sat there, I almost smiled. Maybe that was it. Maybe they were scouring the apartment to remove all traces of the bus man. It made sense. What if Robie had been beaten and burned because he had given me the bottle? What if he had been beaten and burned to make him tell that he had given me the bottle? Then they would know that I probably had a fingerprint. The bus man, Mantis, would know. If the print would identify him, maybe he'd have to run. But if he ran, would he want to leave any evidence that he had been there? Would he want to vanish without a trace, except for the trace on the bottle of Pepsi?

I sat there and sipped and watched. A pickup truck pulled into a driveway behind me and I could see the guy get out and look over, wondering what I was doing there. Was I a thief? Was I a weirdo? Should he walk over and tell me to beat it, threaten to call the cops? He stopped, then walked inside the house.

I'd give it five more minutes, and I'd move. I looked at my watch, then back at the lights.

If they were, indeed, scrubbing the place, what good would it do for Mantis to cover his tracks if one track were already in police custody? Maybe he didn't know that? Maybe Robie was tougher than we thought. Maybe he hadn't told them about the bottle. Maybe Mantis didn't know.

Maybe Mantis wasn't up there at all.

I felt like it had just landed in my lap. That was a reason why someone would scour the apartment: to remove evidence that Mantis had been there. Why would you do that? Because you didn't want anyone to know he'd been there. Why wouldn't you want anyone to know?

There were lots of reasons.

Because Mantis was a fugitive and you didn't want to be hit with a harboring charge. Because Mantis had convinced you to do something illegal and you didn't want to be tied to him. Because something illegal had been done in the apartment—Robie's beating and burning came to mind, cutting a kilo of coke—and you didn't want any evidence left behind.

Or maybe, just maybe, because Mantis had been there but he wasn't anymore. He wasn't there because he was dead. He was dead because you'd killed him. Behind the sheets, Howard and Damian, Robie and Rob-ann, and in the spirit of a country barn-raising, their relatives and friends, were on their knees trying to get bloodstains out of the rugs.

It fit, more or less. What if Howard and Damian had befriended Mantis? What if he'd been befuddled? What if they'd taken him to the apartment and rolled him? What if he'd tried to rip them off in some way? What if there'd been a fight and Mantis had been killed? A drunken, stupefied argument that ended with a kitchen knife in the back. A broken neck on the stairs. Hell, Damian had almost strangled me in the parking lot at McDonald's. Lord knew what he could do in private.

Had Robie told? Burn him and find out. What did I know? Shoot me and it wouldn't matter. If the cops had a fingerprint, scour the place. They could connect him to the

Pepsi bottle, but not to the apartment. Where'd Robie get the bottle? He collects them by the side of the road. How did he know that there was a fingerprint on that one? Prove that he did. McMorrow must've made the whole thing up.

Some of it made sense. It would explain why Howard and Damian had gone berserk when they'd found me in the apartment. Maybe Mantis had been sitting in the closet, awaiting burial. It wouldn't explain why they'd jumped me in the parking lot. If you'd killed someone, wouldn't you lay low? Even if you were Howard and Damian, and not given to prudence and restraint? And what about that remark? Howard saying, ''I told you these guys are trained.'' Who or what did they think I was?

I sat there a few minutes longer, the same questions running through my mind. There were no more answers, but all of the questions and theories and speculation pointed to one thing, and that was death. And only one person was unaccounted for and that was Mantis, whoever he was, whatever he was doing in—

Headlights rounded the corner behind me, two blocks back. I started the truck, put it in gear, and took a quick right, drove past Robie and Rob-ann's apartment, still all lighted up. I took the next left, then the next right, then the next left, and headed east out of town. In the rearview mirror I saw a Scanesett police cruiser emerge from the same street but turn back toward the station.

With a long sigh, I headed home to Prosperity. After fifty minutes in the truck, alone with my questions, I had the same few answers. After a half hour alone at home, I fell asleep in the big chair, with the lights out, a half-full ale in my right hand, and my loaded rifle beside me on the floor.

I woke up to the blat of cicadas and the glare of the rising sun. It was eight-thirty and the dew had already burned off. My neck was stiff and my mouth was full of glue. When the phone rang, I knocked the ale off the arm of the chair and onto the floor. It sprayed and foamed as I grabbed for the receiver and a towel.

"Did I wake you?" Roxanne said.

I coughed.

"No. Why does everyone keep asking me that?"

"Because you sound like you're kind of out of it."

"Thanks a lot. Hang on, will you?"

I bent and mopped up the ale, but the place still smelled like a fraternity house.

"What's the matter?"

"I spilled a beer."

"Starting kind of early, aren't you? Or are you just getting in?"

"It's the other half of the one beer I had last night," I said. "What's the matter?"

Roxanne seemed stiff, a little bit cool.

"I thought you said you were going to call last night."

"I didn't get home until late. Then I fell asleep in the chair. I feel rotten."

I tossed the rag in the sink and opened the refrigerator.

"How are you?" I asked.

"Okay. I'm about to leave. I wanted to catch you first."

"Everything all right? What happened yesterday that you were so upset?"

I took out a half gallon of orange juice and drank from the jug.

"I hate it when you do that," Roxanne said.

"Do what?"

"Drink from the bottle."

"I'm all by myself. Who can get my germs?"

"It's just a bad habit. When I get up there, you'll still be doing it."

"But you'll have my germs anyway," I said. "Remember?"

Roxanne gave a little snort. She was softening.

"Vaguely," she said. "When I think of sex I get nostalgic."

"I think that was a previous incarnation."

"Good thing we came back as Jack and Roxanne," she said.

"A very good thing."

I hesitated.

"So did you want to talk about what happened yesterday?"

I drank more juice. Stood and faced the screen and the sun and the woods and waited.

"You don't have to," I said.

"Yesterday," Roxanne said. "God, it seems like weeks ago. Oh, Jack, I don't know. What was it? Oh, yeah. God. I don't know, I just had this weird thing happen, another one. I was talking to Mom and it was in the afternoon and we were having this conversation and she seemed pretty good. She was talking about Florida and the traffic, and then she asked me how I liked Maine."

"Really."

"Oh, it was like getting her back, and I know, they've warned me. It isn't going to get better, it'll just have little moments of remission, sort of. But, oh, Jack, she was talking about Maine, and how did I like the beaches and oh, the water was so cold, and she could never stand the water so cold."

"Yeah," I said softly. I could feel it coming.

"And I was getting into it, telling her about Jordan's Beach and Higgins, and the islands, and she was nodding and we were, I don't know, having a conversation again, and I know I shouldn't have. I shouldn't have thought—"

"It's all right."

"So she said, 'Well, we'll be up there soon enough.' And I thought, 'Great, I've been talking about the nursing home and selling the condo, and she's been understanding, even though I thought she didn't seem to.' So I said, 'Yeah, we'll leave in the next few days.' And she said, 'We have the same house. We always have the same house.' You know, we had that house in York when I was little. And I thought, 'Oh, no.' And she said, 'You know who used to love that house?' I said, 'Who, Mom?' She said . . .''

Roxanne's voice broke.

''She said, 'My daughter. She lives in Maine, too. What did you say your name was?' ''

Roxanne started to cry. I tried to console her. She said she really just needed me to hold her, and I said I'd do that. I said I loved her and I'd come there, and again she said, no, but I'd have to be ready to help her when she and her mother got back. I said I would and she said she loved me, too. She asked about Québec, how it was. I said it was very European, very old-fashioned out in the countryside, but somehow it had made me sad.

''A lot of things do that to me now,'' Roxanne said. ''I think it's an emotional overload. More and more things become triggers. I know this is hard on you, too. What did the police find out?''

''About the guys with the gun?''

''Yeah.''

''Stolen license plate. From Scanesett. That's about it. And Robie, the guy with the bikes, somebody beat him up yesterday.''

''Somebody in that town?'' Roxanne asked.

''Yeah. Well, actually they don't know. He said it was an accident. There were cigarette burns on his arm and he said he did it, I don't know, heating up a part for a bicycle.''

''He's afraid of them.''

''I'm sure. Maybe afraid for his sister.''

''Strange,'' Roxanne said.

''Very.''

I thought of sharing my revelation from the previous night, but decided against it.

''Are you still going to be able to meet your magazine deadline?'' Roxanne asked.

''I think so,'' I said, but I was really thinking that there were two things I was going to have to finish before Roxanne and her mother came back. The Benedict Arnold story was one.

So we rang off with a pledge to call that night, and I was free to tackle Benedict. I shucked my dirty clothes and showered, setting the rifle by the sink while I shaved. The heat already was working its way into the house, baking through the roof, seeping in the windows. I put on running shorts and a loose T-shirt, and made a pot of tea. I drank it while I transcribed my notes, listening to my own voice on the tape. I sounded resigned and dispirited as I described the wild Dead River reaches, the shorn hills of southern Québec. It wouldn't do for that to come through in *Historic Touring.* "Relive Arnold's defeat and come home depressed."

Come on, Jack, I thought. Pump yourself up.

So I did, in a way. I drank more tea. Transcribed my notes. Called a small hotel in Québec City, recommended by somebody who worked with Roxanne at the Department of Human Services. The woman who answered grappled with my French and finally said, "So that's one night. Thursday, right?"

I called the phone number for the museum in Stratton and left another message. I did the same for the museum in Pittston, downriver, and a woman answered. She said she'd open it up at my convenience. I said I thought I could come that afternoon, but I asked if I could call her back. I didn't tell her why. I didn't tell myself, but I knew.

At eleven o'clock, I checked the answering machine, and then walked down the road to the Varneys'. The sun was searing hot, and the dirt road was dry. A car went by, a beat-up hippie Volvo that I knew from town, and I waved. The woman driving waved, too, and I walked on in a cloud of dust.

At the Varneys' big white farmhouse, I unlocked the back door and went into the cool silence. The house was still as only an empty house can be, and I walked through the halls, the rooms, up the stairs. The beds were made, with Mary's quilts folded neatly at their feet. Not for the first time, I looked at the photo album on their bureau, at the pictures of Clair as a marine at Quantico, in Vietnam. The neat printing on the margin of the barechest picture said, "Hue Jan. '69."

There were pictures of Mary as a pretty young girl, standing by a dappled horse. Fountain pen writing on the back: "Mary and Camp, 1943." Pictures of their daughters in tap-dancing outfits, in gowns with gawky dates before high school proms.

A lot of life in those pictures. A lot of life lived in this house. I nosed around a little more, then went downstairs. Locking the back door behind me, I went out to the barn, a big immaculate cedar-shingled ark. Barn swallows were slipping in and out of the hayloft door, left hooked open for them per Clair's instructions. I watched them for a moment, then opened the padlock on the big door at the ramp and slid it open. It was cool and dim inside, a big dark space even in the sun. I walked through to the empty box stalls, the empty sheep pen, the cow tie-ups, to the back door. All secure.

Back at the front of the barn, I climbed the ladder to the loft. It was warm up there, with a few stray bales left, and smelled of bird droppings. The swallows were in full swing, and when I cupped my hands around my eyes, I could see fledglings in nests on the beams. They chittered when parents swooped in, were quiet as their gullets were stuffed. I watched for a minute and then climbed back down.

Clair's truck, a spotless green three-quarter-ton, four-wheel-drive Ford, was parked beside the tractors, facing the front door. I climbed in and started it, listening to the easy rumble for just a moment, then pulling out and down the ramp before the exhaust fumes asphyxiated the baby birds. Climbing out, I walked back to the door and took a last step inside. Stepping back outside, I slid the door shut, slipped the lock through the hasp, and snapped it fast.

As I turned toward the road, an old Ford pickup passed,

with two guys inside. The driver was clean-shaven, wearing a baseball hat. The truck was spray-painted camouflage, green and tan.

Over black.

I climbed up into Clair's truck and snapped it in gear. Rolled down the gravel driveway past the cedars and out into the road. The camouflage truck was almost to my house. The brake lights came on. Both heads turned left, looking toward my truck, parked in the dooryard. The truck slowed almost to a stop, with both of them still turned. Then, as I approached, the brake lights went out, and the camouflage truck sped up, kicking up dust. I thought I saw the driver glance up at the rearview mirror. He sped up some more and kept on going.

As I got closer, I grabbed a John Deere hat off the gun rack and put it on, pulling it down over my forehead. I rested my chin in my hand to cover my face. The camouflage truck held steady at thirty-five, slowed at the intersection at the end of the road, and turned left, toward the village. I got close enough to check the license plate; it wasn't the same number as before.

At the main road, they turned left again, away from the village, toward the town of Albion. I followed, staying back, and we both cruised along at about sixty. I looked at the rusty bumper ahead of me, the way the truck listed slightly to the right. Had the shooters' truck listed like that? Or would I have noticed, seeing it mostly from the front? I could try to get in front of them, pass them on the next straight, but I didn't want them to see me. I also didn't want them to know that I was driving Clair's truck, or even to take note of it. Clair's truck was my disguise for the next trip to Scanesett. Should I blow that cover now? Would I know them if I saw them? Would they be more likely to know me?

We drove past dairy barns and hayfields, slowing as we came into the center of Albion. It was almost noon and quiet on Main Street: a car at the gas pumps at the store, two guys loading two-by-fours onto a pickup. The camouflage truck slowed as if to pull into the store, then kept going. They drove the length of Main Street, then pulled into the parking lot of the town's other store, driving right up to the front door. As I passed them, I saw the passenger pop out and go in. I cut across the little intersection, and pulled into the lot of a repair garage.

I sat. Watched the mirror. Tried to get a better look at the driver.

He didn't have a beard. He was wearing sunglasses and a red hat. A dark T-shirt, with his arm out the window.

I eased around to get a better look. As I was turning, the passenger came out. I caught just a glimpse: Jeans and a white T-shirt with a picture of something on the front. No beard. Dark hat. A twelve-pack of Budweiser.

They pulled back out, cutting straight through at the intersection, heading toward East Winslow. I gave them a bit of a start, then pulled out and followed.

East Winslow was flattish fields and big farms, with narrow, twisting roads branching off through the woods to the south. I kept the truck in sight from a distance as we crossed the open flats, but then they took a left, into the trees where they could disappear behind a trailer in an instant. I sped up, but there was no other traffic and they were sure to notice if I dogged them through these twisting, potholed lanes.

I slowed. Tried to think it through. If they were the shooters from Scanesett, where would they be going? Back home? To find a place to pull off into the woods and drink their beer? If so, what would they do when they were good and buzzed? Load the rifle and come back?

I drove more slowly, letting the truck loaf along. The road was in thick spruce and pines, pitching up and down. There was an occasional house, a trailer hidden in the woods, marked only by a mailbox. I looked left and right, into the trees. Saw a junk car. More woods. An old blue bus, resting on its chassis. More woods. A homebuilt shack.

More woods. A plain ranch house with a yard full of red four-wheelers. Then more woods.

And then the truck.

It was right there, to my left, backed into a shaded space between the pines, fifty feet from the road. I glanced up, saw the driver lifting a beer to his mouth. The other guy was reaching down, so that I only saw the top of his hat.

That was it.

I couldn't turn around. If I passed them twice, I might as well get out and introduce myself. And getting another look wouldn't do me any good. I needed to know what they had in that truck. I needed to know who they were. I needed somebody who could ask.

Hitting the gas, I sped up, bouncing over the last mile before the road ran into Route 137. I needed a telephone, but the nearest pay phone probably was in downtown Winslow, five miles away. I turned right and slammed through the gears. A few hundred yards down the road, a woman was out in front of her trailer, sitting in a lawn chair in the heat. I braked and pulled in. Made sure to smile as I got out and strode toward her.

"Hi," I said. "Could I ask you a big favor? I just got almost creamed by what I think was a drunk driver. I need to call the police before he hits somebody. Could I use your phone for one minute?"

She looked at me. She was seventyish. Wearing big blue shorts and a sleeveless blouse. Tinted shades stuck under her glasses. Under the chair was an orange cat on a leash.

"Hell almighty, yes," the woman said. "They blast by here all hours of the night, drinking and drugging. Oughta lock 'em all up. Getting so you take your life in your hands if you run downtown to get a gallon of milk. My husband, he passed away, but he used to be a part-time deputy, he used to say you take your life in your hands on the roads after dark. That's why we hardly ever went anywheres at night. Stopped going to beano. He used to say, 'If people knew what was out there, they'd sit behind locked doors with a loaded gun.' God almighty, just the things they have on the TV are enough to—''

"Is the phone close by?" I said, interrupting but still smiling. "I don't want you to have to get up."

"On the counter by the sink. It's one of those cordless ones. You got to pull up the antenna thing and then talk or it's all static."

I opened the screen door and went in. The phone was on the counter, next to a crocheted dog that held Brillo pads. I pulled the antenna out and started to dial 911 but stopped. That wouldn't be right, I thought. There was a phone book in a set of cat-head bookends and I took it out and looked up the number for the Winslow police. Dialed it. A woman answered.

"I don't want to give my name, but there's a truck driving around East Winslow. Old Ford. Camouflage paint on it. Guy driving it's drunk as a skunk. They've got beer in the truck, and right now they're sitting on the Pond Road a mile in from the China Road on the right, pulled into the woods. You'd better get somebody out here before they kill somebody. License plate number six-nine, thirty-three, S as in Sam. But I'll bet it's stolen."

"And where are you calling from, sir?" the woman asked.

I hung up, put the antenna down, and put the phone back by the Brillo pad dog.

"Thanks," I said, coming through the door.

"Well, hell, yes," the woman said, still sitting. "I hope they catch those scumsuckers and lock 'em up. 'Course, then they get some lawyer who dresses 'em up all nice and says they're good boys and the judge gives 'em a pitty-pat on the head. Oh, my husband, when he was living, he used to get so steamed up about that."

I walked to the truck and climbed up and in.

"Thanks, again," I said, starting the motor.

"Oh, he used to say, 'I catch 'em, but just as fast, they

let 'em out. They beat me home.' That's why he finally got out of it, you know.''

I backed out. She still was talking. The cat hadn't moved.

Past the corner of Pond Road, I pulled over and waited. The sun beat down on the truck, and perspiration trickled down my temples. After five minutes, a cruiser appeared in the distance, blue lights and headlights flashing. It slowed as it approached, slid around the corner. The lights went off. I counted to one hundred and then backed the truck up and turned down the road.

One of the luxuries of small-town life is that the local police take small crimes as seriously as do the victims. By the time I passed the camouflage truck, a big uniformed cop had the truck blocked in with his white Winslow cruiser and the driver outside, digging in his pockets for ID. I slowed and looked. The driver was fortyish, about my size, wearing jeans tucked into work boots. He didn't look familiar. I drove on, and at the next rise, an oncoming cruiser passed me.

I sat back in the seat and smiled.

When I got back to the house, I trotted inside and grabbed the phone. Bell's number was on the cover of the notebook on the counter. I dialed. Asked for her. She came on the line.

''McMorrow, I just tried to call you. I left a message.''

''I just got in. I didn't check the machine. But listen, a truck came by here, checking the place. It was an old black Ford, painted camouflage.''

''Yeah?''

''I think it might be the guys from Stratton.''

''You get a plate number?''

''Better than that. I got the truck stopped. As we speak, Winslow police have them for drinking in the car. Maybe you could get their names. When I went by, the cop was taking the driver's ID.''

''I'll call them,'' Bell said. ''But I've got one for you.''

She sounded pleased.

"Yeah?"

"I got a name. Off the print on the bottle."

"No kidding. And it isn't Robie?"

"And it isn't Mantis, either."

 I stood there at the counter, feeling wired.

"What is it?" I said.

"You didn't hear it from me," Bell said.

"Come on."

"It's Marvin. K. That's K-A-Y. That's the middle name. Surname is Maurice."

She spelled it. I wrote it down in a reporter's notebook.

"Mor-ris? Mor-reese? I don't know how you pronounce it."

"Mau-reese, maybe," I said. "Who is he?"

"He came back a hit."

"For what?"

"He was indicted for theft by deception. That's all it says. I've got a call in. But he never showed up for his arraignment so a warrant went out."

"So he was indicted and he took off?"

"Looks that way."

"And went all the way to Boston to take a bus to Québec?"

"Maybe he thought it would be a good way to cross the border," Bell said. "Then he got cold feet."

"Where's he from?"

"NCIC lists him as from Winslow. Sixteen Dan Avenue, Winslow, Maine."

I scribbled that down, too.

"But I thought you said he was from Gardiner."

"No, the checking account was in Gardiner, but that was phony."

"So he's local. Sort of."

"I guess."

"Maybe when he got off the bus, he was just going home. Twenty miles down the road."

"But there was a warrant out for him there," Bell said. "Winslow isn't a big place. He couldn't hang around long before he'd get picked up."

I stood there with the pen in my hand, trying to put myself in the place of Marvin K. Maurice. Had he just been covering his tracks? Leaving a phony trail?

"What do you know about this guy?"

"That's it."

"When are you going to talk to Robie and Rob-ann? And Howard and Damian?"

"I'll try to fit it in today. Chief isn't gonna let me spend hours and hours finding out. That's why I told you."

"You think I'll spend hours and hours finding out?"

"Yup."

"What do I look like? Some sort of gofer?"

"Yeah. You're my research assistant."

Bell gave a little chuckle.

"Yeah, well, maybe I'm busy," I said. "I've got things to do."

"You kidding, McMorrow? As soon as we hang up, you'll be on the phone to Winslow. You'll be on your way over there to knock on doors. You've got the bug."

"What bug's that?" I asked.

"If you don't know something, you have to find out. You're just one of those curious types. Some people are and some people aren't. Probably what made you get into being a reporter."

"I don't know. I suppose."

I paused. Bell had considered me, and that was startling.

"You probably would have made a good cop," she said, "except you'd have trouble with the drudge stuff."

"You don't think I could write a parking ticket?"

"Or a speeding ticket. Or write an accident report for some stupid fender-bender. You'd be running off to Winslow or someplace on some investigation."

"But you're the same way," I said.

"I would be if I could," Bell said. "But this has to be a job, you know? We got a mortgage."

There was something wistful in her voice. And then other voices in the background. The crackle of a police radio.

"Yeah, ten-four," Bell said. She sounded resigned.

"Listen, I gotta go."

"Fender-bender?"

"No. Nothing that exciting."

"You'll call Winslow? Get the names of the guys in the truck?"

"Yeah, I will."

"I'll bet you coffee they know Howard and Damian."

"Probably swing from the same family tree," Bell said.

"I'll be in touch," I said.

"Be careful knocking on doors in Winslow."

There was concern in her voice. Maybe even a little affection.

"Oh, yeah. As always."

"And McMorrow?"

"Yeah?"

Her voice was a whisper. I braced myself for something more unexpected, more intimate.

"Yeah?"

"Everything I just told you is totally off the record."

So where to turn, which lead to track down first?

I stood there in the kitchen, felt a hot breeze blow in through the screen door. Outside, the field was jittery with butterflies, flitting cabbage whites, and the woods were green and lush and still as a rain forest.

Things were heating up.

I stood there and listed them in my mind. There was Marvin K. Maurice and his background in Winslow. The two guys in the camouflage truck. Robie, with his cigarette burns, Rob-ann with who knows what. There were Howard and Damian. What did they know about Mr. Maurice? What did they know about the guys in the truck?

There was Benedict Arnold, who, like the Kennebec, was always lurking in the background. I had to go to Québec City the next morning, and then I had to come home Friday and chain myself to the computer and write the story. I just had to. There was no wiggle room left, but then, Winslow was on the way to Scanesett. And Scanesett was on the way to Québec. I could spend the night in a motel in between, someplace cheap. It was five after one. That gave me the afternoon and evening to knock on doors, roust Robie, touch base with Hope Bell, and find out who had shot at me and why.

And be in Québec City for croissants in the morning.

Alone.

As I mounted the stairs to begin to pack, I felt a twinge of remorse and regret, but just a twinge, like a passing wave of nausea. Roxanne hadn't been on my list at all, not even to call. But she couldn't be here, I told myself, pulling open the bureau drawers. I couldn't be there, not until my story was done. She couldn't help me with what I had to do, so the best thing to do was to plunge in and get it done as quickly as possible. Clear the decks for her return. Write the Marvin K. Maurice story, and sell it and use the money to take both of us away for a day and a night. A night in a little inn on the Maine coast. Or a weekend on an island. Vinalhaven or Monhegan. Someplace where we could both get away from the rest of the world.

That would do it, I thought, stuffing my canvas duffel. I even allowed myself a small smile, though a nagging thought was bumping around in the back of my mind. It tapped and tugged, but I kept it back there until I was well on my way to Winslow and it was too late to revise my plan.

Too late to consider whether what I was doing—chasing these stories, consoling Roxanne long distance—was wrong, whether a weekend in an inn was just a way to try to tidy things up. That possibility gnawed at me the whole way, and it was beginning to break through.

Luckily, Winslow was only a half hour away.

And Dan Avenue was in the directory. It was a neat street of small ranch houses with attached garages, in a development of other streets with small ranch houses with attached garages. Each of the streets had a name like Dan, or Eileen, or Joseph, probably all relatives of the developer. All of the houses on the namesake streets faced the road squarely, and the lawns were respectably mown.

The development was on a hill a mile or so from the Kennebec. I drove in from the river side, threading my way left and right, stopping Clair's big truck in the road to peer at my map. Once I looked up to find a woman pushing a stroller, peering at me. The next time it was a boy on a bike with a baseball mitt hung on the handlebars.

This was middle America, where Marvin K. Maurice lived, and I didn't quite fit in. I wondered whether he did, and when I finally turned onto Dan Avenue, I parked, got out and went to ask.

Number sixteen was a gray-blue ranch with a tattered hedge running across the front of the yard, and shades pulled down in all the windows. The lawn was parched and had turned a khaki color. A chubby blond guy was out in his driveway watching the sprinkler on his grass, which was as green as Ireland. I slipped my notebook out of my back pocket and sauntered over.

"Hi, there," I said. "Looks nice."

He turned and looked at me. His shirt was open. I saw a good-sized belly, a long surgical scar on the left side.

"Gotta keep after it," he said.

He turned back to the sprinkler, which was the kind that chit-chit-chits like a machine gun.

"I'm Jack McMorrow," I said. "I'm a reporter. A free-lance reporter. I'm working on a story about one of your neighbors. Mr. Maurice."

The guy turned slowly, leading with his gut.

"Why you want to write about Maurice?"

He pronounced it "Morris."

"Well, it's sort of an odd reason," I said.

I smiled. He looked at me warily.

"Well," I said, "it could be that the police are looking for him. He's sort of disappeared. You seen him lately?"

The man's mouth visibly hardened. He shook his head. "Nope."

He turned back to his lawn.

"But he lives right there, right?"

"Yup."

"But you haven't seen him?"

"I said that, didn't I?"

"Yeah, but when was the last time you saw him? I mean, even if it wasn't lately."

The man turned to me.

"This isn't for the local paper, is it?"

"No," I said. "I sell stories to magazines. Sometimes to the *Boston Globe*. Places like that."

He looked at me, and his lips seemed to meld.

"So has Mr. Maurice been around?"

The man shook his head.

"I mean, when was the last time you saw him?"

"Don't remember," he murmured, barely opening his mouth.

I paused. This was odd, but maybe he was just shy.

"This can be off the record," I said. "Just background. I don't have to use your name."

He didn't react. We both watched as the sprinkler suddenly chittered and raked the lawn with a drenching fire.

"So, you've known him a long time?"

He nodded, barely. That was it. I tried again.

"So what can you tell me about him? Does he work? Have a family? Live alone?"

"Just him," the man said, teeth clenched, turned away.

"Has he lived here a long time?"

He shrugged. I moved in front of him.

"Is there something wrong, sir?" I said.

He looked at me, then away again.

And then he walked into the garage, through a doorway and into the house. The door slammed shut behind him. I stood there in the driveway, bewildered.

I walked slowly down the driveway and into the street, stuffing my notebook back into my pocket. There had been other people outside but they were gone. As I stood there, a woman came out of the house across the street, walked briskly to a van in the driveway, backed out and drove away. What did they think I was selling?

I stood by the truck for a minute, then went to the house on the other side of Maurice's. I thought I'd seen a kid on a bike in the yard, but when I got there, the garage door was closed and no one was in sight. I rang the bell at the back door. Nobody answered.

I kept going.

Across the street, I heard a television on but no one answered the door. Next door to that house, a car pulled away as I approached. Two houses away from that one, three houses down and across the street from Maurice, I saw a white-haired man in the backyard. I walked across the lawn and around the corner of the house.

He was sitting in a lawn chair, legs stretched out. A little white dog yapped twice and he said, "No" and "Sit," and it fell to the grass. He looked up at me—he had a narrow face with metal-framed glasses—and smiled as I gave my pitch.

"And you want to write a story about Maurice?"

He pronounced it "Morris."

"I'm thinking about it."

"I saw you pull up," the man said. "That your truck?"

"Well, no. Actually, I borrowed it from a friend."

He grinned again. This time gave me a little wink.

"I'm sure," he said. "And I suppose you have a card, too."

I took out my wallet, dug one out, and handed it to him. Still smiling, he looked at it.

"Jack McMorrow. Prosperity, Maine," the man said. "That's it?"

"Yeah," I said. "That's my name."

He almost chortled.

"Can I keep this?"

"Sure. I've got plenty."

He eyed me conspiratorally.

"I'll bet you do."

I looked at him. He looked at the lawn.

"So you're looking for Maurice, huh?"

"Well, not really. The police are looking for him. I'm just looking to find out more about him."

"Like when he left?"

I paused.

"That's a start."

"Don't know. He just hasn't been around," the man said.

"For how long?"

"I don't know. A week or so. I don't keep track."

He still was smiling.

"And you guys can't find him. Well, well."

"Us guys?"

He ignored me.

"Well, can't help you, Mr. McMorrow. Sorry about that. I don't know anything about Mr. Maurice."

"I beg your pardon, but how can you not know anything? You're neighbors, right? You must have—"

"I was in the service," the man said suddenly, still staring at the lawn. "Infantry. Chief. Saw Sicily. France. Even got into Africa. So I know you got your orders. It's nothing personal. But I'm seventy-four years old. Wife's sick, and I'm too goddamn old to get involved in something like this.''

He lifted himself out of the chair and turned toward the house. As he walked away, I noticed the webbing on the seat had left a crisscross pattern on the back of his legs. It was the last thing I saw as he went through the doorway, the dog scurrying after of him.

I stood there for a moment. What was going on? What was wrong with these people? I had my orders? Us ''guys'' couldn't find him? The winks and the grins? Were they all nuts? This was like Scanesett, with Howard and Damian in the parking lot.

''I told you these guys are trained.''

What guys? Trained for what? Of course, I had a card? Was that my truck? I walked around the other side of the house and down the driveway to the street. At two-thirty on a Wednesday afternoon in the summer in the little mill town of Winslow, Maine, there was nobody around. Maurice's deserted house fit right in.

I walked across and up the street and looked at it.

''The hell with 'em,'' I said, and went across the lawn to the front door. I pulled the screen door open and banged. Nothing. I went around to the side door by the driveway but that screen door wouldn't open. I rang the doorbell, which showed an orange light. Nothing. I went to the garage and, shielding my face from the sunlight, peered in the windows. My eyes slowly adjusted.

There was a motorcycle parked inside. It looked fairly new. It was a Harley-Davidson. To the left of it, along the wall, were tires and rims. Four of them. Fancy alloy rims and low, wide, white-lettered tires. I pressed my hands closer to my face and peered. Goodyear Eagle GTs, which were very expensive.

Where was the car to go with them? If Maurice had the money to buy a car that warranted a thousand dollars' worth of wheels, why was he riding a bus? Was this stuff stolen? Where was the car? Who was this guy?

I walked around the garage and into the backyard. It was plain and parched, like the yard in front. There was a big gas grill on the cement block patio: both looked new. I went to the sliding door and gave it a tug. It was locked so I pressed my face to the glass again, peeking through the space between the curtains. It was a den sort of room with a big-screen television and a stack of electronics. More bucks. What did this guy do?

Circling the other end of the house, I walked back to the truck. Stood for a moment and then climbed in. There still was nobody in sight, so I started the truck and rolled slowly down the street and around the corner. It was time to take a look at the indictment, to see just what Maurice was accused of stealing. Was it all that stuff in the house? If so, why hadn't somebody come and hauled it off?

But Augusta was the wrong direction. I didn't feel like driving another fifty miles, but then, I probably didn't have the connections to get it over the phone. I could give it a try, hope to catch some court clerk in a good—

Some kids came around the corner, swinging along on Rollerblades. I pulled the truck over and got out and said, ''Hey, guys. Could I talk to you for a second?''

Two of them went by me and kept on going. A third pulled up. A fourth kid, smaller and slower, stopped fifty feet away and bent to tug at his skate. I smiled at the third kid. Thanked him for stopping. He whirled around me, feet spread, showboating a little. I told him I was a reporter, that I was doing a story on Mr. Maurice, down the street. Bang, his expression became the same mask I'd seen on the blond guy with the sprinkler.

''Nahhh, sorry, can't help you,'' the kid said, and he with a kick, he was gone.

I stood there in the street, then turned to kid number four. He'd flopped down on the grass by the street, still working on one of his skates. I walked over.

"Hey," I said.

He looked up, then back down at his skate. He looked like he was about ten. He had glasses and was wearing a Nike T-shirt, baggy Nike shorts.

"Hi," he said.

"Having a little trouble there?"

"Blisters. I don't have socks on, or I could keep up with those guys."

"They didn't wait," I said.

"They never do."

I squatted next to him, hoped he hadn't been drilled too much about talking to strangers.

"You live around here?"

He was loosening his skate, then easing his foot out and then back in, trying to find a position that didn't hurt.

"Oww. Yup."

"I'm a newspaper reporter. I'm doing a story on a guy who lives around the corner. Maybe you know him. Mr. Maurice?"

On the skate, his hands froze. The rest of him, too. He lifted his head slowly and looked at me.

"Mr. Maurice?"

"Yeah."

He gave me an assessing look. The polo shirt. The khaki hiking shorts. The lightweight hiking boots.

"You don't look like a reporter," the kid said.

"I know. But I'm a freelancer. I can look however I want, if I get the story. So, you know Mr. Maurice?"

"Um, I don't know if I'm supposed to tell you."

I stopped. Looked at him. Sat down on the strip of grass beside him.

"You don't know if you're supposed to tell me? Why do you say that?"

" 'Cause I don't know."

"Don't know what?"

"If I'm supposed to talk to you."

"Because you don't know me?" I said. "Well, that's

reasonable. Sometimes you shouldn't talk to people you don't know.''

''Not about him.''

I paused.

''Not about Mr. Maurice?''

''I don't know. I don't think I'm supposed to.''

I smiled—reassuringly, I hoped.

''Why not?'' I asked.

'' 'Cause it's classified.''

''Classified?''

''Yeah,'' the little boy said. ''People could get hurt.''

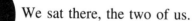 We sat there, the two of us.

''Who told you that?'' I asked him. ''Mr. Maurice?''

''Yeah. A lot of what he did was classified. He wasn't supposed to talk about it. Not ever.''

''But he did?''

The boy hesitated.

''Sometimes. But he said not to tell anybody about it.''

''Because—''

''It was classified.''

He looked at me seriously, his skate hanging loosely off of his right foot. His legs and arms were thin and white. His right ankle was chafed.

''You're not a reporter.''

I looked back. Smiled again.

''Why don't you think so?''

"I can tell."

"How can you tell?"

"I just can. I talked to Mr. Maurice a lot. No names, though."

The boy looked at me to make sure I understood. I didn't, but I didn't admit it.

"Just kind of overall stuff."

"Overall stuff?"

"Different places. Different operations. I promised I wouldn't tell anybody. And I haven't told. Swear to God."

He held up his right hand, as if to take the Boy Scout oath.

"Swear to God."

"I believe you," I said.

"Good. I don't want to get in trouble. I don't want Mr. Maurice to get in trouble, either. You're not gonna hurt him, are you?"

"No," I said. "I'm not going to hurt him."

"He's a good guy. He just was in the covert stuff too long."

A car went by, and the woman at the wheel looked at us but kept going.

"The covert stuff will do that," I said.

"Yeah. But he'd never do anything to hurt his country. He told me that."

"He did?"

"But he said when you were in covert operations, after a while things weren't black and white as much, you know? They were sorta gray."

I looked at him. Skinny, glasses, skating by himself. He probably read a lot of books.

"How old are you?"

"Twelve."

"You talked to Mr. Maurice a lot?"

"Yeah. My backyard leads to his backyard. There's a space between the fence."

"So you'd go over and talk?"

"Yeah. He didn't have a lot of friends or anything. He wasn't married. You know that."

"Uh-huh. So you guys would talk?"

"Yeah, but nothing specific, if that's what you're worried about. I mean, some of this stuff may've been classified, but only just barely. I guess the CIA doesn't care, though, right? I mean, something's classified or it isn't, right?"

I stretched out my legs and rested back on my hands.

"I don't know," I said truthfully.

"It was just that we kind of liked the same stuff. I read all of Tom Clancy. When I found out Mr. Maurice was in covert ops, I was, like, blown away."

"And you're twelve?"

"But I read on, like, a twelfth-grade level. Other kids in my class, they're reading these baby books. I've always been way ahead. It's a problem for my teachers. Keeping me stimulated. Motivated. My mother has to go into school a lot."

"Well, that's good. You don't want to just coast along. What's your name, anyway?"

"You need it for your report?"

"Well, maybe."

"Jeremy. Jeremy Jackson. That's my father's name. He lives in Virginia."

"You live with your mom?"

"And my stepdad. He's nice but he works a lot. At the mill. We need the overtime so I can go to college. If I go to a good college, it could cost a hundred thousand dollars."

"Yeah," I said. "It's expensive. But it's worth it."

"Where'd you go?"

"A college in New York."

"I don't want to go too far from home."

"Oh," I said. "So where is home?"

"Thirteen June Street. Like the month."

"Gotcha. So listen, Jeremy. Did you tell Mr. Maurice

that you liked Tom Clancy's books? Espionage and all that?''

''Oh, yeah,'' Jeremy said. ''I think that's why he started talking about it. 'Cause he knew I was interested. I'd like to get into covert ops someday.''

''So he told you about his experiences?''

He looked at me.

''Not specifics. Like I told you. No names. He'd name a country, or, like, an area. But he never, like, told me cities or dates. It was always, like, 'When the company was in Southeast Asia,' or 'When I was working in Chile.' ''

Jeremy pronounced it ''Chill-ay.''

''He knew I could be trusted. I mean, who was I gonna tell around here?''

I looked around. It was a plain little street in a plain little Maine mill town. He was a plain little kid with glasses.

''So you didn't tell anybody?''

He didn't answer.

''You kept this all your own secret, Jeremy? You and Mr. Maurice?''

Jeremy licked his lips. Inhaled deeply and let it out.

''I told my mom,'' he said quietly.

''You did? What'd she say?''

''She said not to tell anybody else.''

''Probably good advice,'' I said. ''So nobody else knew? In the neighborhood, I mean.''

''Oh, they just knew he was with the CIA. But they knew that 'cause Mr. Maurice's mother told them.''

''His mother told them.''

''Yeah, but then she went in a nursing home and then she died. But when Mr. Maurice came home to live in her house, like, everybody sorta knew.''

''When was that?''

''I was in fourth grade. It was right after tryouts. Baseball.''

''You play baseball?''

He turned solemn.

"Yeah. Well, sort of. I didn't play much."

I paused. The subtle cruelties of childhood.

And now you're in what grade?"

"Going into seventh. Middle School."

"That'll be interesting," I said. "So, Jeremy, everybody knew he was in the CIA?"

"Yeah, but nobody really talked about it. I mean, he was just Mr. Maurice. He didn't go on about it or nothin'."

"Except to you."

"Well, yeah."

"But you told me."

Jeremy looked worried.

"But I had to. I mean, he told me you'd be coming."

I stared at him.

"I'd be coming?"

"No, no. I mean, he told me somebody like you would be coming. Looking for him."

"And why did he say I'd be looking for him?"

" 'Cause you decided you wanted the money back."

I thought for a moment.

"The money he took with him when he left the company?"

"Yeah," Jeremy said. "But Mr. Maurice said that was one of those gray areas, too."

I hesitated, framing the question in my mind.

"So did you know he got in trouble?"

Jeremy nodded.

"It was part of the plan. Take him into custody and then disappear him."

"But he disappeared first?"

"He had to save himself."

Another car went by, swinging wide past the truck. Hot exhaust and grit blew over us.

"So Jeremy, did he tell you where he was going?"

He shook his head.

"Nope. He said I was better off not knowing."

"He say anything else?"

"Just to cooperate," Jeremy said. "Cooperate fully with the investigation."

"And that's what you're doing?"

"Yeah," he said, struggling to his feet on his skates, and wincing. "But now I gotta go home."

I sat in the truck feeling, as Jeremy might have put it, like, blown away.

Could Maurice really have been in the CIA? Could that have been the theft? Could that have been the reason he was trying to get to Canada? Because Jeremy certainly was telling the truth, as he knew it. As told to him by Mr. Maurice.

That question hovered in the back of my mind as I taped everything I could remember of our conversation. I stopped, then started again, as bits and pieces of it surfaced. The space in the fence. Chile, correctly pronounced. The mother in the nursing home. The man in the chaise, with his knowing winks and grins. Had that been what he had meant?

It had to have been because it all fit. My "orders." His army years. The amused look he'd gotten as he looked at my business card and read its brief message. Nobody wanting to say boo about this guy who lived in their midst. Why?

Because it was Mr. Maurice. He was in the CIA.

I tried to recall the way he'd been described by the woman on the bus. No glasses. Shorts. Pale legs. Nothing much distinctive about him. Could that be a guy in the CIA? Well, I supposed they didn't look like Sean Connery. They probably looked like accountants, insurance brokers, college professors. Did they come home to Winslow, Maine? Did the CIA come after them?

Could it be true? If it were, how did Maurice of the CIA end up with Robie and Rob-ann of Scanesett?

I leaned down and picked up the cellular phone, which

I'd unplugged from my truck, and plugged it into the cigarette lighter. It lighted and beeped and I punched some
numbers. Directory assistance answered and I asked for Su-
perior Court in Augusta. The clerk's office. I scribbled the
number in my pad. Punched and waited. A woman answered.

"Criminal or civil?"

"Criminal," I said.

The phone clicked. Another woman answered. I told her
my name. I told her I was a reporter. I told her I was
interested in the indictment of Marvin Maurice of Winslow.
She told me I could come in and see the file. I told her I
was on my way north, that I was just trying to make sure
that this was the charge I thought it was.

Silence.

"It'll just save me half a day if I know it's not the right
charge," I said.

I waited.

"Well, we're really not supposed to give out that kind
of information over the phone," she said. "Oh, gosh."

It was a burden trying to be accommodating, especially
when it meant breaking the rules.

"Well, just a minute."

The phone clicked. I sat and waited, the cellular seconds
ticking by. But still, it was cheaper than driving fifty miles
in Clair's ten-mile-per-gallon truck. I waited. She came
back on, whispering.

"What do you need to know?"

"He was indicted on a theft charge. I just want to know
what it was he's charged with stealing."

I fibbed.

"Is this the stolen car?"

"Oh, no," the nice clerk said. "This is, let me see."

I heard papers rustling, her voice as she read to herself.

"On or about the date of . . . Marvin K. Maurice did attempt to defraud . . . knowing this to be false and mislead-
ing . . ."

She paused.

"The case we have here is a credit card thing," she said.

"Stolen credit cards?"

"Hmmm, I don't think so. Let me see. No, you'd have to come and see the file for yourself, but it looks like this is more like a fraud thing. 'The state charges . . .' I think they're saying he applied for credit cards and then charged all kinds of things . . . 'cash in the sum of ten thousand dollars . . . cash in the sum of seventy-five hundred dollars . . . ' No, I think he maxed out a bunch of credit cards all at once. For cash."

"I see. So what's the total?"

"Oh, gosh, I don't have time to add them all up. I don't know. Twentysome thousand? Thirtysome thousand? No, that's the same as the other one. I don't know. You'd have to come in, Mr. . . . what did you say your name was?"

"McMorrow," I said. "Jack McMorrow."

"And what paper are you with?"

"I'm not," I said. "I'm on my own."

And I was, even more than usual. Living alone, working alone, delving into a story that became more bizarre by the day. Alone. It was the kind of story that required perspective, the kind that left you wondering if you were being snookered. But by whom?

By Maurice? Robie? Or maybe the little kid was off his rocker, maybe he told the CIA story to anybody who would listen. Maybe his name wasn't Jeremy. Maybe he didn't know Maurice at all. Maybe Maurice told CIA stories, but only when he was off his medication. Maybe Robie picked up that Pepsi bottle by the side of the road. Maybe to all of the above, but I didn't think so. No way.

I started the truck, then on a chance, reached for the phone again. I punched in the number of Scanesett P.D., which I no longer had to look up. It rang, the same dispatcher answered. Yes, Officer Bell was working. No, she was not in the station. Yes, he'd give her my message.

As I thanked him, a small red car slowed beside me. I tensed and looked over. The white-haired man from the backyard was at the wheel. He saw me with the phone in my hand, gave me a crisp salute, and grinned.

I didn't, but I followed.

He drove through the development and out onto the road by the river. I followed him through the strip-mall main drag, wondering if I made him nervous, the big Ford looming in his rearview mirror. I hoped so. And then he turned left, over the bridge into Waterville. I continued straight up the hill and pulled up at the Winslow municipal building.

It was just south of the sprawling, steaming mill complex, a one-story brick building sitting high above the river, next to a pretty little park shaded by old oaks. I pulled into the parking lot, then saw a police cruiser out behind the building. I parked next to it and went through the station doorway. The door led down a hall, the walls of which were lined with souvenir insignias from other police departments. The hall led to a room with a wooden counter. Behind the counter, a woman was typing at a computer.

She smiled and got up.

I told her who I was and what I wanted. She was matronly and pleasant, but she said I'd have to talk to the chief or one of the detectives. The detective in question had grand jury all day in Augusta. The chief was at a meeting of the state chief's association in Bangor. I'd have to come back, she said, apologetically. I thanked her and said I would, and then started to ask about the guys in the camouflage truck, but caught myself.

How would I know about that? Why would I care?

So I left, but outside the door, I stopped. The municipal offices were above the police department. I opened the door and soon found myself in front of another wooden counter, behind which another woman, fortyish, hair tightly permed, smiled and got up. I told her who I was, that I was a reporter, doing a story for the *Boston Globe,* and I wanted to

double-check a fact in a story. The story was about Marvin
Maurice.

Her expression changed. It was still friendly, but knowing. Maurice, or at least his troubles, were known here.

"I'd like to know what vehicles he has registered here,"
I said.

"Oh," she said. "That we can do. It's all public."

She went to a bank of file drawers and slid one open.
Thumbed through them and lifted out white registration
slips.

"You want the plate numbers?"

"No. Just the make and model. And if he owns or leased
them."

She put the slips on the counter. Two of them. I dug out
my notebook and leaned over.

A 1995 Mustang GT. A 1990 Harley-Davidson. The
Mustang was leased from a dealer in Waterville. The Harley he owned. The registration on the bike was expired.

I scribbled in my notebook, copying down numbers, giving myself an excuse to stay.

"So he's in a bit of trouble," I said without looking up.

"I heard," the woman said.

"You know him?"

"Knew who he was. He was in my brother's class in
school. Pretty quiet, I guess. But he didn't stay here. Joined
the service and was gone for twenty years or something."

"What, did he come back here to retire?"

She leaned on the counter.

"I don't know. I saw in the paper when he was arrested
for whatever it was."

"Indicted. Credit card fraud."

"Yeah, well, I don't know. I heard he was all over the
world in the service. He came in here once and started
talking about how they drive like maniacs in Vietnam or
someplace."

I kept scribbling, copying the numbers for the third time.
An old man in green work clothes came in and stood at the

counter beside me. Another woman rose from a desk to help him. The woman waiting on me rested her chin in her hand.

''I heard he was in the CIA,'' she whispered. ''Is that right?''

I looked up at her.

''I heard that, too,'' I said. ''Where'd you hear it?''

She thought. She had long eyelashes. Green eye shadow. The skin at the top of her chest was very tanned, almost leathery.

''You're not gonna quote me, are you? I mean, I'd get fired.''

''No,'' I said. ''I won't quote you.''

''Promise?''

''Promise.''

She settled in.

''Well, I don't know. I guess I heard it around town. And I think he said something when he was here once. He called it Army Intelligence. Made some joke about how many Army Intelligence people it takes to change a light-bulb. Something like that.''

I looked at her.

''Is that right? Seems like somebody in that wouldn't really talk about it,'' I said. ''I thought they had to promise they wouldn't.''

''I don't know,'' she said. ''Maybe he figures it doesn't matter, now that he's back home. I mean, who're we gonna tell?''

I smiled.

''I suppose.''

She leaned, apparently in no rush to go back to her terminal.

''So what was he like? Nice guy?''

I kept scribbling.

''Well,'' she said, ''I guess. In a pathetic sort of way. Trying to put on airs. He'd pay for, like, his registration for his car and he'd have this big wad of bills. I don't know. And the car.''

"The Mustang?"

"You seen it?"

"No."

"It's a red convertible. Goes, like, a hundred and forty miles an hour or something. My brother said it was a car for somebody who wanted everybody to look at him, think he's a hot—hot stuff.''

"Married?"

"Who, me?"

"Uh, no. Maurice."

"Nope. I mean, not that I know of."

And she would know, I thought.

"Seeing anybody?"

"Who, me?"

I smiled. She did, too.

"No, I don't know. He's kind of, well, it isn't that he's really ugly or anything. It's just that, I don't know, at least when he was in here, I guess he just tries too hard. You know what I mean? He seems kind of desperate for people to notice him. Tries so hard it makes him kind of, I don't know. Kind of dorky.''

"Yeah," I said. "I know what you mean."

"But don't quote me."

"Wouldn't think of it."

"So you all set?"

"I guess," I said, putting my notebook in my shorts pocket. "Thanks."

She started to turn, but lingered.

"So you live in Boston?"

"No. I live in Maine. Waldo County. I just write for them sometimes.''

She seemed glad to hear it.

"Oh, really. Well, I don't know if I should say this . . .''

I waited.

"But your shirt's turned in. The collar."

I looked down. It was, and I straightened it.

"Don't know how your wife let you out of the house like that," the woman said.

"Just slipping up, I guess."

She gave me a long look.

"Time to trade her in for a new one," she said, and turned and walked slowly away. I turned, too, smiling to myself, and pushed through the door out to the parking lot, where a car drove past me, and pulled into a space.

It was an Chevette. Copper, with a blue door.

Howard was behind the wheel, Damian in the passenger seat. I kept walking toward Clair's truck, which was parked at the end of the building, fifty feet away. As I got to the truck, I turned and looked.

Damian was still in the car. Howard was going into the town office. I waited until the door closed behind him, then followed.

When I got inside, Howard was leaning against the counter, his logger boots tapping on the floor, his baseball hat in his hand. My friend was in an alcove off of the main office, looking through a file drawer. The other woman was looking up from her desk at Howard. I turned and perused the bulletin board.

"Yeah, I got this friend of mine," Howard began. "And he, like, he's sick, and he couldn't come in but he wanted me to check for him to see if, like, his car needs plates. I mean, stickers. It already has plates.''

The woman, fifty-five and no doubt hardened by years of waiting on the moronic public, looked at him skeptically. My friend still was occupied at the files.

''So you want to know if your friend's registration needs to be renewed?'' the woman said from her desk.

''Right,'' Howard said hoarsely. ''He asked me to check for him, on account of he couldn't come in. 'Cause he's sick.''

''Why doesn't he just look at the license plate and see what the date is?'' the woman said.

Howard looked down at his hat, then around the room.

''Well, he would, but he don't have the car. A buddy of ours took the car and went out of state with it. Borrowed it, I mean.''

''Why don't you just call him and ask him to look at the plates?''

She was grilling him. I wondered if Howard would be able to curb his natural reflex, which probably was to leap over the counter and beat her head against her desk until she was unconscious. It was good that he'd left Damian in the car.

''Yeah, well,'' Howard said, ''our buddy, he ain't got a phone. But my friend, he just don't want the cops, like, stopping the guy for a taillight or some bullshit, and the car's not registered and the shit hits the fan, you know what I'm saying?''

She looked at him with unbridled disdain, let out a long, disgusted sigh, and heaved herself and her chair back from her desk.

''Okay. What's your friend's name?''

''It's Maurice,'' Howard said. ''Marvin Maurice.''

My friend turned from the files and started toward the counter, her mouth half open, ready to speak. I put my finger across my lips, and she saw me and caught herself.

The other clerk stomped over to the car registration drawers.

"Well, the next time have your friend think of this before he goes loaning out his car," she said. "We've got plenty to do without this sort of thing."

"Yeah, well, he got sick awful fast," Howard said, relaxing now. "It was that flu that's going around. Sick as a dog. Usually he keeps track of this sort of stuff pretty good. I mean—"

"Okay. Which vehicle?" the clerk barked, holding the slips in front of her.

"Um, I guess . . . I'm not sure what one—"

"The Mustang or the Harley-Davidson?"

"Um—"

"The Mustang is good till September. The motorcycle ran out last April. You said the car, so I guess your friend is okay for another couple months."

"Hey, thanks much," Howard said. I put my face into the bulletin board as he started to turn toward me, but then he turned back.

"This is the right Marvin Maurice, ain't it? I mean, it ain't his father. 'Cause his father—"

"Marvin K. Maurice. Sixteen Dan Avenue. Only one we've got."

"Oh, great. Thanks. I mean, thanks a lot. I know you're busy and all that, so thanks much."

Howard brushed past me, slammed through the door and trotted to the car. I came out in time to see him exchange high fives with Damian. The car backed up and Damian flicked a burning cigarette out onto the pavement.

"A friggin' Harley?" I heard him say. "What year?"

They pulled out and took a right. I hopped in the truck and followed. They drove down the hill past the park and made the first light, rolling through on the yellow. I sat and waited as they drove along Route 201 and out of sight. I wasn't worried.

When the light changed, I drove through, past the strip

mall and used-car lots, to the next light, which was green. I continued straight, past more used-car lots, and on into the drab little developments. Retracing my route, I threaded my way through the little ranch-house streets. As I approached Dan Avenue, I slowed. Eased up to the corner.

The Chevette was in front of Maurice's house, stopped at the side of the street. Howard and Damian were both looking up at the house. I rounded the corner, and drove slowly past them, my hand against my face. Three houses down, I pulled over and stopped and watched. They were talking. Looking. Looking toward me. I put the truck in gear and, picking a house that looked particularly empty, drove into the driveway and up to the garage.

I waited. Nobody came to the door. The curtains didn't move. There was a chain tied to the handle of the garage door but there was no dog. No barking. I reached for a pad and started leafing through it, as if looking for a work order or an address.

Howard and Damian got out of the car and started for the house.

I thought of calling the cops but changed my mind. As I watched, they went to the front of the house and Howard knocked loudly, rattling the aluminum storm door. Then they went toward the back door and disappeared from view. I slipped the truck into neutral and rolled it back until I could see the garage. They went to the door, leaned down and heaved it open. Disappeared inside. I figured they were fondling the Harley. I wondered how long it would take for the neighbors to call the cops.

They came back out, pulling the garage door down behind them. It slammed closed.

I started the truck as they got back in their car. There was another high-five, a muffled whoop of jubilation. Maybe Maurice had joined a monastery. He'd left them all his earthly goods.

As they drove by, I leaned down to the glove compartment, counted to five, and then rolled back out and followed. They exited at the other end of the development, and I followed, a quarter-mile back. At the next light, they took a left, driving back down the hill toward the river and the center of town. They cruised slowly down the main drag, then signaled left and pulled into a convenience store. I sat in the lot of a gas station and waited as Damian went in, and returned a moment later with a twelve-pack of Bud.

It was, after all, after three o'clock.

They took the back way, following the road on the east side of the river. As they passed the town office, a police car pulled out and headed in the other direction. They slowed and I got too close. Damian passed Howard a can of beer. They seem to ease in for a leisurely ride; I backed off and followed.

It wasn't easy because they followed the back road up the river all the way to Scanesett. Most of the time we were the only cars on the road, so I had to let them out of my sight for three or four minutes at a time. I counted six empties along the road, and then we were coming up on Route 2, the main east–west highway. They pulled out to the left, three cars and a tractor-trailer went by, and I followed and picked up the phone receiver.

I called the Scanesett P.D. My dispatcher friend answered and I asked for Bell. He said she was on the road. I identified myself and asked if she'd gotten my other message. He said no, she'd been "right out straight." I asked if he could tell her I called again. He said he would, but I knew I couldn't count on it.

Howard and Damian turned right.

I wondered if they were going to lead me to Maurice. Would they say, "Hey, Marv. How 'bout the keys to that Harley? We'll just borrow it." Or would it be, "Hey, Marv. We checked on the Harley for you. It's still there. Want us to snatch it for ya before the cops grab it?"

What was their relationship? Who was in charge?

I tried to picture it. Robie and Rob-ann and a dorky doughboy guy from Winslow. Howard and Damian, who sensed vulnerability like wild dogs. The other two guys in the camouflage truck, who thought nothing of trying to put a bullet in me in broad daylight.

Something told me Mr. Maurice was not in command.

The Chevette slipped through the back streets, circled the block beyond Robie and Rob-ann's and then came home to roost. Howard whipped the car up the driveway but pulled it around behind the house, out of sight from the street. I drove past, craning to see in the mirrors, but they'd disappeared. I took two rights on to the next block and parked.

It was a street of square plain houses, four dingy to every one well kept. I got out and walked along the broken side-walk until I could see Robie's house, the second-floor land-ing above the roof of a sagging garage. There were kids down the block, two guys under the hood of a pickup across the street. I looked both ways, then walked up the driveway, past the porches and alongside the garage. At the corner of the building, underneath a squeezed clump of sumac, I leaned and watched.

The Chevette was parked alongside Robie's bikes and carts. The grim little yard was silent, and no one was in sight. I checked the time; it was three-forty. I decided I'd give it until four o'clock, then go find Bell myself. Maybe if I drove fast up and down Main Street, she'd get me on radar.

I stood. Watched. Nobody came out. I watched some more. Looked around the driveway of the garage. There was an old black Camaro with four flat tires and a blue tarp instead of a hood. An overturned shopping cart with three wheels. Pieces of broken plastic toys. Red and blue. I watched some more. Still nothing.

Paper wasps buzzed by me and I looked up. There was a sunflower-size nest under the eaves over my head. I watched the wasps come and go for a moment, then looked over at the apartment. I looked down. The ground at my feet was sprinkled with broken glass, trodden into the mud.

I looked more closely and saw what appeared to be a dissolving page of a *Playboy* magazine. This was a place where kids hid. If they came by, maybe I could join the club. Maybe I—

There was a rattle. The door flung open. Robie came through it, carrying a cardboard carton. It was heavy and he grunted as he kicked the door shut behind him. It shut, then swung back open. Robie lumbered down the stairs and they creaked under his weight and the weight of the box. He came off of the stairs and turned toward his bike, walked the fifteen feet and placed the carton in the attached trailer. His armpits were stained dark.

Robie went back up the stairs and into the apartment, closing the door behind him. I could heard muffled voices from inside; then he reappeared with another carton. He clumped down and put it in the trailer next to the first, then went back up. I leaned against the garage and watched, and the door opened again. Robie had a third carton and he shifted it in his arms, then descended the stairs. Halfway to the bike, the door swung open. Howard came out, carrying two paper bags.

"Numb nuts," he barked from the landing.

Robie looked up.

"The car. Put the shit in the car. C-A-R."

"Yeah, but—"

"The car, you friggin' zipperhead."

I saw Robie purse his lips, then turn and walk resignedly to the Chevette. He waited while Howard came down the stairs, walked to the car with the bags, and put them on the hood. Howard opened the passenger door and flopped the seat forward, and Robie leaned in and put the carton in the backseat. Howard put his bags back there, too, then stood and lighted a cigarette as Robie went to the bike trailer twice and moved those cartons to the car, too. Howard stood there in his jeans and boots and black T-shirt and smoked.

The door upstairs opened. It was Damian, hat on backward, hand and forearm in a cast.

"You goin'?" he called down.

"Yeah," Howard said. "And no bullshit while we're gone."

"Hey, what do ya—"

"No bullshit."

Howard walked to the driver's side. The door opened with a sagging creak and he got in. Robie stood there.

"Hey," Howard snapped.

Robie lowered himself into the seat and the car settled closer to the ground. He closed the door and Howard started the motor, ground the gears and backed up fast. Damian gave the car the finger as it pulled away. I turned, and walked quickly, then trotted, to the truck.

The risk was that I'd meet them head-on on the little side streets, then have to turn and follow. I'd rather come up behind them but which way had they gone? I backed the truck into a driveway and turned around, with some dirty-faced little kid watching from a rickety second-floor porch. I waved, then drove to the corner and sat.

I looked both ways. No sight of the Chevette. If they'd come this way, they would have shown up by now. I turned left and drove the block over to Robie's street. Looked left and right again.

Nothing. This was easier on television.

I could go left or right or straight. Left would take me by the house, where maybe there'd be something to see. I turned and hit the accelerator, roaring through the gears. The house was still. I blasted past to the next stop sign, where I faced the same choice. Where would they go with a bunch of cartons? How far could they have gotten?

Left led downtown, where at least there were traffic lights. If they'd gone that way, at least they might be sitting in what passed for traffic around here. I slammed through the gears again, hitting forty-five, then slowing down so I could look left and right up the driveways and cross streets.

All the way to Main Street, nothing.

Damn it.

At the stop sign, I sat behind an old man in an old pickup. He probably came to town once a year for supplies, and was in no hurry. I sighed. Cursed again. Clenched the shifter and waited.

The old man wasn't going to pull out with another car anywhere in sight. He peered to the right, started to move, then thought better of it. I looked up the street and saw a delivery truck a quarter-mile away.

"Goddamn," I said, slouching into the seat. The delivery truck approached slowly between the old brick blocks. As it finally rumbled past, a woman came out of a shop, pushing a baby carriage, and headed our way. The old man turned gallant.

"Son of a bitch," I said.

He sat there with his brake lights glowing. The woman, short and plump, eased the stroller over the curb and smiled at him. He waved to her. She smiled, and said something, then veered toward the truck and stopped. They were talking. They knew each other.

Goddamn small towns.

Suddenly she looked up and noticed my truck sitting there, rumbling, ten feet away. She gave me a coquettish grin and an apologetic wave, leaned in to say good-bye to Grampa in the truck and scampered away. But now traffic had picked up. A dump truck. A van. The Chevette.

It rolled by, and the old man pulled out behind it. I followed and the procession moved down Main Street. At the end of the block, the van turned left and the Chevette sped up. The old man looked left and right, at the stores, the people, at who knows what. The dump truck pulled over and stopped and the Chevette pulled farther away. The old man continued at his leisurely pace. I stayed on his bumper and bit my lip.

And then he pulled over, into a parking space. I sped up

until I had the Chevette within range, and followed it, past the municipal building, past the Catholic church, past a stretch of drab little houses, past a big house turned into a rest home. After the rest home, the Chevette turned right. It was a side street that led to a parallel block of even smaller houses, barely more than shacks. The street was narrow and the big Ford felt glaringly conspicuous. I saw the Chevette disappear to the left. I coasted to give them some distance, then followed.

The Chevette was a couple of hundred yards ahead. I slowed and a couple of women stared as the truck passed. I ignored them and watched the car. The brake lights came on and it turned right.

I approached warily. It had turned into what appeared to be a driveway, but was really an alley, a lane between a garage and a brushy lot. The lane led toward woods, through which I could see the Kennebec, the sun flickering off the water. I considered following, thought better of it, and pulled past the lane. In the lot was what had been a driveway, which led to the remains of a foundation. I pulled in, tires crunching broken glass, and parked. Got out and started walking.

The lane was gravel and rutted. It went downhill toward the river, bending to the left past the bigger trees, which were pines. The edges of the lane were strewn with beer cartons, and an occasional brandy bottle. It narrowed as it reached the woods, and then began to peter out as the woods gave way to heavier undergrowth.

I walked slowly, staying on the edge of the brush and stopping every twenty or thirty feet to listen. I heard birds: a flicker somewhere behind me, kinglets up high in the pines, gulls toward the river. Then a car door slammed. I froze. Heard voices. Another door closed. I eased my way into the brush and waited.

After a minute, it was only the birds. I slipped out of the brush and walked. The river was to my right, a band of dappled light through the trees. The lane tipped downhill toward it, two hard-packed ruts between trampled grass. I inched along, then stopped. The Chevette was pulled nose first into the brush, into a space that must have been used as a turnaround. The lane ended here. A path marked by more beer cartons led into the brush, toward the river. The trail was blazed by Budweiser.

But it was narrow, an Indian-file path. I stood at the top and peered in. Listened for voices but heard only the woods sounds. A distant cicada, whining in the heat. A subliminal buzz of bird and bees, flies and bugs.

I waited. Listened. Looked behind me. Started down.

The path wound between trees, then steepened. I stepped on exposed roots that served as steps. Every ten feet I stopped. Listened. Heard the hum of mosquitoes. The chitter of birds. Warblers in this low growth. I kept walking, and the path led into a grove of old pines. The pines hung out over the Kennebec.

I stood there and looked out at the river. The water was still and silvery, banded by dark reflections of the tree line on the far bank. I turned away from the river and looked around.

This was a party spot. The hard ground was littered with pine needles, cigarette butts and broken glass. A charred pile of burned branches and beer cartons was circled by blackened stones. A smashed liquor bottle lay just outside the circle. Coffee brandy. There was no sign of Robie and Howard.

I stood and listened again. Nothing. I walked back to the river and looked up- and downstream. Just upstream, there was a long island, like a grounded ship bristling with trees. The downstream end was low, with marsh grass leading to low shrubs, then small birches. Upstream were bigger birches, and, at the highest point, a stand of big pines. I wondered. I looked around.

Walking to the far edge of the clearing, I picked at the brush. There was a slip of a path into the bushes, like a place more prudish partyers would go to urinate. I pushed the branches aside and followed it, found the spot where guys stood. There were cigarette butts here, too, and a couple of flattened Budweiser cans. The path seemed to end here, but when I looked closer, I saw that it didn't.

Stepping through the tangle, I kept going. There was a path, but it was like an animal trail, most discernible at ground level, where the branches were trampled. I followed it along the river for forty or fifty yards, and then it stopped at an open spot along the bank. White birches hung drunkenly over the water. The bank sloped steeply to shallow water showing a sandy bottom. There were footprints at the water's edge, partly washed away. Hanging from one of the birches was a frayed piece of yellow nylon rope.

I stood and looked out at the river. A great blue heron wafted by the island on big, heavy wings. Gulls followed, faster and higher. Nothing else stirred on the water. I turned toward the woods and looked, listened.

They had to be here somewhere. Where had they gone? Into the water? Into a boat? Deeper into the woods?

Something clanked out on the water. The answer.

I crouched by the tree as a small rowboat came around the north end of the island. There were two people in it: one rowing, one sitting in the stern. As the boat came out of the shadow of the island and into the light, I saw that it was Robie manning the oars, his back toward me. Howard was perched in the stern and the bow was wallowing with Robie's weight.

They crossed above me and disappeared into the growth on the riverbank. I waited and thought, for a moment, that they'd turned back upstream or put in somewhere else. Then I heard the oar clank again and it was close, then a voice.

"Goddamn it. You didn't tell me this thing leaked."

I backed away from the river, into the brush beyond the path. The twigs snapped underfoot and I still was backing when the boat suddenly nosed out of the leaves. Robie looked over his shoulder as the boat grounded metallically on the sand.

''Only leaks a little,'' he said.

Howard clawed at branches on one of the birches and pulled the stern of the boat into the bank, then scrambled up onto the bank.

''You wait here,'' he said. ''And don't go floating off on me, neither. You done enough to frig things up.''

''I didn't do . . .''

Robie's words trailed off.

''Yeah, why don't you just go to the friggin' cops and turn us all in? See how your sis likes jail. You know what a bull dyke is, Robie? Huh? I'll get you one of those movies so you can find out. Ever seen one of those movies, Robie? Probably learn you something, you goddamn virgin.''

Only Robie's head was visible above the riverbank. He sat glum and silent. Howard lit a cigarette.

''Stay here,'' he said, and started off through the bushes.

Robie sat in the boat. I crouched twenty feet away and watched. The boat was parallel to the bank and he was staring straight ahead. At first his lips were clenched in a pout, and then I could see them moving as he mumbled. As mosquitoes hovered around my head, I tried to listen. The words came in fits and starts, at first just sounds, then louder and pronounced.

''Jerk . . . he don't know . . . Rob-ann said . . . jerk . . . stupid jerk . . . ain't his money . . . it's Marvin's money . . . I ain't going to jail . . . he can go to jail . . . jerk . . . I ain't never done anything to him . . . didn't hurt him . . . you leave him alone . . . Rob-ann told him and he laughed . . . don't hit him, he didn't do nothing to you . . . jerk . . . I hope he goes to jail . . . I hope he ain't never coming back . . . jerk . . . . . . I hope he kills him . . . he's a secret agent . . . he'll kill him . . . I bet he's a secret agent, like Marvin said . . . Marvin said they got guns . . . I hope Jack Morrow's a secret agent . . .''

20 A secret agent? Like Marvin said? I tried to make sense of it, while my thighs cramped and the mosquitoes had a feast. Then there was a crashing to my left, and Howard, the cigarette down to a butt in the corner of his mouth, came through the brush with a carton in his arms.

He put it down on the bank.

"You get it," Howard said. "I ain't your servant."

Robie swung around and heaved himself out of the boat and up on the bank. He leaned down and grabbed the carton and when he lifted it, the bottom tore and everything spilled out.

The carton was full of groceries.

"Goddamn it," Howard said, standing there as Robie gathered up cans and jars. "We need that and you're throwing it all over the ground. It's gotta last, too. Don't you and Junior get any ideas about pigging out. You could both stand to lose a few pounds. This goddamn tub better not sink when he and you get in it at once."

He stepped down and into the boat, and Robie had to shove off.

"My feet are soaked," he said, stepping over the gunwale.

"Stop your whining, little girl," Howard said, and Robie slipped the oars into the locks and pulled right and headed upriver under the trees, the blades making a slurping sound in the water.

I counted to ten and lurched to my feet.

At the bank, I leaned out to see. The boat had disappeared as it hugged the bend in the river, and I waited for it to reappear upstream, where the shoreline came to a point.

And it did, the boat with the two of them in it. They continued along the riverbank, just out of reach of the overhanging branches, and then they swung away from the shore. They were above the island and the current took the boat, which looked to be small and aluminum, downstream toward the island. Robie rowed rhythmically, as though he had done this many times before, and they disappeared into the trees just below the island's upstream tip.

I ran for the truck.

When I got to the top of the path, I was breathing hard but I kept to a trot until I swung up into the cab. I waited a minute to catch my breath and then I dialed. The dispatcher answered in his mechanical monotone.

"Officer Bell there?"

"She's on the road, sir. Is there something I can help you with?"

"No. Is she on a call?"

"I can't tell you that, sir. But I can give her a message when she calls in."

I thought.

"Yeah. Could you tell her to call Ja—. Call Sam Alexander. Could you tell her it's very important?"

"Is this an emergency, sir?"

"Well, sort of. Not life-threatening or anything like that. Not a 9-1-1 kind of thing. But—"

"Sir, I'll give Officer Bell the message. Does she have your number?"

I said I thought so, but I gave it to him again. He said he had an emergency call coming in, and he hung up.

Damn it, I thought. I'll find her myself.

I backed the truck out and swung it back to the main road, then took a left. A secret agent? Marvin said I was a secret agent? I pondered it as I drove, west to the downtown, around the Main Street block. What was it Robie had said. He hoped I was a secret agent, like Marvin said. Who? Just me? Had he tied me into his CIA thing? What kind of crazy stuff had he told Robie?

I looped the block again, then swung across the Kennebec on the bridge above the downtown, looking for a police cruiser. On the east side of the river, I turned and cut through the parking lot of a supermarket, then out the other side, still looking.

And now they were going to bring Maurice-Mantis down to the river? Why, to hide him? What was the scam? It wasn't his money, Robie had said. It was Marvin's. What money? Were Howard and Damian and friends holding Marvin up for the cash in his wallet? For the proceeds of his credit card thing? Why didn't Marvin get out of there? Was he tied to a chair?

Looking left and right, I drove past drab little stores built on false hope, a flea market set up in front of a boarded-up gas station, a swimming pool business, of all things. If Bell were somewhere on the outskirts of town, I'd never find her. Scanesett was just too big, too sprawling. When the houses and trailers thinned out, I pulled into a driveway and turned around.

What I needed was a police scanner, not a cellular phone.

I drove back into town, down Main Street to the police station. There was one marked police car parked outside, but it was an older one, not the one Bell used. The sergeant's unmarked Caprice was there, and I toyed with the idea of going in and spilling my guts to Nevens, but kept driving. That was a last resort. I wasn't there yet.

Swinging through the side streets, I circled back to the downtown. I'd seen a pawnshop on the back side of the downtown block and I parked on the Main Street side and cut through an alley. The shop was three doors down from where the alley emerged. It had a window full of pawnshop stuff—a couple of off-brand electric guitars, a CB radio, a cassette player—and it was open. I went in, and a faintly shifty man looked at me from a chair behind the glass case. His hair was wrapped around the top of his head like a coiled snake. His legs were crossed. His shoes were black and his socks were white. In the corner behind him, rifles leaned in the corner like umbrellas in a stand.

"Hi," I said.

"How can I help you, sir?" he said.

He didn't get up.

"I need a police scanner. A little one I can run in the car."

The man looked at me, caught the tension in my voice.

"The law in hot pursuit or what?"

"No."

I forced myself to smile.

"I'm just looking to talk to a cop and I can't find her. If I had a scanner, I'd at least know what part of town she was in."

I smiled again to make my request seem benign. Then again, if I'd said I was looking for a cop and I needed a rifle, he probably would have sold me two, with armor-piercing rounds.

"I got a hand-held programmable. Hundred channels."

"How much?"

"Eighty-five."

"Too much. I want cheap."

"Don't we all."

He lifted himself from the chair and bent to the bottom shelf of the glass cabinet between us. When he stood up, he put an old portable scanner on the counter. Realistic from Radio Shack. Wrapped in electrical tape.

"It works. Twenty bucks."

"Does it have the Scanesett P.D. channel?"

"Both of 'em. And county and state police. Statewide and car-to-car. Don't know how good the batteries are."

He pronounced it, "battries."

"Fifteen."

"Fine."

I took out a twenty and handed it to him. He scribbled out a receipt, which I stuffed in my wallet for the IRS, and a five. On the way out the door, I turned the thing on and it squawked and then there was the dispatcher's monotone, Bell's response. I closed the door and listened.

The dispatcher again. He said something about Myrtle Street, number 93. Second floor. Subject wanting to remove his belongings from his girlfriend's apartment. Myrtle Street. Where was that?

I turned back to the pawnshop and opened the door. The guy was back in his chair.

"Where's Myrtle Street?" I said.

He thought for a moment, savoring the authority.

"You know where the Kmart is?"

"Yeah."

That was the shopping center where Robie had ridden his bike to scrounge metal.

"Two streets this side. On the right. What you want Bell for?"

I closed the door.

Halfway there, the dispatcher said the parties at number 93 Myrtle were having a verbal altercation. When I turned onto the street, he said he'd gotten a second call. As I approached 93, a gray apartment house with the front steps torn off and overturned on the lawn, a woman came to the railing of a second-floor porch and flung something into the air. Then something else.

I parked and waited.

The woman, really just a girl, was throwing the guy's clothes. She looked about sixteen, too young to have a guy's clothes in her apartment. He didn't look much older, standing there in the driveway, screaming obscenities as his briefs fluttered like confetti to the ground.

By the time Bell pulled up, a handful of neighbors had gathered to watch. The guy was using very bad language, and little kids were laughing. Bell got out of the police car and I got out of my truck. She glanced at me, then strode by, stopping in front of the guy.

"One more word, Eddie, and you're gone," she said, pointing her finger at his chest. "That'll violate your probation. You want to go away? Don't think I'm kidding. And Lanie, anything else comes out of that apartment, you're going with him. The rest of you, clear out. Show's over. I'm gonna count to three. One . . . two . . ."

I thought of her, kneeling in her garden.

The crowd drifted away, but in good spirits. The guy picked up his clothes and shoved them into the cab of a Nissan four-wheel-drive truck with a rusted bed. Then he and Bell went inside the building. I waited. Waited some more. What were they doing? Divying up the silverware?

Finally, they came out. The guy, long hair, knotty biceps, was carrying stereo equipment, with a few cassettes lying on top and electrical cords trailing on the ground behind him. He put the stuff in his truck, slammed the door and went around and got in, slamming that door, too. Bell and I watched as he sped off, squealing his tires.

"Damian's uncle," she said. "Elbert Flagg."

"That guy?"

"No, the owner of the truck in Winslow. Winslow got him for public drinking."

"Arrest?"

"Summons."

"Was there a rifle in the truck?"

"Yeah, but that's not against the law in Maine."

"Who was the other guy?"

"His cousin. Donnie Morrison."

"At least it's a close family."

"At any one time, half of them are in jail. The other half's on probation."

"Anybody ask them about taking a shot at me?"

"Not yet, but I will."

No rush, I thought. I'll just keep ducking.

Bell reached for the microphone on her shoulder. She

told the dispatcher she was all set at 93 Myrtle.

"I got a better one than that," I said.

She started for her cruiser. I walked with her.

"What's that?"

"Howard and Robie are moving Marvin Maurice to someplace down by the river. An island. Twenty minutes ago, they were bringing groceries out there in a boat."

Bell stopped and turned to me. There were beads of perspiration on her upper lip.

"You saw Maurice?"

"No, but I heard them talking. Howard was saying he hoped the boat didn't sink because they were both big. Marvin and Robie."

"So he is still here."

"They're down there now. I just left them. They were going back out to the island. It's this long low sort of island just south of town. You get to it off those little side streets past this nursing home. Looks like people party down there."

"And they're there now?"

"They were. They're in the Chevette."

"But Maurice wasn't there?"

"I think he's still in the apartment. Damian's with him. From what Robie was saying, I think they're squeezing money out of him."

Bell looked at me.

"Where was this?"

"At the river. He was sitting in his boat, waiting for Howard to get the last carton of food. He hates Howard but he's afraid of him. From what he was saying, I think Howard smacked him around, and Maurice, too."

"Robie told you that?"

"No. He was talking to himself."

"Where were you?"

"In the bushes."

"Doing what?"

"Watching. Listening."

She shook her head.

"Jeez, McMorrow. You are one ballsy reporter. Excuse my French."

"Also you should find out what Maurice did in the service. His neighbors in Winslow all think he was in the CIA or something. At the river, Robie said something about that, too."

"In my spare time, McMorrow."

"Well, soon," I said. "But the thing is, I think they're going to move him tonight. And I'll bet you anything he's in the apartment. Can you get a search warrant?"

"A warrant? I don't think—"

Her radio blurted. The dispatcher wanted to know if five-nineteen was ten-eight.

"Shortly," Bell said. "I'm finishing up here."

"Well, let's go," I said. "At least knock on the door. If Robie's back, I think he'll blab everything if you just ask him."

"McMorrow, I don't think—"

"So just make something up. You got a tip that there might be something wrong at this address. You're a cop. You figure it out."

I headed for the truck before she could say no.

"Where'd you get that truck?" Bell called after me.

"I borrowed it."

"What was wrong with your other one?"

"It had a bull's eye painted on the side."

She pulled out of the little side street first. I followed, three cars back. We passed the car wash, the Burger King, the auto parts store, a used-car lot and a place that sold lawn tractors. After the tractor place, Bell took a left, I heard her tell the dispatcher she was going to be out of the car for an investigation. We stopped at stop signs, zig-zagged through the back streets toward Robie's. A block away, the dispatcher's voice came over the scanner.

See a Mrs. Somebody about a harassing phone call. In

front of me, Bell threw up her hands in resignation. At the next intersection, I pulled alongside.

"I'll try McMorrow, but I'm the only one on, until ten."

"In the whole town?"

"Yeah," Bell said. "Then the next officer is alone until six. They used up too much overtime on the Fourth of July. The parade and everything. We're bare bones."

"What if something big happens?" I called across the seat.

"Nevins gets a call at home. But he goes home at four."

"That's screwy."

"That's Scanesett."

"So you're not even going over there?"

"I'll try to clear this quick."

"I'll wait."

"Where?"

"Up the block. I've got a scanner."

She looked at me curiously for a moment, then her car pulled away.

It was five thirty-five, and I'd been in the truck all day. I stretched my legs in the parking lot of a corner pizza place, two blocks from Robie's. Then I went in and bought two slices of cheese pizza from the illuminated plastic oven thing on the counter, a big bag of pretzels, a quart of orange juice, and a six-pack of Molson ale because the store didn't stock Ballantine.

I jumped back in the truck, looped the block and parked by my spot next to the garage. A couple of guys were sitting on the porch of the place, drinking beer. They eyed the big Ford, and me. I couldn't see the Chevette from the truck so I got out and walked up the driveway, notebook in hand.

"Somebody here order deluxe cable?" I said.

They looked at me without expression, and didn't answer. I looked past them into Robie's yard. The Chevette was back in its place by the stairs.

"Too bad," I said. "First six months are free."

I smiled. They stared. I got back in the truck and drove around the block, parked, ate and listened.

Bell's evening went like this. First the threatening phone call. Then a dog hit by a car. Kmart security apprehended a juvenile shoplifter and Bell had to go and collar the kid and deliver her to her parents, such as they were. At seven-ten, there was a minor car accident in the parking lot at Scanesett Shoe, and Bell had to go and take the report. At seven twenty-five, the same lady from earlier in the day reported she'd gotten another harassing phone call. Bell told the dispatcher she'd try to get to that one, but then somebody else reported a logger had cut timber on his property without permission.

This was somewhere out in the country, and Bell told the dispatcher to tell the guy to call in the morning and talk to the sergeant. He did, and then he told her a lady on Maple Street said neighborhood kids were sitting on her car and used foul and abusive language toward her when she told them to get off. Bell drove there and reported that she'd talked to the juveniles and told them to go home. Then a truck hit a deer on Pressey Ridge Road. The truck's windshield was smashed and the deer was killed. The driver wanted to know if he could keep the deer for venison. Bell said yes. The Maple Street woman called and said the kids were back.

At nine o'clock, the lights went on in Robie and Robann's apartment, but otherwise nothing stirred. I'd eaten the pizza and pretzels, and the beer was warm. I went to find a place to sleep.

The choices were the motel on the south side of town and the motel on the north side. I chose the north side because it was closer to Québec City by almost three miles. But then, Québec City, like a lot of things in my life, seemed very far away, in more ways than one.

Benedict Arnold loomed like a long put-off term paper. Roxanne seemed like a lover from long ago. Clair was a friend from another life, Mary his distant relation. I was adrift in this odd sort of oblivion, chasing a guy I didn't know, for reasons that were starting to escape me.

I needed a beer.

So I left Robie's and drove out past Kmart to the Scanesett Motel, where several rooms were occupied and tractor trailer rigs were parked in two lines between the motel and the road. The guy in the office had the TV on with no sound, and as I signed the registration forms, he kept glancing toward it and smiling. It was a sitcom. At one point, he laughed out loud.

The room was on the end, clean and spartan, like a well-kept truck cab. I dumped my duffel on one of the beds and opened one of the warm Molsons. It went down in two gulps. I opened another and sipped it, a study in moderation. Sitting on the bed, I dialed Roxanne's number, the AT&T charge number, my credit card number. It rang. She answered.

"How's it going?" I said.

"The same. How 'bout you?"

"Kinda wild."

"You in Canada?"

"No. Scanesett."

Silence.

"You still going to Canada?" Roxanne asked.

"Tomorrow morning. From here. You still coming back next week?"

"I don't know."

"Why not?" I asked.

"I don't know. Nursing home people in Maine are playing games. I thought Mom was in line for the next bed in the Alzheimer's unit, but now they're saying she's number three."

"How can that be?"

"I don't know," Roxanne said.

She sounded discouraged.

"Anything else?"

"Good news, you mean? No. I thought I had a buyer for this place but they started playing games, too. As soon as they get wind of the situation. Oh, I just want to come home. That's all I want."

"Well, then—"

"I can't, Jack. I can't. That's all there is to it."

"Then I'll come down there," I said. "I'll finish this story this weekend."

"Which one?"

"The Arnold trek."

"I thought you meant the one in Scanesett, or wherever it was. Find your man yet?"

There was a hint of irritation in her voice. I paused.

"No. But I'm close."

"Anybody helping you? I mean, you're not wandering around all by yourself. Police in on this?"

"Yeah. The Scanesett cop. Bell."

"The woman?"

"Yeah. I talked to her about it tonight but she couldn't break free."

"Where did you talk?"

Another pause.

"Where? I don't know. On the sidewalk. She was at a call, and I stopped to talk to her. Some girl was throwing her boyfriend's underwear out the window."

I took a long pull on the ale.

"She's married, right?"

"Who, Bell? Yeah. Husband's a contractor. They have a nice little baby."

"Good," Roxanne said.

"What's the matter?" I asked, trying to break through.

"I don't know. Sometimes I just have to take inventory."

"Of what?"

"Of the important people in my life. The people who care about me."

"And I'm at the top of the list?" I said.

"Yup."

"So what's the matter?"

"I'm not sure," Roxanne said. "Something."

I leaned down with my elbows on my knees, straining to listen.

"Is it more like everything?"

Roxanne paused. I heard the soft jarring sound of a glass settle on a table.

"It's a Bordeaux," she said. "Mom always kept good wines."

"You sound tired."

"I'm okay. You know, I was reading in the paper today, they did this study of nuns that said people who have low linguistic ability when they're young seem to have more likelihood of getting Alzheimer's when they're older. If they have a lot of language ability, they're less likely to get it."

"Reason to *parle français.*"

"I know. An advertisement for Berlitz. That's what I thought, too."

"Great minds . . ."

She didn't say anything. I waited. Stared at the cigarette burns on the nightstand.

"So what is it, Rox?"

For a moment, she didn't answer.

"I don't know," she said, but I knew she did, so I waited. "I don't know, it's just that you know how they say? How bad things come in threes?"

I didn't say anything. I heard her glass on the table.

"Well, gee, I've got all this going on. My mother turning into a vegetable right in front of my eyes. That's one. And I suppose I could get in a car accident down here. Or get mugged or something."

"Rox, don't."

"That's two. And that leaves you."

"Nothing's going to happen to me," I said.

"I don't know, Jack," Roxanne said with detached matter-of-factness. "I used to think so. Now I'm not so sure."

21 She'd never talked that way before. She'd told me to be careful. She'd said she worried about me. She'd said she wondered why I seemed to always find the messiest stories, the scroungiest characters. I said it was a matter of self-discipline. Sometimes she laughed, but not recently.

This was new, though. Roxanne had said it as though none of this was in our control, not the decay racing through her mother's brain, not the bus man and Robie and Rob-ann. If bad things come in threes, then I was on the list, Roxanne had said. There was no number four.

And what was she thinking would hurt me, or take her from me? Howard and Damian? The bus man himself? Officer Hope Bell, with her big blond husband and toddling daughter? What was Roxanne thinking?

I could blame the wine, but Roxanne probably had sipped half a glass and lapsed off to sleep. No, it wasn't the wine. It wasn't just her mother. It was me, leaving her in her faraway limbo while I went looking for what in her mind was nothing but trouble.

A guy trying to disappear. A sister and brother living in their slow-witted, small-town world. Their brutally feral relatives. And me, two thousand miles away, navigating in the dark.

I was fueling her worries, calling in every day or two with a new bit of troubling news. Somebody took a shot at me. His name isn't Mantis. He's wanted in Kennebec

County. Somebody burned Robie with a cigarette. No, I'm not in Québec City. I'm in Scanesett, in a trucker's motel, waiting to talk to a cop.

And I hadn't even told her about Robie and the river.

It was time to finish things off, for Roxanne's sake, if not for mine. I finished the Molson and left the bottle on the nightstand, the lamp turned on beside the bed. Some sort of mayfly-type bug was swarming and when I opened the door, a bunch of them fluttered past me. I left them to badger the light, and locked the door behind me.

The night was muggy and still. At the Kmart parking lot, kids were standing around their jacked-up trucks, wiling away their lives. I drove past them into town, and down Main Street. I followed Main to the municipal building, turned in and met Bell's cruiser as it started to pull out. She sat behind the wheel. I got out and walked over.

''Been busy?'' I said.

''Right out straight.''

''What do you have going now?''

''I'm afraid to say it, but nothing. Usually that means all hell's about to break loose.''

''How 'bout stopping at Robie's?'' I said. ''Can't you just say you'd like to talk to them about your investigation?''

''Yeah, but Robie might not be there,'' Bell said, still at the wheel, the cruiser huffing hot exhaust into the warm night air.

''What do you mean?''

''I saw him a few minutes ago. Riding his bike down Main Street, pulling that cart. He waved.''

''He waved?''

''Yeah. Gave me a big smile. Like he was glad to see me.''

''What's that about?''

''I don't know, McMorrow. You tell me. You're the primary investigator on this case.''

I turned away, then back to her.

"Hell with it. I can guess, but I'm sick of guessing."

"Can't fill a story with guesses, huh?"

"No, I've got enough to write twenty-five inches now. I just want to know where this guy is. I just want to know."

Bell shook her head, reached up, and put her cruiser in gear.

"You're in the wrong business, McMorrow. Come on. You can tag along."

The scanner didn't make a peep the whole way over to Robie's. Bell parked her cruiser at the curb out front, and I parked in front of the house next door. The curtain in the front window pulled back and the shoe-shop lady stared out, shielding her eyes with her hand. I walked over to Bell, who was standing by her car, looking up at Robie's apartment. All of the lights were on.

"You want me to come in with you?"

"Sure. You've met both of them, right? I'll just say you happened to come along behind me."

"Never saw me before in your life, right? And you know who else you should talk to? That lady in the window next door. She doesn't miss a thing."

Bell nodded. We crossed the grass and walked up the driveway to the back of the house. The Chevette was gone. Robie's bike was there, trailer and all. Bell went up the stairs first, and I followed.

She rapped on the aluminum screen door with her flashlight. We could hear a TV, then heavy footsteps. It was Rob-ann, in gym shorts and slippers.

When she saw us, her eyes showed no surprise. She swung the door open wide.

"Hey," Rob-ann said. "Hi, Officer Bell."

"Hi, Rob-ann. I'm sorry to bother you but—"

"No, come on in," Rob-ann said. "Come in. You, too, Mr. Morrow. I was watching a movie but I can stop it. I've seen it before, like, five times. You like Mel Gibson? This is the one where he's not a cop or anything. He's just this guy, but he's got this face, and it's Mel Gibson on one side but the other side is all gross. But there's this little kid, and he . . ."

Her voice trailed off from the other room. I looked at Bell and shrugged. She shrugged back and we followed.

We walked down the hall, the same hall where I'd wrestled Howard and Damian. It led past the kitchen, and I glanced in as I walked by. It looked neat and clean. Canned goods were stacked on the shelves next to bags of Doritos. I followed Bell into the living room, and that looked picked up, too. Bike parts set out in rows on newspaper. Cinderblock shelves packed with row after row of videos. Movie posters on the walls. All the lights on. All of the doors open. Shades up.

Rob-ann was bent over the VCR, waiting. It popped out a cassette, and she put it in a cardboard sleeve and placed it in an empty space on the top shelf.

"You guys hungry?" she said, smiling an unsettling hostess smile.

"No, thanks," I said. Bell shook her head and started her pitch.

"I just wanted to talk to you about—"

"Thirsty? We got Coke and Pepsi and Orange Crush."

"No, Rob-ann," Bell said, putting her hand on her gun belt. "We just wanted to ask you. Well, I did. Mr. Mc-Morrow was coming in when I pulled up. I think he wanted to talk to you, too. You mind if he's here?"

"No," Rob-ann blurted. "He's welcome in my home." She looked at Bell and smiled.

"You got a baby, right? I think that's great. Does she have blue eyes or brown eyes? I figured, if I ever had a baby, which I won't 'cause I'm not married, I figured I'd like it to have blue eyes. 'Cause I have brown eyes and maybe my husband would have blue eyes and she'd get his. I'd like it to be a girl, too."

I looked at her curiously. What was this? Rob-ann on

nitrous oxide? When we'd talked before she hadn't even looked at me.

"You sure don't want a Pepsi? I don't have any diet. I think it leaves, like, this aftertaste? You know what I'm saying? Some people think it's okay, but not me or Robie."

"Where is Robie?" I said.

"Robie?"

"Yeah. Your brother."

She hesitated, as though she'd forgotten her lines. And then she smiled, as though they'd suddenly come to her.

"Robie's downtown. He went for a ride. Didn't you see him?"

"Yeah, I did," Bell said. "He waved."

Rob-ann beamed.

"Yeah, he went downtown. And he'll be back soon. It was just hot, you know? Even with all the windows open it gets wicked hot in here. Like even in all the bedrooms, it's like steaming."

She turned and walked out of the room and into the room to her left. From the other room, we heard her talking.

"So I opened the window all the way to get the wind in here, but the air is like, dead. You know what I'm saying? I told Robie, I said, 'Robie, we gotta get a fan or something,' and he's like, 'Yeah, I'll get one.' So he brings this fan home but it's, like, from the dump or something, and when he plugs it in, it starts this wicked screeching sound, and then it smells like something's on fire. . . ."

I looked at Bell.

"Are we supposed to go in there?" I whispered.

She looked puzzled, but she led the way.

Rob-ann was standing by the window, facing the door. The window overlooked the driveway. In front of the window, there was a beat-up stuffed chair with wooden arms, a rusty red girl's bicycle with one flat tire, a brown vinyl couch with a seat cushion missing. The floor, flaking paint. The light was a bare bulb hanging from the center of the ceiling. From the light, a string hung.

"Yeah, well, we don't really use this room," Rob-ann said, that odd smile still fixed in place, like it was painted on with lipstick. "See what I mean about the heat? Whooo, it's hot in here."

She wiped her forehead with her forearm.

"But we keep some stuff in here. Things Robie might need someday. And we have the couch."

"So it's like a guest room," I said.

"No," Rob-ann said, dropping her smile. "It's nothing like that."

"Is this where Maurice slept?" Bell said.

Rob-ann's mouth hung open. She stood there in her shorts, her big slippered feet splayed out.

"No," she said, shaking her head. "Uh-uh. Nope."

"So where did he sleep?" I said.

"He . . . no, nobody slept here. I sleep in my room and Robie sleeps in his room. They're on the other side."

She brushed past us, out the door. Bell looked at me and followed her. I looked around. The carpet, dirty brown wall-to-wall, looked like it had been vacuumed. I bent down and looked under the couch. It was gritty, and I could see dusty potato chips and a piece of what looked like a crust of bread.

Standing up, I scanned the rest of the room. Buckled paneling. A blotchy brown stain on the ceiling tiles. There was a door in the corner, away from the windows. I opened it to a closet. It was shallow, with a single shelf. On the shelf were coffee and juice cans. I took one down; it was full of screws and nuts and bolts. I took down another. Washers, a pencil and blades for a saber saw.

I looked at the floor. A coil of electrical cable, attached to nothing. In the corner, a bunched-up piece of cloth. I bent down again. Picked it up. It was a sheet, white with pink roses, with elastic corners. I ran it through my hands, caught my finger on a tack. I found three more, a couple a foot apart. I went to the window and checked the frame.

Every foot, there was a tiny hole. The sheet had gone over the window.

I stood in the middle of the room and flipped the sheet open. It was dingy gray. In one corner there were three brown flecks.

Blood?

I folded the sheet, stepping out of the room and listening for Rob-ann's voice, I walked down the hall and out the door to the porch. The sheet went over the railing and fell softly to the ground.

Rob-ann and Bell were in Rob-ann's room. It was decorated with pictures of dogs and cats, some clipped from magazines, some on greeting cards. The bed had four low posts, three of which still had wooden balls on top. There was a bureau, with faded pink paint, and the name Rob-ann scrawled on the side in marker, in a child's printing. A bathrobe hung from a hook on the wall. Under the bed were several pairs of sneakers and shoes, lined up in a row.

When I walked in, they were standing in silence.

"You don't have to tell me, Rob-ann," Bell said suddenly. "But I wish you would."

"Nothing to tell. I can't tell something that isn't true, right? That would be lying."

She looked at me for confirmation.

"That's right, Rob-ann," Bell said, leaning right into Rob-ann's face. "I don't want you to lie. I want you to tell me what really happened here. I want to know where Maurice is now."

"I don't know any Maurice," Rob-ann said.

"Mantis, then. Whatever he was calling himself."

"He isn't here," Rob-ann said.

"But he was here?"

"He left a long time ago. He didn't stay. He said he had to go."

She thought.

"He said he was late."

"For what?" Bell said.

"I don't know," Rob-ann said. "He didn't say."

"How did he leave?" I said.

"He just left."

"In a car?"

"I don't know."

Rob-ann was standing by her bed, staring between us. Bell was watching her almost sadly.

"Oh, Rob-ann," she said. "What have you guys gotten yourself into?"

Rob-ann stared.

"Was he a nice man?" I asked.

"Yup," she said. "I mean, I guess so. I don't know. Who?"

"Then why'd you let Howard and Damian hurt him? Why'd you let them hurt Robie?"

"I didn't," she blurted.

"They did it anyway?"

"Yeah. I mean, no. Nobody got hurt."

"Robie did. We all know that."

She didn't say anything.

"If Maurice was hurt here, you could get in trouble," Bell said.

"I didn't do nothin'."

"Doesn't matter, Rob-ann. If something happened, and you knew about it and you didn't call the police, you're in trouble."

"Nothing happened. Nobody did nothing. That guy left. You guys shouldn't be saying these things if they're not true. You shouldn't—"

There were steps on the stairs outside. The door rattled open. Bell started to move to the bedroom door, but Robie appeared there first.

"Hey," he said. "How come you're here?"

"How was the river, Robie?" I said. "Did you and Junior sink the boat?"

•   •   •

After a minute of stammering that dwindled to a pudgy, stubborn frown, Robie said he had to go to the bathroom. He walked toward the kitchen, his big sneakers making a gritty sandpaper sound on the floor. We heard a door close and the toilet seat bang. Then it was quiet.

I turned to Rob-ann, who had sat down on the bed as Robie stalled. She was rocking almost imperceptibly, brushing at her hair, picking at her ear, her nose, her ear again. Her feet brushed through the line of shoes and slippers.

''Did you know Robie was down at the river with Howard?'' I asked.

''Yeah,'' Rob-ann whispered.

''Why did you say he was downtown?'' Bell said.

''Because he was.''

''After he was at the river with Howard.''

''I guess so.''

She seemed to have withdrawn, like a child who tuned out while being scolded.

''Please don't play games, Rob-ann,'' Bell said. ''You're the one who's going to get hurt by it in the end. You and Robie. Do you want that?''

Rob-ann shook her head, but still stared, her mouth settled into a vague half smile. Suddenly she seemed to focus.

''We weren't supposed to talk about Howard,'' she said.

Bell looked at her, half smiled back.

''Why not, Rob-ann?''

'' 'Cause he's hiding out.''

''From what?'' Bell said. Her expression hadn't changed.

''From a guy.''

''What guy's that?''

''A guy from Bingham or someplace. Howard danced with his wife. The other guy's wife, at a bottle club place. And then they went outside and they were kissing in the car, and the guy's friends saw them.''

She paused. Her smile was building, like a breeze.

''And then what happened?'' Bell said.

"And then the guy, he was really big and he came out and he tried to get them out of the car but Howard locked the doors and, he, like, started to drive away."

"With the wife in the car?" Bell asked.

"Yeah, but he let her out down the road. Now the big guy is looking for Howard. The big guy and some of his friends."

"Who is this guy?" I asked.

"I don't know. I think his name is Dave. But don't quote me on that. But he's got Howard scared. Like, really scared."

Rob-ann was grinning now, showing her teeth, which were small and needed cleaning. I stood there and listened.

"So he's hiding out down by the river to get away from this guy from Bingham?" Bell asked.

"Yeah. But I'm not, well, maybe it wasn't Bingham. It was someplace like that."

"But that's why he went down there?"

" 'Cause he's scared of this guy. The guy's really big, I guess. And he's got all these friends, and Howard oughtn'ta kissed his wife but he did. And he's gotta hide, on account of—"

Bell's radio chattered. She put her hand to it and turned it up. A car accident. Route 2. Possible injuries.

"Gotta go," Bell said, and she turned toward the door. Rob-ann kept talking, something about the wife telling her husband not to beat Howard up but the husband was really mad and he'd always hated Howard. Bell looked back at me, then at Rob-ann.

"Yeah, well, Rob-ann. If the guy catches Howard, you let us know, okay?"

She went into the hall and I followed her.

"You don't believe that, do you?" I whispered. "That isn't what Robie was talking about down there. He was talking about 'Marvin's money' and both of them going to jail, and all this. It didn't have anything to do with—"

"Who knows, McMorrow?" Bell said over her shoulder.

"I don't have time to sort through it. I just know I gotta go."

"Yeah, but—"

She went out the door, and I heard her steps going down the stairs. To my left, I heard a toilet flush. A door rattled and Robie came around the corner saying, "They gone, Rob—"

His belly bumped mine.

"Hey, Robe," I said.

Robie took a step back in the narrow hallway. Rob-ann came out of her bedroom and stood behind me. I turned sideways to her. She looked away.

"What a crock that was, Rob-ann. We both know what's going on here. You both do. How deep do you want to get into this? 'Cause you'll all hang together, you know. You have Marvin down there, don't you? Don't you? You know what people get for kidnapping?"

They both looked at me, their faces expressionless; neither of them answered.

"Twenty years. You know what they get for extortion? Twenty more. You'll have gray hair when you get out of jail, you know that? Robie'll be an old man when you see him next, Rob-ann. Doesn't that bother you?"

"Well, yeah. It would. I mean, he's my brother."

"And you guys are sort of best friends, aren't you?"

"We don't have anybody else," she said.

"Right."

"Nobody's here," Robie said suddenly, his voice oddly animated. "You can look around. There ain't nobody here, and you can look in all the rooms. He isn't in the living room. He isn't in the bedroom. He isn't in mine, and I'll show you, too. I'll show you—"

"Robie," Rob-ann said sharply.

"Yeah, it's too late for that one, Robe. He isn't here because you guys moved him to the river. Didn't you?"

They both stared. Standing against the wall in the hallway, I looked at both of them, settled on Robie.

"Why do you want me to kill Howard?"

Robie's eyes popped open.

"I didn't say—"

"You said you bet I was a secret agent. 'Like Marvin said.' You said, 'I hope he kills him.' "

"Then you are a secret agent. How'd you hear me if I—"

"I was at the river, Robie. Down by the Kennebec. I heard you talking to yourself."

"You're gonna get Marvin, right?" Robie said. "Don't kill him, okay? He didn't mean it."

"Robie, shut up," Rob-ann said. "Just shut—"

"But I like Marvin. He's a nice man. Couldn't you, like, just take him back to headquarters and, like, make him say he won't talk about your secret stuff? I don't like that you think you have to kill him. That doesn't seem—"

"Robie. What did Howard do to Marvin?"

"Robie, just shut up," Rob-ann said.

"You know what both of you should do? You should go down to the police station and tell Bell the whole thing. I'm telling you. Just tell her the whole thing, or it's just going to get worse. I think you're caught up in something that's—"

I stopped. Listened. A motor roared on the driveway side of the house. I squeezed past Robie and hurried to the back door. Pushed it open and stepped out on to the porch. Peeked over the railing as headlights swung across the garage and the house out back.

It was a truck. It was brown and green and black. Camouflage.

22 I heard the truck doors slam as I backed across the porch and slipped back inside. Rob-ann and Robie were standing side by side, filling the hallway.

"Does this place have front stairs?" I said.

"No. I mean, well, yeah, but they're sorta boarded up," Robie said.

"This is the only way in or out?"

They nodded. I heard footsteps on the stairs behind me. Men's voices.

"Get out of the way," I said, and I shoved my way through them, and trotted down the hall to the living room. To the right was the empty room. I stepped into it and swung the door closed behind me. Reaching for the string that hung from the light, I pulled it and the room went dark.

I stood against the wall beside the door and listened.

"Hey, numb nuts," a voice called. "What was this sheet doing on the ground? Where's the other one? There was two. And we need twenty bucks so we can get some beer."

"There's beer in the refrigerator."

It was Rob-ann's voice. There was a pause, then muffled voices, unintelligible. I concentrated and listened.

"Three beers? That'll last about a goddamn minute and a half. Cough up the cash. Come on. Don't be shy."

I heard Robie's voice. It sounded like he was protesting.

"Well, Howard ain't here, is he? Yeah, he got beer for himself. But what does that got to do with me? Think about it, Robie. Don't strain yourself, but think about it. Howard's down on the friggin' Kennebec someplace. I'm right here. Me and my buddy Elbert is drinkin' two beers now. That leaves how many? Come on, Robe, you can do it. Yes, one. Very good. Give the man a Twinkie.''

The voices dropped. I heard the back door open, then close. Damian called, ''Get my cigarettes.'' I stood in the dark, my back against the wall, and waited.

They talked in the kitchen. And then the voices got louder. I heard Elbert's voice, low and raspy, but I couldn't make out the words. Then Rob-ann. Then Damian again, saying, ''You think I wanta get eaten by friggin' bugs?''

Then more mumbling, then Damian: ''What do you mean, the cop was here? Right here? Well, why the hell didn't you say so? Jeez . . . Well, what did she want?''

Rob-ann answered. They were coming down the hall.

''So did you show her? I mean, like Howard said. Have all the doors open. Be the friggin' welcoming committee?''

''Yeah,'' Robie said. ''We told 'em. Just us here. You can—''

''What do you mean, 'We told 'em'? I thought it was that friggin' bitch cop?''

''It was,'' Rob-ann said. ''Officer Bell. Robie just don't think of her as a girl.''

''Robie don't think of anybody as a girl, do you, Robe,'' Damian said. ''Someday we gotta do something about that. You gotta come with me to Lewiston.''

''So what'd she say?''

That was Elbert. Elbert with the rifle in the truck. Now they were moving closer, coming into the living room. The silence in the darkened room was humming in my ears.

''She didn't say much,'' Rob-ann said. ''She just looked around and left.''

''That bitch,'' Damian said. ''Well, she ain't gonna find him now. She can come around with her bitch nose in the air all she wants. I hate that bitch. I told her, too. That time she put the pepper spray to me over at Larry's. I told her,

'You won the battle, but my time will come. You better watch your friggin' back, 'cause—' "

"Hey," Elbert said, "I thought Howard told you to leave all the doors open. Lights on."

"They were—" Robie started to say.

"But you don't have to pay the light bill here," Robann interrupted. "She went all through the place. I mean, what do we gotta do? Leave all the lights on all night?"

"Howard said to light up the place. Show 'em there's nothing here. That means—"

I tensed. Clenched my keys in my fist, fingering the metal bottle and can opener on the ring, the closest thing I had to a weapon. The door banged open, swung into my face, bounced off the ends of my running shoes. I gently grabbed the knob to keep it from swinging back. The light clicked on. I held my breath. In the crack between the wall and the door, I saw Elbert pass.

"You ain't seen the secret agent around town, have you?" he said, back in the living room.

Nobody answered. I prayed they were shaking their heads.

"If he comes back to town again, I think we gotta get rid of him. I don't know. I mean, you take a shot at a guy and he keeps coming back, that's no newspaper writer."

"That ain't what he is," Damian said.

"Marvin said the CIA don't give up," Robie said. "They follow you for years and years. They don't ever give up."

"First thing I do, I catch that son of a bitch, I break both his friggin' arms. Then I'll break his legs, too. Cold-cocked me, the son of a bitch. We'll see how he likes it when I got him crying like a puppy. I'll have him screaming for mercy."

That was Damian. There was a pause, then the sound of a can being crumpled.

"I gotta get drunk," Damian said. "Let's get outta here. Fork it over, fat boy."

"I don't got any money."

"Okay then, Sister Sue. A twenty-dollar bill."

"It's in my room."

"Well, hustle your butt. I'll pay you back."

"Yeah, right," Rob-ann said, her voice fainter, from her room. There was a footstep as she came back.

"That's it for this week. You drink it all away, don't come looking for more."

"I won't. I'll shake it outta your brother."

"He don't have any money, either."

"What's the matter, Robe? Ain't finding enough bottles, you beggar?"

He paused.

"Oh, come on, Robe. Just bustin' your nuts. Don't get all bent outta shape. We're family, right, man? We're gonna be all set anyway, we sell that Harley. That Mustang. It's gonna be gravy train for all of us. You'll be able to get a new bike, Robe. Get a new set of trainin' wheels, man."

Damian had the twenty. Now he was Mr. Nice Guy.

"Let's roll, Bert," he said, and I heard them move out of the living room, down the hall. Behind the door, I closed my eyes, and exhaled slowly. Their voices receded. But then somebody came back. Damian.

He was in the room. In the closet. I heard the sheet flap.

It flipped into view. Damian's hand, too. He was in the middle of the room.

"That's the blood?" he muttered.

Damian moved into view, his back toward me. His left arm, in the cast, hung by his side. With the right arm, he was holding up the sheet, tossing it up, and gathering it into a ball. If he turned to his left, he'd be looking right at me.

The sheet fell to the floor to my left. He knelt and began bunching it up. He was going to turn toward me. I moved out and took two quick steps, then jammed the bottle opener against his back.

Damian froze.

"You make a sound, I'll slice your spine," I whispered. "One sound."

I waited. He was silent.

"On your belly, hands behind you."

I pressed the bottle opener between Damian's vertebrae. He eased his way on to the floor. Crouching over him, I reached out and took the sheet from above his head.

"Lift your head," I whispered.

He did. I slipped the sheet under his face, then gave it two quick wraps around his head. I could smell him. Beer. Cigarettes. Sweat. Maybe the sweat was mine.

He was on the floor between my legs. The door was open and the light was on. I could hear the others talking at the other end of the apartment.

"Dame," Elbert called. "Hurry it up."

I pressed harder, felt the opener find the crack between the bones.

"Not a word."

I thought of Robie and Rob-ann. What would happen to them if Damian and Elbert thought they'd been set up? Oh, God. How did I get out of this? I looked around. The window was five feet to my right. The screen was the kind that fit between the sill and the sash. I took hold of the sheet and pulled Damian toward the window, sliding him across the floor with the opener still pressed against his spine.

"I'm going out the way I came in," I said. "You tell anybody I was here, you're a dead man."

I switched hands on the opener and reached for the screen. I pushed but it didn't budge. I pushed harder. Still, it didn't move. Standing up quickly, I pressed my foot against the back of Damian's neck, and with both arms, pushed up on the sash. It went up an inch and I pushed the screen out. It fell to the ground with a soft metallic shush.

I reached down and gave the sheet another tug, then went headfirst through the window, rolling my torso out, hanging for a moment and dropping for what seemed like a very long time.

Damian started yelling before I hit the ground. I landed and half rolled, half sprawled, on the grass, jamming my right knee. But I hung on to the keys, then was up and half running, half limping for the truck, two houses away.

As I pulled away, lights off, Damian and Elbert came down the driveway at a full run. I floored the truck, slammed through the gears, and took a left at the next intersection. Three blocks up, I turned again. Two blocks after that, I switched on the lights. When I eased my grip on the steering wheel, my hands shook.

I drove through the back streets, watching the rearview mirror. It was quiet and still on the streets behind me, but my knee was throbbing, my mind racing.

Would Damian believe that I'd come in the window? Would he go after Robie and Rob-ann? How were they going to get Maurice to sell his car and motorcycle? What had they done to Marvin Maurice that left blood on the sheet?

I turned on the police scanner and listened for Bell's voice. The scanner hissed. I picked it up and slapped it with my hand. It hissed some more. Finally, a weak, crackling voice, speaking in police code. State police, calling Augusta. Then the Waterville dispatcher. State police again. Then a voice, loud and clear. The Somerset County sheriff's office dispatcher, calling a deputy out in the boonies. I drove on and waited.

Finally I picked up the receiver and dialed the Scanesett police number. The Somerset dispatcher answered. I asked for Bell. He said she was on the road. I asked him where, and he called me "sir" and asked me about the nature of my problem.

"It's sort of complicated. Bell knows—"

"Is this an emergency, sir?"

"Not at the moment, but—"

"Then you can call the Scanesett police department first thing in the morning, sir."

"But can't I leave a message?" I said.

"Yes, sir. I'll give Patrolman Bell the message when she clears the scene."

"Of the car accident?"

"I'll give her the message when she clears, sir," he said.

"Could you ask her to call Jack McMorrow. I'm at the Scanesett Motel. I don't have the number right here but—"

"Thank you, sir," the dispatcher said, and he hung up.

As I put the receiver down, his voice blurted from the scanner on the seat.

"Somerset to five-forty one . . . when you clear, could you call Jack McMorrow at the Scanesett Motel. Subject wants to speak with you regarding unknown matter."

"Oh, no," I said aloud. "Why don't you tell the whole world?"

In this part of Maine, police scanners were like talk radio. You listened to hear who the cops had pulled over and why. You knew who's license was suspended, who locked their keys in their car. When there was a car accident near town, you could get there before the ambulance. If a man and wife quarreled, the whole town would hear the blow-by-blow. Was he summonsed? Was she hurt? Were the kids home? What a shame. You know, the cops were there three times last night.

And now they'd know Jack McMorrow was staying at the Scanesett Motel, that he wanted to talk to Officer Bell.

This wasn't a town. It was an amphitheater, and I was onstage.

I called the dispatcher again and asked him to Bell another number to call. He wasn't happy about it, but after I hung up, his voice came on the radio again. This time he called me, "the same subject." Bell said "ten-four." She sounded irritated.

So I drove through the back streets of Scanesett, making my way north toward the main drag and the motel. I made one pass, and looked up toward the building, but I couldn't see past the tractor-trailers lined up out front. I drove a hundred yards up the road, past the kids hanging out at Kmart, and made a loop through the Burger King parking lot. The second pass didn't show much more, but I didn't see a camouflage pick-up or a beat-up Chevette.

On the third pass, I pulled in. The light was on in the unit that served as an office, and the red neon sign said "vacancy." Lights showed in two-thirds of the rooms, including mine, on the end. I drove past slowly, rounded the end of the building, and drove out back.

There were trash cans back there. A Plymouth Reliant with two flat tires. An orange cat that slipped through my headlights. No truck. No Chevette. Nobody.

So I circled the motel again, this time pulling in and parking at the end, out of sight of the road. I waited a minute in the dark, with the lights and motor off, and watched and listened. Cars passed out on the road. A kid squealed his truck tires as he roared out of the Kmart lot. Somebody whooped and then it was quiet again. I made myself sit for five minutes, watching the front of the building by my room. Clair's truck ticked as it cooled. Mosquitoes hovered above the hood, attracted by the heat. Nobody passed, except the cat, which padded by with a mouse or a small rat in its mouth. When it disappeared around the corner of the front of the building, I followed.

Easing the door open, I found the room as I'd left it. My duffel was on the bed. The Molsons were on the bureau. I chained the door behind me, pulled the curtains tighter. Then I went into the bathroom, turned on the light over the sink, and sat on the toilet seat to examine my knee.

It was scraped and bruised, sore and stiff when I flexed it. I ran the water until it got warm, and then wiped the knee with a washcloth. It stung. I unwrapped a bar of soap and rubbed it on the cloth and wiped the knee again. That stung more, and I gave up and tossed the cloth in the sink. A dirty knee was the least of my worries.

Turning out the light, I went back into the room and

stood and listened. It was quiet. I went to the lamp and turned it off, then felt around the table for a warm Molson. I flipped the cap off with the same opener I'd threatened to use on Damian's spinal cord. Shaking my head at the thought, I drained half the beer in four long gulps.

Damian had wanted to get drunk. That made two of us.

But I couldn't get drunk any more than I could go to sleep. Not here, not this night.

They'd seen Clair's truck, at least from a distance, and it was distinctive enough, and the town small enough, that they'd spot me in no time, even just driving around. In Scanesett, there was no place to hide, unless, of course, you went out in the woods or down by the river.

I had to tell Bell what they'd said about the river, and Marvin and the blood, and selling the Harley and the Mustang. Somebody had to get out to that island, and somebody had to make sure they didn't hurt Robie and Rob-ann. How many loose ends would Howard tolerate? He'd already shown that he wasn't above hurting his own relatives. And what were we talking about here? Ten or fifteen thousand dollars? To Howard, that was a once-in-a-lifetime score. It probably was enough money to kill for. It probably was more than enough.

So I finished the ale but didn't have another. I sat on the edge of the chair and looked out of the crack between the curtains, and after a quiet minute or two, I got up. I grabbed my duffel and stuffed the three remaining beers inside. After a quick look around, I slung the duffel over my shoulder, opened the door, and shut it behind me. I slipped around the corner and walked to the truck. The duffel went on the floor of the cab. I started the motor and drove behind the motel, past the trash cans and out of the driveway at the far end of the building. Stopping, leaving the truck running, I trotted to the office and dropped the key inside the screen door. As I pulled onto the road, I turned on my lights.

I drove a half mile north, until I came upon a used-car

lot, closed for the night. There was a line of cheap compact cars and a row of trucks, none of which were as nice as Clair's. I parked on the end of the row of trucks, and killed the lights. Sitting in the dark with the motor idling softly, I dialed the Scanesett police number. The sheriff's department dispatcher answered. I asked for Bell.

"She's gone off duty, sir," he said.

"But she told me she'd be on until ten."

"She's gone off duty, sir. Is there anyone else who can help you?"

"Who's on duty in Scanesett now?"

"Reserve Officer Marcel."

"Just one officer?"

"I can't divulge that," he said. "If this isn't an emergency, I suggest you call Scanesett P.D. in the morning, sir."

"I guess—"

"Excuse me, sir, but I have another call," the dispatcher said, and he hung up.

So I dug out the phone book, looked up Bell's number. She wasn't listed. But her husband's business, Bell Bros. Construction, was listed at their home address. I dialed.

It rang. The answering machine clicked on. It was Hope Bell's voice, but more silky, like somebody on television. She said I could leave a message for Bell Bros. Construction. I left one for her.

I started to tell her the whole story, until the machine beeped and cut me off. I called back, and started in about everything Damian had said, but the machine hung up on me again. I called one more time and blurted that I was worried about Robie and Rob-ann. I said Howard wasn't hiding from anybody from Bingham. She could call me in the truck. Or the next day in Québec City. I left the car phone number again. The machine beeped, and I hung up, weary. I pulled out of the car lot and drove due north.

23 In Madison, there was a crossroads with a flashing yellow light. In Solon, eight miles to the north, there was a gas station and a store, where the Budweiser sign glowed reassuringly. Nine miles north of Solon was Bingham, where, from a store window, another Budweiser signed beckoned with its soft rosy glow.

And then there was darkness.

I followed the twisting route along the Kennebec, the truck's headlights making little stabs at the blackness all around me. A couple of tractor-trailers passed, coming south, but then their pinpoint taillights slipped beyond the next bend and disappeared. I was alone.

To my left, somewhere, was Wyman Lake, the dammed, swollen stretch of Kennebec that lay in the trough between the ridges. I drove on, rumbling along at fifty-five, with the windows open, the radio off. It was still warm, but there was no moon and there was a haze that dimmed the stars, too. At Caratunk, there were two houses with lights on, but they were soon left behind, and, again, only the headlights picking feebly at the darkness, like flashlights pointed at the sky.

As I drove, I pictured the map. To the west were the Carry ponds, and ridges and hills that were there when Arnold staggered through all those years ago. It was blackness then. It was blackness now. Hills that had been logged and left, bogs where fishermen ventured, paper company roads that cut jaggedly through the back country. Still, it was all dark. All quiet.

But then I was in The Forks, where the Dead and Kennebec rivers did just that, and there was a restaurant and lounge that gave the white-water rafters a lighted place to go at night. There was something about this impenetrable darkness that could make you uneasy, make you ask questions, make you ask yourself what you were doing with your fast-passing life.

Beyond The Forks and West Forks, I could feel it set in, this feeling that something was out there. This was country that could swallow you up, where you could vanish without a trace. For some reason, I thought of a news story I'd read about a man who killed himself up here somewhere. He hung himself from a tree, fifty feet from a logging road. A couple of years later, they found his belt buckle under the tree, the rope around the branch. The rest of him had been carried off by animals, bone by bone.

I shivered and reached for the radio.

This was past West Forks, past Parlin Pond, which the sign said was somewhere off to my right. The only station was country and western, drifting in and out like a static-filled dirge. I turned up the scanner but heard nothing at all. I looked down at the lighted phone receiver, and the indicator said there was no service here. There was no need.

But then there were headlights ahead, cresting the top of a grade and I was climbing. The headlights came at me faster, and a chip truck roared by like a freight train passing a crossing, leaving a cloud of dust and grit. I wiped my face and drove on, until I finally came into Jackman, where there was a health center, a high school, small houses gathered along the main street, and two Budweiser signs. The store sold gas and I stopped, filling both tanks with cheap American gas. The kid who took my money was wearing a T-shirt that said Forest Hills High School basketball. It must have been a long ride to away games.

The kid said thank you. I said he was welcome.

And then I plunged on, slipping into the terminal darkness beyond Jackman, where the road pointed straight at the border and where signs warned of moose. There was a frontier feeling here, a sense that the road was somehow one-way, like a highway crossing a desert, that there was no turning back.

But then, I felt that way already.

I'd been operating in the dark for days. I was trailing people I didn't know, who thought I was somebody else. The man I was pursuing was pretending to be somebody else, too. It was a crazy game we were playing, and a dangerous one. And the odd thing was, I couldn't wait to get back to it.

What was it Roxanne had said, one night in bed? She'd said that she tempered my self-destructive impulses. I'd joked that she just made me trade one impulse for another.

So this was what I did when I was left alone. Look for a missing man, on the chance that he might not want to be missing. Haunt his acquaintances, on the chance that they might be his captors. Duck, on the chance that they'd shoot high. Press a can opener into somebody's back, on the chance that he might not call my bluff.

Roxanne was right. But she was far, far away. As I passed the sign saying I was approaching the customs station, I made a mental note to call Roxanne. I wouldn't tell her about the can opener.

I knew the drill. I knew I had to *attendez dans l'auto*. I knew they'd want to know if I had liquor, guns or cigarettes. But I hadn't considered how I might be received, pulling up to the Canadian border, a man alone, at midnight.

With a skinned knee.

This was the border station at Armstrong, Québec, a lonely outpost backed up against miles of monotonous paper company forest. In the little cluster of buildings there was a duty-free shop that sold T-shirts and beer by the case.

The brick inspection building, with its beckoning carport. A couple of connected buildings and a line of cars with Québec plates. I pulled up, shut the truck off and waited.

For a minute or two, nobody came out. I sat and watched moths swoop at the lights, and then a bat swoop at the moths. Suddenly the glass door swung open and a man in a uniform swished through it. He opened the passenger door and said, *"Bonjour."*

"Bonjour," I said.

He was short and slight, maybe thirty, with a stubble of beard and darting eyes that said he was all business. He looked at me with an intense gaze that brought me to attention after my solitary ride north.

"And what is your name?"

"Jack McMorrow."

"Where are you from, Monsieur McMorrow?"

"Prosperity, Maine."

"Why do you want to come to Canada?"

"I'm a writer. I'm going to Québec City to do research for a story."

"Yes," he said, eyes scouring the cab. "And do you have anything in your truck?"

"No liquor," I said. "No cigarettes. No firearms."

He paused, leaning toward me. I could smell cigarettes on him, see acne scars on the left side of his chin.

"You have been in Canada recently?"

"I came in at Coburn Gore last week. Stayed one day and came back into the United States here."

"Oh," he said. "Now you are going back?"

"I didn't go to Québec City that time."

"But you are going there now?"

"Yes."

"You will go there direct?"

"Yes."

"Where will you stay?"

"I don't know. There's a place called Manoir sur la Terrace. A friend recommended it. I'll probably try there first.

But any place right in the old city will be fine.''

A large pale moth fluttered in on his side and flung itself against the inside of the windshield. The customs man didn't appear to notice.

"You will arrive at early morning hours," he said.

"Yeah. I figured I'd walk around. Get a feel for the place at night, because what I'm writing, it's about—"

"Could you step out of the vehicle, *s'il vous plaît*. Come inside and fill out the form. The customs declaration. Leave the keys in the ignition."

He backed out of the cab, stepped to the glass door and opened it, then waited. I heaved myself out, wincing as I put weight on my left knee. He noticed my limp as I came around the front of the truck.

"You are injured, sir?"

"No. I just twisted my knee. It's stiff from riding so long."

I went by him. He followed. Motioned toward a doorway to my left. I went in and saw a table and three plastic chairs.

"Assiez, s'il vous plaît."

I sat. He went to a shelf, slipped a form off of a stack and put it in front of me. I patted my shorts pockets for a pen, but he whipped one out of his breast pocket and clapped it down on the table.

"It is a short form. A few questions."

I picked it up. Outside, I heard the truck start.

"Oh, yeah," I said, starting to read. "Another thing. It's not my truck. It belongs to a friend, Clair Varney of Prosperity, Maine. I borrowed it."

I looked up. The customs man was standing by the door, watching me closely. He didn't answer.

The form took five minutes to complete. It asked who I was, where I was from, my driver's license number, whether I had anything to declare. I checked no, and then I got up. The inspector had left, telling me to wait for him to come back. I did, for two or three minutes, and then got up from the table. From the other room, I could hear a woman speaking in French. I stepped into the corridor and looked through the glass door. My truck was gone. I walked to the door to see where it was and heard a sound behind me.

"Please remain inside, *monsieur*," a woman's voice said.

I turned. She was in the same uniform. Fortyish and small, smiling, but with the same intense dark eyes.

"You would like a cup of coffee?" she said.

"Sure," I said. She turned and I followed. At the little room, she stopped, holding her arms out to direct me in. I went past her and stood by the table. She disappeared and I stood some more, and then she came through the door with the coffee in a foam cup. She handed me the cup and two creamers and a packet of sugar. I put the creamers and the sugar on the table and sipped.

"So are they tearing the truck apart?" I said.

I smiled. Standing in the doorway, she smiled back.

"The vehicle has been moved from the primary lane for inspection."

"What are they looking for? Drugs?"

"Contraband."

"They aren't going to tear it apart, are they? I've heard they do that sometimes. Take the tires off the wheels and all that."

"You don't want them to tear it apart?"

I shrugged.

"No, I don't care. I just don't want it damaged. The guy who owns it, he's pretty meticulous about his truck."

"Uh-huh," she said. She wasn't impressed.

I waited in the room for forty-five minutes and two cups of black coffee, enough time to read all of the forms on the shelf, and whatever I could glean from a day-old copy of *Le Soleil,* the Québec City newspaper. There was a story about an increase in the use of the drug PCP. One about a dispute over restoration of an auditorium at a library in the old city, which, from what I could tell, was some sort of cultural rallying point. I was halfway through a story about a guy who was accused of *du meurtre au premier degré de sa mère,* murdering his mother, when the customs man came back in.

"The owner of the truck, sir? He can be reached by telephone?"

I put the newspaper down.

"In North Carolina. He's visiting his daughter. I'm using the truck while he's gone."

"And he can be reached?"

"Yes."

I dug in my wallet for the number. Found the piece of paper and handed it over. It was almost 1 A.M.

"You're going to call right now?"

"Yes," he said, and he left the room.

Clair and Mary, Susan and hubbie, would all be pleased. Another call to make in the morning.

I sighed and finished the story about the guy who was supposed to have killed his *mère.* The story said he killed her with *un coup de hache à la tête.* I read the phrase again, and for some reason thought of Mantis. How would they kill him? I asked myself. Would they use an ax? And then I wondered at my own question. Did I really think they'd do that? I supposed I did. After all, the question had to have come from somewhere. And it was true. They couldn't hold Mantis and they just turn him loose. Certainly, the longer they held him, the less likely it became that they'd let him go. He'd talk, but they couldn't let that happen. But Robie and Rob-ann would talk, too. What would they do to them? How could they—

"Mr. McMorrow."

It was the customs man and the customs woman. I put the newspaper down and got up. They were standing side by side between me and the door. For the first time, I noticed they didn't carry guns.

"You were not honest entirely with us, Mr. Mc-Morrow," the customs man said.

"Did you get hold of Clair?"

"Were you aware that you must declare all liquor?"

"Oh," I said. "The three beers in the bag. I forgot about that."

"Next time, you must remember to declare all items. The keys are in the truck."

"Enjoy your stay in Canada, *monsieur*," the customs woman said.

And then they turned and left.

When I walked outside, a tractor-trailer was in the entry port and the customs woman was standing on the step on the side of the cab. I didn't see my truck, so I walked to my right, and the back end of the truck appeared, parked next to a garage with a lift. I walked over and got in. The keys were in the ignition, the seat cover was rumpled, and the floor mats were askew. I opened my bag and everything was rumpled. But then, it probably had been rumpled when I'd put it in. I shuffled through it and shrugged, then zipped the bag closed. They were doing their job; I was doing mine. Well, sort of.

I turned the key and the truck started. At least they'd left the motor.

As I drove north in the cool quiet, I told myself I had some patching up to do. I hadn't called Roxanne that night, and Clair, good friend that he was, still might be wondering why his truck was being searched at a Québec port of entry. I wondered what he'd said to persuade the customs people that I was okay. Perhaps something military. There's a bond between people who wear uniforms.

In Linière, the sawmill town just north of Armstrong, I looked down at the phone. The cellular signal was getting stronger, roaming among the Canadian towers, and occasionally jumped to a level of two of a possible five. I looked at my watch. It was twenty after one. I decided waking Clair once was enough for one night, more than enough for his daughter and her kids. And Roxanne, I'd let her sleep. Call before breakfast.

So I drove the four-lane highway north, past the steaming sawmills, the darkened houses that lined the road on both sides. Even in the dead of night, they were as I remembered them from a Québec trip with a woman from long ago. The houses were neat and brightly painted, and stood proudly alongside the highway, like people watching a parade. The houses I hadn't forgotten. If I chose, I could remember the woman, but the memories were mostly of the arguments that had followed the infatuation. Rolling into St. George-de-Beauce on Route 173, I cringed at the thought.

St. George-de-Beauce was a service town, the shopping center for all of the sleepy hamlets that were scattered among the fields and farms to the east and west. There were strip malls, supermarkets, places to buy tires. At a traffic light at the center of town, there was a blue-and-white police car. The cop showed as a pale face with a dark mustache. He looked at me in passing. I drove on.

The traffic was light, mostly little compacts that whizzed around the lumbering Ford. I drove through Notre-Dame-des-Pins, and into Beauceville, a little bigger town, with more car dealers, more malls, more places to buy cars and tires. I pulled into a McDonald's and ordered *thé* at the drive-through window. The girl behind the window had a musical voice that made me pause when she said, *"Merci."*

I smiled at her and she smiled back, all high-school confidence, and I drove out onto the highway and continued north.

The road followed the Rivière Chaudière, Arnold's highway, somewhere below me to the left. The river was at the base of a valley that rose on both sides, with hills and farmland to the west and this commercial corridor to the east. When Arnold had come through, the French farmers had gladly plied him with food, and he and his recharged troops had churned down the Chaudière to the St. Lawrence like criminals newly pardoned.

I felt a little bit like that, too. The foreignness of the towns, the French signs, even the girl at the McDonald's window had made me feel like Scanesett was a continent away. And if I were to do a decent job on the Arnold article, I had to let myself be transported by the country, the history, the distances in kilometers, the language and the people. To do the job, I had to be in the spirit of the assignment.

Digging on the seat beside me, I found my tape recorder and held it to my mouth. I began describing the valley of the Chaudière, the lights glimmering in hamlets in the western hills. I described the immaculate and colorful houses, the shrines on the lawns, the Gallic feel that seemed to permeate even McDonald's. I even smiled to myself as I did my running commentary, following the signs for Route 173 as it jogged to the east at St. Joseph-de-Beauce, then turned into a real highway with exits that said Vallée-Jonction and Ste. Marie. I would suggest my readers take the time to explore the smaller towns, savor the trip rather than rushing to Québec City. After all, Arnold spent time along the river here, too. Pausing from my soliloquy, I reached for the radio.

And the phone rang.

It was seven minutes after two.

It rang again.

Clair unable to sleep? Roxanne lying awake, worrying about her mother? Bell up with the baby?

Slowing, I reached for the receiver. Picked it up.

"Hello," I said.

"McMorrow," a man said.

"Yeah."

"You want this guy or what?"

The voice was low and ragged. A little slurred. Elbert.

"What guy's that?"

"The guy you been friggin' chasin'. I can make your job a little easier, you know what I'm sayin'?"

"I don't know. Depends on which job you're talking about."

I held the tape recorder up to the phone receiver and pushed the record button.

"You wanna deal or not, McMorrow? 'Cause it don't make no difference to me."

"I just want to talk to him, I guess," I said. "That's all."

"Well, that's fine, but you want to talk to him, you gotta talk to me."

"Who are you, his agent?"

"Hey. Don't get friggin' wise. You go ahead and get friggin' wise, you don't want to see him again. You just go ahead. You just see. There's a lot of cedar swamps in Maine, mister. And don't you—"

The words were lost as a tractor-trailer passed. The highway was widening as it merged with Route 73, and everything was bathed in a surreal orange light.

"Take it easy," I said. "I couldn't hear you. A truck just went by."

"So you wanna talk a deal?" the guy said.

The slur was more pronounced, punctuated by the sound of lips coming off a bottle. He was drinking. There were noises in the background. A faint murmur. Closer than the murmur, I heard somebody whistle, then the noise was muffled, as though he'd covered the receiver.

"You still there?" I said.

"Frig, yeah."

"Well, I don't know. I don't usually do deals. I usually just ask and we go from there."

"Well, friggin' A. Let's just say I ain't too easily impressed, McMorrow. I don't care who you are. I ain't gonna friggin' kiss anybody's ass. You got that? I don't care if you're friggin' Rambo. You hear what I'm saying?"

I drove slowly, in the right lane. Cars whizzed past. The sign said "St. Rédempteur."

"So you want to see your little buddy, you talk to me,

McMorrow. And I'm talking about five grand, nothing bigger than a twenty-dollar bill. For finding him for ya. Like a reward.''

"Hey, this isn't—''

"You got the money," he barked. "The goddamn government has twenty friggin' trillion. This is friggin' cheap, man. I'm giving you a deal. Your man for twenty thousand.''

"You don't understand," I said. "I can't—''

"Don't give me that shit!" he screamed. "I ain't no friggin' rube that you're talking with. I know what the friggin' deal is. I know the friggin' scene. So get the money and you get your little buddy and he's all yours and you can friggin' shoot him full of shit and put wires on his balls or whatever it is that you do.''

"Hey, listen—''

"No. Hey, you listen. You want him, that's the price. Or something close to that. You don't want him, hey, shit if I care. But you won't never know what he told and who he told it to, or where the money is or nothing.''

"Hey, I don't know—''

"You got a couple of days. Forty-eight hours. I'll call you. You don't want him, I'll friggin' waste the guy. How's that for tough? Five grand or he comes back in pieces. What do you want first, his hands? How 'bout his feet? I'll friggin' whack 'em off, I kid you not. Whack 'em right the hell off.''

Un coup de hache.

As the lights of the St. Lawrence bridge came into sight, he hung up.

24 Actually, it's called le Pont Pierre-Laporte, and I crossed it in a distracted daze. Red navigation lights flickered here and there on the wide blackness of the river, and the lights of the Québec City suburbs, *les banlieues* Sillery and Ste.-Foy, sprawled away to the northeast. I looked but my mind was in Scanesett, the voice still playing in my head.

I'll friggin' waste the guy. How's that for tough?

The voice was still ringing as I scanned the cluster of highway signs that suddenly rushed toward me. I didn't want Route 73, or 540, but there was 175 again, a sign that said Québec, and I changed lanes and swung off to the right. The highway ended and I was on a broad boulevard lined with hotels and restaurants. I watched them pass: Auberge du Boulevard Laurier, Hôtel Plaza Québec, Motel L'Abitation, Motel Louise. They were all likely places to spend the night, especially as I was arriving at two-thirty in the morning.

I let the truck drive on.

The hotels and restaurants gave way to shopping centers, on the left, a hospital on my right, and then the campus of Laval University across the boulevard. This was Sillery, with houses close on both sides of the road, occasional cars. At the lights, the Québecois looked skeptically up at the truck, with its gun rack and Marine Corps decal on the back window. At the light before Haute-Ville, a young guy in the passenger seat of a white Toyota leaned out and said

something to me and laughed. I caught an American ob-
scenity entwined in his French.

I looked at him and looked away. I had more serious
matters to consider.

As I drove east on the Grand Allée, Benedict Arnold rode
with me, telling me to pay attention because we were getting close. Elbert and Howard rode with me, too, and said
the same thing, with Damian taunting in the background.
We were getting close. Close to death? Close to killing
someone because I wasn't a secret agent, no matter what
Marvin had told them.

And so I rolled through the Porte Saint-Louis and into
the old city, with its cobblestone streets, and eighteenth-
century stone buildings that hunched on the sidewalks on
both sides. The shops were closed, the restaurants dark behind dimly glowing signs, and in the apartments and town
houses, only an occasional light showed. The road pitched
down toward the river and I let the truck idle as it squeezed
between the tightly parked cars. For a moment, I felt a
tremor of déjà vu, as though I'd liberated France in another
life, been at the wheel of a half-track or a tank that had
rumbled through a city's narrow, winding streets.

But these streets were silent, and I was more like an
intruder who had slipped through the city's walls. But now
that I was in, what would I do?

I drove down Avenue Saint-Louis and suddenly there
was the Château Frontenac, the old city's castle hotel.
Lights winked high above me, and I craned my neck forward to see. And then there was a little square, Place
d'Armes, and people walking toward the Terrasse Dufferin,
the long boardwalk that overlooks the St. Lawrence, and
the steep roofs of the oldest part of the city. I stopped and
looked at the Terrasse, up at the Château again, and then
there was a car behind me, high beams flicking on and off,
and I put the truck in gear and drove on.

For a half hour I circled the old city, driving outside the
walls to the east, then back up the hill and through the

winding streets again. Couple walked arm and arm on the Côte du Palais, wobbling side by side. Teenagers stood in a huddle outside a movie theater on Rue St. Jean. I slowed and found myself leaving the old city through Porte St. Jean, so I circled again until I found the Grand Allée again, and came back in Porte St. Louis.

I took a right and followed Avenue Ste. Genevieve down to the little square next to the Château Frontenac, looking for a place to park, but all of the legal spaces were filled. I looped around the Parc des Mont Carmel and then back up Ste. Genvieve, and right again on a narrow side street, Rue Ste. Ursule. A guy was getting into a van and I double-parked behind him. When he pulled out, I began pulling in, parallel parking the truck like it was an oil tanker sidling up to a wharf. After five minutes, I'd jockeyed the truck into the space, or less. I shut off the motor, leaned back in the seat and began to make plans for the next day.

Call Bell, first thing. Call Clair and Roxanne. Find the historic sites, at least the ones that related to Arnold. Make a list of photo possibilities, and maybe call the magazine to check in, maybe not.

I closed my eyes, and when I opened them, the next day was here.

It was raining and my shoulder was damp, my neck stiff and my mouth gummy. The water poured off the roofs of the stone buildings onto the cobblestones in a steady patter, and English sparrows chittered in the ornamental trees that lined the curb. I groaned as I pushed myself up in the seat, then opened the door and got out to see if I could still stand. My right leg was stiffer than my left, but it took a minute to get either of them to loosen up. I twisted my torso, scratched my head and yawned. As I stood there, the door of the stone building across the street opened and a little fuzzy dog came out, pulling a young woman behind it on a leash.

The dog ignored me. The woman was wearing running

shorts and shoes, and a bright green slicker. She glared. Leave the city gates open and all kinds of riffraff wanders in.

Good morning to you, too, I thought.

Climbing back in the truck, I turned the rearview mirror and looked at myself. I glared, too. My empty stomach grumbled. I started the truck, and still sitting there on Rue Ste. Ursule, picked up the phone receiver.

I got Bell's husband first. He said she couldn't come to the phone, in a way that suggested, not now, not ever.

"This is Jack McMorrow," I said.

"I know. You called last night."

"Yeah, I'm sorry if I called too late but it's sort of an emergency."

"That's why they have nine-one-one."

"Well, it's not really that kind of emergency."

"I'll tell her you called," Bell's husband said. "I gotta go to work."

"Could you ask her to call me on the car phone?"

I winced inwardly. It sounded effete.

"Yeah, right. Whatever. Listen, I gotta get going, so—"

"Could you tell her they want money for Maurice?"

"Hey, buddy. I'm not—"

"Or they said they'll kill him."

Bell's husband paused.

"They called me early this morning. I really need to talk to Officer Bell."

He hesitated.

"Yeah, well, she's with the baby and . . . God almighty, wait a minute."

There was a clatter as Bell's husband put the receiver down. I waited as the truck idled. This phone bill was going to be expensive, I thought. Oh, well. I sniffed myself and decided I needed a shower, badly. The woman with the dog came down my side of the street, carrying a newspaper and a bakery bag, and peered at me curiously. I smiled. She crossed the street and went inside.

"McMorrow," Bell said suddenly. "What's going on?"

"I called you last night."

"Yeah, well, I got a life, you know?"

"I do, too. It's just on hold."

"So what's this emergency?" Bell said.

She called away from the phone, "Don't give her zwiebacks. That's her outfit for the baby-sitter."

"Sorry," Bell said.

"It's okay," I said.

"Well?"

"I got a call last night. In the truck. I think it was Elbert. He was drinking."

"Those guys are always drinking."

"Well, he was drinking while he talked."

"Yeah?"

"He said he wanted five thousand dollars for Marvin."

"What?"

"Yeah. They've got this idea that I work for the government. He said that. 'The government's got the money,' or something like that. Then he said I could 'shoot him full of shit.' Like I'd drug him for interrogation or something."

"What are these guys on?" Bell said.

She paused. I heard the baby in the background. Bell's husband said, "Hope. I'm sorry, but I gotta go."

"Listen, McMorrow, can I—"

"One more thing. This is really why I called. It wasn't just wanting money. It was Elbert. He said he'd kill Marvin if I didn't come up with the money. It's like they've kidnapped the guy."

"And they're holding him for ransom?" Bell said.

"And I'm supposed to be the one with the ransom."

"Hope," Bell's husband was saying, "come on."

"And I think they'll kill him," I said. "I really think they will. Once they get the Mustang and the motorcycle. Did I tell you what I heard Damian say after you left the apartment last night?"

"When?"

"He came in after you left. With Elbert. He told Robie something like, 'After we sell the Mustang and the Harley, we'll all be in fat city.' Or rolling in money or something. You ought to have the Winslow police take the bike and the car out of there."

"Where were you?"

"When?"

"When you heard all this."

"The car and Harley stuff, I was in the empty room. The one with the sheet. And Damian came in and said Howard told him to get the sheet out of the closet because it had blood on it."

"Jeez, McMorrow. I'll talk to the chief today. This is going too far."

She paused, said, "Bye," and I heard something that sounded like a kiss.

"Listen, I'll let you go," I said. "But I'd do two things. I'd check the islands in the river. And I'd find out what Marvin did in the service. And another thing: If I saw Robie or Rob-ann on the street, I'd take 'em for a ride. They're into something, or at least on the edge of it. That's no game."

"Okay," Bell said. "Okay, honey."

She wasn't talking to me.

"McMorrow, I'll call you later. I mean, you going to be home?"

"No," I said. "I'm in Québec City. Calling from the truck."

"Québec City?"

"Benedict Arnold. This is where he stormed the city. I'm finishing up my research."

"So how do I call you?"

"You can call the truck, but I don't know if I'll be in it. I'll be here tonight, but I don't know where. I'll call and leave a number, when I get one. If I don't hear from you, I'll call you. What time do you get off?"

"Five."

"I'll call at four."

"Okay," Bell said. "Yeah, it's all right, honey."

"Hope," I said, "just so you know. He said he'd cut off Marvin's hands and feet. Stuff like that. In forty-eight hours."

"Probably he's bluffing, McMorrow. He'll wake up and won't even remember talking to you."

"Oh, good," I said. "I won't worry about it."

"I didn't say that," Bell said.

So I did worry. I worried as I tried to call Clair, but the number rang busy. I started to call Roxanne, but then reconsidered. If we talked long, a credit card call from a hotel would be cheaper, and there was a chance Roxanne would want to talk to me. Not 100 percent, but a chance.

With the rain still coming steadily, I circled the block, past the Château Frontenac, still majestic in daylight, and back up Avenue Ste. Genevieve. Across from the park, the street was lined with *manoirs,* stone guest houses with colored awnings. One, Manoir sur le Parc, had a sign in the first-floor window that said, *"vacance."* There was even a parking space. I pulled in, grabbed my bag, and went up the steps.

The couple in the office was gray-haired and plump. They both got up from seats in front of a television, where they were watching the news in French. The man said, *"Bonjour,"* and I said, *"Bonjour,"* and the woman said, in English, "You look like you drove all night, uh?"

I said I had, from Maine, and could I check in early?

"Oui, monsieur," the man said, and I said, *"Merci beaucoup,"* and took the pen and registration form that he slid across the table. I signed and gave him my Visa card, which he ran through his machine. I carried my own bag up the stairs, and in five minutes was standing under the spray of a hot shower. In a half hour I was getting into clean, if customs-rumpled, clothes, fastening my khakis as I listened to the phone ring at Roxanne's condo.

And ring, and ring.

I tried the nursing home, but the woman who answered said Roxanne hadn't been there yet. I left the number of the *manoir,* and a message to call.

"Could you tell her I'm fine?" I blurted at the last moment, but the woman had hung up.

So I sat on the edge of the bed and again called Clair in North Carolina. The number rang once and a woman answered.

"Hi," I said. "Is this Susan?"

"Yes," she said.

"This is Jack. How are you?"

"Fine," she said. "How are you?"

The emphasis was on the "you." The implication was that there was reason to think I was not fine. Nothing like a late-night wake-up call from Canadian customs.

"Hey, Bones," Clair barked suddenly, his voice genial as ever. "Where the hell are you?"

"Behind enemy lines. Thanks for talking me in."

"Well, hell, I told 'em you hadn't smuggled drugs in a coon's age."

"Thanks."

"And you turned over a new leaf last time you got out of state prison. And also you sweat when you're nervous."

"They came in and felt my palms."

"Good," Clair said.

"Hey, Clair, I wouldn't have taken your truck without asking, but things sort of started happening in a hurry."

"And you needed a real truck, not that Toyota."

"I needed a truck nobody had seen me driving in Scanesett."

"Don't tell me," Clair said. "Now they've seen it."

"Well, yeah, but only from a distance."

"Uh-huh."

"With the lights off," I said.

"And this was at night, I suppose."

"Well, yeah. But I could see fine. You know I wouldn't take any chances."

"Hell, no. Haven't had to run any roadblocks or anything?"

"Nope. Truck's sitting out front right now. Avenue Ste. Genevieve, in Québec City."

"So everything's fine?" Clair said.

"Oh, yeah."

"How's Roxanne?"

"The same. But I haven't talked to her in a day or so."

"What about you?"

"Good. I'm doing the Québec end of the research today. The historic stuff. It's a beautiful place."

I walked to the window and looked out. The myriad angles of the Château Fronterac's copper roof were gleaming in the rain.

"A lot of history there," Clair said. "But I think you'll find there's more about Montcalm and Wolfe than about Benedict Arnold. Arnold got shot and went away. English were in charge when he got there, and they were in charge when he left."

"Thanks, but I'm trying to make a living here, if you don't mind."

"No, go to it. I think it's great that you work once in a while. If you can call it that."

"I'm slaving away."

"No doubt."

Clair paused. I looked out at the park, with its rain-soaked benches, and the cars coming out of the courtyard at the Château.

"So what's really going on, Jack?"

I turned from the window and stood by the bed.

"Oh, the crazies in Scanesett say they have this Marvin guy."

"Uh-huh."

"And they've got this idea that I work for the CIA or something."

"Naturally."

"And, well, they want five thousand dollars or they say

they'll kill Marvin, or at least chop him up.''

"If you don't pay the money.''

"That I have because I work for the government.''

"Well, historically, the CIA has had many agents pose as journalists,'' Clair said.

"You're a big help.''

"But I don't think they run too many covert operations in Maine.''

"Only when they're hunting for some guy who retired from the service and came home and told all his neighbors he was into some clandestine stuff,'' I said. "And told the kids somebody from 'the company' was coming looking for him.''

"LeCarré.''

"Probably where he got it all.''

"But the local kids believed him?'' Clair said.

"Yeah. And the local hoods in Scanesett believe him, too. Near as I can figure out. I still don't know what the hell he's doing there. Unfortunately, they've got me dragged into it. And it's funny, but I think they've got this macho kind of thing where they want to show me they're not afraid of the CIA.''

"Could be their only chance,'' Clair said.

"Yeah, and they've grabbed it.''

"You told the cops all this?''

"Yup. They're looking into it. Supposed to be finding out where the guy really was in the service. Looking for him down by the river. Then again, they might just decide I'm a crank.''

"I decided that a long time ago. So what'd this guy do? Call you?''

"Yeah,'' I said. "In your truck, on the way up here, two this morning. I have my phone with me.''

"How'd you leave it with them?''

"I told them I just wanted to talk to the guy.''

"What'd they say?''

"They said I had a couple of days before they started

chopping him up, but I got the feeling that was negotiable.''

''The chopping or the money?''

''I don't know. Maybe both.''

''Well, hell,'' Clair said. ''At least they're being reasonable.''

And Clair was, too. He told me that if he were me, he'd put the whole thing out of his mind, for the day, anyway. He'd concentrate on the job at hand, and when he got back to Maine, see what the police had found out. It could be just some drunken, half-baked extortion attempt, Clair said. A lot of nonsense.

I didn't think so. And I didn't think he did, either.

But I had no choice but to follow Clair's advice. I'd come this far, and the Arnold story had to be done. I'd promised. I needed the money.

So I called the Scanesett P.D. and left the *manoir* number for Bell. The dispatcher took the number and the name of the *manoir* without a glimmer of reaction, as if CIA agents called from Québec every day.

I hung up and took a deep breath. Then I unzipped my camera bag, took out my old Nikon and loaded a new roll of color slide film. I put a new cassette into the tape recorder, put that and the camera back in the bag. From my duffel bag I took an issue of *Historic Touring* and a couple of history books. One of the books had a map of Arnold's attack, and I looked it over, considered taking the book with me, then tore the map out. There was a guidebook on the nightstand and it had a street map of the old city, too. I compared the two. The place hadn't changed much since 1775.

I put on an anorak, and with a wave and a *bonjour* to the gray-haired couple, out the door I went. Outside it was raining steadily, and I went to the truck and grabbed a John Deere baseball hat from the gun rack. I put it on, then stood on the sidewalk for a moment and tried to orient myself, as much to the task as to the city. I decided that the first order of business was to eat, so I walked across the street and cut across the park, through the courtyard of the regal entrance to the Château Frontenac and out onto the Place d'Armes. There, I turned back up Rue St. Louis and walked along until I came to a café with small-paned windows, the mullions of which were painted red. There were people inside and they were eating. I went in and stood among them.

The waitress, who was small and fair, with knotty, muscular legs and bright, red lipstick, said *"Bonjour"* and trotted off and I followed her. The table was in the back of the room, and I sat and she gave me a menu and trotted off someplace else. I perused the menue and when she trotted back, I ordered in my pidgin French: *"Je voudrais les crêpes avec jambon, s'il vous plaît. Et aussi thé, et* orange juice. *Merci."*

I handed her the menu. She smiled but didn't laugh.

"That will be just a few minutes," the waitress said.

So I sat and waited with my maps of the walled city, and thought how simple it would be to be able to keep bad guys out by building a wall. Today, the wall would just keep the bad guys in.

The old city was built on a point overlooking the St. Lawrence, where the river narrowed to just a kilometer wide. The point was marked by steep bluffs, atop which the French had built massive stone walls to keep out the English, Indians or anyone else who might come out of the woods. Below the walls, on the river side, the city had spilled over, forming what was called Lower Town. It was here that Arnold had attacked on New Year's Eve, sneaking with his men along the outside of the walls from St. Roque, to the northeast, and storming the barricades. It hadn't worked out, of course. Arnold had been wounded at the first barricade, and his detachment of troops didn't even make the second.

This all took place on the Rue Sault au Matelot, which, according to the map, still was there, a ten-minute walk away.

After just a short wait, the waitress brought my *crêpes* and ham, with a garnish of orange slices and what looked like some sort of *pêté*. She hurried off and I began to eat. By the time, she'd come back with the tea, I'd decided I'd give myself until one o'clock, and then I would go back to the Manoir sur le Parc and check for messages. If Bell hadn't called, I'd call her. Maybe by then, she would have found Robie and Rob-ann. Maybe they would have led her to Maurice. He would be alive and well. Howard, Damian and Elbert would be arrested. Robie and Rob-ann would testify after being granted immunity. It would all work out fine, and I'd write my story, and Roxanne's mother would get better.

"How is your meal?" the waitress said, suddenly appearing over me again.

I looked up into her scarlet smile.

"Fine," I said. "That much is just fine."

25 I spent the morning in the eighteenth century. From the café, I walked down St. Louis past the Château, and stood at the railing on the terrace. The Quartier Petit Champlain was below me, a close-packed warren of stone buildings, their metal roofs all steeply pitched, painted different shades of gray. This was the oldest part of the city, and it had been resurrected from dilapidated oblivion. Now tourists clattered down the cobblestoned streets, foraged in the restaurants and shops.

I walked down Rue Petit Champlain with those tourists,

who moved slowly in little umbrella-topped groups that looked like clusters of colored mushrooms. Stopping in a gift shop, I bought postcards of the quarter, paying with an American ten-dollar bill and getting pretty Canadian bills and change in return. In the doorway of the shop I looked at the Arnold map again, holding it beside the map in the guidebook. Arnold had circled the city from beyond the Palace Gate, by Rue LaCroix. I was on the southwest side of the point, and if I wanted to try to retrace his steps for the readers, I had to start at the northeast.

So I did.

I walked up a steep, winding street, Côte de la Montagne, and cut through a park where there was a statue of Champlain. The statue was flanked by cannon that pointed over the wall, and out over the gray mist of the St. Lawrence. I stopped for a moment and looked out over the jumble of roofs and into the windows. Below me, in a room that fronted a narrow, railed terrace, a man was reading a newspaper. A child, a toddler, came in and out of view. The observer in me, the voyeur in all journalists, could have watched the man and his family for hours, but it was raining, and I had a job to do here. After I did this job, I had to get back and finish another.

With the rain dripping off of the bill of my cap, I walked past the courtyard of the old Laval University, and along the wall on Rue des Remparts. The Palace Gate was gone, of course, and in its place was a steep intersection across from a bank of restaurants and shops. I stopped and looked at my maps again, and then pocketed them, and walked down until the wall was above me.

Even in modern times, it loomed ominously, slick and black and impenetrable.

As I walked along Côte de la Canoterie, Rue-Sous-le-Cap, I tried to picture this walk in the dead of night, in the dead of winter. I would have been wearing wool blankets, carrying a heavy musket. I would have trotted down these very streets. This was the street where Arnold was wounded. I looked up at the wall. Here on Rue Sault-au-Matelot, his men were shot down. From behind the shuttered windows of these very houses, women and children had heard the musket blasts, the screams.

Does a soldier scream when he's shot with a musket? Raked with grapeshot? Was there a moment when they realized it had all been for nothing and they had lost?

In the rain, these streets were deserted, and somehow ominous. I walked into a little square where the cobblestones were set in a widening circle. The stones lay like a carpet in front of the church of Notre-Dames-des-Victoires. The sign said it was built in 1688. I stood for a moment, whispered into my tape recorder.

And then I walked the old streets, down to the Place Royale, where a replica of the stockade had been built. There were cannons here, too, and at that moment they were trained on a ferry that was approaching the wharf just upriver. I looked at the river, then up at the city wall, and made my way back through the old narrow streets, where the restaurants were still closed and the galleries were dark.

There was something heavy and solemn about all this history, about knowing that so many people had lived here once and were now gone, forgotten, disappeared into the hereafter, or maybe just into oblivion.

Or maybe it was just me.

As I walked those streets, with the rain pattering the stones, soaking through my hat, the ghosts of the dead were backed up by the living. As I made my rounds, where was Maurice? Where were his captors? Or could they be his cronies? Would I have to see his body to find out? Touch my fingers to his wounds?

If I thought about it, I lapsed into a distracted silence, like someone burdened with a terrible secret. But if I were to get this story done, I had to put my secret aside, at least for the day. Travel stories can be dark. They can't be morose.

So I took photos of the old port, the lower city, all of

which dripped with rain and history. I had lunch in a café across from Notre-Dame-des-Victoires Church, ordering broccoli soup and more tea. The man behind the counter was efficient but quiet. I sat in the window and scrawled notes of the morning. When I'd finished my tea, I asked the man if there was a pay phone. He scratched at his thinning hair, then patted it back into place, the way balding men do. Then he sighed and reached below the counter and took out a portable phone and handed it to me.

"Québec?"

"*Oui.*"

I held up my notebook and showed him the number of the *manoir*.

"*Mais, oui,*" he said again. I dialed, and it rang in that buzzing European way. The *madame* answered. She said, "*Bonjour,*" and I did, too, and then I said it was Jack McMorrow.

"*Messages pour moi?*"

"*Oui,*" the *madame* said. "Roxanne. You must call her. And Hope."

Hope. Hope for—

"Officer Hope, uh? She said you must call her, too. You are police, uh?"

"No," I said. "*Je suis un journaliste. Pas police.*"

"Hope *et* Roxanne. Roxanne *et* Hope. *C'est tous.*"

The phone clicked. I handed it to the balding man, who took his hand out of his hair to take it.

"*Merci,*" I said.

He nodded and resumed stroking.

Back out in the rain, I decided to walk to the truck or a pay phone, whichever came first. The pay phone did, in the doorway of a restaurant near the Escalier Casse-cou, the stairs leading up from Rue Petit Champlain. I stood and dialed the many numbers that would connect me, in my world in Québec, with Roxanne, in her world in Florida. A nursing-home person answered. I asked for Roxanne and the nursing-home person said she'd gone. She asked if I was Jack. I said yes. She said Roxanne asked her to tell me she had appointments but she would call back.

"When?" I asked.

She said she didn't know.

And there in the rain, I felt a pang of loneliness, followed by the urge to run. Fill up the truck and drive south until everyone spoke English, and I could be in my own house, on my own road, in my own bed. And then I remembered that I'd be alone there, too. Standing there with the receiver in my hand, I sighed. Dialed. The dispatcher answered in his world-weary monotone. Sam Alexander, from Québec. Area code 418 . . .

"I'll give her the message when she clears," he said.

"Merci," I said.

And that left no alternative but to work.

I decided to tackle the restaurants. Travel stories always talk about restaurants, raving about the exquisite this, the delicate that. I didn't know much about cuisine, but I could wing it with the best of them.

My approach was to ask for the restaurant manager and then explain, with varying degrees of difficulty, who I was and what I was doing. It had never been an easy task. But I showed the magazine and, once they understood, they all wanted to feed me. I declined, saying I only wanted a menu, and they called to the kitchen in French, bringing out the chef and pastries, and I had to take tiny bites and smile and say, "Mmmmmm," so that they would give me menus and wine lists, and I could leave my card in exchange, flinging it behind me as I inched my way toward the door.

All of this took time, of course, and after three restaurants it was twenty to three. Loaded down, I stood under a gift-shop awning on Rue Cul-de-Sac and looked at my map. What else should I say? What else would they want to do? The Musée de la Civilisation was down a block and over three, on Rue Dalhousie, along the river. Perhaps a chaser of culture after their meal, I thought, so I shouldered my bag and trudged over. There were lots of people in the cavernous glass-sided atrium, and I stood in line for a half hour to buy a ticket to the featured exhibit. After I paid, they handed me a brochure. The exhibit was, *"La mort à vivre."* It was all about death.

It figured.

I wandered for two hours among coffins, hearses, and theories of the afterlife, nicely packaged, interestingly told. If they killed Marvin, now I knew where he might go.

When I emerged, it was after five and still raining, but the lower city was beginning to light up. In the streets near the Old Port, the restaurants were opening. I walked along and noted the plaques on the buildings—1688, 1693, 1704—and wondered if I had enough old stuff. When an entire city is a museum, where does one draw the line? How much information did I need? How much was too much?

I hadn't set foot in the Château Frontenac, which wouldn't do, so I made my way up the steep streets to the terrace and around to the courtyard. Porters were swarming around cars, and patrons were flowing in through the heavy brass doors. I followed them, a bit soggy and still rumpled, and spent a half hour gawking in the stately lobby, talking into my tape recorder outside the elegant shops. I heard French, German, Japanese. Standing by the check-in line, I eavesdropped on a couple whose carry-on tags said Zurich. They were fortyish, well-dressed, attractive, glowing with anticipation. I watched them wistfully.

Roxanne would have loved it. I would have loved it with her.

I went to the phones and dialed the *manoir,* again. The *madame* answered, again. Roxanne and Hope had called, again. I called Roxanne, again, first at the condo, leaving a message, and then at the nursing home. The woman who answered said Roxanne was "around somewhere." She went to find her. I waited. Waited some more. Looked around at the old oak, the chandeliers, the porters in full dress.

"She was here, but I can't find her," the woman said suddenly. "Is this Jack?"

"Yeah. Could you tell her I called? Tell her I'll keep trying."

I paused.

"Tell her I'm thinking about her," I said, "and I'll be back in Maine by tomorrow morning."

She stifled a giggle.

"You're thinking about her," the woman said. And then she snorted.

What was funny about that?

I stood in the lobby of the Château, and felt disoriented. Tell her I'm thinking of her. Was that too much to ask? I scowled. Felt thwarted at every turn. Tired. Ready to get out of here. Ready to go home.

But instead, I walked over to a cluster of leather chairs in the lobby and sat down. A regal white-haired woman looked at me from the next chair and got up, high-stepping away across the thick carpet. Hey, I thought. I'd like to see what you'd look like if you'd slept in your truck.

I sighed, and dug out my map. I felt as though this story was getting away from me, that Allison Smythe at *Historic Touring* would say, "You mean you went all the way to Québec and you didn't see the . . . ?"

Citadel, I thought, scanning the soggy, dog-eared map. I hadn't been to the Citadel, the massive emplacement overlooking the river and the Plains of Abraham, where Montcalm and Wolfe slugged it out. Wrong war, but the history buffs would want to know. So I heaved myself out of the chair, out of the Château Frontenac, and into the interminable rain. I dodged the water sluicing down from the rooftops to the sidewalk, and made my way back to the terrace, along the boardwalk, and up the three hundred and ten steps to the walkway in front of the Citadel. The fort's walls were behind me. Below me, somewhere, was the spot where an

Arnold team member, General Montgomery, had exhorted his men to victory, only to be killed while his words still hung in the air.

So I stood at the wall, by the separatist graffitti, and spoke into my recorder. There were ferries scuttling to and fro on the St. Lawrence, and a Canadian Coast Guard cutter waiting at its berth. The rain flattened the water, moving across the gray surface like brush strokes. I noted this, and watched some more, and then headed off past the sunken armory walls toward the city, mumbling to myself like some mad tour guide who'd lost his group.

Past the Citadel, down Rue St. Louis, a detour for the Ursuline Convent, which showed on the map from 1775. After more talking to myself, it was back down Rue St. Louis, where people sat in the restaurant windows. Couples. Groups. Families. And me.

The club was called "Jazz" and you could hear the saxophone out on the cobblestones. I walked in, saw the restaurant tables upstairs, heard the music coming from downstairs. Down a short flight of stone steps was an open room with stone walls and exposed beams in the ceiling. There were tables, half full, a man playing sax alone on the little stage. There were empty seats and instruments on their stands, and a small dance floor. I went to the end of the bar and sat, heaving my sodden bag up onto the stool next to me. The bartender was a young woman in black slacks and a white blouse, henna-colored hair longer on one side than the other. She came over and smiled.

"Bonjour."

I said hello, too tired for biligual.

"You look like you need a drink," she said, her accent very French.

"A beer," I said, my accent very American.

"How would you like to try one of Québec's beers? You like dark beer?"

"I like all beer," I said.

She smiled and brought the beer and a glass and poured.

I put a twenty-dollar bill, U.S., on the bar, and the bartender brought back Canadian.

The beer was Mautide, very dark, fermented with the yeast in the bottle. A winged devil stared at me from the label. I took a long swallow, felt him take a little piece of my soul. With the second swallow, I closed my eyes.

I drank slowly after that, listening to the sax player, who was old-fashioned and very good. He quit and sat at the other end of the bar, and then the seats in the middle began to fill, too. The band must have a following, I thought. I was trying to get the bartender's eye when a voice behind me said, *"Pardon,"* and I turned and a woman smiled. She said something in French that I couldn't understand.

"Pardonnez-moi," I said. "I'm American."

"You're excused. This chair, is someone seating here?"

I said no and took my camera bag onto my lap. The bag left the stool damp and I wiped it with a Labatt's napkin from the bar. She climbed up, arranged her dress underneath her and sat down.

"Merci," she said.

"Pas de quoi."

"You speak French?"

"That was most of my repertoire."

"Thanks for trying."

"Pas de quoi," I said. "I can also say, 'I'm sick. Please call a doctor.' "

"How did you learn that?"

"I studied French for four years in high school."

She smiled. Ordered a glass of chardonnay, and when it came, turned toward the stage, where the band was assembling. I turned, too, and couldn't help noticing that she was attractive, that her dress was black and it was short, or maybe it was just the barstool. I slapped myself inwardly for noticing.

She turned back.

"My husband is a doctor," she said.

"Oh, really."

"A surgeon. Cardiac."

"I could learn to say, 'I'm sick. Call a cardiac surgeon.' "

"Add another one to your repertoire."

"Get a job translating at the U.N.," I said.

She held out her hand. I took it and squeezed it. It felt small and soft. I let go.

"I'm Chantal Ricard," the woman said.

"I'm Jack McMorrow."

"Very nice to meet you."

She was pretty. Small, with short, sort-of-feathered dark hair, and dark eyes. Greenish brown, against pale, finely grained skin. Her legs were tanned, and the diamond on her left ring finger was a rock. She looked like money. Canadian money.

"Where are you from in the States?" she asked, sipping her wine.

"Maine. Not very far away."

"When the children were little, we used to go to Cape Cod. You are in Québec on vacation?"

I took a swallow of Mautide.

"Working."

"Business?"

"Sort of. I'm a writer. I'm doing a magazine piece."

I glanced over. She looked interested, or maybe was just pretending.

"Oh, how interesting. What about?"

She leaned toward me expectantly.

"I'm writing about Benedict Arnold."

"Le traître?"

"I don't know. I've come to like him, in a way."

"How can you like a traitor?" she asked.

"Well, it wasn't quite that simple. Part of it was that the Revolution sort of changed. It swung to the left and he was pretty conservative. A businessman. Also, the lefties in the group mistreated him in a lot of ways. No excuse, of course."

I glance at her, saw that she appeared to be listening intently. Maybe she was in the theater.

"So, he was still a traitor, right?"

"Right," I said.

She smiled, recrossed her legs and turned to the band. The bartender brought me another beer and poured it. Chantal Ricard turned back.

"Are you waiting for dinner?" she asked.

"No," I said. "I just stopped for a beer. I heard the music outside."

"The music's good. The dinner's good, too."

"You come here to eat often?"

"Whenever we're in Québec City. We're from Montréal. My husband likes music and good food."

"Is he coming?" I asked.

She turned away, then turned back. There was a new tautness to her smile, and to her back.

"No. He was supposed to come but he had to go to the hospital. I'm here with another couple. Two of them and me. That makes three. He was supposed to meet us, but he called the hotel and said he would be delayed."

"Surgery?"

She shrugged.

I sipped my beer. The band honked and thumped as it got ready for the first set. She turned back to me.

"You should do a story on Montcalm and Wolfe."

"So I hear."

"The French against the English. That battle is still raging."

"Do you think Québec will secede?" I asked. "The last vote, I was really rooting for them. I like people who act on principle."

"It will happen in time. They say it will mean economic disaster, a Great Depression. You should hear my husband go on about it."

"He's English?"

"No, he's just a businessman doctor. He knows what's good for business. He's probably right."

"So you agree?"

"Oh, no. On this we disagree. This and other things. The separatists? That's minor. Are you married?"

I looked at her as she looked away.

"Yes," I said. "More or less."

"Someone for a long time, huh? I've been married twenty-one years. We have two children from his first marriage, one from ours. She's in college. In the States. She goes to Columbia."

"How does she like it?"

"Johanne loves it. She's studying Greek. Her father thinks it's a waste of time, but he doesn't say much. He dotes on Johanne."

But he didn't dote on his wife?

"I grew up around New York," I said. "It's a great city, despite what you hear."

"Yes, but I worry about her. Kids do foolish things sometimes. You have kids?"

"No," I said. "Not yet."

"You should try it. If you don't, you'll always wonder. If you can, of course. I mean. Well, children are great. I didn't mean . . ."

"I know what you meant," I said. "I love kids. I just don't own any."

I smiled. She smiled, but more sheepishly, then turned away.

The band started in. The song was "Summertime." Some jazz buff said, "Yeah," from one of the tables, the way some jazz buffs do. I sat there and watched and listened, but I was very aware of this woman, very aware of my own awareness. Her legs were crossed. I was aware of them, too.

It had been a long time since I'd been in this situation, whatever this situation was. I felt energized in spite of myself. Probably some hormonal reaction. Everything is hormones, when it comes down to it.

She turned back, held her wineglass up to the bartender. The bartender came over and poured. She looked to me and I started to say no, but then shrugged. Another Mautide, *s'il vous plaît.*

We sipped and listened. After a song with a long bass solo, she turned back to me.

"You like writing? You write short stories or poetry or anything?"

I shook my head.

"No, not in a long, long time. I'm really a reporter. A newspaper reporter. That's what I did in New York."

"Let me guess. The *Village Voice*?"

"No, the *Times.*"

"My daughter gets the *Voice.*"

"A lot of people do."

"So you were a reporter at a big paper. You like writing about history now?"

"I write about all kinds of things. Before this, I did a story on puffins."

She shook her head.

"You know. The seabirds? The ones that look like clowns?"

It didn't ring a bell with her. I wondered at that. How could somebody not know what a puffin was?

"So you are a freelancer. Is that what you call it?"

"Yeah," I said. "I freelance."

"How did you get that scar on your face?"

I looked at her, wondered if she was becoming emboldened by the wine. Alcohol affected some people like that. I took a swallow of Mautide and hoped alcohol didn't do that to me.

"Doing a story," I said. "I fell down."

Next thing, she'd want to know how I skinned my knee. I could tell her about Damian. About Marvin Maurice. She'd be glad her daughter hadn't gone to Maine to school.

The band kicked in, something zippy, with trumpet and saxophone playing in unison in rapid scales. Somebody said, "Whoo," and somebody else said, "Yeah." The horns paused and the drummer started his solo, and the same guy said, "Yeah," again. Chantal Ricard turned to me.

"You like what you do?"

"Most of the time," I said. "I like people. I like studying the things they do. And I like arranging the words, too. How 'bout you?"

"I like to paint," she said, turning away.

"Paint what?"

"Watercolors, for the most part."

"That's nice. Do you do it just for yourself?"

"Oh, I've had a couple of shows, but I think it's just because of my husband. He's very well known, and it rubs off on me. They throw me his crumbs. Hang my pictures in the corridors at the hospital."

It was a sad thing to say. I didn't know how to respond, so I didn't. The band played a couple of more numbers and took another break. The breaks were at the end of the bar, and they seemed to be frequent.

Chantal Ricard turned to me. Her cheeks had taken on a faint flush, like makeup subtly applied.

"So, have you seen much of the Québec City?" she said.

"The oldest parts. Lower town, mostly. That's as far as Arnold got."

"It's a beautiful place. A lot of art, you know."

"I guess I missed that."

"How long are you in town?"

"I don't know. I'm staying on Rue St. Genevieve. I have to be back tomorrow."

She seemed to mull that as she sipped her wine, her pinky rubbing against her diamond.

"How 'bout dinner?" she said, turning toward the band. "I'd rather talk to you. You could tell me about New York, because of my daughter. Then I would not have spend the whole evening with somebody who knows.''

I looked at her.

''Knows what?''

''That my husband didn't have surgery. That he's seeing a very pretty, very ambitious, much younger woman. A nurse. A surgical nurse. Her name is Almanda. I'm gone so they can go to her apartment.''

''Huh,'' I said. ''They know that? The people you're with?''

''The guy's a doctor, too.''

''Huh,'' I said again.

''So how 'bout it?''

''I don't know. I might leave tonight. I'm pretty much through here. With my research.''

Chantal Ricard gave a little shrug. Then she turned to me brightly.

''Okay. You can think about it. While you're thinking, we'll just have one dance. One dance, to mark our acquaintance. A Canadian-American friendship. Come on.''

She reached out and took my hand in hers and stepped down from the stool, and pulled me after her. Mercifully, there were other couples dancing slowly, off to the right of the little stage. As if on cue, the band slipped into another song—a soft, sensual number, with the sax drifting in and out.

Oh, God, I thought. She turned to me and smiled and pulled me toward her. I stood there stiffly, like a junior-high boy on Sadie Hawkins night. She draped her arms over my shoulders and stared up at me with those big dark eyes. I gingerly put my arms somewhere near her waist.

''Are you afraid of me, Jack?'' Chantal Ricard said, rocking slowly to the music.

It jarred me to hear her speak my name.

''No,'' I lied. ''Why should I be?''

''You shouldn't be. I won't bite. I just want to dance. You know that in the old days, a woman, a lady, would dance with every man at the ball. It was a courtesy, not seduction.''

''That's good to know.''

I looked away. When I looked back, she was still staring up. I could feel her hips through the thin material of the dress. They were different from Roxanne's hips, harder or something.

''You're a better dancer than this, I think,'' she said.

''It's been a while.''

''You should relax. Come here, I'll show you.''

I didn't come to her, but she came to me. She slid close to me so that I could feel her belly and breasts against me. Her dress seemed to be dissolving. The band played on, interminably.

''The dancers should move as one,'' Chantal Ricard said. ''When I was young, I did ice dancing. Like on the Olympics?''

Quick, I thought. Talk sports.

''You were in the Olympics?''

''Oh, no. I gave it all up to get married and have a baby. But the coaches always told us. You are one *organisme*.''

She pronounced the last syllable, the French way.

''Not separate. You move as one.''

I looked down at her, down between her breasts. As I looked away, the band stopped playing. I stopped my almost imperceptible movement. Started to back away, off the dance floor. The bass started up again, mercilessly. The brushes swished on the drums.

She pulled me to her again, then began to guide us deeper on to the dance floor, away from the minimum-security perimeter. I stared straight ahead, over her hair at the stone wall. Roxanne was taller and this was odd, this different fit. As I thought about that, Chantal Ricard nestled closer, her head resting against my chest. I could smell her perfume, her fragrance. That was very different from Roxanne, too. Then I could feel the rest of her pressing against me, her breasts and thighs. I moved back but she stayed with me.

I heard her exhale heavily. The song was endless, played by this pack of voyeurs.

Chantal Ricard leaned away from me, just her head and shoulders. She looked up.

"I have a suite at the Frontenac. The ninth floor, over-looking the river. It's very elegant."

"I'm sure."

"We could get some bottles of champagne," she said. "We could have dinner sent up."

She kissed my neck very lightly, her hair brushing my chin.

"Get even with the doctor, eh?"

"This isn't him. This is us. I like you. I could tell right away. So we have a night of complete bliss. No strings."

Chantal Ricard looked up at me, with her big, wet, im-ploring eyes. She dropped her arm from my shoulder and ran a finger over the scar on my cheekbone.

"You know, I like your cut," she said.

I smiled down at her.

"You know you're the second woman to say that?"

I took her hand away from my face and gave it a squeeze.

"Thanks for the dance. Good luck with your life."

I left her on the dance floor and didn't look back. On the way out, I grabbed my bag. I went up the steps two at a time, and out into the rain on Rue St. Louise. The *manoir* was a block over and I trotted there, went upstairs and got my duffel. The *madame* poked her head out of the office door as I came back down the stairs, two at a time. She looked perplexed.

"Is something wrong?" she asked.

"No, I'm sorry," I said. "My plans just changed. You can still charge for the room."

"Then you have to sign."

She went back into the office. I followed her and waited

as she rummaged under the counter for the credit card machine. She reappeared and plopped it down.

"We only charge you twenty-five dollars Canadian, because you couldn't stay. But you come back here again, uh? And tell the other officers."

"Officers?"

"The drug agents. My husband and I, we figured it out. You're undercover. But don't worry. We don't tell nobody. *C'est confidentiel.*"

The machine went ka-chunk. I signed and took my receipt. She gave me a big wink. I smiled and went out the door, threw the duffel on the floor of the cab of the truck, and in five minutes, fueled by Mautide and guilt, was blasting down the Grande Allée toward home.

When the phone rang.

Roxanne. Should I tell her? This weird thing happened. A woman tried to sort of pick me up. Asked me to dance. I'd make it funny. Or maybe I wouldn't. Maybe I'd make it sad. Her husband has a mistress. She seemed very nice, but lost. . . . Maybe I wouldn't say nothing at all.

I picked up the receiver.

"Hello."

"McMorrow. You got the money?"

 I said no, I didn't have the money.

"The friggin' clock's ticking."

Elbert's voice was faint. I didn't say anything.

"And a deal's a deal."

"There was no deal."

"Hey. A man's word is his word. I said you could have Marv for five grand. You got my word."

Great, I thought, pulling up to a red light in St. Foye. Honor among drunken, bullying scum.

"You should just let him go. It's going to go to hell on you. It's going to unravel. These things almost always do."

"No. We got a deal. Don't frig with me, man. Don't try to frig with my head."

"I'm not. I'm just telling you the odds. They aren't good."

"You get the money, Morrow. I'll worry about the odds."

The light turned green. I started off, holding the receiver in the crook of my neck as I shifted. I passed the shopping plazas, the motels, a McDonald's where the sign said, "*Jouer à* Muppet Mania."

I waited for Elbert to say something else, but he didn't. He didn't hang up, either.

"You're in over your head," I said. "And you know it."

"I ain't in over my head, Mr. friggin' CIA. I did a tour in 'Nam. Eleven friggin' months, man. I seen guys get blowed away. I seen some serious goddamn shit. Hey, you spooks think you're hot shit. Yeah, well, buddy, I ain't impressed."

I waited while he rambled. Heard the telltale pause and gulp as the beer bottle was raised and lowered. Should I tell him? Tell him I know his name? Tell him the cops know, too? That it was over? Or would he panic? Kill Marvin for sure, to cover his tracks, if I uttered that one word?

Elbert.

The ramp for Route 75 was approaching. I changed lanes, the receiver still in my hand. I weighed it. Decided to stall.

"How's Marvin now?" I said.

The phone got fuzzy.

". . . fine. Eats like a pig."

"How do I know you haven't whacked him?"

Whacked him. I thought he'd like that gangster talk.

"I ain't gonna whack him unless you frig things up," he said.

He did like it.

"How do I know this isn't just a bunch of talk?"

"I'll send you his finger," he said. "You can check his prints."

"No," I said quickly, driving up onto the bridge, the St. Lawrence down below. Oh, God, I thought. "No, he's got to be perfect. Not a scratch. No damaged goods."

"Yeah, well . . ."

He hesitated.

"You haven't hurt him, have you? If he's all beat up, he's going to be worth a lot less. A lot less."

I was in now. I was playing along, no longer the innocent bystander, the honorable guy pulled onto the dance floor. I came off the bridge, onto the other side.

"You hear what I said?"

"Yeah," he said. "He's fine."

"I'm going to need some time," I said. "The bureaucracy, you know. Requisitions are handled out of Langeley. That's in Virginia. It isn't like the movies, but you probably knew that, right? If you were in 'Nam."

"Hey, I seen it. My friggin' discharge pay took for-friggin'-ever to pry out of those bastards."

So he could be stroked. But he could turn on you, quickly and easily. "You're getting the money, I can wait. But I ain't gonna wait forever, McMorrow."

"I know," I said. "I'm not, either."

"I'll be talking to you," he said.

"I'm counting on it," I said, but he'd already hung up.

I drove down the Canadian interstate in a distracted daze, my mind flicking through the scenes. My hands on Chantal's hips. The silent cobblestone streets. Elbert's voice on the phone as I drove over the St. Lawrence. Roxanne, my memory of her fading, like the image of someone who has died. Damian on his belly. The smell of him. The feel of the can opener against his spine.

And my own voice: *Requisitions are handled out of Langeley . . . I'm going to need some time.*

Over and over, the order shuffled, the scenes played as I drove in the yellow-lit highway haze. Roxanne in bed, straining on top of me. Roxanne in tears, breaking down as I listened, paralyzed on the other end of the phone. The feel of Chantal's breasts against my chest. Damian taunting Robie. Rob-ann's voice, *This is my house.* That little kid, Marvin's neighbor, talking about "the company" in Chile. In Southeast Asia. Marvin, whom I'd never seen, but could picture. Flabby. Balding. Soft, doughy hands.

Elbert, so matter-of-fact: *I'll send you his finger. You can check his prints.*

And then it was nine-fifteen. The rain had stopped, and a steamy mist rose from the pavement. I looked up, startled to see the sign that said Route 173 and St. Joseph-de-Beauce were to the right. I turned, then pulled into a variety store that sat alone on top of a hill. Parking at the gas pumps, I went in and exchanged *bonjours* with the made-up woman behind the counter, eyed the menu above the pizza oven, and ordered a turkey sandwich and orange juice. She bustled about, handed them to me, and I paid her for the food and twenty dollars, Canadian, worth of gas. A teenage boy wearing a Yankees T-shirt appeared to pump the gas for me. I thanked him and he said, "Nice truck," and walked away, leaving me to my sandwich and my reveries.

Such as they were.

But at least in this stretch of Québec, there were distractions. As I drove and ate, I could eye the shopping centers and stores in Beauceville; the sawmills in Jersey Mills and Linière. But then the wrappers were on the floor of the truck, and I was through Armstrong, and the border station reared up out of the mist. The stubble-faced guy from the previous night was replaced by his American counterpart, also stubble-faced but distracted and disinterested. I told him I had nothing to declare, that I lived in Prosperity, Maine, that I'd come through the night before. I was a writer. The truck's owner was in North Carolina.

Standing beside the driver's door, he gave me a single long look, right between the eyes, waiting for that flicker of nervousness that betrays the guilty. It wasn't there.

"Go ahead," he said, so I did.

South into the United States I drove, with the road slick and wet, and blackness on both sides. In the quiet, my demons began circling again, taunting and demanding. What was I going to do now? Why did I dance with another woman? Why did I say I was in the CIA? Would that be enough to save Marvin? Was I deserting Roxanne in her time of need? And I couldn't forget that I still had to write my story.

Jackman was a respite. I looked at the stores. Both of them. I wondered what it would be like to grow up in such a remote place, or was remoteness just a relative state? But then it was another hour and a half of darkness, with the blackness punctuated by little settlements, twenty miles apart. My mind was still whirling when the lights of Scanesett showed up ahead, glowing against the clouds.

It was after eleven. The kids were still standing beside their cars and trucks in the Kmart parking lot, as their parents had done, as their children would do. They looked up at the truck as I passed and I stared back and drove on, past McDonald's and the Scanesett Shopping Center. I considered taking side streets through town, but the situation had changed since I'd jumped from the window. I was getting the money. There was no reason to give me a hard—

The bike crossed the road, swerved and turned off. The bulky figure. The heavy legs, knees splayed out slightly.

Robie.

I followed.

He pedaled down the side street, on the right. There was something white in the milk crate on the carrier over the back wheel. I hung back, then gave the gas pedal a punch and coasted closer. The bags were from McDonald's. A midnight snack?

I stayed behind him for two blocks, past little bungalows, a garage, a mobile home, until Robie came alongside a wooded lot. He turned to look back and I sped up, passed him, and turned hard to cut him off. Something bumped the side of the truck and I slammed the brakes on, and flung the door open.

''Robie,'' I called, running around the back of the truck. ''It's okay.''

He was still on the bike, which was wedged in the burdocks and brush.

''I can't talk to you. I can't talk to you,'' he jabbered.

''Come on, Robe. We need each other. We need each other now.''

I put my hand on his back, my other hand on the handlebars.

''I need to talk to you, and you know why.''

''I can't. They'll—''

''They won't do anything. But if we don't talk, something bad's definitely going to happen. Get in the truck.''

He looked at me, his eyes wide, his thick mouth set.

''Come on. Put the bike in the back.''

''They'll—''

''Robie,'' I barked. ''Get in.''

''But my sister, she's gonna be—''

''She's gonna be in big trouble, that's what she'll be. Now get in.''

He got off the bike on the brush side, lurching into the burdocks. I rolled it onto the pavement and he held it up as I dropped the tailgate. Robie took the bags out of the crate and I lifted the bike up and in, and laid it down. I closed the tailgate and Robie tentatively opened the passenger door. I climbed in the driver's side, and only then did he climb in, too.

Robie sat forward on the seat, McDonald's bags on his lap, like a kid anxious for the bell to ring. His thighs were big and pale, even in the dark. His right sneaker was jiggling, which made the bags rustle rhythmically. Robie alternately picked at his eyelashes, and turned to look at his bike in the back of the truck.

"McDonald's open late?" I said as I started off.

"Till twelve. I been riding around."

"Don't want to go home, Robie?"

"Um, I don't know. You think it'll be okay?" Robie said.

"It'll be fine."

" 'Cause it's my best bike. I got others, but that's my best one."

He looked back again.

"You sure it's gonna be okay?"

"Yeah, Robie. I'm sure about the bike. I'm not sure about you or your sister."

He ignored me.

"Yeah, well, that's bike's my best one."

Robie switched from plucking at his eyelashes to digging at his scalp, so deeply that I could hear a scraping noise. I coasted to the stop sign at the end of the block, rolled through, and went to the right. Robie went back to his eyelashes. I could smell the french fries, and then his odor began to fill the truck cab, too. Not a foul odor, but the smell of sweat and dirt, like a kid just home from playing baseball. Even Robie's bodily functions were frozen in preadolescence.

I shifted from second to third, let the truck loaf along. He turned again, his big hand on the back of the seat.

"The bike's okay, Robie," I said, pulling up to the next stop sign. "That's the least of your worries."

"Yeah, well, that bike's my—"

"Where is he, Robie?"

He kneaded the folded tops of the McDonald's bags. Didn't answer.

"Do you know what they're doing, Robe?"

I looked at him. Shifted the truck.

"I'll tell you in case you haven't heard the latest. They're trying to extort money from me for Marvin. Like kidnappers, you know? Five thousand dollars. They think I'll get it from the CIA."

Robie looked straight ahead. His foot was still. His hands kneaded the bags more slowly.

"And you know what people like that do a lot of the time?"

I rolled through another stop sign, headed south for the downtown.

"They kill the person, Robe. So that person can't testify against them. Say right there in court, 'Yeah, it was Howard and Damian who held me captive and beat me up. It was them that stole my car and my motorcycle. It was Howard and Damian, and Robie and Rob-ann.''

"I ain't done nothin'," Robie blurted.

"You haven't done anything to help, either. And you're running out of chances, Robe. Running out of chances to get off this runaway train before it crashes."

He was staring straight ahead.

"You know what I mean?" I said.

Robie didn't answer. I drove down a street of big old houses chopped into apartments. Most windows were dark. Up ahead, there was a glow from the lights of a corner store. A truck approached, then passed us, country music blaring for a moment, then fading.

"When did your mother die, Robie?" I said.

I waited, wondering if he'd answer.

"June eleventh, nineteen-ninety," Robie said.

"You remember that, huh?"

"Uh-huh."

"My mother died in '85. Not in June. January. I have a

friend whose mother's sort of dying now. It's hard.''

''Uh-huh.''

I paused as the truck rumbled on.

''Your mother drank a lot, didn't she?''

Robie shrugged.

''I don't know.''

''And you and Rob-ann took care of her.''

''I guess.''

''You think you're mother loved you, Robie?''

''Uh-huh. People said she didn't, but she did. I know 'cause she was my mother. She wasn't their mother. She was my mother. Me and Rob-ann.''

''So you had to defend her? To other people?''

''You mean, like, fight?''

''Or just take her side.''

''Uh-huh.''

''A lot?''

''Yeah,'' Robie said. ''When we went to school. After we stopped going to school, not so much.''

''Was that better, not having to go to school?''

''Yeah. I didn't like school.''

''What didn't you like about it? The work? The other kids?''

''Yeah,'' he said.

''So you stayed home?''

''Uh-huh.''

''Took care of your mother, right? You and Rob-ann?''

''Yeah.''

I looked over. His fingers were still moving. The tops of the McDonald's bags were starting to shred.

''You remember times when your mother was nice to you?''

Robie didn't say anything for a moment.

''Uh-huh.''

''Because she did love you, right?'' I said.

''Yeah, and people didn't know her, because she was our mom and we was the ones who knew her. They said stuff but they oughtn't of 'cause they didn't know.''

"Do you think she wanted Rob-ann to end up in prison?''

I glanced over. Robie swallowed. His lips parted and his mouth hung open.

"No.''

"Do you think she'd be mad if she knew you were the one who let Rob-ann go to prison?''

He didn't answer.

"You believe in Heaven, Robe? You think your mother is up there, looking down at us right now?''

"I guess,'' Robie said softly.

"A lot of people think that. Or maybe they'd like to think that. What do you think your mother would think of this mess? She loved you, right? You said that, didn't you?''

We were approaching the downtown. Cars passed on Main Street, their headlights and taillights passing from left to right, right to left.

"You ain't gonna put my sister in prison, are you?''

Robie seemed disbelieving.

"It's not up to me, Robie. Out of my hands. But I know if they hurt Marvin, then you're both sunk. You could never see her again. What if something happened to—''

"She didn't do nothin'.''

"But sometimes doing nothing is doing something be-cause you could have helped but you didn't. You know what I mean? You're walking along and you see somebody killing somebody and you just keep going and you don't call the police or tell anybody. What I need you to do is tell the police everything that's happened. Just tell them.''

He stared stolidly ahead, then shook his head.

"Howard would—''

"Then tell me. Tell me what Marvin said. At least tell me where they are on the goddamn islands down there, Robe. You have a place you go out there? Tell me where he is so I can get him out, or have the police get him out, or something.''

"You'd bring a helicopter?"

I paused.

"A helicopter?"

I was turning onto Main Street, driving past the appliance store. The clock said 1:05.

"The government. The CIA. Howard said they got—"

"Robie. I'm a reporter. That's all. I'm not even on staff. I'm not . . ."

I stopped. Let the words trail off.

The car coming toward us. The headlights.

"Get down," I said.

"What—"

"Down."

I reached over and grabbed Robie's T-shirt at the neck. Yanked him hard down on the seat. The top of his head brushed my thigh.

The Chevette passed. Howard's face. One frozen glance. Brake lights went on in the rearview mirror.

"Hey, I ain't done nothing to—"

"Shut up, Robie. Stay down. Stay right the hell down."

"Why?"

"It's Howard. And Elbert, I think."

"Oh, jeez. Did they see me?" Robie said, his head still jammed against my leg. "Howard'll kill me, he sees me, he thinks I been talking to you."

"No. I don't think so. They saw me, though. They're turning around."

One back-up light flicked on, then off. Then the head-lights swung back out into the street. Robie started to lift his head.

"Stay there," I said. "Don't get up unless I tell you to. Don't."

The Catholic church was ahead on the right. I sped up, turned into the parking lot beyond the church building, drove to the back of the lot and wheeled the truck around.

I backed it up so the tailgate was against the bushes at the edge of the lot. Then I shut off the light and the motor, left the keys in the ignition.

"Get on the floor," I said. "Don't move and don't make a sound."

And then I got out, went to the front of the truck and waited.

The Chevette appeared. It passed the first driveway, and had almost reached the second when the brake lights went on. Howard backed up fifty feet in the middle of the street, then turned hard into the lot. The car bucked as it hit the ramp, underside scraping, then Howard drove straight toward me. I walked right into the lights, away from my truck, until the car stopped. The lights went out. The motor was stilled.

Howard got out on the driver's side. Elbert, the same guy I'd seen being rousted by the Winslow cop, the telephone negotiator, stayed in the car. Howard walked toward me. He was wearing a long-sleeved flannel shirt. His jeans were muddy on the knees. Six feet away, he stopped and grinned.

"Hey," I said.

"How's it goin'?" Howard said.

"Fine. How 'bout yourself?"

"Can't complain. Where you been?"

"You missed me?"

"Nope."

"I didn't miss you, either," I said.

He looked at me, then turned and cleared his throat and spat. Stroked his beard.

"So," Howard said.

"So what?"

"So I heard you left town in a hurry last night."

"Where'd you hear that?"

"Friend of mine. He said you went out a window."

"Is that right?" I said.

"He said you put a shiv in his backbone. Said you'd friggin' cut his spine."

"Quite a story. Sounds like bullshit to me."

"My friend ain't a bullshitter."

I looked toward the Chevette.

"That him in the car?"

"No. That's another friend of mine."

"I didn't think you had two," I said. "They like you for your money, or what?"

I grinned. Howard tensed, his lower jaw pressing forward.

"What goes around, comes around, McMorrow."

"The grass is always greener," I said. "Early bird gets the worm."

Howard scowled.

"You do something to my friend, it's like you do it to me. Ain't no difference."

"That's noble."

"I don't give a shit what you think it is."

I shrugged. Elbert stared from the Chevette, his face partly hidden by a baseball hat, pulled low. Howard looked past me toward the big Ford.

"What, you get another truck out of the motor pool?"

I ignored him and looked at the car.

"Your buddy shy or what?" I said.

Howard still stared at the truck. I hoped Robie had patience. Robie was my only chance.

"He don't say much."

"I guess not. What do you have him around for? His good looks?"

Howard shook his head slowly.

"Friggin' A, man. Someday. Just you and me, man."

"A little red wine. Candlelight . . ."

"You're one lucky son of a bitch, McMorrow. You didn't have the government to hide behind, I'd shred you."

To my right, Elbert sat still as stone. Howard took two

steps toward the Ford. I thought I heard a muffled thump
from inside the cab.

"There's always an excuse, isn't there, Howie?"

He took two or three more steps, until he was beside the
left front wheel. Another step, and he'd be able to see inside
the cab. But then Howard stopped and turned. Walked toward me slowly, so that he was between me and the truck.

"You got something to say?"

"Not really."

"Go ahead, McMorrow. Here and now. Face to face."

"I thought your style was more like a bullet in the
back."

He stared. Seemed to stop breathing.

"I thought you were more like a leech, you know? Sucking up to your cousins. Bleeding them dry. You ever have
a job? Or have you always been a mama's boy? That's what
I picture. Lived off Mommy, and then some girlfriend on
welfare, drinking up her check until she tossed you out and
you found another one. Then you found Robie and Rob-
ann. That's why you wanted Marvin, right? Same thing.
Suck him dry 'cause you can't make it on your own. Is
that right? Is it?"

I paused. Our eyes were locked, like the eyes of two cats
about to spring. And then Howard looked past me, toward
Elbert, and he seemed to relax. He pursed his lips, then
started to turn away from me, toward the truck.

"Small-town loser," I said.

He spun around and came off of his feet, and his elbow
caught me in the chin, his forearm turned my head, and I
was falling backward, almost going down, almost, but then
staying on my feet.

But I was staggering, and he was bulling against me,
kicking my shins, stepping on my feet. I wrapped my arms
around his neck and he bit my shoulder, and I started
pounding on his ear with my left fist, as hard as I could,
over and over, harder and harder. But he didn't let go, and
I could feel his teeth sinking into me, those dirty yellow

teeth, and I wrapped a leg around his and tripped him, heaving both of us to the pavement, landing on my elbow with a jolt. I was on top and he fell back and there was blood in his mouth, probably mine, and he was smiling, like a vampire.

"Aaahhh," I screamed, and I grabbed his beard and slammed his head against the asphalt, not hard enough to smash his skull, but hard enough to wipe the smile off of his face. He pulled his fist to the side, and swung hard at my crotch, but got mostly hip. I grabbed his arms and pinned them back and he spat blood in my face, and I let go with my right hand and leaned back and punched him as hard as I could, right above the belt. Once. Twice. Three times. He gasped and sagged, and a motor roared.

The Chevette.

Elbert.

I rolled off of Howard and lurched to my feet, facing the car, backing away, but then it started to back away, too, lights still off. Howard got to his knees, his backside to me, and said, "Wait," and then ran, still in a crouch, to the car. He yanked the passenger door open, then stopped, and took a few steps toward me. I backed toward the truck, looking to see if he had a gun or a knife or a club, but he stopped.

"Get the money, McMorrow," Howard said hoarsely.

And then he turned and trotted back to the car, his boots clumping on the pavement, and climbed in.

"Oh, Jesus," I heard him say, and then Elbert drove out of the lot, right over the curb, scraping the Chevette's underside, and leaving a piece of metal jingling on the road. I walked to the truck, pulled open the door, and heaved myself up and in. The dome light came on, revealing Robie, laying on his side on the floor on the passenger's side.

"They gone?" he said.

"Yeah," I said.

I pulled my shirt away from the bite, which showed as a splotch of blood. HIV, I thought. Tests for, what was it? Six months? Six years?

''Damn,'' I said, turning the key.

And then headlights swung into the lot, first one car, then another. Then both cars slammed to a halt in front of me, one to the left, one to the right.

''Damn,'' I said again.

 ''I thought I told you to clear out,'' Chief Dale Nevens said.

''I don't remember that.''

''I told you there wasn't any story here,'' he said.

''I guess you were wrong.''

''Guess again.''

The patrolman, the young kid I'd seen before, was sitting in the marked car with Robie, running my license and Clair's registration. We were sitting in the front seat of Nevins's unmarked police car, a black Ford, in the parking lot of the church. The chief was wearing a cream-colored sports jacket and dark brown slacks. His brown tie was on the dashboard next to his cigarettes. The motor was running. He'd been drinking. He was a walking fossil, a living dinosaur who'd somehow survived in this isolated little town.

''Working late, aren't you?'' I said.

''I'm always working. I had to attend a function in my official capacity, and I was on my way home when I heard the call. I often assist my officers.''

''I guess I just haven't run into you on the streets.''

''I wish you had. I woulda told you, we don't want no

stories in the *Boston Globe*. All we need. Goddam TV cameras all over the place."

He blew smoke my way.

"Maybe I'll sell this one to the *New York Times*," I said, my breath stirring the cloud.

"What story? A buncha wingnuts telling fairy tales and you believe 'em."

"They've got him, and they want five thousand to give him back."

"There ain't a brain between 'em," the chief said. "Who's the mastermind? Bicycle boy over there?"

"He's an innocent bystander, so far. They kill Marvin, he's an accessory."

"Who are you? The district attorney?"

"Elbert could pull this off. So could Howard. Damian is in it up to his neck. You tell me those three aren't capable of kidnapping somebody."

"They're capable of feeding you a line of shit, that's what they're capable of. If my department tried to investigate all the cockamamie stories these half-wits told us, we'd need all the cops in the state."

"You put a boat in the river in the morning, Chief," I said. "Fifty bucks says you find one Marvin Maurice camped out on one of the islands with Howard or one of them."

"Guy wants to go on a bender with a bunch of lowlifes, that's his friggin' problem," Nevins said. "My department isn't chasing him."

He flicked his cigarette butt out the window onto the pavement. A june bug rattled into the car, and he crushed it against the inside of the windshield with his big, fat thumb, then flicked the carcass out the window, too.

"Car's getting cleaned tomorrow anyway," he said.

"Who does that? Your valet?"

"You got an attitude, you know that?"

"I know I'm tired and I'm beat up, and you can never find a cop when you need one."

"You keep harassing my officers about this bullshit, and I'll haul you into court."

"For what?"

"Obstructing government administration."

"I'll write about that in the *Boston Globe*."

That seemed to give Nevins pause, and he reached for his cigarettes. Just then, the patrolman got out of his car and walked over.

"No history on the license, Chief. Truck comes back to a Clair Varney, post office box, Prosperity. Dispatch is trying to call Mr. Varney to see if the McMorrow subject has permission to possess the vehicle."

Nevins scowled, then opened the door and heaved himself out. He and the patrolman walked ten feet away and talked in whispers for a few minutes. Then Nevins turned back to his car.

"Tell Robie to take his bike and hit the road," he told the kid. "You, too. I'll deal with Clark Kent here."

The patrolman looked over at me and then walked back to his cruiser. Robie got out, hurried to the truck and lifted his bike out. He pedaled about twenty feet, then made a loop and pedaled back. I thought he was coming to tell us something, but he rode past and went to the truck and got off the bike. Opening the door, he reached in and took the McDonald's bags out and put them in the milk crate. And then he left, without looking at me or saying a word.

"Deal for you, McMorrow."

"Oh, yeah?"

"You get in your truck and go back to Waldo County and don't come back."

"I can go where I please, Chief."

"You go and don't come back, and I forget the public lewdness charge."

"The what?" I sat up.

"Robie says you asked him to come with you for a ride in your truck. He didn't want to, but he's of limited mental ability, and you insisted. You drove him to this parking lot, where you parked your truck in the dark. Then you told him to lie down on the seat with his head in your lap. His relative came along and intervened, just in time.''

''That's crap.''

''D.A. won't think so, McMorrow. Fifty bucks says I get an indictment. Another fifty says I get you convicted. Juries around here hate perverts. They really hate perverts who take advantage of the handicapped. And another fifty says you get jail time. The judge hates perverts, too.''

''But I didn't do anything to Robie. He was afraid of Howard. That's why he was hiding in the truck. He didn't tell you that story.''

''Robie'll say what I want him to say. If not today, then tomorrow. Or next week. Or the week after that.''

He flicked ashes on the floor of the car. I looked at him.

''Even if it were true, you've got two consenting adults.''

''What you do in the privacy of your own home is your business, mister. What you do in the parking lot of a Catholic church, on the town's main street, mind you, is my business. I know some people get off on these sorts of public displays, but—''

''You're a liar, Chief.''

He leaned toward me, close enough to see the yellows of his eyes.

''Ever been in jail, McMorrow? You could write about that in the *Boston Globe*. What it's like to be a sex offender behind bars. I hear it isn't much fun.''

I looked at him.

''How do you live with yourself?''

Nevins smiled, dimpling his booze-flushed cheeks.

''Very quietly, most of the time,'' he said. ''I like things quiet. I like small-town life. That's why I don't like characters like you.''

The chief left me in the parking lot alone. I sat in the truck for a few minutes, watching the moths and flies swarm around the floodlight on the wall by the back door of the church. Every once in a while, a bat slipped through and picked off a few bugs, but they kept coming out of the darkness, inexorably and instinctively drawn to something that didn't do them much good, that put them at risk.

I knew the feeling.

But I pulled out of the parking lot and headed east, out of Scanesett. My shoulder stung, and I kept pulling at my shirt to keep it from sticking to the scabs. That bastard. Dirty-fighting bastard. What if he was HIV-positive? What if he had TB? What about Roxanne? Could we make love? Oh, this was just what she needed to hear.

I thought about that on the long, dark ride along the Kennebec River, back to Prosperity. It was as though I'd gone upriver to fight and had lost. I was one of Arnold's survivors. Worse than that, I was one of the deserters, slipping away in the night, skulking all the way home, leaving others to die, inventing a tale to cover up my cowardice.

What happened to the story about the guy on the bus? Clair would ask. Roxanne would ask. Bell would know, or would she?

I could tell Clair and Roxanne that it hadn't panned out. It wasn't worth the time it would take to put it together. The guy wanted to be missing. Just some check bouncer trying to disappear. Some jerk playing games.

But what would Bell think? That the sergeant put the muscle to me and I ran? That this McMorrow guy turned out to be some kind of weirdo, hitting on poor Robie, of all people? He seemed okay, Bell would tell her big, blond husband. I never liked him, he'd say. Pushy bastard, always coming around.

Those were the choices. Turn tail and run, and let this small-town bully beat me. Leave Maurice hanging, after leading Howard and Elbert and Damian to believe that I really was from the CIA. What would happen to Maurice? Would fingers start arriving in the mail?

Or I could call Nevins' bluff, see if he'd really go to a

grand jury with some trumped-up story about me forcing myself on Robie. Except I didn't think he was bluffing. Not in the least. He'd probably arrest me, based on a complaint dictated to Robie in the back room at the Scanesett police station. He'd make sure the local weekly got that story. Maybe a mug shot. A photo as I walked out of the police station, or into court with my lawyer.

God, I would need a lawyer. That would cost money. Once word got out, my freelance jobs would dry up. The boys at the Prosperity General Store would turn deaf and mute, giving me that silent, icy stare. And what if I were convicted? Jail? A record as a sex offender?

I would become the people about whom I had always written. A perp. A name in the police blotter. Jack McMorrow, forty, of Prosperity.

And on top of all that, I had a story to write.

"Oh, God," I said with a sigh.

That said, I lapsed into silence, driving through the black streets of downtown Waterville, past the locked shops, the vacant storefronts, over the bridge and the dark presence of the Kennebec, which rolled along just as it had for my buddy Benedict. Oblivious. Relentless. Not caring whether you lived or died or burned in Hell. As I drove through Winslow, past the sprawling, steaming paper mill, past the used-car lots, the darkened McDonald's, I wondered whether Maurice could hear the river where he was. I wondered whether Chantal was sleeping alone. Whether Roxanne would ever be the same.

I wondered all those things, over and over, came up with no answers, and then I was home, on the dark road in Prosperity. It was after three. I sat in the yard with the headlights on for a moment and scanned the house. The door was closed. The windows weren't broken. I shut off the motor and waited another minute. Listened to the nighthawks, an owl. Took a flashlight out of Clair's glove compartment and shut off the headlights. Walked around the side of the house, past the shed, and into the backyard. Only then did I turn on the light. The slider was closed. The windows were intact. The house was dark, except for the green glow from the clock on the microwave. I stopped and listened. The nighthawk screeched.

My bags went on the kitchen floor. I hit the flashing button on the answering machine and it began blurting out the usual messages.

Sandy, brightly asking me if I'd called Lon or Don or whatever his name was, about the Cadillacs.

Right. At the top of my list.

Allison Smythe at *Historic Touring,* just making sure everything was still a go with the Arnold piece. Elbert, asking me when I'd have the money. Roxanne, saying she was okay but sounding like she wasn't. Allison Smythe, asking me to call as soon as possible. Elbert again, saying he couldn't wait forever. He didn't leave a number. Roxanne, not even bothering to pretend she was okay. Clair, asking me if his truck had been impounded.

I didn't feel like talking to him. At that moment, I didn't even feel like talking to Roxanne. Maybe I'd say it with flowers. Maybe in the morning, except it was the morning. In a half hour, the birds would begin. I emptied my pockets on the counter. Keys. Canadian change. Receipts. I went to the refrigerator and opened it, but there was no beer, so I went to the bathroom and took off my shirt. The bite marks were arranged in the crescent shape of a jaw. Only two teeth had broken the skin, and the rest showed as dark red bruises. I washed it with warm water and soap, then coated it gingerly with some sort of antiseptic ointment.

Had it been his blood in his mouth? My blood? In the morning, I'd call the hospital. In the morning, I'd call Roxanne, Clair and Bell. In the morning, I'd start my story. In the morning . . .

I raised the toilet lid and seat, and stopped. The toilet hadn't been flushed. A cigarette butt floated in the yellow pool like a dead minnow. I heard myself swallow. Turned slowly back toward the door. Listened. Listened harder.

Nothing.

I left the bathroom light on, and carefully and slowly walked out into the main room. Stopped. Walked along the walls to the kitchen. The cupboards were closed. There was another cigarette butt in the sink. Next to it was a gob of saliva. I swallowed again.

Slowly, I walked up the stairs to the loft. I looked at the bureau. The table. The bed. The covers were rumpled. I lifted the blanket and sheet. Didn't see anything. Reached under.

Felt something cold.

I pulled it out. A photograph. Shiny.

A Polaroid.

I turned toward the light from the bathroom. Felt my stomach go taut.

It was a photograph of a hand. The pinky finger was missing.

The hand was pudgy, with dark hair just below the wrist, a skinned knuckle on the index finger, and a nub where the little finger had been. The nub looked like uncooked chicken, reddish-pink against what appeared to be a dark gray rock. With the thumb and three fingers, the hand looked like a starfish that had lost one of its arms.

I sat on the edge of the bed and stared. So they'd done it. But they hadn't sent me the finger. They'd sent me a photograph, instead. Except they hadn't sent it. They'd dropped it off, slipped it between my sheets. They'd been here. Right here.

Looking up from the photograph, I listened. The house, the only occupied dwelling for a mile in any direction, ticked and creaked. A bug buzzed against a screen. Somewhere outside, a night bird chirped. I listened some more, then got up from the bed, the photograph still in my hand.

I stopped at the edge of the stairs and listened again. Then I eased my way down the stairs and went to the counter to get the flashlight. Padding quietly in bare feet, I went to the closet and took out the rifle. Holding the rifle in the crook of my arm, I went to the silverware drawer, pulled it open all the way, and reached back for the shells. I loaded the rifle on the counter, in the flashlight beam, with the bolt clacking loudly. Then I pushed the safety off and, leaving the photograph in the kitchen, walked to the door to the shed. I opened it and played the light over the firewood, the chainsaws, the gas cans and tools. I listened.

All was still.

I did the same for the storage room under the loft, kicking the door open, and pointing the rifle at the darkness as the beam searched among the skis and bicycles and sleeping bags. Then the bathroom, pushing the shower curtain aside with the rifle barrel. There was a beetle stranded in the bottom of the tub. Nothing else.

So I turned the light off, and went to the kitchen and picked up the photograph. Then I went to the big chair and sat in front of the sliding door, with the Remington across my lap. I held the photograph by the edge, in case there were prints.

But they hadn't sent me the finger, to check the prints, as Elbert had said. They were smarter than that. This could be anybody's hand. There was no way to link it to Maurice unless you could find the rest of him. As long as Maurice couldn't be found, there was no way to tie any of it to Howard or Elbert or Damian or anyone else. Unless, of course, I paid the money. But would they be dumb enough to just hand me the guy after this? Maurice, with his little finger in a plastic bag?

I turned the photograph over. There was nothing on the back, just the hand on the front. No moles or freckles. No ring mark. Just a hand, with three fingers.

Why had they done this now? To show me they meant business? To prod me into dealing with them? If I wanted Maurice alive, and not dismantled, then I'd have to pony up the cash. For the first time, I considered it. I had five thousand dollars. Not much more, if you didn't count the

Times-era IRAs, but I could put together the money. Maybe if I did that, I could save Maurice's life. But was that crazy? What if they just took the money and told me to get lost? What if they never produced Maurice? Even with the photograph, I couldn't even prove they'd had him. It would be my word against theirs, and I knew what mine was worth in the town of Scanesett, at least with Nevins, and he called the shots.

"Oh, my God," I said. I'd said that a lot lately.

I put my head back in the chair and closed my eyes. Outside, the darkness had turned into a deep blue, and the birds were tuning up, readying for their morning crescendo. Red-winged blackbirds. A cardinal. Chirpy sparrows. A phoebe. Mourning doves. I opened my eyes and looked at my watch. It was five of four.

Who could I call at that hour? Nobody, except maybe the dispatcher in Somerset County. And then I'd have to explain the whole story, from the bus to the finger. That wouldn't accomplish anything, except maybe get me committed.

No, I'd have to wait, at least until six. Then I could call Bell. And Clair. Did Roxanne need this, on top of all of her own problems? Probably not, but she'd want to know. I'd call her last. Maybe.

But when it came down to it, this was my problem, mine and Maurice's. I looked at the photograph and wondered how they had done it. A hatchet? Who had held his hand down? Had they gagged him, so his screams wouldn't be heard across the river? From where they were, could screams even be heard? You would think so. You would think that the sound would carry across the water, like the pained cry of a loon. But it wouldn't be a loon this time. It would be Maurice and he'd screaming and then they'd throw his finger in the river and fish would nip at it, perch in the shallows.

My head lolled back, and then someone was fishing for the finger, and I knew for a moment that I was dreaming, and then I'd slipped back to the other side. I was kissing Roxanne, kissing her belly and her breasts and then looking up and it wasn't Roxanne, it was Chantal, and my mouth had left lipstick on her breasts and her belly and I was trying to wipe it off, all the little red kisses, because Roxanne was coming, I could hear her voice, she was close, and Chantal was pulling my shirt up over my head, so I was trapped. And Roxanne was coming closer, and she was saying that Maurice had wanted to call but he couldn't, because he didn't have any fingers, and did I know where his fingers were?

I was saying, no, I didn't know, but Roxanne said I was the only one who could help, but I had to say it in French. *"Le doigt,"* I said, but she couldn't hear me, and Bell was saying, "We need his fingers and we need his toes, too, to see if they match, because if they match he can go." And Bell was in a police car, but it turned into a bicycle, except it still had windows and seats, and Rob-ann was telling Bell, "You have to pedal, too." Roxanne was there, instead of Bell, and was saying, "I know how to ride a bike," to Rob-ann, and then she was pedaling, but with her arms, lying on her stomach, and I was saying, "Good thing this is a police car, because it still has a radio." Clair was in the backseat, and he was saying, "You don't have a license, Jack. You can't call on the radio, you have to use the access." I didn't know what that was, and when I tried to ask him, the words caught in my throat, like moths stuck in syrup, and the alarm was going off, and Clair was saying, "Use the access, Jack," and the pedals were going backward, all by themselves, like a giant flywheel, and Robie was putting his legs against them to slow them down. Big chunks of his thighs flew off, like hunks of clay, and I said, "No, Robie," but those words didn't come out, either, and the alarm was ringing and my mouth was full of the moths, and I heard my own voice, like I was a robot . . .

"This is Jack McMorrow. Feel free to leave a message."

My eyes opened. The room was bright, as though it had

been bleached. I tried to get up and the rifle started to slide off of my lap, and I caught the barrel but the butt slid down and caught the top of my foot.

"Ohhhh," I said, but I got out of the chair, put the rifle down, and hobbled to the phone. The machine beeped and a voice said, "McMorrow. Where's the goddamn money? You think you—"

I picked up the receiver, left the answering maching running.

"Yeah," I said.

"That you?" Elbert said.

"Yeah. The one with the teeth marks in his shoulder."

"Yeah, well. You pushed him too far."

"I haven't pushed at all yet," I said. "You'll know when I start pushing."

Elbert paused, apparently taking me seriously. But to me, the words sounded as though they were someone else's. Who was this guy I was becoming?

"Where is it?" Elbert said.

I could hear traffic noise in the background. A truck starting up, shifting through the gears.

"I don't have it," I said. "It's Saturday, you know? The banks are closed in Washington."

"For the CIA?"

"What do you think? The CIA prints its own money?"

"You get some good mail?"

"I got a picture," I said. "Somebody stuck it in my bed."

"Is that right?"

"Yeah. He's damaged goods, now."

"Get the money, and you'll get him good as new. Almost."

"You keep chopping and you won't get a penny."

"You get the money, McMorrow."

"What are you gonna hand over? A walking hospital bill? You ever hear of the federal deficit?"

Elbert paused again. I heard a voice in the background.

A loud echoing voice, like something over a loudspeaker. A name, then "Line one."

"Gimme a time," Elbert said.

"Can't."

"A friggin' day, then."

"Can't do that, either."

"You're friggin' with me, McMorrow."

"No, I'm not. I'm telling you straight. You want me to make up some date and time?"

"I want the money."

The loudspeaker again. The woman's voice said, "Gary. Gary to Home and Garden."

Home and Garden? Presuming Elbert was in Scanesett, where could you find a place with a home and garden department? Kmart?

Was Elbert on the pay phone outside Kmart?

"Time's running out, McMorrow," he said with a growl.

"Not from my end. These deals aren't done in an hour. This isn't TV, man."

"No shit, Sherlock," Elbert said.

"So you've got to be patient."

"I don't gotta do anything."

"If you want the money you do. And I'm going to have to add one more thing. Maurice, in one piece, plus Howard gets an HIV test."

"So talk to him," Elbert said. "I'll be talking to you."

And he hung up.

I hit the button with my finger and dialed the Scanesett police. My stolid dispatcher friend answered. I asked for Bell. He said she was with somebody. I said I'd wait. He put me on hold. I waited. He came back on.

"She may be a while. Who's this?"

I told him. He put me on hold again.

I waited, my elbows on the counter. Closed my eyes and waited some more. The phone clicked.

"She's gonna be—"

"I'll wait."

I did. Outside, the cicadas already sounded like chain-saws, and the heat was building, radiating through the windows. The trees were becalmed and the birds already had quieted. When I took the receiver from my face, it was clammy with perspiration. I put it back.

"This is Officer Bell. Can I help you?"

"Hi, this is Jack."

She didn't say anything.

"Jack McMorrow."

"Yes, sir. How can I help you?"

Yes, sir?

"Well, I just wanted to tell you. They left a photo here. Last night, maybe yesterday. Here at my house. It's of a hand, and one finger is missing. Maurice. They've cut off one of his fingers."

"Well, you can bring this photograph in and an officer will look at it."

"An officer?" I said. "What do you mean, 'an officer'? What's the matter with you?"

"Nothing, sir. If you want to come in and file a report, you're welcome to do so. But I've got somebody waiting and—"

"Somebody waiting? Are you nuts? They're gonna kill this guy and you want me to drive forty miles and make a report? Elbert just called me from Kmart. The pay phone in the parking lot. In Scanesett. Demanding the five thousand dollars. I've got the conversation on tape. If you get up there, you can follow him and then you'll know—"

"Mr. McMorrow. I made an inquiry regarding Mr. Maurice. He was discharged as a master sergeant, spent most of his army career at Fort Devens. He spent several years as a baker. He made bread and muffins and doughnuts. Later, he bought supplies for the food service on base. Flour and stuff. He was as far from the CIA as you can get."

"Right."

"And I talked to one of his neighbors. She said she

thought Mr. Maurice had gone to visit relatives in Québec.''

''Which neighbor's that?''

''I'm not at liberty to—''

''God almighty. Maybe that's what Maurice told her.
The guy's on the lam. Right? He's a thief. What, he tells
a neighbor he's going to visit relatives, so you just forget
everything else? The CIA stuff is his fantasy. It's—''

''You may be right there,'' Bell said, her voice as cool
as the day was hot. ''But I'm not sure whose fantasy it is.''

''What's that supposed to mean? What's your problem?''

And then I knew.

''Nevins talked to you?''

Bell didn't answer.

''He made that whole thing up,'' I said. ''I had Robie in
the truck so Howard wouldn't see him. If Howard had seen
him talking to me, he would've beaten the hell out of him.''

''In the back of the parking lot,'' Bell said, her voice an
antiseptic monotone. ''At two in the morning. Robie lying
on the seat.''

''He was hiding, for God's sake. What do you want him
to do? Stand on the roof? Are you going to believe Nevins?
He doesn't want you to investigate anything? You know
what he's like. He's—''

''I know what the chief is like. And I thought I knew
what you were like, McMorrow. Listen, I'm very busy. If
there's nothing more, I've got to go.''

''If there's nothing more? Nothing more. Just a guy getting his fingers lopped off one by one. A bunch of lowlifes
in your town trying to stick me up for five grand because
they think I'm in the CIA. And don't think they'll stop with
Maurice. You think they're gonna let Robie and Rob-ann
walk around, knowing that—''

But Bell had hung up.

I flung the receiver onto the counter, and it banged off
of the wall and knocked a glass into the sink. The glass

broke into three pieces. I picked the receiver up, almost threw it again. Slammed it down, instead.

So who did I go to now? State police? County sheriff? One call to Scanesett and they'd file me under fruitcake. "McMorrow? The reporter? Oh, yeah, he's got some crazy idea about the CIA and a kidnapping and all this crap. Other night, the chief caught him in a truck in a back alley at, like, two in the morning, with a local nitwit. Yeah, you got it. So, how you like those new Chevys?"

I picked up the receiver. Put it down again. What did I do now? Forget the whole thing ever happened? Sit here and wait for the Polaroids to be delivered, one by one?

I had to try.

Standing there in my shorts, I opened the drawer, started to reach for the trash can when something cracked. I jumped back, staggered. Stood and looked. No blood on me. No smoke from the drawer. I walked back and peeked in. There was a piece of pale wood on top of the books and papers. I took a fork from the sink and poked it. It didn't move. I flipped it over.

A rat trap. A scrap of paper bag under the heavy steel bail. Printing in pencil: *Get the money.*

28 So Maurice lost a finger, and I would, too?

I slid the drawers open, slowly. Gingerly opened the cupboards. On my knees, I peered into the darkness under the couch. With a broom, I swept under the bed. I didn't reach in with my hand.

The toilet seat. The toilet tank. The bathroom cupboard, carefully lifting the stacks of towels and sheets. The bureau drawers. The armoire thing where a couple of Roxanne's skirts hung alongside my one suit, which was stored like a wedding dress.

Still in my boxers, I padded outside. Knelt on the ground and looked under my truck, parked next to Clair's. Eased the hood open. Nothing. Opened the doors. Nothing there, either. Looked in the glove compartment, under and behind the seat.

I looked around, up and down the dirt road, across the road into the woods. And then I brushed off my knees and went inside.

The rat trap went on the counter next to the picture. I picked the picture up as I waited for the state police to answer in Augusta. They did, in the form of a man whose every syllable said he'd heard it all before.

I told him about the photograph. I said I'd found it in my bed, that I was sure it was of a guy who'd been abducted in Scanesett. He asked me if this had been reported to the local police department.

Grudgingly, I said yes.

Then it was already under investigation, he said. I said the Scanesett police didn't seem to understand the urgency of the matter. His tone changed. I said I knew it all sounded crazy, but I had the photograph. The finger was missing. He took my name and number, said he'd have a trooper call me when one was available.

And maybe he would. And maybe the trooper would take me seriously.

Maybe.

I went through the same routine with the sheriff's office, but the dispatcher there was more skeptical. If the Scanesett P.D. was already involved, why would the sheriff's office be needed? Because Scanesett didn't seem to think it was important, I said. And who was handling the investigation for Scanesett P.D.? Officer Bell, I said. Had I notified Officer Bell? Yes, just a few minutes ago. Oh. And where was this photograph? At my house, in Prosperity. The tone changed. Well, sir, we don't usually duplicate efforts with local police departments. We have enough to do trying to keep up with our own cases. Yes, I know, I said. But this could be life-threatening. It was a serious matter. Yes, sir, you said that. I'll have a deputy call you. Will you be at that number all day? Yes, I said. But even as I said it, I knew it wasn't true.

Let me give you my car phone number. I may have to go out. I may have to go to—

I hung up, discouraged and dirty.

The phone rang while I was in the shower, and the tea water was coming to a boil. I let the answering machine take the call, and standing in the middle of the bathroom floor, gently patted my bite marks dry. They didn't look infected, at least not by bacteria. My own words echoed: This could be life-threatening.

"One life at a time," I said aloud.

With the towel in my hand, I went to the phone. Hit the button on the machine. Allison Smythe's bright voice rang out. "Jack, this is Allison. Be a peach and call me right back."

I put the towel around my waist and dialed. She answered and asked how everything was going.

"Good," I said.

"Well, I hate to tell you this, but I might be able to give you another week."

"Great."

"Change in the production schedule. Sorry to jerk you around, but these things happen. But listen, I was thinking, Jack. I was trying to conceptualize the art. And I was picturing this photo of the Kennebec River, with nothing modern showing. You know, the woods, a bend in the river. Kind of like what Arnold would have seen as he stroked his way upstream."

"Okay," I said. "I can do that."

"I didn't know if you had a boat or something."

"I can get one."

As I said it, I knew.

"Maybe you can find a stretch of river that would work. I know it won't be autumn, but what the heck. I still think it would work, don't you?"

"Sure, Allison," I said, my own voice far away, my mind leaping forward, picturing the canoe, the river, the islands. "I know a place. I'll do it today."

"Oh, fantastic. I had this idea—I don't know if you'll be able to do this—but I pictured the river has having this tremendous portent, you know what I mean?"

"Portent. Sure."

"That it looks beautiful and idyllic, but it's really a beast, malevolent and threatening. Arnold looking out from his canoe with a sense of foreboding, like somewhere in the back of his mind, he knew what he was getting into. Something lurking under the surface. Someone hiding in the trees. Danger on the Kennebec. Can you picture that?"

"Yeah," I said. "I think I can."

"Do you think you could bring that concept to the art?"

"I don't know," I said. "It depends on what I find."

A lot depended on that.

I knew where I was going. I knew why. I knew it as I got dressed, in dark green shorts and a dark green T-shirt. I knew it as I called Clair, and was relieved to learn that he was out, at the pool club with the kids. I knew it as I left a message with the son-in-law: Tell Clair his truck was fine. I knew it as I called Roxanne. It was ten o'clock and she would surely be at the nursing home. I called the condo and left a message. I was fine, working on my story and thinking of her. I loved her, and I'd call later.

I knew it as I did all of things I was supposed to do. I called the hospital and asked for the emergency room. A cheery E.R. doctor answered and I told him about my bite. He said chances of transmitting the HIV virus were very slim if the other guy's mouth contained only saliva. But if his mouth was filled with his own blood, as sometimes happens in a fight, then that's a different matter.

I pictured the fight. Howard had bitten me before I'd slammed his head against the pavement. I hadn't hit him in the mouth, and I told the doctor that.

"Just to be safe, you should be tested now, then six months from now," he said. "And the sooner you get the other fellow tested, the better. If it's a month from now, you won't know whether he contracted the virus after his contact with you, or before. Can you persuade him to come in?"

"I don't know," I said. "I'm going to try to meet up with him later today."

And then I sat down at the big table by the window and turned on the computer. I rummaged through my notes, separating them into file folders with labels such as "lower Kennebec" and "Coburn-Gore to Lac Megantic." I shuffled papers, sorted tapes, and then, with my mind about forty miles away, I actually started to write.

If your planning is as poor as mine, and like me, you arrive in Québec City in the early morning darkness, you can console yourself with this thought.

You've accomplished, after just a few hours' drive, what Benedict Arnold couldn't after three months of marching, starving and fighting: pass through the gates of old Québec.

I read it over. Did it work? I couldn't tell. Should I delete it and try again? I didn't know. Would Clair mind if I borrowed his canoe? Not at all.

So I shut off the computer and picked up the rifle and a box of cartridges. I took my sheath knife out of the kitchen drawer, and dropped it in my camera bag. Then I slung the bag and binoculars over my arm, and went out to the Toyota and loaded the stuff in. I started the truck and drove up the road to Clair's barn, backing up to the front door. Unlocking the padlock, I slid the door over and backed my truck into the cool darkness.

The canoe was a sixteen-foot aluminum Grumman, painted camouflage for duck and goose hunting. Clair said he'd hunted deer from it, too, but had given up on that idea after spending a whole day trying to tow a dead buck up a stream. It was like hunting moose, Clair had said. Shooting one was easy, but hours after its death, as you hauled and tugged and cursed, the moose was still getting its revenge.

I backed the truck another ten feet, until I was directly under the canoe, which hung on a wooden trapeze from the joists of the loft. Standing in the bed of the truck, I lifted the bow off of the wooden dowel and lowered it onto the two-by-four behind the cab, and tied it down. Then I dropped the stern onto the truckbed and tied it to the trailer hitch. The paddles and cushions were hanging on the wall. I put them in the bed, rolled the truck back out and locked the door.

Back at my house, I pulled in to get the phone from Clair's truck. And while I was at it, I decided to grab some food. Stepping inside, I heard a man's voice. On the answering machine. I grabbed for it as the guy said, ''Thank you.''

It was the trooper. He'd hung up.

I grabbed the receiver and called the State Police dispatcher, said the trooper had just returned my call. He said he was on the road and he'd try to reach him. I waited. When the dispatcher came back on, he said the trooper had gone on a call. He'd try again later.

I hung up, and hit the button on the machine, listening as I took cheese and mustard from the refrigerator, a loaf of bread from the freezer. The trooper's name was Smith. He sounded relieved that I wasn't home. But then the machine beeped again, another call.

''Jack,'' Roxanne said. ''Is there something wrong? I know you said you're fine, but I know when you're not, so don't try to fool me. I'm at the nursing home. You have the number. Please call me. I love you.''

A hissing pause.

"Oh, yeah. I'm okay. Things here are the same. But I'm worried about you. So call. I love you. I'll try the other phone."

I stood there for a moment, with the food in my arms, listening to Roxanne's voice. Sure, I could talk to her. Something to take her mind off of her troubles. Tell her the whole messy story, as she sat beside her mother's bed. Maybe she had five grand she wasn't using. I shook my head, and then I walked out the door, out to the truck, and tossed the food on the passenger seat. I started the truck, but I didn't plug in the phone.

"Portent," Allison had said.

29 I parked in a brush-lined turnoff just below downtown Scanesett, loading the rifle in the truck and then backing the truck into the brush. Then I stopped and paused.

If I took the rifle, that would mean I was ready to shoot someone. I wasn't, so I jacked the shells back out and, looking around, slid the rifle under the truck seat. I took the canoe off the truck, slid it through the bushes to the bank and shoved off. The canoe scraped and then was silent, slipping quickly across the Kennebec and into the shadow made by the trees on the opposite bank. I figured I had only a half mile to go before the islands began, and for a few minutes, the going was easy.

Too easy.

The water was the color of strong tea, the bottom littered

with silt-coated limbs and logs. Snags lurked just under the surface like crocodiles, grazing the bottom of the canoe with long, metallic creaks as I paddled along the western shore.

I paddled kneeling, in front of the stern seat, gliding past the overhanging birches and swamp maples. Then a perverse afternoon breeze had come up, rippling the water and turning the bow left and right. There was little current in the summer, and as the river widened, it turned into what seemed like a long, placid pool. The wind, a hot blast, picked up, and if I stopped paddling, it turned the canoe broadside and pushed it back upstream.

"Goddamn wind," I said.

After a half mile, I was losing it. Arnold would have drummed me out of his army.

But I dug in harder, still hugging the west bank, away from the island side of the river. If the idea was to reconnoiter, I didn't want to come around a bend and find myself staring them in the face. I just wanted to see if I could pinpoint their camp or tent or whatever it was. Once I'd done that, I'd . . . I'd keep paddling.

I did, flushing a kingfisher that led me downriver, dropping from a tree and dipping along the water, then perching until I approached again. I watched the kingfisher, and a lone black duck, a female, and the far bank, a quarter mile away.

There was a bristle of pines, hardwoods in the hills to the east, rock outcroppings at the top of a ridge. Under an overhanging birch I pulled in my paddle, took the binoculars out of my camera bag and scanned the far shore. Trees hung densely over the water, with no break in the vegetation.

I paddled on.

It was slow going, following the shoreline. I bent low for branches, maneuvered the canoe around fallen limbs and sunken pulp logs, relics of the now-banned log drives. From somewhere in the distance I could hear the whine of a tractor-trailer. I bent to the paddles, fell to the rhythm of my strokes, thought of Arnold and his men as they—

There was an explosion from the shallows.

"Jeez," I said.

A great blue heron, all legs and wings, flapping out of the trees and around me, across the river, where it flew low toward the bank, and then to the right, disappearing behind . . . an island.

From this distance, it blended into the far bank. But when I looked again, with the binoculars, I could see a channel, then two walls of trees, one behind the other, differentiated only by a slight change in color.

I looked upstream. There appeared to be a point, a place where the first island ended, and then another island, higher, with bigger trees. I put the binoculars back in the bag and paddled on.

Slowly. Hugging the bank.

It took patience to stay under the canopy, to wend my way among the branches. But I fought off the urge to break out into more open water, where I'd be seen, where the paddle would flash like mirror. With the kingfisher leading the way, I picked my way downstream, stopping to scan the shore. The southern island began to take shape. It was a quarter of a mile long, with a big pine at the downstream tip. Beyond the big pine was a point of marsh grass, like the prow of a ship, and there were smaller pines at the center, behind birches and brambles. Both above and below the islands, the far bank was all unbroken vegetation, a strip of woods as dense as Arnold might have seen.

Maybe this was the stretch of river Allison Smythe wanted. I could go downstream farther, then turn and shoot. Kill two birds.

So to speak.

So I did, sticking to the shoreline, flushing some small songbirds: cedar waxwings, and what looked like a wren. I paddled slowly and then the river started to veer to the west, bending away from the island side. I followed it for another half hour, looking back until the islands had disappeared beyond the bend.

The sky was a hazy pale blue to the west, turning slowly to gray to the east. The wind was like someone's hot, fetid breath, and perspiration ran down the middle of my back, darkened the front of my shirt. I sat for a minute, still along the bank, then dug out the camera. I shot upstream, showing the bend in the river, framing the picture with an overhanging birch.

It felt ominous to me.

And then I knelt again and eased my way out, paddling slowly as the wind caught the canoe broadside and sent it scudding like a leaf up and across the river.

I stayed low, squatting on my haunches. I kept the paddle down, too, stroking on the upstream side, quartering the wind. In minutes, the far shore was taking shape. A few minutes more and the trees were distinct, and I was coasting into the overhanging branches.

The island had just come into sight.

I watched for a moment, and everything was still. The haze was darkening behind me, and the blue sky had turned a pale gray. Mosquitoes broke from the branches when I brushed against them, and lit on my neck and arms, but I tried to brush them off slowly. I didn't want to look like I was waving.

Picking my way upstream, I kept the paddle on the side of the canoe away from island. The wind tried to swing the stern around, toward the river, and I had to work to keep it along the shore.

The island drew closer, the big pine standing like a mast. I had to make a decision here. Run through the passage between the island and the shore? Paddle out into the river to meet the island's tip? Paddle along the side of the island on the main channel of the river?

Paddling along either shore, I risked coasting right into them. Landing on the tip of the island, I could work my way down. Look for some sign of life, or some sign of . . .

I held on to a sheaf of branches and watched. Gulls passed overhead, but other than that, everything was still. I let go of the branches, and used the paddle to shove off of the bank.

It wasn't a wide crossing, maybe two hundred yards, but I felt naked. The wind gave a little gust, sending me into open water, and the canoe bumped over a barely sunken tree, balancing for a moment until I reached forward with the paddle and pulled it over.

I stroked faster, harder, deeper, and then the island was rushing at me, and the canoe ground into the marsh grass. I shoved twice with the paddle, then shipped it, and stepped out.

And sunk.

The bar wasn't sand, it was silt, and my left leg plunged into the dark gray muck up to my calf. I tried to pull it out, one leg still in the canoe, and the mud started to suck my shoe off, and I fell to one knee, and it hurt again.

The shoe came out as I pitched forward, out of the canoe, my hands disappearing halfway to the elbows. Mosquitoes came out of the grass in a cloud, and I could feel them on my face and neck, hear them in my ears. I got one muddy hand out and swiped them away, then, getting to my feet, started dragging the canoe over the grass to the low bushes on higher ground.

And then I stopped. Crouched and listened. I heard the drone of the bugs, felt something crawl across my hand. I looked down to see a wolf spider, an inch across, spring off my hand into the grass. I shuddered. Dragged the canoe ten more feet. Listened again.

To the birds. Bugs. The wind in the trees.

I was covered with mud. It was smeared over my arms and legs, and my running shoes were black-gray clumps. The mosquitoes, tiny, humming sentries, were still rising up to meet me, and I wiped again, muddying my forehead, my temples, behind my ears. They were in my eyes, in my mouth, and I had to fight off the urge to run into the trees, flapping my arms. Instead, I took my pack from the canoe. From the pack, I took my sheath knife, then slung the pack on my back.

Still in a crouch, the knife tucked into my shorts, I eased my way into the brush.

It was dense, red-twigged stuff that scratched at my face, tore at my pack. But after twenty feet, I was on higher ground, and the red-twigged brambles gave way to alders, with broom handle–size trunks and openings between them like tunnels. I eased my way through, the branches making a slashing sound against the nylon pack.

I stopped. Listened. Counted to thirty. Continued on.

The ground rose steadily and, after another fifty yards of alders, I was climbing over a rock outcropping, then walking, almost upright, toward the trunk of the big pine.

I leaned against it. Waited.

On the far side of the trunk was a shaded opening where the ground was covered with pine needles. There was trash there, too: faded and flattened twelve-pack cartons, a vodka bottle, its neck broken off. On the edge of the clearing, in the brush, was a pair of men's briefs, dirty and gray.

All of it looked like it had been there for a long time.

I crept through the clearing, staying low, and stopping every few steps. The ground sloped downward to another tangle of alders and I had to push and pull the branches aside. For a moment I thought of Arnold's men, fighting their way through the brush. And then I didn't think of Arnold at all.

Through the alders, I walked, whining mosquitoes rising to meet me. I slashed at my face and kept moving, slowly, step by step. Then I was on higher ground, with a big birch to my left, over the river. Two pines showed up ahead, through the foliage. I stopped to listen.

Heard a grunt. A moan.

I froze. Held my breath. Listened.

Didn't hear anything. Waited. Mosquitoes whirled around my head. Motionless, I listened.

Nothing.

I moved in slow motion, listening after each footfall. A branch snapped, and I started, but it was me. I'd stepped on it. I listened. Thought I heard a rustle, ahead and to the right. This time I waited a fifty count. Started to move, peering through the trees. Somewhere up ahead, a red squirrel chittered.

At me? At somebody else?

I waited, and the squirrel quieted. Mosquitoes whined. The trunks of the pines, joined at the base, showed through the trees. I eased my way along. Another five feet. Five feet after that.

And I smelled it.

Feces.

It passed as the breeze wafted from behind me, but then the breeze faltered, and I smelled it again. And as I silently sniffed the air, I spotted the clumps of white. Toilet paper in the leaves, scattered like mushrooms in the brush on the slope that between the pines to the riverside bank.

Someone had been here.

I counted the clumps. Eight that I could see. But how many people? How many were here now?

Sixty feet from the pines, I dropped to a crouch. Peered through the branches. Then closed my eyes and listened.

Heard it again.

It was a rattling groan, like the noise a sleeping person makes when turning over. It came from beyond the two big pines, which I could now see had two-by-fours nailed to their sides, butt ends toward me. I reached into my shorts and took out the knife. Slipped it out of its sheath. Flicked the blade open, holding it in my fist to muffle the click.

I wished I'd brought the rifle, thought for a moment that I should go back and get it.

But I was this close. I wanted to see who it was. I wanted to know.

I crept forward, out of the trees and across the pine needle–littered opening. There were empty cans in the bushes,

Budweiser bottles, a yellow-and-white potato chip bag.

And another moan beyond the trees.

There was a creak, a muffled knocking, as though boards were being moved. I was ten feet from the pines, crouched close to the ground. I had to decide which side to approach, and I picked the left, because it was closer to the river and I could always swim if I had to escape. I could run and then I could swim if the person . . .

I stood up, the knife in my right hand against my thigh. Watched my feet as I placed them, one after another, on the pine needles. And then I was against the tree. I waited. Started to sidle around. Saw that the two-by-fours, silvery and old, were the frame of a hut. The roof was head high, covered with pine needles and mossy shingles.

The sides were rough boards, and the nails were rusty.

I listened. Thought I heard someone exhale. Inside the hut. There was a crack and I took two slow steps until I could put my hand on the roof. I peered through the crack. Saw something light, like a rag. I held the knife tighter. Swallowed. Inched toward the corner of the wall.

Stopped.

I tried to crane my head forward just enough to see, but I could see the other wall. A plastic milk jug, filled with water. An empty soup can. Campbell's, vegetable beef. I leaned toward the corner.

An inch. Another. I stopped. Stared. Eyes met mine.

"Mr. Maurice, I presume," I said.

30

I could smell him.

He was stretched out on planks, filthy legs poking out of shorts. One wrist was handcuffed to a rusty eyebolt, which was screwed into the wall of the shack. The other hand was wrapped in a filthy gray bandage, streaked with old blood, the color of chocolate. The bandaged hand was on his chest. He was on his back. His face was a mass of scabs. Arms and legs, too. His mouth gaped open, and he began to stammer.

"But you can't . . . No, because . . . Why did you . . . I was never . . ."

"You were a cook at Fort Devens," I said, moving toward him. "You weren't CIA."

"Then . . . then why—"

"I'm a reporter. I'm not CIA, either."

"But you . . ."

His puffy eyes looked me over, and I realized what I must look like. My arms and legs were smeared with mud. My face, too. I was carrying a knife.

"I'm not an agent, Marvin," I said. "I'm just going to get you out of here. Where are they?"

"Gone," he said weakly, as if he might cry.

"Where? Off the island?"

He nodded.

"To get food."

I stepped closer and stood over him.

"How long?"

He looked up at me.

"I don't know," he said.

"Today?"

He nodded his bloody, stubbled chin.

"Will they be back soon?"

Maurice nodded again. I squatted next to him. Pulled the handcuff by its chain. The eyebolt, screwed into a two-by-four, held. I reached up and tried to twist it. It didn't budge. I looked back at Maurice, then down at his other hand.

"Your finger?"

He nodded slowly.

"That's the smell, isn't it?"

He nodded again.

I felt my stomach roll. The odor, a foul, sweet stink, was Maurice's rotting flesh.

"No antiseptic or anything?"

"No," Maurice said.

"You've got a fever?"

He didn't answer, and I reached and touched his forehead. Under the scabs, it was burning.

"We've got to get you out of here," I said.

I stood and stepped around the wall to see what was holding the eyebolt. It was a lag, the screw end of which stuck out an inch from the board. All I had to do was twist it back out.

Coming around to Maurice again, I leaned over him and tried to twist the eyebolt with my fingers. It didn't move, so I looked for something—a nail, a stick—to use to get better leverage.

I looked around. There was trash all over the ground, Budweiser cans stomped flat.

"They bring any tools?" I asked him.

"No. A big . . ."

He hesitated.

"Knife," Maurice said.

The knife they used, I thought.

"Who did it?" I asked.

"Damian. But Howard. He held it."

"God almighty," I said.

Maurice, his hand on his chest like he was ready for a last Pledge of Allegiance, just stared.

I leaned over him again and tried to fit the butt of my knife through the hole in the eyebolt. It wouldn't go, so I tried the blade. With the ring of the handcuff through the eye, only the point and two inches of blade would fit. I tried turning the bolt, and the blade started to bend. The bolt didn't budge. Maurice's hand hung limply by its chain.

Under the cuff on his wrist, there was a green ring.

I scanned the campsite. Broken glass. Cigarette butts. Wrappers from balogna. A plastic bread bag. A white plastic pail, with green lettering. Drywall compound. I walked over to it, saw and smelled the urine.

"You can't reach this, can you?" I said to Maurice.

He shook his head. I noticed the dark stain on the front of his shorts.

"Damian thought it was funny," Maurice said.

I turned the bucket over and let the urine drip out on the ground. Then I put the pail on its side and pulled at the metal carrying handle. Twisted it. It held.

The handle was attached to plastic housings on each side of the pail, inserted with some sort of knob on the ends that I couldn't see. But if the hole that the handle went through could be widened . . .

I took my knife and started stabbing and gouging at the plastic. It was hard and the blade bounced back. I stopped. Looked over and saw that Maurice had his bandaged arm over his eyes. I looked back at the knife and understood.

But I had to get the handle off to get him out. I knelt with the pail between my legs and jabbed away. The sound was dull, but still I paused every few blows and listened.

The wind blew through the trees. A crow cawed somewhere off of the island. Maurice still had his hand over his face. I resumed chopping.

Finally, after five minutes of chopping, I stuck the tip of

the blade into the hole and twisted it, drilling the knife through the plastic side of the pail. The blade ground against the metal handle and I twisted, and then yanked the knife out, and put it on the ground. I took the handle in both hands and pulled.

It came away. I fell back. The bucket dangled by one end of the handle. I thought I heard a splash.

I froze and listened. Maurice had taken his hand from his eyes and was looking toward the east side of the island.

"That where they come up?" I said.

He nodded slowly. I listened again. Heard nothing.

I took the handle and bent it double. Then I leaned over Maurice again, and inserted the doubled handle into the bolt. He looked up at me, eyes wide but weary. The bucket rested on his arm as I turned the handle. It bent, and I took both ends in my hands and turned again. It bent more, so it was half of a swastika. I flexed my hands, gripped it again, and twisted.

With a squeak, it turned. I heard another splash, like a fish jumping. Then a faint voice.

I turned the bolt faster.

The handcuff chain pivoted. The bucket swung. The bolt had come out an inch, and I stopped and pulled. It didn't give. I kept turning.

"Can you walk?" I said, in a half whisper.

"I hurt my ankle. I think I broke it."

"Can you limp along?"

"I think so," Maurice said.

"Get ready. Move your legs or something."

He did, pulling his pudgy legs up and down like a baby.

There was a rustle. A branch snapping. Down by the shore. They were here.

I twisted and pulled again, and the bolt still held. I twisted one more time, pulled hard, and it came loose, bolt, bucket and all.

Maurice's arm came with it, and I yanked him off of the planks as I pitched to the ground.

"Get up," I said.

He did, but stiffly, as if his feet were tender. I tried to pull the handle out the eyebolt, but it was twisted around it, and it wouldn't come, so I held it, and pulled Maurice.

"Let's go."

We went around the pine, and into the brush. I shoved Maurice ahead of me, but at the first bramble, he stopped and looked back and I pushed by him, and kept going, dragging him through the branches behind me.

I kept the white pail in front of me, trying to cover it. It caught on the saplings, clattered against the branches. The handcuff chain rattled. A branch whipped back and hit Maurice.

"Oww," he said.

"Shut up," I said with a snarl.

I was trying to be quiet, but in the stillness on the island, we must have sounded like elephants moving through the jungle.

"Ohhh," Maurice said as another branch slapped him. I dragged him faster, through the alder thickets. Left, right, looking for the openings, hoping we wouldn't hit a dead end, because there was no time to backtrack.

This was a race. There was no place to hide, nowhere where they couldn't find us within fifteen minutes. They could start on one end of the island and walk toward the other, drive us like deer.

We had to get to the canoe. We had to get out into the river. Cross to the far side.

"They have guns?" I said.

We were in the red-twigged brambles, bulling our way through.

"A little one," Maurice said, panting. "A little pistol. Elbert had it yesterday."

A little pistol. That was better than a big rifle. But we had to get out of range.

I pulled Maurice along faster, still holding the stupid pail in front of me, like Jack in the Beanstalk, running for the vine. The chain caught, and I yanked hard and heard branches tearing and cracking, and then we were in the open, under a big birch, and Maurice fell. Hard.

He lay there, like he wanted to think about it, and I turned back and yanked him to his knees. Blood was running from all over his face, as though he'd been scourged.

"I can't," he panted.

"Come on," I said, and dragged him, stumbling, into the alder thicket.

The alders were dense, with trunks growing in clumps. The pail jammed against them, and they held, and I had to stop and turn back, drop to my knees. Maurice watched, his arm outstretched, jerking as I twisted the pail to get it free.

"Goddamn thing," I said, and then I was on my feet, pail in my gut like a football, Maurice's arm against my thigh.

We crashed along, stopping again, kneeling again. I heard a shout behind us, maybe back behind the birch, then another shout to my left, abreast of us, from the water.

Were they paddling around?

"Damn," I said.

A footrace and a rowing race, a biathlon with me towing Maurice.

"Jesus," I said.

The alders were thinning, and we crashed through, into the clearing under the last pine, and Maurice was panting and he stepped on my heel and my left running shoe came halfway off.

"Sorry," Maurice said.

I dragged him into the red-twigged brambles. He was grunting now, and falling against me when I slowed. I felt his chin on my back, his right hand on my waist. The brambles thinned and the mud began. My left shoe was coming off and I reached back to try to shove it back on, and Maurice piled into me, getting his blood all over my arm, and I thought, goddamn it, I'd have to get him tested, too.

And then we were out of the red-twigged stuff, and into the grass, and the mud was pulling at my feet, but I sprinted, leaning forward against Maurice and the chain. And there was the canoe, and I reached in and grabbed a paddle. Maurice started to step into the boat, right on dry land, and I yanked him out, and said, "Wait. And stay down."

He crouched and I shoved the canoe through the mud and marsh grass, and I looked back and he was thirty feet behind me, still waiting.

"Come on," I called, and I heard crashing and voices, saw somebody back at the pine. Maurice lurched toward me, and I shoved the canoe over the mud, my shoes slogging, the canoe sliding, and then the stern was in the water.

I ran in, up to my knees, sinking into the silt. Maurice splashed in, and I pushed the canoe, and said, "Get in," and he took one gunwale and started to climb in, almost turning the canoe over. I grabbed the other gunwale and shoved him in, he fell to the bottom of the canoe. I tossed the pail in on top of him, stepped in and shoved off.

I started paddling, desperate, deep strokes. But he was heavy and the wind was in my face, and we didn't seem to be moving at all, and I dug in harder, one side, then the other, putting my arms into it, my shoulders, my back and legs. We were ten yards out, then twenty, and the canoe felt like lead, and then I heard the shouting behind us.

"Get 'em. Get 'em."

I turned to my left and looked back, and saw Robie's little aluminum boat coming around the tip of the island, except Robie wasn't in it. It was Elbert, rowing, and Damian sitting in the bow. Elbert couldn't row, and the boat was twitching left and right. Damian was smiling.

"Get 'em," I heard again.

I looked behind me. Howard was on the shore. There was no gun in sight. I turned and dug in, heading downstream, toward the far shore. The canoe was too heavy.

Low in the water. How much could Maurice weigh? He couldn't be this—

"Hey," Maurice said.

He raised himself to his knees. His shirt was wet. Dripping.

I looked at the bottom of the canoe. Water was gushing in.

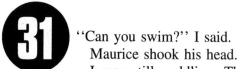

"Can you swim?" I said.

Maurice shook his head.

I was still paddling. The water was three inches deep in the bottom of the canoe, flowing through a four-inch gash. It looked like it had been made by an ax.

"You're in the army and you can't swim? What the hell kind of army is that?"

"I was a baker," Maurice said, staring down at the hole. "I did muffins."

"Then why'd you say you were in the CIA?"

Still looking down, Maurice shrugged.

Behind us, Damian and Elbert were fifty yards back and closing. Flotation in the bow and stern would keep the canoe from going to the bottom, but we'd soon be swamped. Immobile.

I could swim for the far shore, leave Maurice behind. Elbert and Damian had switched places, and now Damian was still grappling with the oars, and I might be able to outrun him. Maybe overturn him. They'd both drown. On the island, Howard would starve to death. Or maybe I'd stand on the shore and shoot him.

A happy ending.

"We're sinking," Maurice said.

"We won't sink. There's foam under the seats. You'll have something to hang on to."

"You aren't gonna leave me here are you?"

I looked at him.

" 'Cause they're gonna be ripshit. Damian'll . . . I don't what he'll do, but . . ."

He looked down at his bandaged hand. I kept paddling and glanced back. They were thirty yards away, still veering left and right like a waterbug. There were no other boats in sight, and the far shore was all woods. I looked back again. Elbert was scowling.

"Give it up, McMorrow," he called over his shoulder. "You ain't going nowhere."

Damian gave a long, maniacal cackle. I kept paddling. The canoe was filling like a bathtub, the water over my knees.

"Last chance, McMorrow," Elbert said.

"Yeah, CIA man," Damian shouted. "How smart do you feel now, smart-ass?"

"Don't let him get me," Maurice said. "I'll try to swim. I don't know if I can do it, but I'll try. Don't let him get me. Okay? You won't let him get me?"

I considered it. I could flip them over, and Maurice could dog-paddle toward shore. Or he could hang on to the canoe and kick. But in the water, the bucket on his arm would be like an anchor.

"Can you swim at all?"

He looked out at the dark chop like it was boiling oil.

"Um, well, I never really learned. But, I don't know. I could try."

They were twenty yards away, the waves slapping at the bow of the aluminum boat, oars flailing like legs on an injured bug. The water in the canoe was six inches deep and tepid. Maurice was still kneeling in it, the pail beside him, his eyes fixed on Albert and Damian.

"Oh, no," he was murmuring. "Oh, no. Oh, no, please God, no."

I stopped paddling.

"Just sit there and don't say anything," I told him. Then I turned to my left as the rowboat pulled closer.

"We had a friggin' deal," Elbert said.

"He's infected," I said. "He's got to get to a hospital or he's—"

The canoe pitched. I grabbed for the gunwales as Maurice rolled over the side.

"Hey!" I shouted.

"What the—" Damian said.

There was a sound like "kashoosh," and Maurice disappeared in a roil of bubbles.

"Goddamn idiot," Elbert said.

The pail bobbed on the surface of the water, then filled and sunk into the brown murk. I leaned forward and half-dove, half-spilled from the canoe, went in head first and opened my eyes.

It was brown water, like varnish. So dark my hands faded in front of me. I kicked twice and pulled myself deeper. A white form drifted below me. The pail. I tried to dive, kicking and stroking, but it was still sinking. The pressure was building in my lungs, a weight on my chest, my throat, inside my head. I took a last look and shot, five kicks, to the surface.

I broke through and gasped.

"Where the hell is he, you mother?" Elbert screamed.

"He killed himself!" Damian shouted. "I didn't do it. Morrow did it. I ain't gonna—"

I took two deep breaths and dove again.

It was dark, no whiteness, no shape to follow. I kicked down into the murk, feeling in front of me, seeing nothing but my arms, my fingers. The water was colder, and I could feel current, gentle but relentless, pushing my head, my torso, twisting me so I didn't know which way was down. My lungs were squeezing outward, upward and I stroked and kicked and something gouged at my belly, and I jerked away.

And saw the white shape ahead of me.

But my lungs were ripping, tearing, and I had to surface again, had to, and this time it was seven kicks, and on six I blew out like a silent scream, breaking through the surface like it was ice. There was light and then sky and I gasped and panted and swallowed.

"He's dead and you friggin' killed him," Damian was saying from the boat, twenty feet away. "You still owe us, don't you—"

Sucking in air, I dove again.

I aimed at a point downstream, heading for the bottom at an angle. One stroke. Two. Three. Four, and something glanced off my right arm, scraped at my face. A tree limb, slick with algae. I pulled at it, and then it was gone and I was going down, down into the cold blackness, and then slam, I hit bottom.

It was mucky, and I recoiled, almost gasped, but caught myself. Kept stroking, with the current, blind in the darkness.

And there it was again.

The pail emerged five feet in front of me, a light blot, then a whitish shape, then the cylinder, bottom toward me. I kicked hard, and caught it in two hands and put my feet down into the mud and pushed.

The pail, and Maurice, held me down.

I kicked against the bottom again, but it was too soft, and my feet plunged into the silt, sticks scratched at my legs. I kicked again, pushed harder, twisted as I flutter-kicked, hard.

My lungs were beyond the other times, like there was a scream caught inside me. I felt like it would blow out of the top of my head, out of my eyes and ears. But I could feel myself rising.

My legs kept lifting, so I was prone, and I pulled on the pail, and my legs sunk deeper. But I was moving, and I was kicking, then stroking with one hand, and then the brown syrup of the surface was above me. I could see Maurice's hand, outstretched like it was being offered for a kiss, and then his shirt, and his legs, splayed and bent, in that space-walk position.

I pulled and kicked, and we rose toward the surface, and then it was close, the light, and the air burst from my lungs, bubbles against my face, and I held my breath still, jaw clenched, one hand on the pail.

And broke through.

I gasped and pulled, over and over. The bucket came to the surface, but Maurice was still under.

"I got him!" I yelled. "Help!"

Treading water, I yanked the pail up over my shoulder, and Maurice's hand and arm appeared. I grabbed the arm, the slick, wet flesh, and then the shirt at the neck. It tore and Maurice's head went back under and I had to go under, too, putting my arm around his neck and frog-kicking upward, harder and harder.

And then my face was out of the water, and Maurice's, too. I gasped and said, "Help!" but the word barely came out and nobody answered. I went under again, then clawed my way back up. Maurice was on his back, half beside me, half on top of me.

I twisted around, sputtered "Help!" again. And then I saw them.

Elbert and Damian, in the distance, rowing toward the tip of the island, toward shore.

Towing the canoe behind them.

My legs ached. I was panting. I spun around, kicking to keep us afloat. How did lifeguards do it? With a sort of sidestroke. A frog kick and a one-arm reach. I looked around. Elbert and Damian had disappeared around the tip of the island. The west shore was farthest away. The east shore was closer. The island, just upstream, was closest of all.

But was Howard there? Would he be waiting?

Frig it, I thought. And I started swimming.

It was slow and hard, and the pail was like a sea anchor. I kicked, and stroked with my left arm. My legs kept tangling with Maurice's, and his weight pushed me under. Every ten strokes, I looked up and sighted the big pine on the island. It wasn't until I'd done thirty strokes that I knew I was moving closer.

My legs ached, first a pain in the thighs, then a numbness. My arm reached out, but grew weaker and weaker. I kept stroking. Kept counting. Stayed in rhythm. By inches, the pine drew closer. By the minute, I wanted more and more to stop. To rest. To release this awful weight.

I felt my arm start to relax around his neck, felt myself coasting longer between kicks.

"No," I said between clenched teeth. I took a mouthful. Coughed. Kept going.

The island was closer, the pine bigger. My legs were burning and my arm reached out limply. It was like Maurice's arm, trailing in the water, dragging the white pail. I couldn't keep going. I had to let him go. He was dead. He was dead, anyway. It wouldn't be like—

It hit me in the armpit. A tree limb, just under the surface. I grabbed for it and missed, and plunged under. It was against my chest and I reached for it and pushed myself up. It wavered but it held.

I lay on my side across the limb, with Maurice laying beside me, his hair in thin bangs on his forehead, eyes closed, mouth gaping like a fish. I looked toward the island, now just twenty yards away. I shouted.

"Help! Help me!"

The words drifted away with the wind.

Time was passing. Maurice was growing more dead with each minute. But didn't they revive people after a half hour underwater? Didn't they revive people who had fallen through the ice?

What was it they did? Pumped the chest and blew into the lungs? Something about keeping the tongue from blocking the air passage?

I looked at Maurice. His tongue was lolling in his mouth, lifeless as tripe. I reached over and touched the tongue. Tried to pull on it but it was slippery. I leaned toward him.

And we both rolled into the water.

I let go, and for a second, didn't know where he was. But then the pail bumped my head and I grabbed his arm and surfaced. Yanked and heaved, and coughed and sputtered. Finally I had him by the throat again, and I started for shore.

My legs were fresh again, but only for a dozen kicks. My arm was limp again; Maurice was heavy, like a sandbag on my hip. I kicked and stroked, kicked and stroked, and the island drew into sharper focus. It was closer, and I could see the marsh grass on the point, the dragonflies. My knee scraped something underwater, and I started to put my foot down.

And sunk. Struggled to the surface again.

It wasn't shore.

The bank was there, it was close, but the water was still too deep. I was panting, huffing into the water, fighting the urge to put my feet down. If I went down again, I might not be able to bring Maurice back up with me.

I kept kicking. Kept reaching. And then I felt more branches with my legs. A pause, and more branches after than. Then my knee hit a rock. My hip, too. I knelt, felt the ledge scrape my shins.

Maurice was floating above me now. I sat under him and stood up. The water was up to my waist. I took him under both arms, and his head lolled like a baby's. Walking backward, I dragged Maurice through the water. Stumbled but didn't go down. Slipped on the mud, saw the mosquitoes light on Maurice's face.

Did that mean he was alive? Did mosquitoes bite a dead man?

I jerked him along the ground until his sneakers were out of the water, then dropped to my knees. His mouth was open and his head rested on a rock. I moved him over six inches, then flipped around to straddle his chest. I checked for a pulse on his neck, and thought I felt something, but maybe it was the pulse in my fingers. I reached into his mouth and stuck my fingers down his throat. What was it they said? Clear the air passage? It seemed clear, hard and sort of bony, but how far down did you go?

"Okay," I told myself.

I took a deep breath and clamped my mouth over his and blew out. His lips were big and cool and coarse, and I could feel the stubble on his face, and then that breath was gone. I leaned back, inhaled deeply, and locked onto him again. Was I supposed to pump on his chest, too? Christ, I didn't know. The Heimlich maneuver. How did that work? You pushed hard under the lungs, didn't you? Was this the same thing?

"Oh, Jesus," I said, lifting from his mouth. "Oh, Jesus, Jesus, Jesus."

I leaned back and pressed down, just under his rib cage. He was chubby and soft, and I felt like I could press right through him. I did it again, then a couple of more times, then bent to his sour mouth.

Blew. Took a breath. Blew. Took another breath. Blew again.

"Oh, my God," I murmured, then locked onto his mouth.

I kept going, because to stop was to declare him dead. If I kept going, he wasn't dead yet. He wasn't alive, but he wasn't dead, either. He was . . .

Gagging.

A faint jerk. Then still again. Then another jerk. He was still for a moment, and then he made a gurgling sound, and his abdomen jerked under me in spasm, like a cat about to vomit.

32 Maurice did vomit, and greenish watery stuff came out of his mouth and spilled down his chin and neck. I heaved myself off of him, and turned him on his side so he wouldn't choke. He coughed, over and over, and then spat repeatedly. And then he turned so that his head was on the ground, and I heard him take short, jerking breaths.

I knelt behind him, felt a long, draining shudder of relief. My own.

"You okay?" I said.

Maurice moaned. Vomited again. Said, "Oh," as though in pain, then coughed and was quiet. I knelt and waited, brushing mosquitoes away from both of us. The island was quiet; even the birds had hushed. I listened for Howard, for Damian and Elbert, but didn't hear anything, just the bugs. Something told me they hadn't gone for help.

So I waited, watching Maurice's back move with each breath. That reminded me of Roxanne's back, curled against me, her breathing in the morning, when she slept and I lay awake. That was in another life, another world. I vowed to go to her when I left this one. I'd go directly. I'd say to hell with Maurice and the *Globe* story, and all of this, and I'd go to Roxanne, and tell her I loved her and . . .

My legs started to cramp. I winced and eased myself to my feet, trying to straighten up. The cramp peaked and subsided, and, in my soggy running shoes, I stepped around to see Maurice's face. His eyes were open. His mouth, too.

A blood-filled mosquito hung from his chin. I brushed it off. He didn't blink.

Was he brain-damaged? How long did that take? How long had he been under? Three or four minutes? It couldn't have been much more.

I crouched in front of him.

"You okay?" I asked.

Maurice still stared.

So I waited again, this time watching his eyes. They stared, and I stared back. The bugs hovered and the river shimmered behind him. But after twenty minutes, I decided they weren't unseeing. A robin shot by, giving a little cluck as it passed, and Maurice's eyes moved with it. I asked him again.

"You okay?"

He swallowed, and didn't answer, but he seemed more alert. Finally, a mosquito flew into his eye and he jerked, and pawed at it with his bandaged hand.

Rest time was over.

"You tried to kill yourself, didn't you?" I said.

He didn't answer.

"Come on. Talk. Can you talk?"

Maurice's eyes slowly swung up so that they met mine. He nodded.

"So talk. Go ahead."

"What . . . Where are . . ."

He stopped.

"They're gone. They took off when you didn't come back up. If you were dead, they didn't want to be blamed. That's my guess."

Maurice tipped his head to the ground and spat, and the saliva dribbled onto his cheek and chin.

"The water . . . my mouth tastes terrible," he said.

He sounded groggy.

"Tell me about it."

"My stomach, it really hurts."

"It was full of water. I had to pound on it a little."

"It's this pain," Maurice said. "When I breathe. Where are we?"

"Back on the island."

"How'd we get here?"

"We swam."

"I don't know how."

"I noticed," I said.

There was a moment when neither of us spoke. The river rippled and flickered. Birds chirped. Mosquitoes hummed around my head.

"Where'd they go?" Maurice said.

"Back to shore. Except Howard was here. I don't know if he still is. I don't think so. I think they swung around and picked him up."

He paused.

"What if he's still here?"

"I don't know. One thing at a time."

Maurice paused again. Spat.

"So you're sure you're not . . ."

His voice trailed off.

"With the CIA? No more than you are, or were," I said.

"They used . . . they used journalists, you know. As covers. I read that."

"You read a lot of stuff, didn't you? That's where you got all of it, isn't it? All the stuff you told that kid on your street. Told your mother. Told these guys, too, right?"

Maurice didn't say anything.

"Answer me, Marvin," I said. "You owe me."

I waited.

"Yeah," Maurice said.

" 'Yeah,' what?"

"Yeah, I read it in books."

"And then you turned it into your life. What's the matter? Didn't want to tell the kids back home you baked cookies? What, did it sound too wimpy?"

He shrugged.

"And the bike and the car? That was all part of it, wasn't it? The retired secret agent. But you spent more than you had, keeping up the image. One credit card after another, all maxed out."

Not even a shrug this time, just his head falling a little lower.

"What, your parents withhold their approval or something?"

Maurice didn't answer.

"And you told Howard and Robie and those guys, too. Why'd you bother with them? I mean, how did you end up with them?"

He took a deep breath. Winced at the pain in his chest.

"I didn't. I fell."

"You fell?"

I could see him looking at his bandaged hand. It was starting to smell again, or maybe it was my imagination.

"After I got off the bus."

He paused. Took a shallow breath. When he exhaled, it was with a soft, "puff" sound.

"I was gonna hide. Just until it got dark. But I fell, climbing down."

"Climbing down what?"

Maurice waited. I did, too.

"Down to the river," he said. "From this parking lot. I fell and I hurt my ankle. And then this guy found me. Robie. He was looking for bottles. So he helped me."

"You went to his apartment."

"In this trailer thing on his bike. At night. And his sister, she was there."

"Rob-ann. But what about the rest of it? Howard and Damian and all that? The CIA? You didn't tell them you were running from bad checks and credit cards, did you?"

Maurice didn't answer. I waited, then got to my feet and looked down at his face. It was pudgy and pouting. A little kid caught in a lie. He looked down at the ground.

"So what'd you tell them?"

He closed his eyes, then opened them.

"I told them I was running away. From the CIA. I told them the CIA wanted this money that I had from when I'd been working with them. I told them I needed to disappear so the CIA wouldn't find me."

I almost smiled.

"And then I showed up."

"Looking for me. You were looking for me," Maurice said. "Just like I said, this guy was looking for me, this stranger guy, and you hit Damian and broke his hand, and you kept coming back. And you said you were a reporter, and—"

"The CIA has agents pose as reporters."

"Yeah. I read that. I mean, it wasn't true, but it was like it was coming true. It was really . . . I don't know. It was weird."

I looked down at him. He held his bandaged hand out in front of him.

"And then things turned sour?" I said.

Without looking at me, Maurice nodded.

"But you never told them the truth?"

He shook his balding head.

"Why not?"

Maurice shrugged. I knew the answer, but I waited.

"Why not?" I said again.

"They were, I don't know, counting on it. It was what I was worth. The car and the bike. And the money. The money from you."

It was what he thought he was worth, too: not much, without the fabrication, the frills from his imagination. I looked out at the river, the green foliage on the far shore.

"Was Robie in on this? Rob-ann?"

"No. They said, 'No. Leave him alone, leave him alone,' but Howard and the other guys told them to shut up, and then, after a while, I didn't see them much."

"The other guys held you? I mean, against your will and everything?"

"I couldn't leave," Maurice said.

"That's kidnapping," I said. "Aggravated assault. Extortion. They're in serious trouble."

"If we—"

"When we get out of here."

"But I can't—"

"I know," I said. "You can't swim."

The shore was two hundred yards away. I left Maurice and went to the other side of the island and gazed across. It was four-thirty, and the wind still was blowing and the sky was white. There was no sign of activity on the shore, but that didn't mean they weren't waiting. That they hadn't come back. That it hadn't occured to them that maybe, just maybe, we hadn't drowned after all.

I looked back through the woods, then across the rippling waters. I felt an urge to wade in up to my waist, then dive and swim for the other side. An easy breaststroke would do it. I'd be across in five minutes, up on the road in ten. I could run back to my truck; there was a key under the seat. In a half hour, I could be away from the river, heading south, heading home.

Like Arnold's men. Like the deserters.

I took a last look at the river, and turned and made my way up the bank, and back to Maurice, my charge.

He had moved twenty feet away from the river. He was sitting against a birch tree, his head back against the trunk, his eyes closed. I stood in front of him.

"You all right?"

"I'm sick," he said, his eyes still closed. "I feel sick."

I felt his forehead. It was hot. I took a deep breath and reached for his hand. I meant to unwrap the bandage again, but then I noticed his arm. It was red and swollen. I held it up to the other arm, which was pale and slim by comparison. The veins in the infected arm stood out darkly, like purple vines.

"We've got to get you to a hospital, Marvin. You could lose your arm."

"I'm sick," he said again. "I'm sick."

I lowered his arms and looked around. I could just stand on the shore and scream for help, and hope that someone heard me. But what if that someone was Elbert or Damian or Howard? They'd be sure to come to our aid. Maybe they'd bring their little gun.

Or I could swim for it and go get help. If I called the cops . . . God, the cops. The sergeant. Well, they'd still have to send an ambulance. The fire department probably had a boat. I'd just have to convince the cops, Bell or the chief, that Maurice was real, that he was on the island and was very sick.

Or maybe I could float him off myself. Gather up some logs and make some sort of a raft that he could hang on to, and I could tow. Or maybe I could just heave him over my shoulder again. Get that stupid pail off of his arm, tell him to kick his legs.

The pail. My knife. I patted my shorts. It was gone. I'd have to just untwist it, with a stick or a rock. Or just pound the crap out of the thing until it came loose.

I looked down at Maurice, lolling now against the tree. I crouched in front of him and picked up the pail, with the eyebolt attached. I tugged at the metal handle, and the pail and arm twisted.

"Ow," Maurice said.

He opened his beady little eyes.

"Oh, shut up. I'm not taking you anywhere with this thing on you. It was like—"

And I heard it.

I listened. Heard it again.

A metallic knock. It was their boat. It was coming.

"Get up," I said with a snarl, and yanked Marvin by the arm.

He said, "Hey," but he got to his feet and shuffled after me as I dragged him into the woods. Bent low, I pulled him twenty yards into the poplars, then down toward the riverbank. Ten feet from the water, there was a stump. I sat him down behind it and stuck the white pail in his arms.

"Keep this covered. And don't make a sound. Not a sound. I'll tell them you didn't make it. You're dead. Don't move a muscle."

I slipped up the bank to the bigger trees, then worked my way down through the brush on the other side. The ground was leafy and each step crackled. I slowed and tried to move quietly, peering through the leaves toward the water. I heard the metallic knock again.

It was closer.

I crept all the way to the shore. If they searched the island carefully, they'd find us. But maybe I could get below them, get in the water and let them pass above me. Then get the boat. Or wait and hope they didn't find Maurice down there. Hope he didn't make a sound.

I was at the shore now, my feet slipping into the water. I parted the bushes at the water's edge. Heard the knock, but it was above me, out of sight where the shoreline formed a partial cove. I heard the muffled clang as the hull hit the rocks. A splash. The sound of the boat being dragged up onshore.

Then nothing.

I waited, motionless, hunched low, the water up over my socks. I thought I heard a rustle to my left, but then there was nothing. Birds. The wind. Bugs.

Easing my way along the shore, I made my way around the bend. There was the aluminum boat. The oars were in the oarlocks. Another chance to desert. I crouched near the boat and waited.

Then I took a melon-sized rock from the bottom. Came out of the water and started up the path. I walked slowly, freezing between steps and listening. Ahead of me, I heard a snap. A branch breaking. I was approaching the lean-to now. I moved slowly. Gripped the rock. Heard another snap, then a scuff. It was beyond the lean-to, moving away from me. Toward Maurice. But then another snap. Closer. And another. Moving toward me. I stopped in front of the lean-to. Leaned forward. Readied my rock.

"Robie," I said.

"Hey," he said. "You ain't dead."

 "God almighty, I'm glad it's you," I said, trotting toward him. "We've got to get Maurice out of here. He's sick. Where's Howard and those guys?"

"Gone," Robie said, standing there, a vision in his giant sneakers and a Wily Coyote T-shirt. "Gone away. I was coming to meet them, but they just got outta the boat and they left."

I hurried past him, and he fell in a step behind me.

"So he ain't dead?"

"No. But he came close. Guy sank like a rock. Swims like one, too. His arm's all infected. He needs antibiotics. He needs a hospital."

I made my way into the brush, and I could hear Robie behind me. As I turned toward the river, I called out to Maurice.

"It's Robie. It's okay. We can get out of here now."

Below me, Maurice lurched to his feet, holding the pail against his belly. I took his good arm and led him up through the tangle. He fell a couple of times, and I got him back on his feet, and then we were standing, the three of us, in the big trees.

"Let's go," I said.

Maurice stumbled and started to follow me. Robie seemed to hesitate.

"Don't be afraid, Robe," I said, looking back. "I'm not going to kiss you. What was that all about, anyway? The chief put the screws to you, or what?"

He started after us but didn't answer.

"Well," I said.

"I didn't say nothin'," Robie said. "He said everything. He said he knew what we was doin', and he'd tell everybody if I didn't do what he told me. He said you was nothin' but trouble."

"Oh, well. Can't please everybody. It's not important now."

I kept going, and they followed. Robie started in again.

"He said he could put me in jail for doing what I did, and I told him I didn't do nothin', that we was just talking, and he told me it didn't matter, because you prepositured me."

"Yeah, right," I said, not turning to look. "And it's proposition."

"Uh-huh. And he said you was gonna get me in trouble, and he asked me if you fooled around with my sister."

I turned this time.

"Rob-ann?" I said. "Robe, this guy's a sicko."

I slowed for Maurice, who'd caught his foot on a root and gone to his knees. He reeled slightly as he got to his feet.

"You okay? You gonna make it?" I said.

Maurice nodded. I took him by the arm and started up the path toward the lean-to. Maurice glanced at it, then turned away. We started down the path toward the boat.

"So what're you gonna do?" Robie said behind me.

"I don't know," I said. "Let's get him across and up to the road. Then we can flag somebody down. Ask them to call an ambulance, or give us a ride to the hospital. But let's just get him there first. I'll row if you want."

I could hear his heavy steps behind me.

"Yeah, but what're you gonna do then?"

"About what?"

"About, I don't know. You know, the whole thing."

I turned as we got to the boat.

"What? Chopping his finger off and all that? We'll call the cops at the hospital. Try to get county or state. They're in serious trouble."

"Who is?"

I was standing by Maurice. I looked at Robie.

"What're you worried about? Getting in trouble?"

He didn't say anything.

"You didn't cut off his finger, did you? You didn't beat him up. You didn't hold him against his will. So nothing will happen to you. We'll tell the cops—"

"Yeah, but you said not telling was like doing it. You said I could go to prison if I knew somebody killed somebody but I didn't tell. You said—"

"God, Robie, don't worry. When the cops ask you, just tell the truth."

"You're gonna tell the cops you told me that? About going to jail if you know somebody killed somebody but you didn't tell anybody? Damian said I could go to jail, and Rob-ann would be in a different jail, and I wouldn't see her, maybe ever in my life."

Maurice started to get in, with the boat still on the shore.

"Wait," I said, holding him back, and pulling the boat down the bank by the stern. "Robie. Don't—"

"And she's my only member of my family. My real family, 'cause our mom died when we was—"

"Robie. Nothing's going to—"

"Yeah, well, she's my sister, and she needs me, you know? And I don't want her to go to jail, 'cause Damian said, did I know what would happen to her in jail, and to me, too, and I said, 'No,' and he said, every night, they'll come to your cell, and Rob-ann's cell, and they'll take you and they'll do—"

Maurice looked worried.

"Robie, just shut up," I snapped. "If you didn't do anything wrong, then you won't—"

"What're you gonna tell the police about what I did?"

"I don't know. For God's sake, just get in the boat so we can—"

He hit me as I was reaching for the oars. I heard a bullish roar, felt myself flying backward, saw his face above me, his eyes squinting, his mouth clenched shut.

I was sprawling, arms behind me, reaching for the bottom, water splashing. And Robie kept coming, and he was on top of me and I said, "No," and then my head went under and his hands were on me, gripping and pressing. My head was against the bottom, against a rock, and it hurt, and I could see him, all blurry, through the water above me.

I held my breath.

Twisted underneath him.

Kicked my legs, out of the water, and into the air. Kneed his back.

Held my breath.

I wanted to scream, and I almost did. For a millisecond, I thought, well, this was it, it was over, and what an absurd way to die, but I was dying, and I'd never thought it would be like this, but nobody thought it would be the way it was.

But even as I thought that, I was reaching for his arms, for his hands, clamped on my forehead and my mouth. And I could feel it, the need to breath was rocketing up inside me, exploding, and I felt like I was screaming inside my mouth. I gouged his arms with my fingernails, digging deep, got my hands on his face, felt him try to bite me, then ripped at his nose, at his eyes, scratched and clawed at them as he twisted his face away.

And his hands let up, and I lifted my head with them, felt the top of my head come out of the water, but he was still pressing, and my nose was under, but my fingers were in his eyes, and I could hear him bellow as I clawed and kicked, and he fell back and I came out of the water and gasped, still on my back.

"Get him—" I screamed, and I saw his face, all blood, and I grabbed for air with my mouth gaping, and he fell on me again.

I was under and my eyes were open, and his hands were on my throat and he was pounding my head on the bottom, over and over, and I reached to my right and grabbed, and to my left, and grabbed, and my right, still clawing. Something came loose, and I swung my arms up, like I was crashing cymbals, and the rock in my right hand slammed into his skull.

Once. Twice. My eyes were closed, and his fingernails were in my throat. Three times, I swung. Four times, one hand holding his head up, like a nut to be cracked, and I felt him fall, to my left and off of me, into the shallow water.

I got myself on to my elbows, rolled on to my side. I was gasping and choking, and I felt like the air wouldn't go down, like something was caught in my throat. I got myself up on to my knees, still in the water, and turned back toward Robie.

He was on his back, his head toward shore, out of the water. His face was all blood, diluted and running down into the shallows. I stared to see if he was breathing. I looked back down. The water was up to my elbows. I heard splashing behind me. Started to turn.

And slammed face-first into the water.

He was on my back, and I was stunned, and for a moment, I couldn't believe it, then I could, and I started to lift both of us out of the water. He wasn't as strong as Robie, and I got an elbow around and caught his shoulder and started to turn.

The pail dropped over my head.

Maurice was pushing it down, so the rim was against the back of my neck, and it cut me when I pressed up against it. I felt the plastic against my face, and then a seizure of claustrophobia, the bucket like a plastic bag.

He was pushing down, and I felt him hoist himself up so his feet were against my hips, and all of his weight was on top of the pail. He was on my head, on my shoulders, and I started to scream, but this time the scream came out. It came out underwater, in a gurgling roar, and as it ended, and there was no more breath to blow out, I got my right arm over my head, onto the bucket, and I found the hand, the bandage, and I took it in my hand and dug in hard.

34 They sat in the stern of the boat like woozy sailors after a long night in port. I hadn't said a word since I'd dragged Maurice out of the water, and I rowed in silence.

Robie's face was still bloody, and one of his eyelids looked like it was torn. Maurice held his hand in front of him, and he was crying softly. Every once in a while he whimpered, "I don't want to go to jail."

Robie said softly, "What about my sister?"

The pail was in the bottom of the boat. My rock was on the seat beside me. The bow of the little skiff pointed up crazily, and the stern wallowed, but I made it across and ran the boat up onto the sand. I got out first, took my rock, and stood as they eased their way over the seats and stepped out. Twenty feet away, where the bank turned brushy, was Clair's canoe, full of water, my backpack submerged in the center.

"Pull it out," I told Robie.

He looked at me, then at the canoe, then walked over and heaved the canoe, foot by foot, onto the shore. He tipped it, and the water cascaded out like a dam had burst. When the canoe was emptied, I told Robie to drag it up the path. He took it by the little bow deck and trudged off like an ox.

I gave Maurice a shove, and he took his pail and followed. With my backpack and my rock, I brought up the rear.

Our little procession wended its way up the path, pushing through the brush, with the clouds of mosquitoes all around us. Then the path opened up, and we continued on, past the beer cartons and trash, and up the little lane, until we came out of the alley and onto the street. The canoe ground metallically on the pavement.

At the first house, a woman was sitting in a lawn chair at the entrance to her garage, smoking a cigarette. She stared, open-mouthed. I smiled and said, "Hi." The woman got up and hurried inside. I figured the cops would meet us on the main road.

Actually, we had to wait. The canoe was sitting on the sidewalk, beached. Maurice and Robie sat behind it on somebody's lawn, looking like they'd been shipwrecked.

I stood on the curb, as though I were waiting for the bus. A couple of cars passed, and slowed, and the people inside them stared. An older man in a pick-up truck stopped in the middle of the street.

"You okay?" he asked, looking at me, at Robie and Maurice, at the canoe and the pail.

I heard a siren in the distance.

"Yeah," I said. "I think we're all set."

He drove a few feet and parked. The police car came into view, lights flashing, and when it pulled up, I gave a little wave. Bell got out and came around the car.

"McMorrow. What the hell is this?"

"Officer Bell," I said, "I'd like you to meet Marvin Maurice. He came here on the bus."

The chief wasn't glad to see me, but with a real, live Marvin Maurice in hand, what could he do? In my soggy shorts and T-shirt, I nodded to him in the hall, then went into a drab little room to give my statement to Bell and an assistant district attorney she'd called in. He was pleasant but so gung-ho that I glossed over the part where Robie tried to drown me. He was only trying to protect his sister. She was the only family he had.

Rob-ann came to the police station, feverishly looking for Robie. She was told that he was in the hospital in Skowhegan. Maurice went there, too, and lost some more of his finger. After surgery, he was placed under arrest on the theft and fraud warrant out of Kennebec County. Robie was transferred to the hospital in Waterville to have his eyelid repaired, and his eyes checked out. Bell said he'd be summonsed for assaulting me, and questioned about Maurice's abduction and mutilation.

"Tell him it'll keep his sister out of jail," I told Bell. "He'll spill his guts."

She said warrants would be issued for Elbert, Damian and Howard. They'd disappeared, but not to worry. They were predators, but had limited range. All three were homeboys, and they'd be happier in prison in Maine than on their own in some faraway, foreign place like Connecticut.

I said I wanted Howard to take an HIV test as soon as they found him. Outside the Scanesett police station that night, Bell went to her car and got me a flannel shirt, which belonged to her husband. I took the wet T-shirt off, telling her to close her eyes. She apologized for thinking I was a weirdo. I said it was okay, and wished her the best with her case and her family.

"You're not coming back here?" she said.

"Only if subpoenaed," I said.

"You're not going to write about this?" Bell said.

"Probably," I said. "But the first thing I have to do is write about Benedict Arnold."

Or maybe that was the second thing.

Bell gave me a ride to where my truck was parked. It was still there, tucked in the bushes in the dark, the rifle safely stowed under the seat. I nodded to her, and as she pulled away, she flashed her blue lights. I followed her to the main road, where she took a left, and I took a right. The canoe was still on the sidewalk when I got there, and I tied it on to the truck. Then I got back in the truck and drove out of Scanesett, down the Kennebec, toward home.

On the way, I called the only family I had.

Clair was first, summoned to the phone by a little kid who called him "Grampie."

"Hey, Grampie," I said. "I've got good news and bad news. I borrowed your canoe to go down the Kennebec."

"Okay, Jack," Clair said, his voice distant and fuzzy. "Give it to me straight."

"Somebody chopped a hole in the bottom of it with a hatchet."

"What's the good news?"

"It's a small hole."

"I feel like I just won the lottery," Clair said.

"Don't thank me," I said. "I'll even get it fixed for you. Since it was, in a way, my fault."

"He didn't chop anything else, did he?"

"Well, it's a long story. I'd rather tell it over a beer."

"Your place or mine?" Clair said.

"Maybe yours," I said as children clamored in the background. "I'll be calling you."

Wondering if anyone would ever call me Grampie, I said good-bye, hung up and drove on. But before I made the next call, I stopped. I was near the village of Hinckley, and I pulled off the road next to the Kennebec. I knew the river, and the number, by heart.

It rang. Once. Twice.

Roxanne answered.

"I'm coming," I said.

"Oh, Jack, you don't have to . . ."

And then she stopped.

"When?" Roxanne said.

"Tomorrow."

"What time?"

"I don't know yet."

"Will you be here for dinner?"

"Absolutely," I said. "If that's okay. How are things there?"

"They'll be better with you," Roxanne said. "I really need you."

I paused.

"I need you, Rox. And I love you, you know. And we've got some things to talk about."

"Okay. Not bad things, I hope."

"No. As long as we're together, everything will be fine. Nothing else matters."

"That's right," Roxanne said. "But you know, you don't have to come now. I still love you."

"You're the only family I've got," I said. "Somebody was just talking about that."

"Who was that?"

"Somebody I met. I'll tell you all about him."

"Oh," Roxanne said. "All right. Your Benedict Arnold story going okay?"

"Fine," I said. "I'm bringing it with me."

"What about that other thing? The guy on the bus?"

I sat there, looking out at the dark shimmer of the river, thinking of the desperation it had seen.

"That's okay, too," I said. "I'm learning some things. I'm learning a lot."